THE PILOT'S GIRL

THE PILOT'S GIRL SERIES BOOK ONE

FENELLA J. MILLER

Boldwood

First published in 2012 as Barbara's War. This edition first published in Great Britain in 2023 by Boldwood Books Ltd

Cover Design by Colin Thomas

Cover Photography: Colin Thomas, Alamy and Unsplash

A CIP catalogue record for this book is available from the British Library.

Paperback ISBN 978-1-83518-623-7

Large Print ISBN 978-1-83518-622-0

Hardback ISBN 978-1-83518-621-3

Ebook ISBN 978-1-83518-624-4

Kindle ISBN 978-1-83518-625-1

Audio CD ISBN 978-1-83518-616-9

MP3 CD ISBN 978-1-83518-617-6

Digital audio download ISBN 978-1-83518-618-3

Boldwood Books Ltd
23 Bowerdean Street
London SW6 3TN
www.boldwoodbooks.com

This book is in memory of my grandmother Delia Rikh with whom my brother and I spent many happy holidays in Hastings.

1

The three-mile cycle ride to Hastings took Barbara through familiar lanes and well-loved tracks. She would miss this place; she had spent most of her life here.

She laughed as her front tyre bounced into a pothole nearly unseating her. She was going too fast, but she relished the wild run downhill to the coast. It would be hard, leg-aching work, coming back, but it was worth it. She pedalled more sedately down Castle Hill Road, her fingers gripping the brakes. She dismounted outside the library and propped her bike against the wall. Inside she spotted the leaflet she wanted; she was tempted to take the one for the Woman's Royal Air Force, but that would be futile. As long as she got away from Crabapple Cottage she didn't really care where she went or what she did.

Tucking the information into her coat pocket she ran down the steps to retrieve her bicycle. The sun was out, but the wind blowing in from the sea made it difficult to find somewhere outside to read her pamphlets. She had no choice – she would have to pedal home. Her mother wouldn't come to find her in the stables and the tack room had a paraffin stove.

'Babs, Babs – hang on a minute. I want to speak to you.'

'John, I thought you'd gone. I'm so glad I got a chance to see you again.' She beamed at her best friend and the rangy young man returned her smile.

'Shall we go and have a cuppa out of the wind?' He reached out and removed the handlebars from her grip. 'Here, let me wheel that old rattle-trap for you.'

Barbara was tempted to refuse; she was quite capable of pushing her own bike to the café, but he meant well and he was leaving to fight for his country, so she restrained herself. 'Thank you, John. Now I can put my hands in my pockets and warm them up. Even with gloves they froze on the way down. And anyway, why are you still here? You told me last week you would be gone by now.'

He grinned. 'I'm off this afternoon. My papers had to be processed and it took longer than I expected. I have to report this evening to Lord's cricket ground in St John's Wood, of all places. I think I could be sent to Scotland for my basic training but don't know where I'll be going after that.'

'It's a good thing they're sending you to Scotland, somewhere away from houses and livestock, in case your flying turns out to be as bad as your driving.'

'Cheek! I've only had one accident and that was the cow's fault, not mine.'

Amiably bickering, she walked the short distance to the Copper Kettle with him, a small café they had been meeting in for the past two years. She ordered their usual pot of tea and toasted teacakes from the sour-faced proprietor who guarded her domain from behind a high wooden counter at the entrance. Delighted to see the coveted window seat, which gave an uninterrupted view of the sea, was vacant, they headed towards it.

Hats, gloves and coats were handed to the elderly black-garbed waitress before they sat down.

Barbara pushed her hair out of her eyes. 'I have some news for you as well, John. I'm intending to join the Land Army.'

'Good God! Are you? I thought you would become a stalwart member of the WVS.' He frowned. 'Does that mean you'll be leaving here?'

'Of course – that's the main idea. The boys are going off to boarding school on Monday, you're leaving this afternoon, there's nothing to keep me here. I want to do my bit for the war effort and they won't give me permission to join any of the services.'

'But the Land Army? Wouldn't you prefer the WAFS or the WRNS? I'm sure you would be an officer in no time.'

'I just said, they won't hear of the forces. It's the Land Army or nothing.'

'Fair enough! It's bound to be hard work and you get precious little time off from all accounts. Father's thinking of applying for some girls to help him once I'm gone.'

The rattle of crockery warned them tea was coming. Barbara smiled her thanks. There was silence as she poured the tea. 'Do you realise this might be the last time we ever have tea here together?'

'For God's sake, Babs! What a morbid thing to say.'

The tea slopped into the saucer. 'I didn't mean that...' Overcome, she concentrated on filling the second cup without spilling any before she felt ready to continue. 'I meant we're both moving away from here, not that either of us could be killed.'

'Let's be honest, it's a distinct possibility, at least for me.' He smiled. 'And I suppose you could be trampled by a cow or gored by a bull.'

'I'm more likely to die from hypothermia. Can you tell me anything else about the Land Army? I got some leaflets but I haven't had time to read them yet. I expect your father will have been through his information with a fine-tooth comb.'

She watched him lean back in his chair, closing his eyes in thought. He looked so young, far too young to be risking his life as a pilot. What if he was killed? Would she be able to cope without her best friend to talk to? She studied his face, seeing him clearly for the first time. His fair hair was slicked back; she much preferred it flopping engagingly on his forehead. She frowned. He hadn't had his hair like that since he'd gone to Oxford three years ago.

They stared at each other. His pale blue eyes darkened and his pupils dilated. Fascinated she moved closer. He closed the gap and kissed her. She pulled back, embarrassed, her arm catching the teapot, sending it crashing to the floor.

For a second nothing happened. Then Barbara jumped up nursing her scalded arm. John, his face scarlet, leapt from his chair and dropped to the floor intending to pick up the scattered crockery. Their waitress almost threw their precious teacakes on to the table and the three ladies at the next table exclaimed in a loud chorus of 'well I nevers' and 'whatever nexts'.

The manageress, Miss Whiting, appeared from behind her desk issuing instructions in a strident voice. 'Mary, go into the kitchen and fetch a mop and dustpan and brush.' The waitress scuttled off. No one argued with Miss Whiting. 'Mr Thorogood, there's no call for you to dirty your hands; my girls will clean up the mess. Come along, Miss Sinclair, let me take you into my office and put something on your scald.'

Barbara allowed herself to be ushered into the inner sanctum, aware that Miss Whiting had closed the door in John's face.

'There, my dear, sit down. Show me your arm.'

Obediently Barbara held it out, still too shocked by John's extraordinary behaviour to speak. Whatever had possessed him to kiss her and in the Copper Kettle of all places? She shuddered, knowing a description of the event would be regaled to her mother before the day was out. Her mouth felt dry and her stomach contracted unpleasantly.

For an awful moment she thought she was going to be sick. Frantically she swallowed the bile and breathed deeply through her nose. Sweat beaded her forehead and, closing her eyes, she flopped back against the slippery, polished chair-back.

'Heavens, Miss Sinclair, you've gone quite pale. Here, put your head down between your knees; you'll feel less faint.'

The very last thing she wanted was to lower her head. She would be sick for sure then. Miss Whiting's hands gripped her shoulders. She had to say something. 'I'll be all right in a moment, thank you, Miss Whiting. I feel sick, not faint.'

'Oh dear! That's quite different. Just a moment, my dear.'

Barbara felt the welcome chill of a china bowl being placed between her fingers. Slowly her panic and nausea subsided. 'I'm not going to be ill. I'm feeling much better.' She opened her eyes and attempted a reassuring smile.

Miss Whiting, eyes concerned, pink spectacles slipping down her nose, smiled back. 'Well done! I don't know what young John Thorogood was thinking, to behave in such a way. I'd always considered him a well-brought-up sort of boy.' Miss Whiting removed the bowl from Barbara's hands and placed it with a snap on the chenille-covered table.

Barbara was touched by her rescuer's obvious distress on her behalf. She'd never realised Miss Whiting had a softer side. In all the time she had been visiting the café she could not recall its owner doing more than sitting silently behind her till, grey hair scraped back in a bun, daring her customers to offer anything but the correct money.

'Thank you for your help, Miss Whiting. You have been very kind. My arm's not hurting so much now and my stomach has settled down.' She paused, unsure if she should continue. She straightened, marshalling her thoughts. She couldn't allow Miss Whiting to think badly of John.

'John's leaving for flying school later today, Miss Whiting. We might never see each other again. I didn't mind him kissing me; it was just a shock.' Her cheeks reddened. Why had she started this explanation? 'We are not... err... emotionally involved you see, just very close friends.'

Miss Whiting nodded and pushed her glasses back up her nose. 'Well, my dear, all I can say is that you might not be "romantically involved" as you put it, but young Mr Thorogood definitely has feelings for you. I know we have all been expecting you to announce your engagement any day.'

'I'm sure you're mistaken, Miss Whiting. John and I are just good friends, as I said. It was only the thought of possibly never seeing each other again that made him do it, nothing else.'

The walls of the private sitting room began to close in on her. She wanted to get outside, grab her bike and cycle away from all this. She jumped up. 'I must go, Miss Whiting. Thank you so much for your help.'

'You're quite welcome, my dear.'

The café was empty, the three ladies departed, the window table cleared – even John had left. She snatched her coat from the wooden stand by the door and shoved her arms in, flinching as the burn brushed through the tweed sleeves. Without stopping to do up the buttons, she pulled on her beret and gloves and ran out.

She scanned the street: no sign of him. He hadn't bothered to wait and see how she was, to apologise, to explain his behaviour. She blinked back unexpected tears. She hated to part with him on bad terms; he was her dearest friend and she couldn't bear it if he went away thinking she hated him.

A gust of wind snatched her coat open and she shivered. Hastily she did up the buttons and, stuffing her wayward curls under her hat, grabbed her bicycle and vaulted on. She knew where John would go, where he always went when he was upset, on to the South Downs where he could stand facing out to sea, allowing the wind to clear his head and restore his equilibrium.

He was on foot, but had about half an hour's start. The cable car that took you up the cliffs the easy way was closed. He would have to use the steps. The beach was deserted apart from the occasional fisherman sitting by one of the black wooden huts that marched in a line along the upper shore. He couldn't be far up the cliff. If she was lucky he would still be in earshot and she could call him back.

She pedalled furiously along the seafront, her coat flapping out and her slacks in imminent danger of fouling the wheels. The noise of the seagulls screaming overhead almost drowned out the rhythmic bang of the waves on the pebbles. It was full tide and the fishing boats were in and their catch was being sorted into waiting wooden boxes. The gulls soared and swooped over the boats waiting to steal any fish the fishermen cast aside.

She ignored the cacophony – she'd heard it hundreds of times before. Usually she would stop and watch, but not this morning. She stared up at the cliff but couldn't see John climbing the steep steps. Had she been mistaken? Had he gone elsewhere? She blinked, attempting to clear the wind-whipped moisture from her eyes. Her chest ached and her legs were leaden after covering the distance from the Copper Kettle in record time.

The fishermen's huts interrupted her view of the white cliff face. She redoubled her efforts and emerged, red-faced and sweating, her eyes fixed to the rocks hoping to catch a glimpse of him.

* * *

John had seen her coming and knew why she pedalled so furiously but he couldn't face the inevitable questioning. She didn't feel the same as him; he had always known it really. He had hoped she would, one day, come to see him as a potential lover or husband, not just a dear friend.

His ill-timed kiss had told him what his darling Babs could never bring herself to tell him: that his attentions were not welcome. He slipped between the huts and watched her cycle past then quickly crossed the road and vanished up a side street. She didn't see him go.

2

The journey back to Crabapple Cottage took Barbara almost an hour. She pushed her bicycle into its designated slot in the garage and, without checking to see if her mother was home, walked straight round to the stables. Silver needed exercising; the mare would be wondering why she hadn't appeared to take her out.

'I'll not be a moment, Silver; sorry to have kept you so long this morning,' she called as she hurried into the tack room to change. Her mother insisted her riding clothes remained outside. Barbara also had to wash them herself and hang them on a line in the yard.

In less than twenty minutes she was mounted and ready to leave. The sun was out, and away from the coast it was warmer, the wind less biting. She trotted across the stubble field that ran behind the stables, trying to decide where to go. She had been too miserable and tired on her way back to plan ahead.

The mare's ears pricked at the sound of a car in the lane that ran beside the field. A car! Of course – John must have come into Hastings in his father's car. That's where he had gone, not to the cliff, but back to his motor. How stupid of her! She kept forgetting he was a man in a car, not a boy on a bicycle.

'Come along, Silver. I know where to go. We'll go to Brook Farm. John's not leaving until later; I can catch him there if we hurry.'

Her heels touched and her mount responded, lengthening her stride into a long, easy canter. The few miles that separated their homes took her across fields, over hedges and ditches and in and out of Badgers Wood.

She clattered into the farmyard at one o'clock. Old Tom, the cowman, popped his head out of the milk parlour. 'How do, Miss Sinclair. You're just in time for lunch. Give me your mare – I'll take care of her for you.'

'Thank you, Tom. Is John back yet?'

Tom took the reins and patted the horse's sweating neck. 'No, he's not, so you haven't missed him.'

'Silver's a bit hot. I'll walk her round for a while before I go in.'

'That's all right, miss, I'll do it. You go on in. The missus will have seen you arrive and have your meal on the table.'

Barbara stopped at the yard tap to wash her hands, using her jodhpurs as a towel. In the large back entrance hall she pulled off her boots and stood them tidily next to the jumble of other discarded footwear. She hung her riding mac neatly on a peg. She padded along the flagged passageway to the heart of the Georgian farmhouse: the huge kitchen.

The door swung open as she approached. Aunt Irene greeted her. 'Come along in, Babs, we're just sitting down for lunch: soup and rabbit pasties. Would you like some?' They exchanged hugs.

'I'd love some. I'm starving. I ate breakfast at six o'clock and I've cycled in and out of town and ridden over here since then. And I never even got to eat my toasted teacake.'

Mr Thorogood waved as she came in but didn't stand up; after all she was like one of the family. 'John's not back yet, love, but he'll be here soon. I'm taking him to catch the train and it leaves just after three.'

She walked over and kissed his whiskery cheek. 'I have to talk to him, Uncle Bill. We had a bit of a misunderstanding and I don't want him to go away thinking... well... going away without sorting things out.'

'Guessed as much when I saw you come into the yard. You don't usually ride that horse of yours so hard. Something had to be up.' He pulled out one of the mismatched wooden chairs. 'Sit down and have some lunch. Tell us all about it if you want.'

Aunt Irene ladled out a generous portion of thick vegetable soup and set it down on the table. 'Here; eat first, talk later. Everything seems better on a full stomach.'

'Thank you. This smells lovely. Is it leek and potatoes?'

'You know it is. It's John's favourite so what else could it be on his last day?' Her voice faltered and she busied herself cutting her two thick slices of freshly baked bread before continuing. 'I know John's got to do something, but flying? I wish he'd joined the army instead.'

'I thought the same at first,' Barbara said quietly. 'I kept thinking – what if he crashes the plane? It's not the same as a car, is it? But at least he's not involved in hand-to-hand fighting and he'll probably be based in England.'

'I suppose you're right, dear; if he's stationed here he might get some home leave occasionally.' She almost smiled. 'I think the Navy's the worst. Just imagine – all that water and never knowing when a German submarine is going to send a torpedo into your ship or a plane appear and drop bombs on you.'

'Now, Irene love, that's enough. No point upsetting yourself. Our John is going to be a pilot and he won't even be fighting for a few months. He has to train first, doesn't he? Plenty of time to start worrying when he joins an active squadron.'

She sniffed and patted her husband's shoulder before sitting down. 'You're right, love, as usual. No point in getting het up.'

The marmalade cat curled up on top of the Aga yawned and appeared to wave his paw in Barbara's direction. 'Did you see that? Ginger's waving at Babs. Well I never!' Aunt Irene laughed, her usual good humour restored.

Barbara waved her soup spoon at the cat. 'Good afternoon, Ginger. I expect it's the smell of rabbit pasties in the oven that has woken him up, not my arrival.'

John's mother put three mugs of strong, sweet tea on the table.

'Well, Babs, are you going to tell us why you're here, or is it a state secret?' Uncle Bill said, ignoring his wife's attempt to hush him.

Her cheeks coloured. She could hardly tell them what John had done; they would be as shocked as she was. She bit her lip, buried her nose in her tea to give herself time to think. Did they believe he had feelings for her as well?

'We had a bit of a misunderstanding at the Copper Kettle. My arm got scalded and by the time Miss Whiting had sorted me out he'd vanished. I'd forgotten he must have come in the car and pedalled all the way to the cliffs to look for him.'

'You burnt your arm? How did that happen? Is it bad?'

'No, Auntie Irene, it's nothing really. I knocked the teapot off the table and the tea went over me.' Barbara didn't want to continue this conversation. 'Uncle Bill, John said you were going to get some land girls in to help you. I'm going to volunteer for the Land Army so anything you can tell me would be a great help. I've got some leaflets but I haven't had time to read them yet.'

They exchanged glances, believing the cause of the disagreement was now obvious. 'Why don't you join the WAFS, Babs? Maybe you could get stationed near John then.'

'I'd love to, but Mr Evans won't hear of it. It's this, or stay at home.'

'I think it's possible you'll have to stay at home when you join the Land Army. I read somewhere that country girls can be asked to work locally,' he told her.

'What do you mean? I thought everyone was sent away.'

He shook his head. 'Of course city girls would have to live away, but I'm sure it had something on this in my booklet.'

Barbara had to get away; life at Crabapple Cottage would be untenable after her brothers had gone. 'Are you certain, Uncle Bill?'

He pushed back his chair. 'I'll go and find the pamphlet; it's in the office somewhere.'

After he left Aunt Irene turned to Barbara, her face worried. 'Is it still bad at home, love?'

She nodded. 'Yes, Tom and David are leaving on Sunday for boarding school and it will be even worse then. I try so hard to please her, but nothing I do is right. Sometimes she just has to look at me and that's enough to set her off.'

She patted Barbara's hands. 'You could always come and live with us. Short of locking you up, they couldn't stop that, could they?'

'I can't come here; they'd just cause trouble for you. I must get away. Do you know anything about my father, Charles Sinclair? Maybe I've got relatives somewhere who would take me in?'

'I don't know much, but I'll tell you what I do know. Your mother had a glass too many of cowslip wine at a WI Christmas party a few years ago and let slip a few facts. I know you look like your father and that's part of the trouble.'

'I guessed I must. I certainly don't look like my mother, thank goodness.'

'Do you remember him at all? You must have been about three when he died.'

'I recall my mother crying, and being on a train with all our things, but nothing else.'

'That would be when you came down here; your mother got a job as housekeeper at a house in town. She met Mr Evans soon after that and that's how you ended up at Crabapple Cottage.'

'Did my mother ever say anything about my having grandparents?'

Aunt Irene stirred her tea, lost in thought. She looked up, her plump face wreathed in smiles. 'I remember. She once said that your dad's family were well-to-do and hadn't approved of her marrying their only son. They lived in Essex somewhere. I think Mr Sinclair might have been a medical man, but I'm not sure.'

'Do you think the marriage wasn't happy? That's why she hates me – because I remind her of a bad time in her life?'

'Quite likely. Why don't you ask her outright where your grandparents live and then contact them yourself? I bet they'd be happy to see you. They might not even know they have a granddaughter. If your mother didn't get on with them, she might never have told them.'

They both looked at the far door – the one that led to the front of the rambling house. There were footsteps approaching; John had returned for his farewell lunch.

Barbara brushed the crumbs from her beige jumper and ran her fingers through her curls hoping to restore some sort of order. She held her breath, watching, waiting for the door to open. John's mother hurried to the cooker and bent down to remove the bowl of soup and a pasty from the warming oven.

The door opened and he walked in. His expression immediately changed from smiling to wary. He ignored her and addressed his mother. 'Sorry I'm late, Mum. I went for a drive around. It might be some time before I'm back here. I wanted to say goodbye to the old place.'

Barbara stood up, trying to find the words she needed to ease the tension. 'John, before you eat, we have to talk. Can we go somewhere for a moment?' His eyes narrowed and his mouth thinned. She saw him force a smile.

'All right, but it will have to be quick. I've got to leave in thirty minutes and I haven't eaten.'

He turned and led the way back down the passage but instead of going into the sitting room he opened the door into a large wood-panelled room that the Thorogoods only used for formal occasions. He wasn't going to make this easy for her.

He didn't hold the door open, just strode in leaving her to follow. The overstuffed chintz furniture with well-plumped cushions and matching poufs had obviously not been used for months. The dust was thick on the various wooden surfaces and the mantelpiece.

She closed the door and crossed to stand behind him as he glared out over the walled rose garden, his shoulders rigid, his back firmly to her.

'John, please look at me. I don't want you to go away like this.' He didn't turn; gave no sign he'd even heard her. Tentatively she reached out and touched his arm; he shrugged her off.

'For goodness' sake, John, don't be so childish. I overreacted when you kissed me and I'm sorry, but you shouldn't have sprung it on me like that, and in public in front of those three WVS cronies of my mother's. What were you thinking?'

These words finally achieved her objective and he slowly turned, a rueful smile hovering around his lips. 'I'm sorry too, Babs. It was stupid of me, but I've wanted to kiss you for so long and I just couldn't help myself.'

She tilted her head, considering his reply. 'Well, you can try again now if you want. I promise I won't scream or run away. I'm quite ready.'

He stepped closer and gently brushed away a strand of hair from her cheek. 'That's the problem, sweetheart, can't you see?'

Puzzled, she shook her head. 'See what? You want to kiss me and I say you can. I can't see any problems there.'

'I shouldn't have to ask you, Babs. If you felt the same way about me you'd be here, right this minute, in my arms.'

She saw the sadness in his eyes as he spoke and finally understood. 'John! I never realised you felt like that. I thought we were just good friends. Why didn't you say something, do something, before this?'

'Would it have made any difference? I love you, Babs; you're only fond of me, and it's just not enough.'

She felt tears seeping from the corners of her eyes and brushed them aside angrily. 'I could learn to love you, John. What am I talking about? I do love you; in fact, I love you more than any other living soul. Surely that's enough?'

He rubbed away her tears with his thumbs. 'No, darling, it isn't. I'm in love with you. That's quite different and I wouldn't dream of forcing you into a relationship you're not ready for.'

She ducked her head and sniffed, recognising that she was losing her dearest friend and didn't know how to prevent it. What did he want from her? She loved him; she could learn to love his kisses if it meant she wouldn't lose him. She came to a decision.

Allowing no time for him to retreat, or for herself to change her mind, she jumped forward, flinging her arms around his neck. His arms shot out, gripping her waist, more to steady himself than to reciprocate her gesture. But she tipped her face to receive his kiss. She stared at him and he couldn't resist her appeal.

* * *

John covered her mouth with his own and this time she didn't shy away. To his delight she pressed closer and shyly moved her lips against his. He felt his groin tighten and a surge of heat coloured his cheeks. Had he been mistaken? Did she return his love and it was only her inexperience that had caused her reaction?

He tightened his hold, revelling in her softness, the feel of her breasts against his chest. He ran the tip of his tongue across her lips, hoping she might open them and allow him access. Instead she stiffened and he knew he'd frightened her. Reluctantly he drew back, relaxing his hold on her arms. He scanned her face, searching for signs of distress.

She gazed back, her mouth slightly swollen, her eyes glittering with emotion. Then she smiled and his heart turned over. God! How he loved this girl – he would gladly die for her. A flicker of fear ran through him as he realised he might very well have to.

'Darling, tell me, was that better? I didn't scare you this time?'

'It was lovely, John. I think I'm getting the hang of this kissing lark. Do we have the time to do it again?'

His laugh ricocheted round the chilly room. 'Idiot girl! We have the rest of our lives to perfect the art.' His face sobered and impulsively he dropped to one knee. 'Babs, I love you, say you will be my girl. Marry me when all this is over?'

'Marry you? You mean get engaged before you leave? But don't you have to ask my mother and stepfather's permission or something?'

This wasn't quite the answer he'd been hoping for, but then Babs was ever the practical one, not a romantic bone in her body. 'I don't think I have time to see them before I go, but I promise I'll write to Mr Evans and ask him formally. You still haven't answered my question: will you agree to marry me, be my fiancée?'

She didn't answer and he felt his happiness slipping away. His throat constricted and he scrambled awkwardly to his feet, keeping his head down to cover his distress. 'Doesn't matter, Babs, it's silly idea. Ignore me, I got carried away.'

'I will get engaged to you, of course I will. It wasn't that I was worrying about. I really must get away from here. Will being engaged mean I can't join the Land Army and that I have to stay at home and join the WVS? I'm worried they might change their minds about letting me join up.'

Relief flooded through him. He should have realised how important getting away from her unloving parents was. 'Then we won't mention it to them, but I'd like to tell my parents, if you don't mind? They'll keep our secret, don't worry.'

'We must go and give them the good news, but kiss me again. It might be months before we see each other like this.'

He opened his arms and she walked in. For a blissful five minutes he taught her how to open her mouth, how to deepen the kiss, get even more pleasure from it. Neither heard the first knock. It was not until it was repeated a third time that John looked up.

'Darling, that's enough. I think Mum and Dad are reminding us I have to leave and I still haven't eaten my lunch.'

Her face crumpled. 'Not yet. It can't be time already?'

'It's nearly two o'clock and my train leaves at quarter past three.' He pulled her close, keeping his left arm tight around her waist before he gave permission for his parents to enter. 'Come in, Mum and Dad. We have something to tell you.'

* * *

John refused to allow anyone to accompany him to the station; instead Barbara was forced to watch him drive away whilst blinking back her tears.

'Come inside, Babs dear, we need another cuppa. I can't say how pleased Bill and I are about your news. I know you're still young, but there's not going to be a wedding for a while, is there?'

Barbara wiped her eyes. 'No, we've opted to wait until the war's over. Hopefully it won't last more than a year.'

'I should hope not, and that devil Hitler needs shooting; maybe someone will do it for us before too many of our boys are killed.'

Barbara sat down, not sure how she felt. She had been denying for so long that she felt anything other than affection; now she couldn't understand how she found herself engaged to him. Her mother would have a field day if she found out. The wedding would be planned, the dress bought, before there was time to breathe.

Her lips curved as she remembered John's expression when she'd agreed to marry him. He'd almost glowed with happiness. Yes, she'd done the right thing. And returning his kisses hadn't been as hard as she'd expected; in fact, if she was honest, she'd quite enjoyed them. And it was a year or more before their engagement would become official and by then a lot could have happened. She might even have fallen in love with him and want to go ahead with the wedding after all.

She jumped as another mug of tea appeared in front of her. 'Right you are, love, drink up. You looked so sad just then. You mustn't worry – your John will come back safely.'

'I hope so. Do you mind if we don't talk about him any more? I'm finding it too hard.'

'Sure you are, my love. We didn't finish our chat about your mother, did we?' She sat down beside her. 'Are you going to ask about your grandparents when you get home?'

'I certainly am. If there's the remotest chance I have to stay at home to serve in the Land Army for the first year, I'm not going to risk it.'

'What will you say to her?'

'I've no idea. I'll have to see how she is first. I might just ask her outright. But what if she refuses to tell me anything? I don't know what I'll do then. And she'll want to know why I've not signed up yet.'

'Tell her you're sending off for the forms, that should keep her happy for a bit.'

A grandfather clock in the hall struck three times. 'I must get going – it'll be dark soon. I don't intend to gallop all the way back. Poor Silver would be horrified if I asked her to do it twice in one day. I have to get the boys' tea. I daren't be late for that.'

Old Tom helped her tack up and held the mare whilst she mounted. 'Take care, miss, there's a nasty fog coming in from the sea. You'd best go by the lanes, just in case.'

She looked across to the south and could see nothing but greyness. 'Good grief, that's come up quickly. Thanks for looking after Silver.'

There was too much time to think as she walked and trotted to Crabapple Cottage. She hated deceiving John. They had always been honest with each other, but she had no choice. She couldn't allow him to go away to fight, to risk his life in the air, believing the girl he loved didn't love him back.

All the posters said that everyone had to do their bit. It was her first contribution to the war effort, sending one pilot off to fight in a happy, positive frame of mind. If she had to marry John one day, would that be so bad? Loving someone was almost as good as being in love.

It was dark by the time she dismounted in the stable yard. The blackout regulations made untacking Silver difficult, but not impossible. However, it was five before she was washed and changed back into her slacks and jumper. She should have started cooking tea half an hour ago. She prayed her mother hadn't noticed the time and the boys hadn't reminded her.

She slipped in the back door hoping to get into the kitchen and start preparing the meal before she was discovered. In the dark she groped for the light switch. As she clicked it on her mother appeared at the kitchen door.

'Well, young lady, and where have you been all day? Hiding from me I expect.'

Barbara's mouth opened and closed. What was she talking about? Then she remembered the three ladies in the Copper Kettle and shrunk back against the door, bracing herself, whilst desperately searching for the doorknob, praying she would be able to open it.

Her mother, her narrow face twisted with hate, was approaching too fast. Barbara's fingers closed round the knob and she spun, pulling the door open. Too late. A vicious hand grabbed her hair and she was hauled backwards.

'You little slut! You're a disgrace, no better than your father.' These words were punctuated by a fusillade of open-handed slaps and punches. Barbara crouched on the floor, attempting, unsuccessfully, to ward off the blows.

'Mummy, Mummy, stop it, don't hurt Babs. Please don't hurt her any more.' Tom's scream echoed down the corridor and her mother's rage, as always, vanished as suddenly as it had come. 'Inside, Thomas, I'm coming now.' She turned and followed her son, switching off the light as she went into the kitchen, leaving Barbara alone in the dark, her head bowed, too hurt and angry to move.

3

Barbara straightened her legs, lifted her head and leant against the back door, breathing heavily. The cold from the linoleum seeped through her thin twill slacks and she shifted uncomfortably. Her face hurt; she feared one of her front teeth might be loose.

She ran her fingers across her mouth and flinched as they touched the split that ran from below her nose, across her lips and into the curve of her chin. It was blood in her mouth, not tears. The rings on her mother's right hand had caused the damage. The left side of her face was burning and her collar was sticky. She must have a second gash on her cheek.

She couldn't sit here. She had to get to her room somehow, lock herself in as she always did after one of these attacks, and wait until the cuts and bruises had healed. Once, when she was about ten, she had made the mistake of appearing too soon and her mother had responded by bending her over the kitchen table and beating her with a wooden spoon. She never made that mistake again.

Holding a folded handkerchief to her face in an attempt to stem the flow of blood, she pushed herself upright, pressing her back to the door and inching her feet inwards. Eventually standing, she began to edge her way along the pitch-black corridor. Never, ever put on a light – her mother might see it and come back out.

She negotiated the rear passageway and reached the entrance hall. All she had to do was find the strength to climb the stairs and she would be safe. The sound of a key entering the lock on the front door froze her, swaying, with her hand clutching the newel post for support. It was only five thirty. Her stepfather always came home at six o'clock; why had he chosen today to break his routine? He mustn't see her. This was between her mother and herself. He must not be involved.

Too late. The door opened and closed and Mr Evans switched on the hall light. His sharp intake of breath sounded far too loud in the silence. 'God! What has she done now?' Mr Evans dropped his briefcase; her mother would hear it in the kitchen. Frantically she hauled on the banisters, determined to get upstairs before it was too late.

'No, Barbara, not this time, not any more.' A firm arm encircled her waist and to her horror she was guided into his study. Mother mustn't find her in there. In the thirteen years she had lived in Crabapple Cottage, she had never dared to enter the study. It was forbidden.

She was given no choice; in she went. She heard the door click shut behind her. 'Sit down here. Close your eyes. Don't look so scared – you'll be safe here.' He gave her a gentle pat on the shoulder and her knees buckled; the seat of a comfortable armchair rushed up to meet her bottom.

Obediently she kept her eyes closed; perhaps if she could swear she hadn't seen anything in this room her mother wouldn't be so angry. She heard the sound of a key turning and realised her stepfather had locked her in. She shivered. He was going to fetch her, was making sure she couldn't escape. Maybe she could climb out of the window and go and hide in the stables – the only place she knew her mother wouldn't venture.

Her eyes opened and her jaw dropped. He hadn't been locking her in, but locking her attacker out.

'This is the last time I let this happen, Barbara. I give you my word.' He approached, holding an open first-aid tin. 'Now, let's see if I can sort this out.' She remained silent, wincing occasionally as he cleaned above and below her lips and her left cheek. 'I'm afraid these need a stitch or two, but none of us want to call out Dr Reynolds, do we?'

She moved her head fractionally, indicating her agreement. No one knew about this, not even John; it was the one thing she'd never told him. She knew it was her fault for not trying hard enough. She deserved to be punished for her behaviour. She was a very bad girl and bad girls got beaten.

Mr Evans placed a gauze pad over the gash on her cheek and held it in place with a bandage he wound diagonally, several times, around her head. She heard the faint clink of a safety pin being fastened.

'That will have to do. I think if I put a plaster across the other two cuts, it will do the trick. Your lips will heal themselves in a day or two.'

She heard him closing the tin and moving away. She tried to open her eyes but they were strangely heavy. Everything sounded far away. She was so tired; a little sleep would do her good. She was safe in here. She slipped into a semi-conscious state just as the study door rattled loudly. From a distance she heard a whispered exchange between her stepfather and mother. Was that her brothers crying as they were sent to bed supperless?

She woke several hours later stiff and cold and totally disorientated. Where was she? Why was her left eye covered up? She flinched as she touched her bandaged cheek and the memory came flooding back. The study – she was still in the forbidden room. Her right eye opened and she looked around. The small desk lamp had been left burning and gave just enough light for her to examine her surroundings.

She'd always imagined Mr Evans must have dark, dangerous secrets, hidden vices he wished to keep from prying childish eyes. But it was a room like any other. A plain wooden desk, a plain wooden chair behind it. Bookshelves lined the far wall, containing few books; she had more on her bedside table upstairs. A nondescript grey metal filing cabinet occupied the space beside the door. The chair she was sitting in was next to the fireplace, which held a small two-bar electric fire. It wasn't switched on.

What time was it? Why was it so quiet? Her stomach contracted as she imagined her mother's reaction when she discovered her. Barbara pushed down on the chair arms and managed to regain her feet. She waited a moment for her vision to clear before risking a step. She stumbled in the direction of the door, expecting it to fly open and her mother to burst into the room screaming invectives.

With clammy fingers she turned the knob. The hall was silent, the single bulb left burning. Unheard-of extravagance – everything about tonight was wrong. She needed to pee. In fact no sooner was the thought in her head than the urge became desperate. She doubted she had the strength to climb the stairs and reach the bathroom, her mother's pride and joy, before she disgraced herself.

She had no option. She flicked off the hall light and opened the front door, surprised it wasn't locked. She would go behind a bush; she was past caring about what anyone might think of such behaviour. The fog was so thick she knew she would be invisible to anyone standing a yard from her. The damp was seeping into her clothes; she had to go back inside before she caught a chill.

Although she was scarcely a couple of yards from the front door she couldn't see it. Which way was it? To her left or right? She couldn't remember because she'd come out in such a desperate rush. But the door had to be somewhere in front and not more than three yards away. She extended her hands and shuffled forwards, forgetting she had stepped sideways to avoid the mess she'd made.

The front entrance was flanked by brick pillars supporting a tiled porch roof and her outstretched hands went either side of the right-hand column and she walked straight into it. She was glad she'd not been travelling fast; she fingered her way around the bricks and was back at the front door. This was closed.

She'd left it slightly ajar. Could a draught have blown it shut? She pushed it hard but it didn't budge. Exhausted, she rested her uninjured cheek on the shiny blue paint, trying to decide what to do next. With an ear pressed close to the wood she could hear a soft whispering sound.

Unable to move, to breathe, she knew who was behind the door. Her mother waiting for her. She cringed against the porch, too cowed to speak, expecting her mother to emerge and the pain to start again. As she shivered in the blanketing darkness an unexpected image of John filled her mind, blotting out her fear. She could almost feel his strong arms around her waist, hear his rich baritone announcing his intention to marry her, to take care of her.

Something odd began to happen. Her back stiffened, her head came up and she was filled with a rage to match her mother's. After fifteen years of physical abuse she finally realised she could stop it. She was much taller than her mother, stronger, and tonight she would end it, one way or another. She stepped away from the support of the porch and moved stealthily forwards to stand close, almost touching the closed door. She wanted to be ready when it opened, to strike first, be the one to inflict damage this time.

An almost imperceptible sound told her it was opening. She tensed and clenched her fists. Then her mother whispered through the crack, her sibilant hiss making her meaning explicit although the words were indistinct. Barbara didn't need to understand the words. For a second she hesitated, years of fear holding her back, then breaking free, she threw her shoulder to the door.

Her weight shot the door backwards taking her mother with it, slamming her hard against the wall. She leant on it, trapping the gibbering woman, feeling empowered. 'Don't make a sound, Mother, you don't want anyone to know how bad you've been, do you?'

This was spoken quietly but her mother heard and stopped struggling. Now, roles reversed, for a second she wanted to make her parent suffer the way she had, wanted to seriously injure the woman crying pitifully behind the door.

She stepped back, releasing her prisoner, and watched, impassive as the woman slid ignominiously down the wall, her long fading blonde hair around her face, her flannel dressing gown hitched up exposing her bare legs. A heavy silence hung in the hallway. Was it over?

Then her mother catapulted to her feet taking Barbara by surprise, lashing out, her punch catching her on the shoulder sending her reeling backwards. Pain shot through her head as it hit the wall. She closed her eyes for a second. When she recovered she was alone. Where had her mother gone?

She stared up the empty staircase; it just wasn't possible to have got up the stairs so quickly. She must be somewhere downstairs. Was she waiting to renew her attack? Barbara's hands were clammy, her bravado trickling away as fear took hold. She must go upstairs and hide in her bedroom; naughty girls shouldn't be downstairs where they could be seen.

A gust of chilly air blew in and the front door banged against the wall. The noise shocked her out of her terror; she would not run away, not this time. Quickly closing the door she leant against it, steadying her breathing. Her heart hammered. Cold sweat trickled between her shoulder blades. What if that woman (she couldn't think of her as Mother any more) had taken a knife from the drawer and was waiting for her in the kitchen?

The longer she stood shivering here the harder it would be. She'd done it once; she could do it again. She swallowed hard and shoved herself forward to push open the study door. Not in here, so where? The front room, used only when there were visitors, was the other side of the hallway – she would check in there next.

As she reached out for the doorknob the hairs on her arms stood up. The door was ajar; her quarry must be inside. She rested her fingertips on the panel and pushed. Slowly the gap widened. The room was inky black – she couldn't remember where the light switch was. When she stepped in she would be clearly visible, giving her opponent the advantage.

Scarcely able to breathe, her mouth so dry she couldn't swallow, she moved back and flicked the hall light off. She must wait until her eyes became accustomed to the dark. Two steps and she was inside. She moved rapidly away from the entrance and pressed herself hard against the wall. Where was she? Barbara scanned the three-piece suite, the upright piano (never played), and across to the window.

Yes, there was a faint movement in the far corner; a crouched figure was edging towards her, something long and thin held in one outstretched hand. She thought her bladder would empty. That woman had the poker. If that made contact it would break a bone. Her knees began to tremble. She couldn't do this; she must get out before it was too late.

'I know you're there. I can hear you shivering in the corner. You've been bad – very, very bad. I'm going to teach you a lesson.'

From somewhere deep inside Barbara's rage returned. She wasn't going to let this person hurt her ever again. It would end now. She surged forward, shoulder first, and cannoned into her mother sending her flying backwards. She snatched up the poker and stood over the fallen woman.

'It's over. Get up; I have some questions I want answered.' Her mother remained seated. 'Now, get up or do I have to help you?' The threat in her voice was enough and the broken woman scrabbled to her feet. 'In the kitchen; it's warmer in there.'

Barbara waited until her mother had collapsed onto a chair before positioning herself in front of the stove. She propped the poker against the fireplace. 'I want to know where my father's parents live, who they are and why I never hear from them.' When there was no response she gripped the handle of a wooden spoon and lifted it casually. It was enough to prompt a torrent of explanation.

'I had to get married. Charles Sinclair got me into trouble. He thought himself in love with me and was happy to do the right thing.' She paused, her mouth twisted in a sneer. 'That didn't last. His parents disowned him; I wasn't good enough for them. They never knew about the baby. When it was born he doted on it. He had no time for me at all. He went off to his job in the city leaving me to deal with nappies and the continuous screaming.'

Barbara found it hard to grasp that she was the baby in the story. 'And then, what happened then?'

'He wanted to take the baby away, said I didn't look after it properly. He was going to give it to his parents to raise and leave me. I couldn't allow that. He was mine; he'd said so in his marriage vows. For the first time in my life I was living in a real house, not having to share, and had money to spare at the end of the week. I promised to try harder and make an effort to be a good wife and mother.'

She saw her mother smile and this time didn't prompt but waited for her to continue.

'I got on better with the baby as it grew up and could occupy itself, not demand my constant attention. Everything was so good; I was happy then. I believed he still loved me and then I discovered a receipt for a bracelet in his jacket pocket. My birthday was the next day and I knew he'd bought me a special present. I prepared a celebration dinner; the child went to bed early. I washed and put on my best frock.' She paused and her face contorted with grief.

'He didn't come home until late. The meal was ruined. We had a horrible row and he told me there was someone else. He'd given my bracelet to another woman. He said he'd only stayed with me because of the child, but now he knew I could look after her, be a proper mother, he was leaving me. He ran upstairs and when he came back with his things I begged him to stay but he laughed at me. I was so angry I ran at him and hit him across the head with a walking stick.' Mrs Evans wiped her eyes and stared at Barbara. 'It wasn't my fault. He should never have got on his motorbike if he was feeling dizzy.'

'That was the night he died? After you hit him?' Barbara's head spun at the implications. 'You killed him. It was you! And all these years you've been punishing me for your actions.' She stepped closer to her mother. 'You're despicable. I should report you to the authorities. If it wasn't for the boys I would do it. But I'm going to tell Mr Evans, let him know what a monster he's been married to all these years.'

'I know, Barbara. I'm ashamed to admit that I've always been aware of your mother's reprehensible behaviour toward you, but to my shame I didn't interfere.'

Her stepfather had come in unobserved by either of them. He walked over and put his arms around his wife, offering her comfort and support. How could he have known? How could any decent man allow a child to suffer as she had, and not step in?

'Please don't look at me like that, Barbara. I know I should have done something. But I did send you away to school; I did do that, and I bought you a pony, gave you a bolthole outside. I knew Doreen's fear of horses would prevent her from going down to the stables to find you.'

'Then you can make it up to me now. I want my birth certificate, and the address of my grandparents. I also need some money – enough to get by for at least a few months – a hundred pounds should be enough. Call it compensation if you like. You owe me that, after the way I've been treated over the years. Then I'll be gone from here. You'll never see or hear from me again.' Her chest constricted at the thought of abandoning her brothers, but she had no choice. She had to make a clean break, start a new life somewhere else.

Her cheek burned and her lips felt too large for her face but the pain steadied her, forced her to remain where she was, rigid and disdainful. She nearly relented as her stepfather helped the crying woman, aged beyond recognition, from her chair. No longer the fearsome person who until tonight had held her captive, too scared, too ashamed to ask for help. Always believing the mantra that accompanied every beating. *You're a bad, wicked girl. You deserve to be punished.*

Mr Evans nodded apologetically in her direction. 'I'll take Doreen up and put her back to bed and then I'll come back and find the things you want.'

He half walked, half carried the woman she had once called mother. From tonight she would consider herself an orphan. She disowned them both. Her stomach rumbled noisily, reminding her she hadn't eaten since the soup she'd shared at Brook Farm. Her vision misted as she thought about that haven, about John, whose love had given her the courage to fight back.

There were three eggs in the pantry and half a pint of milk. She would scramble the eggs. She thought she could mumble them down through her swollen lips. The milk she heated to make cocoa, adding three extravagant spoonfuls of sugar to the thick brown paste. She needed the energy.

She had finished her impromptu supper before Mr Evans returned. He held a faded foolscap envelope in his hand. 'It's everything that pertains to you. I never looked inside. It was not my business.'

'Like my beatings were none of your business?'

He shrugged. 'You aren't my child. How your mother chose to treat you was always her concern.'

What he meant was, that as another man's child, she'd always been outside his family parameters, tolerated because of her connection to his wife. Even sending her to an expensive boarding school, buying first the pony, and then Silver Lady, had been to prevent that woman getting into trouble, not to protect her, as he'd suggested earlier.

She took the envelope and undid the blue fastener. She flicked through the contents; there were several photographs, a birth and marriage certificate and some rings. She would look at these more closely later. She dropped it on the table. 'And the money?'

'I'll bring it back with me tomorrow night.'

'No, I don't want to spend another night here. I'm leaving this morning.' She paused, her head aching with the effort to concentrate. 'I'll come with you when you go. You can drive me to the station and I'll wait there until you bring me the cash. I don't want it all in five-pound notes – make sure at least half is in one-pound and ten-shilling notes.'

'Very well. Be outside at eight fifteen.' He didn't say goodnight, merely turned and walked out, his back rigid with dislike.

After so many years of abuse she could hardly believe it was over. She was free of both of them. If it hadn't been for John she would never have stood up for herself. Her eyes filled; the salty tears stung her injuries. How could she bear to leave her little brothers in the care of such monsters? Why hadn't she told John what was happening? Would he have known what do?

She glanced at the clock; it was almost one. There was plenty of time to pack and maybe get some sleep. She picked up the precious manila envelope and flicked off the lights. Mr Evans had left the passage in darkness but she adjusted quickly and found her way upstairs by the faint glow that escaped from under the door of the front bedroom, where they slept.

As she passed her brothers' room she stopped. Should she go in and say goodbye, try and explain why she had to go? She turned the knob and slipped inside, closing the door silently behind her.

'Tom, David, I need to speak to you.' She was tempted to switch on the central light, show them exactly what their mother had done to her, but something stopped her. She didn't want them to remember her like this. She edged her way over to Tom's bed, knowing it was at the far side, under the window. She felt along the pillow until she touched his warm face. Gently she shook his shoulder until he woke.

'What is it? Is that you, Babs?'

'Yes, I have to talk to you and David. I know it's the middle of the night, but I won't get another opportunity.'

Tom seemed to sense the urgency and threw back the blankets. 'I'll go over and fetch David; he can come in with me for a bit.'

She shifted down the bed to sit on the end, leaning against the wall, leaving room for the two boys. She heard Tom whispering to his younger brother and the slap of their feet on the lino as he led him back.

'Get in next to the wall, Dave; I'll go on the edge.' The bed heaved and jerked as they settled. They were waiting for her to speak, to explain her unexpected appearance. 'I'm so sorry, boys, but I'm leaving here forever. I'm going away to Essex to live with my grandparents. I know you understand why I have to go, don't you?'

She sensed them trying to make sense of her words, unravel the reasons behind the statement. David started to cry quietly but said nothing. Tom, his voice a miserable whisper, spoke for both of them. 'We know why. It's what happened tonight, isn't it?'

She felt more tears seeping into the bloodstained bandage on one side of her face and trickling down the other. 'It is, Tom. It can't go on. It will never stop as long as I'm living here. It's better for all of us if I'm somewhere else.'

'Please don't go, Babs. We love you.' There was a rustle and a bundle arrived on her lap and skinny arms clutched at her.

'David, darling, I have to go. But I promise I'll write to you at school. I'll find out where it is from Mrs Peterson and even come and see you when I can. I'm sure you'll be allowed a visit from your big sister occasionally.' She rubbed his shaking back, praying his sobbing wouldn't bring anyone in to investigate.

Tom joined his brother, dragging the blankets up around them all. 'Do you promise you'll come and see us and write to us every week? Cross your fingers, hope to die?'

'I do, Tom. It won't be easy, getting to Worcestershire from Essex, not with the war on, but I'll try my hardest, and you will definitely get letters every week.'

Tom snuggled up beside her and she wrapped her free arm around him. The boys fell asleep hugging her and she didn't have the heart to disentangle herself and return to her own room. She heard the cockerels crowing down the lane and knew she had barely an hour to pack and make the arrangements for Silver Lady to go and live at Brook Farm.

She removed David from her lap and carried him across to his own bed, then eased Tom away from the wall and back on to his pillow. She crept across the room and pulled aside the blackout curtains; pale light flooded in giving her one last glimpse of her little brothers. How could two such perfect children be the offspring of those two fiends? They were loving, kind, intelligent and funny – everything their parents were not. Could it have been her influence? No, more likely to be the fact that babies were born innocent and only learnt how to be bad.

She dropped the curtain, plunging the room into darkness. Being blinded by tears made no difference; the room was familiar. She knew the position of the door and reached it without mishap. She paused, listening. Everything was quiet, and no morning sounds of Mr Evans in the bathroom or her flapping about in the kitchen making his obligatory cooked breakfast.

Back in the safety of her room she pulled down two battered cases, the ones she had taken to Thistledown for almost seven years. Her old trunk was no doubt already on its way to the boys' new school, this time full of their uniforms. She opened the largest case, its leather scuffed and worn, but still serviceable. Working methodically, as she had been taught, she folded her slacks and shirts and rolled her blouses. She tucked underwear, socks and stockings into corners, leaving a large space in the middle for her precious books. Jane Austen, Dickens, Shakespeare's plays – she couldn't bear to leave these behind.

She closed the case, snapping the metal catches and buckling the two straps. She grasped the handle, intending to put it ready by the door, but she couldn't move it. Too many books. She'd have to redistribute the weight, put some in the second case. All this took time and it was almost seven before she was finished. The cases were heavy, but not impossible.

She took them downstairs, one at a time, making sure she didn't bang on the banisters. The front door had not been locked after her exit the previous night so that was one problem solved. The bolts made a horrendous noise and could have alerted the sleepers in the front bedroom.

She wasn't scared of seeing either of them, not any more, but she wanted to use the precious telephone and they would forbid it. She dropped the largest case and her canvas haversack by the car, then took the smaller down to the stables to collect her riding gear. She prayed that somehow she might one day be able to send for Silver.

The horse stamped impatiently inside her box, thinking it was time to be turned out, but Barbara ignored her entreaty. Saying goodbye to her mare would be almost as difficult as parting with the boys. She called out with false cheeriness. 'It's too early, sweetheart; someone will be down later to sort you out.'

The case bulged alarmingly with the addition of her jodhpurs, boots and riding mac and she hoped the leather straps would be sufficient to hold it together. Taking the second case she put it with the first. Indoors she could hear her stepfather in the bathroom and knew she had fifteen minutes, to the second, to make her call. She had to assume her mother was safely in the kitchen cooking breakfast. She was glad she had eaten all the eggs. Mr Evans would have to have porridge with water, which he disliked.

The telephone, the only one in the lane, stood proudly on a polished wooden table by the front door. She picked up the receiver and waited for the operator to respond. She could hear the phone ringing at Brook Farm. Auntie Irene hated it and only answered if Uncle Bill wasn't around.

'Hello?'

'Auntie Irene? It's me, Barbara.'

'Good heavens! Whatever's wrong, love?' She didn't need telling Barbara would only use the phone in an emergency.

'Can you send Old Tom over to collect Silver Lady this morning? I'm leaving here, for good. Going to live with my grandparents in Essex.'

'My, that's a bit sudden. Aren't you coming over to say goodbye, then?' The hurt in Auntie Irene's tone almost broke Barbara's heart.

She choked on her answer. 'I can't, I really can't. Mr Evans is taking me to the station this morning. I'll ring you as soon as I'm settled. Let you know where I am. Could you please tell John, when he contacts you?'

'Of course, Babs love. Did you have a frightful row over things last night? Is that why you're off like this?'

'Yes, something like that. I must go; I can hear him coming out of the bathroom. I love you, Auntie Irene, and give my love to Uncle Bill, and John, as well.'

'Take care; good luck, Babs dear. And don't worry about your little mare; she'll be happy enough with us.'

Barbara replaced the handset as quietly as she'd removed it and slipped outside to wait by the car. She kept her back to the house. Her life there was over. She didn't want to see it ever again.

4

The fog had drifted away inland, leaving a crisp clear morning. Her haversack rested on her right hip, the gas mask hung awkwardly around her neck and her two cases stood by her feet.

She patted the canvas bag, checking it still contained the documents she needed to travel. Her fingers ran round the edges of her newly acquired identity card, a fountain pen and writing pad and the bulky manila envelope. She'd also brought her school reports, photographs of the boys and two snaps of Silver Lady and Brook Farm. It was all there – nothing missing. Anything she left behind would be gone forever.

She wished she could run to Brook Farm but she couldn't do that; seeing her face as it was they would finally understand why she had been so unhappy. They'd be so incensed they'd feel obliged to do something about it. Then John would find out and she couldn't let that happen. She wouldn't allow anything to distract him from his job; she would never forgive herself if he crashed his plane because he was worrying about her. That woman had caused the death of Charles Sinclair; she was not going to be responsible, however indirectly, for doing the same to John.

She heard the front door open and close and slow footsteps approached along the gravel path. She almost turned to see who it was. He didn't sound like any man she knew.

Without a word Mr Evans unlocked the car and opened the back door. He got in the front and waited for her to jam her cases in the car and squeeze in beside them. The engine started first time and he reversed from the garage and drove away. She wanted to glance back, perhaps to see the boys waving from an upstairs window, but was convinced that, like Lot's wife, if she did, disaster would strike her. Perhaps not turning into a pillar of salt, but something equally awful.

The drive to the station was completed in silence. The car stopped outside. As it was a quarter past seven on Friday morning there were already a sprinkling of bowler-hatted travellers, furled umbrellas in one hand, briefcases in the other. She unfastened the door and backed out, taking her cases along with her. He didn't speak. She had to say something – what if he intended to abandon her here with no money?

'If you're not back with my money in thirty minutes I shall come down to the bank and explain to your staff and customers why I need it.'

His head slowly turned and she recoiled at the change the night had wrought. The confident man was gone and in his place was an old bespectacled facsimile, with tired watery eyes and a defeated slump to his shoulders.

Had her actions caused this? Had fighting back destroyed both her mother and her stepfather? She had not wanted to ruin his life, just escape from the prison of abuse she'd lived in for so long. He managed a half-smile.

'I'll be back as soon as I can. This is something I can get right. I won't let you down this time, Barbara.'

Burdened by the knowledge she had caused the disintegration of her brothers' parents, the excitement of the forthcoming journey evaporated. Aware of the curious and sympathetic glances she was receiving from fellow travellers, she headed for the privacy of the ladies' room.

Thankfully it was empty, not even any female service personnel returning from home leave. She dumped her cases in a corner and collapsed on the nearest wooden bench.

What about Tom and David? They couldn't fail to notice the change in their parents and they would know this was her fault and hate her for destroying their family. She wouldn't blame them. If she'd kept quiet for a while longer, not retaliated, everything could have stayed the same. She could have joined the Land Army and the boys would have gone away to school happy. Now all their lives were in chaos and she was to blame.

She dropped her head into her hands and let the tears flow. Salt stung her swollen lips and the makeshift bandage around her cheek was soon sodden. Lost in a misery of self-recrimination she didn't hear the waiting room door open.

'Here, Miss Sinclair, what's up? Don't cry like that, lass – you'll make yourself ill.' The vigilant stationmaster, Bert Adams, had come in to offer sympathy and tea. He believed she was distressed because her young man had gone and she was leaving home too. She was well known to him, having travelled back and forth to school for many years. Barbara flinched at his touch and looked up.

'Good Gawd! What's happened to your lovely face?' The horror and concern in Mr Adams's tone shook her out of her despair.

'I had a nasty fall from my mare – you know how it is, Mr Adams. I expect it looks a lot worse than it is.'

'I bloody well hope so, excusing my French, Miss Sinclair.' He didn't offer her the steaming cup of tea he'd brought, instead placing it on the mantelpiece above the empty grate. 'That dressing and your face needs attention, miss. I think it should be seen to before you leave here.'

She had not bought a ticket or enquired the time of the next train to London. 'I'm going to London, Mr Adams, to find my grandparents. Mr Evans is coming with my travelling money and then I can buy a ticket.'

'You'll not be going anywhere until the doc's seen to your face, miss. I can't allow you to travel like this. It would scare the other passengers.'

What did he mean? She had a split lip and a cut face; why should that scare anyone? She pushed herself up from the bench and turned to stare into the large mirror above the fireplace. A stranger stared back. Her mouth rounded and she swayed.

'Steady, miss, let me help you.'

'No, thank you, Mr Adams. I'm fine now. It was such a shock, seeing my face. I didn't realise how awful I looked.' Her lips were twice their normal size and the cuts above and below them livid and oozing blood from behind the plasters. The bandage that had been applied so carefully last night was dyed red from the gash beneath it.

Her hair had metamorphosed from brown curls to lank flatness and the rest of her face was deathly white. Her visible eye was bloodshot and wild-looking. No wonder Mr Adams had been startled. In spite of her injuries her mouth curved into a semblance of a smile.

'I do look a sight. I'm so sorry, Mr Adams. I should have checked before I left this morning. I don't want to make a fuss. I rather thought I'd go to hospital when I got to London. Perhaps you could put a clean bandage over this one, just for now?'

She saw him hesitate, assessing the situation. 'I'm not happy about this, I can tell you, Miss Sinclair; but if you're sure, and you promise to go straight to hospital when you arrive, I'll let you travel. The next train to London is in twenty minutes. Come with me now and I'll try to make you look more respectable.'

'What about my things?'

'Leave them. There's no one going to touch those cases. I get young George to bring them out. I'll put you in first class; you'll be comfortable in there. I take it it's a single you'll be wanting?'

She nodded. 'Yes. I'm not intending to come back. I'm starting a new life from today.'

The second brown envelope was delivered to Barbara as she sat gritting her teeth whilst Mr Adams applied a clean bandage over the top of the first and then gently cleaned up the rest of her face. She hastily pushed the parcel into her haversack, waving her thanks to young George.

'There, that's better – won't frighten the horses now, Miss Sinclair. You wait in here. I'll nip out and fetch your ticket. The train will be along in a few minutes.'

Barbara slid off the chair and looked around with interest. This was the third 'inner sanctum' she'd seen in the last twenty-four hours. Mrs Whiting's parlour, then the study and finally the stationmaster's office. All three had proved to be no more than ordinary; the air of mystery they had acquired over the years had been of her own making. She smiled, wincing as the action stretched her sore lips. Her fear vanished to be replaced by calm expectancy. Hopefully in a few days her unknown grandparents would be familiar and her father's home her own.

She could hear muted male voices outside on the platform; Mr Adams would be back with her ticket any minute. Hastily she delved into her bag, opening the second envelope. She withdrew two notes and pushed the rest back under her personal items. She could manage if her cases went missing, but not if she lost these precious mementos.

The stationmaster arrived with her ticket and took her money, giving her back so much change she must have been given a special rate. 'Wait in here, love – no need to stand out on the platform. Young George will put your cases on and make sure the guard fetches a porter for you when you arrive in London.' He gestured to her gas mask. 'Don't forget that, miss, never know when them Germans will start attacking us.'

'Thank you, Mr Adams. You're being so kind. I do appreciate it.'

Five minutes passed before she heard the distinctive chuffing of the train approaching. As instructed she remained hidden in the office until it was stationary and the doors were open. Then she hurried across the empty platform and into the first-class carriage. It always stopped by the stationmaster's office so he was on hand to answer questions. It wouldn't do for the wealthy passengers to be kept in ignorance a moment longer than was necessary.

She selected the 'ladies only' compartment and, like the waiting room, it was empty. Too early for the well-to-do to be going up to Town to shop. She'd never travelled in first class and ran her hand across the grey-blue uncut moquette seats, loving the velvety feel. She leant back, her head resting on a clean white antimacassar unsoiled by the residues left behind by previous travellers.

She stretched out her feet, luxuriating in the extra space between the seats. She pulled the armrests up and down, trying to decide if she was going to properly examine the contents of the envelope or stretch out and doze. The train would stop at all stations; it had to as there were not so many running. It might take more than three hours to reach London.

She ought to find out where her grandparents lived, have a destination in mind, but was strangely reluctant to do so. The last day had proved, if nothing else had, life did not always turn out in the way one expected.

At the moment she couldn't cope with bad news; she was still reeling from the discovery her actions had not only turned her own life upside down but also that of her brothers. She didn't need any more shocks today. She would get to London and find the hospital and get her face sorted out. One thing at a time. Then she would book into a small hotel and spend a few days in the capital.

She'd never visited London and there were galleries and museums, monuments and buildings all waiting for her to explore. She placed her haversack on the seat and swung her feet up to rest on it. This way no one could steal it and she wasn't getting marks on the seats with her shoes. The guard didn't disturb her to ask for her ticket. She guessed he already knew she had one, as Mr Adams had promised to talk to him on her behalf.

* * *

The train steamed into the station thirty minutes late which, according to the helpful porter who arrived to collect her cases, was excellent considering there was a war on. 'The taxi rank is this way, miss, but I can't promise there'll be one waiting. What with them being called up and all, most of the younger cabbies have gone.'

Barbara followed him, with some difficulty, as the platform was heaving with people all equally determined to get out of the station and off about their daily business. The start of hostilities didn't seem to have slowed anyone down. The porter led her through the brick archway and out into a side street. The noise, the smoke and smell of London made her chest feel tight and her head ache.

There was one taxi, a huge navy blue vehicle with what looked like a giant pram hood on the back. It had an empty space beside the driver, open to the road. It was here the porter pushed her cases. The driver leant over the internal half-door and checked they were secure before calling out. 'Where to, love? Hospital?' This was meant to be a joke.

'Yes, please, to Guy's.' This was where Mr Adams had suggested.

'Fair enough! Get in then – it'll not take long; it's not far from here.'

She pulled open the heavy door and climbed in. She sat on the long back seat but was tempted to try out one of the clever folding contraptions embedded in the partition between the driver and the passengers.

The cabbie slid open the glass window. 'Local doctor sent you up to see a specialist, did he, love?'

She nodded at the man's reflection. 'Something like that. As I was coming up anyway it seemed the sensible thing to do.'

The taxi lurched its way over the cobbles on to the main road. She sat back holding the leather strap by the door. The pavements were thronged with a mixture of middle-aged men in suits and various khaki-covered military personnel. She even spotted the occasional distinctive grey-blue of the RAF. Seeing so many servicemen and women brought home, as nothing else could, that England was indeed at war.

The windows of offices and shops were crisscrossed with brown tape in exactly the same way as the windows in Hastings. Whether such a rudimentary precaution would stop passers-by and occupants from being covered in glass remained to be seen. All pedestrians were carrying gas masks regardless of rank or status.

The taxi hooted loudly, the driver having to remove one hand from the steering wheel in order to squeeze the rubber bulb of the horn, as it turned into the ambulance entrance of the busy city hospital.

'There you are, love. That'll be one and six.' She scrambled out of the car and waited for him to come round and remove her cases. He remained firmly in his seat, his hand held out expectantly. The exact fare was dropped in his palm but the man frowned.

'That's the exact money, like you said, one and six pence.' The man continued to scowl at her and she quickly removed her cases. Holding one in each hand she stepped back to watch him drive away without another word. Why had he been so cross with her? She would have to find out the correct procedure before attempting another taxi ride.

She stood gazing into the sky at the silvery barrage balloons dancing above the houses. The autumn sunshine made them appear magical – it was hard to believe they had a far more sinister purpose. She shivered as she imagined enemy planes swooping in over London becoming entangled in the enormous inflatables. It hadn't happened so far, but it would. Morrison and Anderson shelters were being erected everywhere.

Three navy-cloaked nurses hurried past her reminding her why she'd come to the hospital. She guessed if she followed them they would lead her to the department she needed.

* * *

Dusk was falling when she emerged, three neat black stitches in her cheek, one above her lip and one below, all covered by small dressings. The doctor had given her spare ones and explained carefully how she was to clean her wounds. She was told to present herself at a first-aid point in six days' time to have the stitches removed.

She walked up and down several side streets before she found somewhere with a vacancy sign. She'd had no lunch and her one cup of tea had been too strong to drink. At last she saw what she was looking for and staggered up the steps into the small vestibule of a commercial hotel. The reception desk was deserted but she spotted a flat brass bell. She banged it and stepped back to wait. The door behind the counter opened and a friendly face appeared.

''Alf a mo, love, I've a pair of kippers cooking on the stove for me Frank's tea.' The head disappeared leaving behind her the distinctive whiff of fish. Barbara smiled. The landlady seemed friendly enough; in fact all the people she'd met so far, apart from the taxi driver, had been nice. Perhaps it was her injuries – everyone felt sorry for her.

There was no room for a chair in the tiny entrance hall so she perched on the edge of her largest case, leaning her back against the high wooden counter. She must have dozed off, for she didn't hear the woman return.

'Gawd help us! Whatever are you doing down there, duck?'

Barbara jolted awake then looked up to meet the smiling face of the landlady hanging over the edge of the counter. She grinned back. 'Sorry, it's been a long day. I do hope you have a room for me. I don't think I could manage to traipse anywhere else tonight.'

'Course I do. How long do you reckon on staying?'

'I'm sorry, I've no idea at the moment. It could be just for tonight; it could be for longer. I'm wondering if I should stay in town until I have the stitches out. I'm going to meet my grandparents for the first time.'

'Crikey! You'd scare them half to death the way you look at the moment. But I expect you'll feel better after a good night's sleep.' She came round to stand beside Barbara. 'Here, love, give them cases to me. I'll take them up for you. I'm Mrs Smith, by the way. I'll put you in a back room, first floor, nice and quiet.'

'Thank you, how kind.' She struggled up the narrow stairs scarcely aware of her surroundings.

'This is it.' Mrs Smith unlocked the door and switched on the light. 'Sorry it's so dark. I leave the blackouts drawn, then there's no danger of being caught out if someone arrives late.'

Barbara vaguely heard the information about the bathroom and WC, about the times for breakfast and what to do in the event of an air raid. She nodded and shook her head as required, and concentrated on staying upright. She was hungry and thirsty, but what she needed most was sleep. Kicking off her shoes, she dropped her coat and gas mask on the floor and, hugging her haversack, crawled in under the eiderdown, too tired to undress.

* * *

She slept for hours, like a corpse, in the large wooden bed. It was the sound of male voices, and footsteps in the corridor outside, that finally roused her. Groggily she sat up and, for a moment, didn't know where she was. A wave of panic washed over her and her lungs refused to work. Then her brain engaged and the tightness in her chest relaxed.

Of course, she was in a hotel room in London. London! She was on her own with a hundred pounds in the capital city of England. She could go shopping, buy whatever she wanted, go to the theatre, to one of the picture palaces to see a film; something she'd not even dreamt of doing two days ago.

She rolled out of bed. She needed to find the lavatory. She didn't stop to put her shoes back on, just opened the door and peered round. A passing soldier greeted her cheerfully.

'Mornin', love. The lav's the third door on the left. The bathroom's next to it.'

'Thank you.' Horrified at being seen in her socks, and by a strange man, she retreated, banging the door behind her. She slipped on her shoes, tucked in her blouse and pulled down her jumper.

There was nothing she could do about the creases in her slacks. They looked as if she'd slept in them. She giggled, not surprising as that was exactly what she had done. She would use the facilities and then worry about her clothes.

Twenty minutes later, washed and changed, she headed for the dining room. This was a breakfast room really, as one thing she did remember Mrs Smith saying was that they only served breakfast in this hotel. If she did stay, she would have to eat out for lunch and tea. It got dark at five o'clock so she'd have to make sure she was back before the blackout. She didn't relish the thought of trying to find her way through London at night.

The sound of rattling crockery and the appetising aroma of bacon led her to the downstairs room where breakfast was being served. The landlady greeted her like an old friend.

'Come in, love. I'll do you a couple of soft-boiled eggs. You'll not manage bacon with your mouth.'

Barbara smiled and looked round for an empty table. Even at six thirty the room was busy and there were no seats vacant. Nor were there any other females; she'd inadvertently chosen a business hotel that catered almost exclusively for men. No wonder Mrs Smith had been pleased to see her.

'Stop stuffing your face and budge up, Billy. Make room for Miss Sinclair.' The young soldier nodded, his mouth too full to speak, and obediently moved his plate and mug of tea along the table. 'Park yourself here, ducks. I'll fetch you a cuppa to be going on with.'

Barbara sat down, unsure how to behave. At Thistledown she'd been told gentlemen stood when a lady came in, that they carried her bags, opened doors for her, but so far she'd found the opposite to be true. Flustered, she kept her head down, not wanting to make eye contact with any of the men.

'Drink this, hot and sweet – it'll perk you up. I must say you look a darn sight better than you did last night.'

Gratefully she clasped both hands around the mug, glad to have something to do. The swelling had gone down by half but her lips were still tender. The tea was so strong it made her eyes water but Mrs Smith was right – the drink was beginning to make her feel better. She heard the chair next to hers scrape back and the young soldier shouted down the room.

'I'm off, Mrs Smith, got to be back by noon.'

'See you next time, Billy, TTFN.'

Barbara felt a light tap on her shoulder and glanced up. 'Take care of yourself, love. Stay away from the bastard what did that to you.'

She flushed scarlet and coughed into her mug. Good grief! Is that what everyone was thinking? That her boyfriend had beaten her? Then the knot in her stomach began to unwind; perhaps that was better than the truth? And it did give her a certain air of mystery and might stop strange men from pestering her.

Breakfast over she returned to her room. She could not put it off any longer. She had to discover exactly what information she'd been given about her father's family. The room had a small deal table and chair underneath the window. She drew back the blackout curtains and stretched up to undo the window catch. She grabbed the edge and it shot up, showering her with pigeon droppings, but at least it was open. She drew in a deep breath and coughed, horrified to discover the air in London was fume-laden and bore no resemblance to what she'd been breathing all her life. Hastily she slammed it shut. The sooner she got out of the city and back in the countryside the better.

She sat down and placed the envelope on the table. Which should she look at first? The certificates. She unfolded the first bit of flimsy paper and saw it was her own birth certificate. Her eyes flew to the column containing her father's details.

She put this to one side and carefully removed the next from its little sleeve. She was holding her own father's death certificate. She didn't want to read it, not yet. Her mother's appalling revelations were still too raw. She unfolded her parents' marriage certificate. Next to her father's name was the name of his father, Dr Edward Charles Sinclair.

She saw that the address given for her father was different to that on her birth certificate. It read: *The Grove, Broomhill, Ingatestone, Essex*. This was the address she needed; now all she had to do was find his telephone number.

Tomorrow she might have a family, others who shared her name, who didn't hate her, whose lives she hadn't destroyed. She stared at the entry again, etching it on her memory. Her elation shattered as reality took hold. It was more than nineteen years ago. Dr Edward Sinclair, her grandfather, could have moved away. She looked at the certificate again, and read the entry relating to her mother – Bertram Durham, agricultural labourer, deceased.

Deceased? If one grandfather had been dead nineteen years ago then it was possible Dr Sinclair was also. What would she do then? Where would she go? She sat numb for several minutes before common sense reasserted itself.

She took a deep breath. If she was alone, then she could please herself, join the WAFS as she'd wanted – become part of a women's unit, do her bit for the war effort. It would probably be quite like being back at boarding school but getting paid for being there.

She would go downstairs and ask Mrs Smith where the nearest post office was. There was usually a public call box close by. The operator would probably be able to find the number for 'The Grove'. The third certificate went back into its cardboard sleeve.

The letters were something else she didn't want to read right now. They could keep until she was feeling more sanguine about the circumstances of her father's death. She glanced at the photographs, intending to put those back too. But they were all of her father holding a smiling toddler. Her eyes filled and a lump lodged in her throat. This happy child was her, the young man her father. The resemblance was remarkable; both had a mop of curls and a mouthful of teeth, all of which were visible in their beaming smiles. How different her life would have been if her father had not died that night on his motorbike.

The landlady directed her to the nearest phone box and with a pile of pennies in front of her she picked up the heavy black receiver and dialled 100.

'Number please?'

'I don't have it. I do have the name and address. Is there someone who can find me a telephone number, please?'

'One moment please, I'm putting you through.'

Several minutes later and Barbara was in possession of the number she needed. She replaced the receiver and stood quietly for a moment, gathering herself. She gave it to the operator and waited for the clicks and whirrs to stop. She could hear ringing; someone picked up the receiver at the other end.

5

'The Grove. Dr Sinclair speaking.'

Barbara's well-rehearsed speech remained locked behind her teeth.

The operator spoke. 'You are now connected, caller.'

'Dr Sinclair, you don't know me, but my name is Barbara Sinclair. My father was Charles Edward Sinclair, deceased, and I believe that I am your granddaughter.' The words tumbled down the line to be received in total silence.

'Good God! Did I hear that correctly? You are Barbara Sinclair and your father was Charles Edward Sinclair?'

'Yes. You did. I'm eighteen, if that helps to confirm what I said. I'm sorry to spring it on you like this, but I couldn't think of any other way to tell you.'

Another long pause. 'Where are you ringing from, Barbara?'

'From a call box outside Borough High Street post office in London.' Was now the time to mention that she was hoping to come and live with them?

'Are you on your own?'

'Yes, I am. I rather wondered if I could come and see you, if it's not too much trouble?'

'I was about to suggest that you did so. Come at once. When I tell your grandmother she will be eager to meet you straightaway. Do you have enough to buy the rail ticket?'

'I do, thank you. I have plenty of money. I'll go back to my hotel and pack. I don't know when there's a train but I expect I'll arrive later today.'

'Get a bus to Liverpool Street and then buy a ticket to Ingatestone. There's a train leaves London around noon. Can you make that one, do you think?'

She checked her watch: almost three hours, more than enough time. 'I'm sure I can.'

'I'll be at the station to meet you. Goodbye, my dear.'

She almost skipped back to the hotel. She'd found her grandparents and they wanted to see her. In a few hours she would meet them, be living with people with whom she shared a name. She'd always hated being Sinclair, when the rest of Crabapple Cottage was called Evans, but now she was glad her name hadn't been changed by deed poll, that she hadn't been adopted. Dr and Mrs Sinclair were her natural guardians, as they would have been if her father had had his way all those years ago.

Mrs Smith was pleased for her, not upset at all about the loss of revenue. 'Never you mind, ducks; the room will soon go. I've got a good name in this part of town and being so convenient for Bridge Street Station means I get a lot of passing trade.'

The bus bumped and clattered, stopping and starting frequently, until the shout Barbara had been waiting for echoed down the bus. 'Next stop, Liverpool Street.'

She was forced to clutch at the handles on the back of the seats, bouncing and jolting her way to the platform. The conductor handed down her cases and the bus trundled off. The ticket office was busy and she had to go to the end of a long queue. An elderly lady in front smiled sympathetically.

The line shuffled forward, each passenger pushing their cases along with their knees, or bending down every few minutes to pick them up. By the time she arrived at the window she was worn out.

'A first-class single to Ingatestone, please. Is there a ladies' compartment in first class?'

'Yes, miss, always is.' She handed over the exact money and slipped the small rectangle of green card into her pocket. There was more than twenty minutes to find the correct platform.

This time her porter had a trolley and travelled more slowly through the station than on her arrival the previous day. The noise of the engines letting off steam, the whistles and shouts of the guards, the clanking and banging of metal against buffers, made conversation impossible. The porter stopped by a smart green carriage and opened the door, vanishing inside with her luggage.

She followed him down the narrow corridor until he halted outside a compartment.

'Right you are, miss, looks like you'll be in here all by yourself today.' The young man slid open the door and hefted her cases inside. 'I could put them up for you, but I doubt you'd get them down again. I'll leave them under the window; they'll not be in the way down there.'

This time she was ready with her tip, dropping a three-penny bit into his eager hand. 'Ta, miss. It leaves in five minutes.'

The compartment was identical to one she'd travelled up in from Hastings, but today she didn't feel like an orphan thrust out into the cold. Today she had a destination and loving relatives waiting to greet her when she arrived.

The train left a few minutes late. She peered out of the window as it steamed between tall, grimy brick walls and squashed terraced houses. Soon there were small farms, green fields and villages, but it was all very flat, not the rolling hills she was used to. However, this was still the country, no smoke or fumes, no smog or fog, just fresh clean country air. She smiled, flinching as the movement pulled her stitches, as long as you liked the smell of fresh manure, of course.

More than an hour later the train began to brake. She slid open the compartment door. Grabbing her cases and checking her haversack and gas mask were secure around her neck, she wobbled her way down to the exit. There was no handle of the inside, but she was an expert at opening the window. She'd unhooked the leather strap that held it, then lowered it so she could lean out and turn the handle on the outside, so many times she'd lost count. It was a knack, and several times she'd seen an unwary traveller swing out with the door, feet dangling dangerously over the gap.

The guard didn't shout out the station name and she prayed she'd not miscounted and was clambering out at the wrong place. She scanned the platform expecting her grandfather to have purchased a ticket and be waiting to greet her. Perhaps the steam from the engine was hiding him?

Outside there was no car, no Dr Sinclair, no one at all to meet her. Her stomach knotted. She must have got off at the wrong stop. She hadn't actually seen the sign with the station name on it. There was a woman coming towards her dragging a screaming child by the hand.

'Excuse me, is this Ingatestone station?'

The woman glanced up, uninterested. 'Well, it ain't anywhere else, more's the pity.'

Relieved, Barbara dropped her bags by the wall. She had only to wait; her grandfather would appear at any moment to collect her, all apologies and welcoming smiles and hugs. She closed her eyes, imagining the scene, feeling like the prodigal son, although she was the granddaughter, and she hadn't really wasted her inheritance.

She checked her watch every five minutes but the hands crawled round. Where was he? Had he changed his mind? Had an accident? Should she find a public phone box? After thirty minutes a small black car turned into the road. She'd stepped forward several times already, only to be disappointed when the car drove past. This time she remained where she was.

The car, a Ford Eight, front and back bumpers painted white, slowed down and a tall grey-haired man wound down the window. 'Barbara?' She nodded, too dispirited to answer. This is not how she'd imagined the meeting would go. 'Sorry I'm so late, got called out – Mrs Appleby's fourth, complications. Shove your things in the back and hop in, there's a good girl. Your grandmother doesn't like to keep lunch waiting.'

She did as she was asked but found there was no room for her to squeeze in beside her bags. She would have to get in beside him.

'Hurry up, my dear – you haven't time to dither. Remember we're expected.'

She ran around and Dr Sinclair leant over and undid the door. She climbed in and banged it closed. She supposed she should say something, explain why her face was disfigured, but was too miserable to bother. She turned her head away so he couldn't see her tears.

The fifteen-minute journey was completed in uneasy silence. She hardly noticed the pretty lanes they travelled down, but sat up as the car slowed and turned in through imposing wrought-iron gates on which the name 'The Grove' was inscribed. It travelled along a wide sweep of gravel and halted in front of a grand Georgian manor house.

She stared in awe. At that moment she grew up – forgot her childish imaginings of besotted grandparents waiting to greet her. She was no more welcome here than she had been at Crabapple Cottage. She was an embarrassment. Being the granddaughter of a farm labourer was more significant than her relationship to them.

She wished she could ask him to turn round and drive her back to the station. But she was entitled to know where she came from, to hear as much as she could about her father. He was the only person who had been pleased she was born.

She undid the door and got out, straightening her shoulders, staring proudly ahead. 'Thank you for inviting me to stay, Dr Sinclair. You can understand my wish to meet my father's parents, see where he grew up. But I will not impose on you for more than a few days. It is my intention to join the Land Army, or maybe the WAFS, and I can do it as well in Essex as anywhere else.' She was pleased her voice had remained steady.

'Land Army, is it? Well, no real harm in that, I suppose. But definitely not any of the services – not suitable and far too dangerous.' He smiled at her expression. 'Not one for sentiment, never have been, but it doesn't mean I don't care. I do. You've made an old man very happy today.' His voice was gruff, his brown eyes damp. 'Whatever Mrs Sinclair says to the contrary, this is your home. You're my only son's child and I'm not having you pushed out like he was.' He strode past, giving her left shoulder a quick squeeze, before opening the rear door and extracting her cases.

'This is lovely old house... err... sir.'

He chuckled. 'Call me Grandpa. I've always wanted to be a grandpa – eighteen years late – but not to worry. And you're quite right: I grew up here. My, or I should say our family go back hundreds of years. We share a common blood, my dear, and don't let anyone tell you differently.'

'I've never thought of that. I suppose children have more of a link to the past than they realise.'

'Bright girl! Well done. I can see we're going to get along famously.'

The handsome panelled front door was flanked by white stucco columns and a flight of marble steps ran down to the immaculate gravel. She could just imagine the carriages pulling up in front and an army of flunkies running out to usher the elegant ladies inside. She received a sharp prod in the back from one of the cases.

'No daydreaming, my girl, there's your grandmother to meet.'

Instead of heading for the steps he veered to the right, following the sweep of gravel under a wide, red-brick archway. She was to go in the servants' door – very appropriate, she felt little more than that at the moment with her grubby slacks, lank hair and battered face.

Obediently she trotted behind the man she was to start calling 'Grandpa'. She tried to judge his age. He could be anything from sixty – it was hard to tell. His skin was wrinkled and leathery as if he spent a lot of time outside, his hair grey, but he still had plenty of it. She looked more closely at the back of his head. Could she detect traces of wayward curls in his fierce crop? Auntie Irene had said she looked just like her father, and the photographs she'd found confirmed that. She would hate to resemble the absent Mrs Sinclair.

He dropped a case in order to open the boot room door. 'Barbara, we chuck our outdoor things, boots, and so on in here, before we go inside.'

She followed him in. This boot room bore no resemblance to the chaotic one at Brook Farm. It reminded her sharply of Crabapple Cottage: every coat hung to attention on its peg, each boot beside its brother.

The waxed and polished floorboards were uncarpeted and shone with the golden glow of years of loving attention. Grandfather didn't pause to hang up his battered tweed jacket or take off his shoes, so she didn't either.

They passed a variety of closed doors. She suspected they led to what would once have been a butler's pantry, and a housekeeper's parlour, linen cupboards and the like. He forged on, cases swinging on either side in his gnarled hands. If he was over sixty, he was jolly good for his age; those cases weighed a ton. The passage branched and he turned right, towards what was obviously the grand entrance hall.

Where was her grandmother? Why hadn't she appeared to welcome her? The sunlight poured down on to the black and white chequered floor from a stunning glass rotunda. She gazed up; she could see the sky arching above. This was like a stately home she had once visited with her school. Slowly she spun, trying to take it in, to understand that she was part of all this ancient magnificence.

A flight of stairs curled up either side of the hall, finishing in a wooden gallery carved with intricate animals and flowers. She gazed spellbound at the glass dome. 'What do you do about the blackout, Grandpa?'

'Good question, my dear. Damn nuisance. We have to use the back door now and keep all the lights turned off. I'm afraid you'll have to use a torch to get to bed every night.'

'Not candles? I should feel like a character from a Jane Austen novel if I used a candle.'

'Your grandmother wouldn't allow it. Candle grease is the very devil to remove, you know. Come along, I'll take you to your rooms. I expect you'll want to freshen up before lunch.'

She grinned. She looked a sight and was delighted to be given the chance to repair some of the damage before meeting the redoubtable Mrs Sinclair.

'I've put you in your father's room. I thought you'd like that. A lot of his stuff is still in there somewhere and you can have fun rummaging through it.'

'Thank you, Grandpa, that's perfect. I'll need a guide to find my way about this house. There are so many doors and passageways I'm bound to get lost.'

'Don't worry about it. You'll understand the layout soon enough. You're like your father: you won't let something as insignificant as an old house defeat you, will you?'

'No, you're right, I won't. I can hardly believe I'm here after so many years of praying and imagining.'

They had walked the width of the huge house before he stopped. 'Here we are. Open the door for me – these cases are bloody heavy.'

She giggled. That was three times her grandfather had sworn and she'd only known him an hour. She was going to love it here after all. She was a Sinclair by blood, like her father and grandfather, and she belonged at The Grove.

Light flooded the corridor as she pushed open the heavy door. The whole of the far wall seemed to be made from windows. She stepped in to stand in the centre of an enormous room, unable to speak, eyes wide, mouth hanging open. She heard the cases clatter to the floor.

'Like it, do you? I thought you would. Gets the full afternoon sun. Charles spent hours in here painting and sketching. He said the light was perfect.'

'He was an artist? I would love to draw and paint but I was... I was discouraged from doing so.' She shuddered, remembering the beating with a heavy slipper she'd received when she'd presented her mother with her first childish drawing.

'You'll never, never, never waste your time like this again.' Each word was accompanied by a vicious slap on her exposed bottom. She had never picked up a pencil to draw since then.

She heard her grandfather talking to her but couldn't quite catch the words. Then she felt an arm around her shoulders and she was pushed gently down on the bed.

'Put your head down, my dear; that's right, rest your elbows on your knees, get the blood back to your brain. The faintness will pass in a moment.'

The comforting hand remained between her shoulders and was then removed. She heard footsteps crossing the room and a door opening and closing.

'Here, child, take this, in case you vomit.'

A china bowl was slipped on to her lap. This was becoming a habit – too many memories – too many shocks. Her head cleared as she pushed the unwanted images back into the darkness with all the other horrors.

She sat up. 'I'm fine now, thank you, Grandpa. I've felt a bit light-headed since my accident a couple of days ago.'

'I expect you're a bit concussed. Excellent!' Startled, she looked up at him. 'If you're unwell you can hide up here for a day or two. Get your bearings before facing your interrogation.'

'Grandpa! Surely Mrs Sinclair is not as bad as that?'

He chuckled, unrepentant. 'My Elspeth could give Hitler a run for his money, my dear. A stickler for propriety, nothing left to chance...'

'No stone left unturned,' she added helpfully.

'Saucy minx! I knew we were going to get on. Now, get undressed, and have a hot bath. Fill it as high as you like.' He sounded almost boyish in his enthusiasm.

'I have my own bathroom, Grandpa?'

'You do, child, we all do. What we don't have is anyone to clean them for us. Well, we have a couple of daily women, and a cook, but they never have time to come up here. I hope you won't mind cleaning your own room.'

She shook her head and regretted it.

'I'll send Mrs Mullins up with a tray in half an hour. Make sure you're in bed by then. And try to look suitably pale. I'll be back to see you after lunch, say around three o'clock? We have a lot to talk about; I expect you have questions and I know I do.'

The door closed behind him, leaving her alone in a bedroom so large her old one could have fitted in four times over.

The huge claw-footed bath stood on a pedestal and was accessed by marble steps. When she saw the lavatory she could see why people called it a throne. This too required a step in order to access the seat. She peered inside and was fascinated to see it was decorated with blue flowers and a paisley-like pattern. The washbasin was big enough to bath a baby and this was also beautifully decorated with matching cobalt blue patterns.

She climbed the steps to examine the bath. She smiled nervously. Swimming was not one of her talents; in fact she hated the water and had never gone in the sea unless forced and then only up to her knees. She bent down to put in the plug, but couldn't find one. She searched everywhere, eventually accepting that its removal had been a deliberate act of spite on someone's part. But she was going to have a bath and fill it as high as she dared. The sink had a plug; all it required was a little ingenuity to detach it from the tap. It fitted perfectly.

She eyed the enormous geyser that dominated the far wall. If this was as old as the bath, would it explode when she put it on? She wondered if it had been used since her father's time. She stretched out and peeked inside the small hole at the front. Yes, the pilot light was burning. She turned on the hot water tap and jumped back down the steps to stand as far away as she could as the heater rumbled into action.

She needn't have worried: in less than fifteen minutes she had a piping hot bath with double the usual amount of water. Her dirty clothes were already tossed into the waiting linen basket and all she had to do was remove her dressing gown, a faded pink candlewick that was more than ready for the ragbag.

The long soak exhausted her and she was glad to climb onto the bed and await the arrival of her tray. A tray! Imagine that. The only time she'd ever had a meal brought to her on a tray was when she been in the san at school with measles and Matron had declared her too poorly to get up.

The door opened and a young woman in a floral wraparound apron, her hair tied up in a headscarf, appeared. 'I've your lunch here, Miss Sinclair. Madam says as you're not well you won't want to eat much so she's sent up some nice consommé.' Barbara's face fell; she was starving. The woman grinned. 'Cheer up, miss. I waited until she'd gone and then gave you a bit of everything they're having in the dining room as well.'

She smiled. She had another ally in the house. 'Do you mind putting it on the table by the window? I want to sit and look out whilst I eat.'

'Don't blame you. It's a grand view across the park. I'm Rosie Mullins, by the way. I live in the village. My husband Graham's volunteered, silly bugger, and he's in France, having the time of his life by all accounts, whilst I'm slaving away trying to make ends meet.'

'I'm so sorry to hear that. It must be such a worry having your husband away.'

'Not a bit! At least I'll not be having another baby next year.' She winked. 'He's only got to hang his blooming trousers over the bed and I'm in the family way.'

Barbara flushed, not used to such frankness. Rosie Mullins didn't notice. 'No, love, it's his wages I miss. He'd got a good steady job at the factory in Chelmsford. Made excellent money and now all I get is a few measly bob from the government. I still have the same three nippers to feed, don't I?'

'You do,' Barbara agreed. 'That looks lovely, Mrs Mullins. Please don't let me keep you; I don't want Mrs Sinclair to be cross.'

Rosie sniffed. 'Let her. It'll be her loss when I leave to work at Farley's – they pay good money down there.'

Barbara was left thinking about the implications of Rosie's last words. If the daily left then she would have to stay and help her grandmother in the house and might not be able to join the Land Army.

6

Barbara pulled out the chair and sat down facing the middle window. There was an uninterrupted view of the park, which ended in a handsome stand of ancient oak trees. There was an ornamental lake with fountains, but they weren't playing. She sighed. Would she ever see them working? The previous war had lasted over four years. Was it possible this one could be as bad? She pushed the gloomy thought away – no, everyone said it would be over by Christmas. Obviously not this year, but, God willing, by Christmas 1940.

One sniff of the watery liquid in the bowl was enough. She pushed it away. There were thick slices of ham and creamy mashed potatoes, exactly what she fancied. Ten minutes later she abandoned any hope of eating the meat and was forced to settle for the potatoes. By crumbling it, she managed to eat some of the hard yellow cheese and fresh bread, but even that had to be cut into tiny pieces. The apple was impossible.

She pushed the tray away, disappointed, and still hungry. At this rate she would starve to death! She would ask her grandfather if the stitches should come out sooner than next Friday because without them pulling, she was sure she'd be able to eat normally. There was half an hour before Grandpa came to see her; time enough to explore her surroundings.

He'd said some of her father's things were still in here, but a cursory inspection had not revealed any. They had to be tucked away in a cupboard. The room was almost twice as long as it was wide but held remarkably little furniture. Apart from the huge wooden bed, and the table and chairs in front of the window, there was only a battered *chaise longue* marooned in the centre of a blue floral carpet.

Her bed was at the far end and the adjoining bathroom opened on the same wall. There had to be a dressing room with hanging space, and shelves for her clothes, as there were no wardrobes or chest of drawers visible. The high white plaster ceiling and four windows made the room appear light in spite of the dark wood panelling that ran from floor to ceiling.

She walked the length of the room, her slippered feet sinking into the deep velvety pile of the rug. At the end opposite her bed she found a door cleverly concealed in the wall. The missing dressing room, but not empty – it was crammed full of boxes, books and canvases, hardly room for her to hang even her meagre wardrobe. She didn't care. She'd found her father's things. She didn't hear her grandfather until he coughed politely in the doorway. She looked up with shining eyes.

'Grandpa, look at all this. I can't believe it. There's stuff my father had from when he was a little boy right up to when he must have left home.'

'I didn't realise there was so much. Shall we move some of it up to the far end, find a bit of space for your things?'

'I'm happy to live out of a suitcase for the moment.'

'I'm sure you are, my dear, but I think it wise if you hang everything up.'

Her pleasure faded at the reminder that even in paradise there had to be a snake. 'I don't have very much.' He raised his eyebrows quizzically. She grinned. 'The cases are mostly full of books and my riding gear. I left my school uniform behind. Apart from the slacks I was wearing when I arrived, I have precisely three skirts, three jumpers, four blouses and underwear.'

'Good God! No evening wear? No smart frocks or afternoon tea dresses?'

''Fraid not! I won't need them as a land girl, will I? They supply a uniform.'

'We have to talk about that, my dear. Shall we leave all this until later?'

She was tempted to insist she needed to hang up her clothes before she could sit down and talk, dreading the inevitable questions about her life in Hastings.

'Shall we sit at the table? It's a splendid view, don't you think?'

'I do. I see why my father loved it. But why did he leave all his things, and most of his clothes behind?'

He didn't answer, but pulled out a chair and sat, his face sad. 'I suppose you have a right to know. He just missed being called up in the last war, by weeks. I think the relief was so great he went a little mad. Got in with the wrong crowd, with others of his age in a similar situation, and started staying out late, smoking and drinking. He'd always been such a well-behaved little boy, had gone to his prep school without a murmur, come home in the vacations happy and compliant. He was everything a parent could hope for.'

He paused and his expression changed. She was about to hear some unpleasant facts and braced herself. He sighed. 'I should have stood up to her. It was only a phase; I'm sure he would have settled down. He was still Charles underneath the temporary wildness.'

'What happened, Grandpa? Why did he leave? Was it my mother who caused the rift?'

'No, my dear. That came later. He was not much older than you, but he had a generous allowance from his trust fund, could afford to live where he liked. He moved to London, got a flat somewhere, and applied to go to art school. Elspeth was horrified. She doesn't approve of artists or actors or indeed anyone who doesn't conform to her standards.'

'Art school? How marvellous, but surely he didn't meet my mother at art school? She hates drawing.' Her stomach clenched.

'I think he met her at a dance hall. I imagine she, like other young people, went up to Town to celebrate the end of the war.'

'I see.' She couldn't imagine that woman dancing – she'd always seemed so staid. 'And then what happened?'

'He came down to see us, to tell us he had met someone, was intending to get married. When Elspeth discovered to whom, she gave him an ultimatum: your mother or us. If I had been there when it happened it would have ended quite differently. I would have put a stop to her nonsense.'

'He chose my mother and never came back here again?'

'That's right. I came back from the hospital to find my son had gone, no forwarding address, nothing.'

'But surely your solicitors could find him for you? Or the bank where his money was paid in?'

'Believe me I tried, but I left it too late. I thought it would blow over, waited weeks for the phone to ring, to get a letter, but when Christmas came and went without a word I finally understood I had lost the most precious person in my life. I went to the solicitors but he'd changed to another firm in London, and moved his account from the local bank as well. I went to the art school he'd been attending, but he'd left.'

'Did you never speak to him again?'

He wiped his eyes. 'No, never. Four years after he left we received a visit from the police telling us he'd been killed in a motorbike accident. At least he's home now, buried in the family tomb, in Ingatestone church.'

'Buried here? How can he be?' She couldn't bring herself to accept the implication.

'I'm sorry my dear, but your mother must have left when she heard Charles was dead. I arranged for his body to be brought here and organised his funeral.'

She was transported back to that first train journey, the click-clacking of the wheels, the cases and boxes piled on the seats and her mother crying in the corner. She had been ignored until she wet her pants and was soundly smacked for doing so. Her hands flew up to cover her mouth as her lunch threatened to return. The spanking on the train had been the start. Her mother had been running away from possible retribution; that's why she had not wanted to arrange a funeral for her husband.

'How sad. She must have been so grief-stricken she couldn't face it. She sent the police here, knowing that you and Mrs Sinclair would want to arrange things. Think how awful it would have been for all of you if she'd been there.'

'True, but I would have known about you, not missed eighteen years of your life.'

'Well, I'm here now, and I'll never lose touch wherever I'm sent in the future. You're my family.'

He stretched out and patted her hand. 'Good girl. It's incredible to think we didn't even know Charles had actually married your mother.'

'Did his trust fund die with him, Grandpa?'

'Ha! I hadn't taken you for a mercenary girl.' He chuckled at her horrified expression. 'Only teasing, my dear. You're right to ask. If I'd known about you, you would have received the money every month as he did. It's your heritage.'

'And now?'

'The fund was frozen. It became part of my estate but I can't touch it. But now, we can reactivate it. You're going to be a wealthy young woman, my dear.'

'I don't want it, Grandpa. That's not why I asked. In fact, I don't know what made me.'

'Whether you want it or not, my girl, it's legally yours. It paid Charles a little over thirty guineas a week. I expect it will be double that with all the interest accrued over the years.'

'That's a fortune! What would I do with so much?'

'Buy yourself a new dressing gown for a start.'

She glanced down. 'I know this is a bit tatty, but I don't really bother about things like that. As long as I'm warm and dry, I'm happy.'

'Good grief! Don't let your grandmother hear that. Appearance is everything in her circle.' He paused, his stare penetrating. 'About appearances, your dressings need changing. Did they give you any spare at the hospital?'

She nodded. 'My haversack, I'll get them.'

'I'll wash my hands whilst you do.'

She sat rigid as he peeled away the gauze pads, his hands gentle, his manner professional.

'Excellent. Whoever did this knew his job. I doubt they'll leave much of a scar. No sign of infection. I can take the sutures out in the middle of next week.' He deftly dressed her injuries, not speaking again until he'd finished. 'Now, tell me, who did this, my dear?' She opened her mouth to deny she'd been hit, but he forestalled her. 'No, don't lie to me. I've been a doctor long enough to recognise a blow when I see it.'

She hung her head, too ashamed to admit it was her own mother. He patted her shoulder.

'Boyfriend? I thought as much. I wondered why you'd suddenly decided to look us up.' He didn't give her time to deny or agree, just assumed he was correct. 'Good move, my girl, he'll not find you here.' His voice changed to a neutral tone. 'Any chance you're pregnant?'

She almost choked. 'No there is not! I don't believe in that sort of thing.'

'Don't take offence, my dear. I had to know. Would have made no difference to me, but it's a relief; too many bastards about already, and not all of them born that way.'

She preferred he thought this than probed until he got to the truth. She tried to swallow her yawn.

'That's enough for today, young lady. You need to sleep. Give your body and brain time to recuperate.'

'But my unpacking? My boots are in with all my clean clothes.'

'Bugger the boots, I say. We'll all go to Brentwood once you're fully recovered and get you kitted out. There's nothing Elspeth likes better than spending money on clothes. When I tell her she can buy herself a new outfit at the same time, she'll be your friend for life.'

'I've my own money, Grandpa. Mr Evans gave me a hundred pounds when I left.'

'Did he by God? Severance payment, was it?' She smiled weakly, unable to deny it. 'Where is it, child?' She pointed to the haversack slung carelessly on the floor under the table. 'You can't leave money like that lying around. Give it to me; I'll put it in the safe in my study.'

He walked over and scooped up the bag one-handed, surprisingly agile for man of his years. 'Shall I shove the whole thing in? Or do you need anything out of it today?'

'No, put it all in, if you don't mind, Grandpa. How old are you, if you don't mind me asking?'

'I'm sixty-eight on January the seventh, my dear, and Elspeth is sixty-three sometime in April. I forget when. She always reminds me so I don't need to know the date. When's your nineteenth birthday, my dear?'

'Do you know, I'm not certain, but it's definitely in March sometime. It's on my birth certificate. I'll have a look now, if you want to know.'

He frowned. 'Never made much of a fuss of you on your anniversary then?'

'At school they used to sing "happy birthday" when it fell in term time. But I always got presents at Christmas, so I didn't miss out – not really.'

'Get some sleep, my dear; I'll look in on you at dinnertime and if you're awake I'll bring something up. We usually have soup to start; you should be able to manage some of that I daresay.'

She giggled. 'Not if it's like the gruel I got at lunchtime. I'd rather go without.'

'That bad? Mrs Brown does her best, but she's not a real chef. We had a chap, a Frenchman, but he shot off when the war started.'

'Never mind. I'm a good cook. I can do it for you if you like, until I join up, that is.'

'We'll discuss it tomorrow; settle down and try and rest. I'm going to close the shutters and draw the blackout curtains. Then if you want to switch on the lights when you wake up you won't get a rocket from the ARP warden.'

'Thank you. I've got my torch under the pillow so I won't have to use any of your electricity.'

She heard the rattle of the wooden shutters as they closed, then the soft rustle of the heavy damask curtains and the room settled into comfortable darkness.

'You want me to shine my torch for you, Grandpa?'

He laughed. 'No, I've excellent night vision. I can see well enough, thank you.'

The linen sheets smelt of lavender and her pillows were the softest she'd ever slept on. She began to drift off into that twilight zone, halfway between consciousness and sleep, feeling safe and wanted for the first time in her life.

* * *

The swish of the curtains and the clatter of the shutters woke her. She screwed up her eyes as sunlight flooded in. 'What time is it, Mrs Mullins? I feel as if I've slept for hours.'

Rosie grinned, showing a gappy smile. 'It's almost coffee time, miss. You've been asleep the best part of a day, I reckon.'

Barbara shot up. 'Am I in trouble? Are they angry with me?'

'No, 'course not. Dr Sinclair's out on his rounds. He told me to bring you some breakfast. He says he'll pop in when he gets back, around one o'clock, he reckons.'

'And Mrs Sinclair?'

'Madam? She's out – gone to a meeting in Brentwood. A right load of nosy parkers most of them are, I can tell you. I can't stop for a chat now; I've got a list as long as your arm to get through before she comes back. Ta for now.'

The door closed, leaving her in welcome silence. Rosie seemed a friendly sort but was rather too talkative. She knew more about her family life after two meetings than she did about people she'd known for years.

The tray on the table contained two freshly boiled eggs and bread-and-butter soldiers. A steaming cup of tea rested beside them and under a linen cloth she discovered freshly baked scones, butter and strawberry jam. She smiled; her breakfast had not been organised by her grandmother.

She devoured the eggs and two scones before she was full. Grandpa must be a very fussy eater if he thought Mrs Brown a poor cook. Her baking was delicious and the jam too.

Her cases were still leaning drunkenly against the *chaise longue*. High time she unpacked. Leaving a case unattended overnight was something she had never dared to do before.

She found a corner of the dressing room to hang her few garments and some shelves to stack her other things. The job was accomplished in fifteen minutes, leaving her an hour and a half to spend rummaging through her father's possessions.

* * *

Barbara remained upstairs in her bedroom and still her grandmother made no effort to come up to meet her. She was relieved, rather than offended. She checked the clock on the mantelshelf; her lunch should be up at any minute. Isolated as she was, she'd begun to relish her conversations with the vivacious Mrs Mullins; no longer finding the torrent of words overwhelming or embarrassing, but entertaining.

She had the door open before Rosie could knock.

'Here we are, love. I'm to tell you it's "vegetable potage and quiche".' She plonked the tray on the table and pulled up a chair. 'But why she can't call it soup and egg and bacon pie like the rest of us, I don't know. And here we have "dessert" not afters!'

Barbara had invited Rosie to stay the second morning and now this was a regular meeting. The tray was brought up with both her lunch and Rosie's sandwich and mug of tea on it.

'Mmm... smells good. I'm ravenous. I can't imagine why I'm so hungry as I'm having no exercise at all.'

'Stands to reason, cooped up in here – you're bored. I expect it's the same in prison, only meals to look forward to.'

'Well, this is a very luxurious prison, and I've plenty to do. I'm only halfway through sorting out the dressing room.'

Rosie glanced round the room. 'Looks a sight more homely in here now. What with the pictures on the walls and the books set out on that shelf.' They munched in unison for a while but it wasn't long before Rosie chipped in again. 'Your face looks better; aren't the stitches coming out this afternoon?'

'They are, thank heavens. Maybe I'll be able to eat something more solid after that.'

'You'll have to meet the dragon first. She'll put you off your food, I reckon, and you'll wish you were back up here.'

Barbara laughed, certain such uncomplimentary remarks were not acceptable coming from a member of staff, but she counted Rosie as a friend, her only one, and she wouldn't dream of mentioning it.

'I'm to come down at six o'clock for sherry in the drawing room.

Grandpa told me so this morning.' She giggled. 'I've no idea what sherry tastes like, but I hope it's nice because I'm going to have to drink it anyway.'

'Ask for the sweet one. The dry stuff's like vinegar, but the sweet's all right. I prefer a drop of port and lemon when I go out.'

Rosie pushed over the second mug of tea; she'd dispensed with cups and saucers after the first trip. 'What are you going to wear? They change for dinner. I had to wait on table a while back; a load of toffs came. The ladies wore long dresses and you should have seen the sparklers on them, and the men looked like ruddy penguins in white bibs and dicky bows.'

'I've nothing like that. All I've got is my best skirt and blouse and one pair of stockings. But even with stockings I still look like a child.'

'Well, let's have a deco then. I'll help you decide, shall I?'

'There's not much to choose from, but yes, please come and look.' She led the way into the dressing room where her six garments hung lonely on the rail.

'Crikey is that all? I've got more things in my wardrobe. You can't go down in any of those; that's for sure.'

'I'll just say I'm unwell and put it off for another day.'

'No, don't do that. What time is the doc coming back?'

'He's at the hospital all day. I won't see him until five o'clock when he's coming to take out my stitches.'

'Righty-ho! It's just after one thirty. If I knock off a bit early, we've time to nip in to Brentwood and buy you something.'

'All my money is in the safe downstairs.'

'Mrs Sinclair has an account at Rosebery's. You could get it on tick, put it in her name.'

'I couldn't do that – it would be like stealing. How much would a suitable dress cost, do you think?'

'I dunno – 'bout a pound. It's not cheap in that place.'

Barbara thought. 'I think I have some loose change in my coat pockets; there might be about that. I'll go and fetch it.' She searched through the pockets and came up with a ten-shilling note, two half-crowns and an assortment of coppers. Rosie counted it.

'Eighteen shillings and sixpence. Not enough for Rosebery's, but there's a nice place I go to – you'd get something smart for half that in there.'

'Is Brentwood far from here? Will we be able to walk or do we have to catch a bus?'

'We can cycle. It'll take us half an hour, I reckon. The doctor has an old one in the shed you can use and I've got me own. I come on it every day. You get dressed, and I'll get these dirty plates sorted. Come down when you're ready. There's no one here; it's Cook's afternoon off.'

Twenty minutes later the two were outside the back door. Barbara eyed the enormous, ramshackle old bicycle. 'It's huge, and it's got a crossbar. I'll never get on in this skirt.'

Rosie looked from one to the other, assessing. 'Nip up and put on your slacks. I'll find you a couple of bicycle clips.'

A further ten minutes passed before she was wobbling unsteadily down the drive beside her friend, the loose gravel shifting under the wheels and threatening to pitch her over the handlebars at any second.

Rosie could hardly steer for laughing. 'Once we get in the lane it'll be easier, but I hope we don't meet anyone. You're a danger to yourself and others on that thing.'

It was easier in the lane and she began to relax. It was almost a week since she'd been outside and she gulped in the crisp autumnal air with pleasure. 'I'll be fine as long as I don't have to stop in a hurry. My feet hardly reach the pedals, let alone the ground. I wish we'd put the saddle down before we set off.'

They bowled through Ingatestone – it was early closing day, so the village was deserted – and began the four-mile pedal to Brentwood. 'I've got the hang of this old jalopy. We can go a bit faster if you like.'

Rosie laughed. 'I've got to be back to collect the kids from their nan's at four o'clock and it's after two o'clock now, so I'm game. Are you sure you're not going to fall off?'

'Never. I'm safe as houses. It's all a matter of balance.'

Recklessly she removed her hand from the handlebar to push her hair out of her mouth just as a car roared round the corner. Rosie swerved into the hedge and vanished in a flurry of legs and arms but Barbara, already unbalanced, rode straight into it.

7

'I say – are you all right?'

Barbara, flat on her back on the ground, gasping for breath, thought this was a particularly stupid question. She glared at the speaker, a young man with laughing blue eyes and heavily Brylcreemed brown hair. He flushed under her scrutiny and his hopeful smile faded.

'I'm most awfully sorry. I was going too fast, but I'm in a frightful hurry you know; should have been in Chelmsford half an hour ago.'

She pushed herself up to her elbows, relieved to have suffered no further damage in her fall. She looked round for her companion. Neither the bike nor the rider were visible, but a large hole in the hedge gave her a good idea where she was.

'Don't stand there gawping at me. Go and help Mrs Mullins; she might be injured. I am obviously not.'

'My word, yes, quite right. The other lady. Good heavens, yes, where is she?' The young man vanished through the gap in the foliage.

The man was an imbecile. Using the bonnet of the car for support she heaved herself upright and flexed her legs and bent her arms; apart from being a bit sore, she was fine. Such a shame about Grandpa's bicycle.

From the other side of the hedge Rosie was telling the driver what she thought of him. 'Bloody hell! Look at my bike – it's all bent. I'm not going be able to use this to get to work.' Rosie wasn't happy. 'Get out of my way, you blithering idiot. This is all your fault. What were you thinking of, driving so fast in this lane?'

'Rosie, are you hurt? I'm a bit shaken, but that's all.'

The leaves shook and her friend appeared with a mud-streaked face but a cheerful grin.

'What a palaver! That's our trip to Brentwood finished.' She ignored the young man.

'Not to worry, I'll go down in my best skirt tonight. It can't be helped.' Barbara kicked the twisted front wheel of the old bike. 'Goodness knows how we're going to get these home. This one won't even wheel.'

'Excuse me, ladies, but I'll drive you home. The bikes can go in the field and I'll arrange for someone to collect them and have them repaired.'

Rosie winked at Barbara. 'More to the point, you can drive us to Brentwood and back; that's the least you can do, Mr Farley, after almost killing Miss Sinclair and me.'

'Brentwood?' He looked confused. 'I thought you would live locally.'

'We do. Miss Sinclair lives at The Grove, I live in Ingatestone, but we were on our way to Brentwood when your bad driving put a stop to it.'

Barbara took pity on him. He was rather sweet, in a hangdog sort of way. 'Please, don't worry; it's not important. I believe you said you had an urgent appointment? We can walk home. But we would be grateful if you could repair and return the bicycles to us.' She smiled. 'You see, Mrs Mullins will have difficulty getting to work without hers, and I borrowed mine from my grandfather, Dr Sinclair, without his permission.'

'Oh, I say! How dreadful! I don't want to cause any more trouble.' He grinned and offered his right hand. 'Simon Farley, delighted to meet you, Miss Sinclair.'

'Barbara Sinclair, and I still haven't quite decided.'

Rosie laughed as Simon's brow crinkled in bewilderment.

'I haven't decided if I'm pleased to meet you, or not, Simon.'

'Oh, jolly amusing, what!' Pleased he understood, he beamed. 'Come on, I'll give you a ride into Brentwood and I'll hang around and bring you back. The least I can do.'

'What about your appointment in Chelmsford?'

'Too bally late for that, Miss Sinclair. I'll tell my father what happened and I expect he'll be pleased I've done the right thing for once.'

'In that case, thank you. What about it, Rosie? We'll be there and back far quicker in a car.'

'Why not? Here, Mr Farley, chuck Miss Sinclair's bicycle in the hedge with mine.'

The young man, eager to atone, grabbed it and almost ran across to throw it through the gap in the hedge.

'Well, if it wasn't broken before, it certainly will be now. Who is he, Rosie? Is he something to do with the factory you keep threatening to go and work in?'

'He is. Nice enough boy but right under his father's thumb. He's a bit deaf so they wouldn't take him when he volunteered, so he's got to stay put and work for his dad.'

He returned and hurried round to open the rear door of the car.

'Coo – very smart. I'll feel like a toff riding in here.'

He scrambled back into the driver seat, rattled, yanked and pushed buttons, but nothing happened. 'Just a tick; I'll turn her over with the handle.' After jumping out he galloped round the car, vanishing from sight for a moment to reappear with the starting handle. It took several turns before the car burst into life. Red-faced from his exertions, he grinned over his shoulder as they finally rolled away.

'Not to worry. We'll be in Brentwood in a few minutes. Where do you want to go?'

Rosie named the shop and he nodded. 'I know exactly where you mean.'

In less than thirty minutes Barbara had purchased her first afternoon-tea dress. It was navy linen, with elbow-length sleeves, a square neck and matching belt. This was perfect for her first appearance as a grown-up and she loved it.

'Navy blue's very smart, miss. That dress has only just come in; I doubt it would have still been there tomorrow.'

'I love it, Rosie. I'm not sure about the white spots all over it. They make me dizzy if I stare at them for too long.'

'I told you, it's all the rage. I'd love one like that, but it's too pricey for me. I was surprised they allowed you to owe them half a crown.'

'As soon as she saw us get out of this car she was falling over herself to open the door, didn't you notice?' Rosie shook her head. 'And then when I told her where I lived, she would have given me anything I wanted on tick.'

'It's lucky she didn't want to see your ID, seeing as you'd left it behind. That's an offence you know. You broke the law today, Miss Sinclair!'

'After seeing the car she didn't doubt my credentials.' She reached across and touched her companion's hand. 'I'm sorry she thought you were my maid. I know you work at The Grove, but I think of you as a friend.'

Rosie shook her head warningly at Simon. 'I know he's deaf, but it wouldn't do us any good for him to hear you say that, miss. Madam would dismiss me straightaway if she thought I was taking liberties.'

'Then it will have to be our secret. Anyway, I'll be joining the Land Army soon and then I'll only be a farm labourer like my other grandfather was.'

The car began to slow down as it reached a neat row of red-brick cottages on the edge of the village. 'Here you are, Mrs Mullins, right to the doorstep.'

'Thank you, Mr Farley,' Rosie shouted. 'See you tomorrow, Miss Sinclair. Good luck for this evening.'

He twisted round in his seat, the leather creaking. 'Will you come and sit next to me, Miss Sinclair? It will look a bit odd, you sitting back there now Mrs Mullins has gone.'

'Of course. I should love to.'

He was out of the car and holding open her door almost before she was ready to exit. It made her feel pampered. This was how a gentleman was supposed to behave towards a lady. He bowed her into the passenger seat, slammed the door and scurried back, to fall in beside her. She grinned at him. She couldn't help herself; he reminded her of an overeager puppy.

'Have you been living at The Grove long, Miss Sinclair?'

'A week, Mr Farley.' She waited for his next attempt at small talk. She could see his mouth thin as he tried to think of something else to say. He cleared his throat noisily.

'I haven't seen you before today, Miss Sinclair.'

She smothered her giggles. 'No, Mr Farley, I said I've only been here a week.'

The car turned into the drive before he could dredge up a third remark. She was out of the car as he pulled on the handbrake. 'Thank you so much for the ride. I must go in – my grandfather will be expecting me.'

His elbow rested casually in the open window, his cufflinks winking against the whiteness of his shirt. With his mouth closed he appeared to be an attractive, wealthy young man.

'My pleasure, Miss Sinclair. I shall have your bicycle returned as soon as it's repaired. Toodle-pip!'

Still smiling, she hurried to the back door, relieved to see her grandfather's car wasn't parked there.

Upstairs she ran the required five inches in the bath and climbed in. She felt a familiar hollowness inside. The excitement of the accident, the car ride, the purchase of the perfect dress, had temporarily blotted out the fact she would have to explain she'd borrowed the bike and crashed it. Her skin erupted in goose bumps and she shivered. She had to get out, so she was ready when he came. She thought he would understand, but didn't know him well enough to be sure. After all, her mother's friends thought she was a good person.

She could lock herself into the bathroom; it had a shiny bolt, but that would only postpone the inevitable. Putting on her knickers and brassiere whilst she was shaking so badly was a major achievement.

She couldn't put on her new dress yet so she pulled the tatty dressing gown on over her new silky petticoat and went out to sit on the bed. She stared at the clock above the empty grate. Ten minutes to five and her hair was wet. She had forgotten to dry it. Should she go and brush it?

She compromised, remaining on the bed but tearing off the sodden towel and running her fingers through her hair in order to remove some of the tangles. At least it wasn't dripping over her shoulders. The bedroom door was ajar. He was coming.

'Barbara, my dear child, whatever's wrong? Good God, you're not worried about those stitches are you? I promise I'll not hurt you.'

She half smiled. 'I'm really sorry, Grandpa, but I took your bicycle without asking and crashed into a car. I've ruined it.'

'Bugger the bicycle, child. Were you injured?' He ran his hands up and down her limbs checking for damage. 'Thank God! A few scrapes and bruises, nothing else. That bike was a death-trap anyway. I'll get you a new one, if I can find one anywhere, and one that's your size.'

'You aren't in the slightest bit angry?'

'No, my dear, of course I'm not. I'm just relieved you haven't hurt yourself.'

She was so moved she flung her arms around him. She rested her face on his tweed jacket, breathing in its distinctive smell, feeling the hairiness on her cheek, nestling into his embrace. His concern, his strength flowed into her giving her the love she'd never had. Briefly he returned her embrace.

'Now, my dear, if you're ready, I must remove those stitches.'

'I'm fine about it, Grandpa. Really I am. I was just concerned about the bike.'

He studied her closely and was satisfied. 'Good. Come and sit under the lights and let's get you sorted out.'

She looked up at him. 'I went to buy a dress in Brentwood, for tonight. I didn't have anything suitable to wear.'

'Tell me about it in a minute. You need to be quiet whilst I remove these.'

There was the coldness of the scissors and the gentle tug as the stitches were removed. 'There, all done. One looks a bit pink, but in a few days they'll be all but invisible.'

She ran into the bathroom to check. She could see the scar across her cheek but the ones above and below her mouth were almost imperceptible. She looked different, and it wasn't just the scars. She tilted her head to one side, trying to decide what it was. Her face was thinner; she must have lost weight. Her enforced diet over the past week had produced an unexpected result.

Delighted, she smiled at her reflection and lifted her hair from her neck. Yes, it was long enough to put up as Rosie had suggested. She'd even bought the hairpins and couldn't wait to have a go.

'Well, what do you think, my dear?' His voice from the door interrupted her preening.

'I can't believe it, Grandpa. They hardly show at all.'

'Now, child, sit down and tell me all about this afternoon.' When she'd finished he was laughing with her. 'Simon's a dear boy, but, as you've already noticed, none too clever. Mind you, I think he'd do a lot better away from that domineering father of his. It's a great shame he's got duff hearing and can't join up.'

'I think he liked me, Grandpa, but I don't want a boyfriend, even one as harmless as him.' She blushed. 'Actually, I have one already; he's in the RAF, away training to be a pilot.'

'Good for you. Serious, is it?'

'We're sort of engaged, but not officially or anything.'

'Sort of engaged? That's a new one on me, my dear.'

'It's hard to explain. John's love for me is different to mine for him. I've always thought of him as a brother, if you see what I mean.'

'I'm beginning to. So why are you engaged to someone you think of as a brother?'

'I couldn't let him go away unhappy. If I did have to marry him after the war, it wouldn't be so bad. I know him better than any other person. We tell each other everything.'

'Not quite everything,' he said dryly. 'You didn't tell him your real feelings, did you?'

'I didn't, but he was so happy, Grandpa, it was worth the white lie. He positively glowed when I kissed him back. Auntie Irene and Uncle Bill – you know, Mr and Mrs Thorogood, the ones you spoke to on the telephone, who are looking after Silver Lady for me – they are the only people we told.'

'Yes, you would have had to tell them. They seem very fond of you. Didn't I post a letter to them as well the other day? And also a thick one to a vicarage?'

'Yes, I don't have the address for my brothers' school. But Mrs Peterson, the vicar's wife, sent her two children away to the same place, and I asked her to post David and Tom's letters on for me.'

'And this John chappie? I don't recall a letter for him.'

'I don't have his address yet. He only left the day before me, and he didn't know exactly where he was going. Neither did he know I was leaving. Auntie Irene will forward his letters.'

'Excellent. I'd better go and get spruced up – doesn't do to be late for drinks. There might be a war on, but here everything still runs like clockwork.'

'I'll be ready. Shall I go down on my own or are you calling for me?'

'Go down. Elspeth is already in the kitchen. It's Mrs Brown's afternoon off as you probably know, so your grandmother's organising dinner. Expect it to be cold cuts, usually is.'

It took longer than she'd thought to arrange her hair into a chignon but the result was worth the effort. She added a quick covering of powder to disguise her scars and she was ready to slip on her frock. She adjusted the shoulders. The pads inside felt awkward, but it did give the dress a certain something. She pulled in the belt and smoothed the linen over her hips, then went back into the bathroom to check she hadn't mussed her hair.

She was too pale, her cheeks lacking their usual glow of health, and she wished she had bought a lipstick to put on to brighten her face. Still, she was meant to be an invalid; looking pale was to be expected.

She turned her back and peered over her shoulder into the mirror checking the seams on her new silk stockings were straight, glad her best shoes were navy and not too reminiscent of school. When she went shopping she intended to buy some with heels like those she'd seen in the window of an adjacent shop.

She glanced at her watch. It was five to six; time to go. She collected her torch from under her pillow. She would need it to find her way through the darkness to the drawing room. She waited for the cold sweat to break out on her forehead, for the shivers to run up and down her spine. For some reason she wasn't terrified. She felt confident, able to cope, even eager to meet 'the dragon' who had been avoiding her all week.

She was a Sinclair by blood, like her father and grandfather. The Grove was her heritage. She paused, shocked. Was she their sole heir? She felt her mouth curving. Whatever her grandmother thought of her, whatever she might say, one day (she prayed it would be a long time in the future) this beautiful house could possibly belong to her.

* * *

Downstairs Elspeth glanced at the walnut longcase clock. 'I do hope Barbara won't be late, Edward.'

'I'm sure she won't. She is well aware how much importance you place on punctuality.'

That was the end of their conversation. Whatever they had to say to each other, over the forty years of their marriage, had already been said. They existed in uneasy harmony, neither happy nor unhappy. It was how things were. You put up with it.

He smiled and straightened his shoulders. After eighteen empty years he had been given a second chance. A delightful, intelligent granddaughter, the image of his beloved Charles, had miraculously appeared in his life. She had problems; had been badly damaged – brutalised by her stepfather was his guess. His first surmise about a boyfriend was obviously incorrect. He'd seen it before: the new husband rejecting the offspring of his predecessor.

But his lovely girl was now safe in his care. He would make certain nothing else hurt her ever again. He scowled. Before the bloody blackout they would have been able to leave the drawing room doors open, giving him a clear view into the entrance hall, but now she'd have to creep downstairs using her torch. Tonight there was a full moon; the light from the rotunda would make it slightly easier for her.

He stood at the far end of the long room, in front of the roaring log fire, in a pool of light thrown by the single standard lamp. This left the door-end of the room in darkness. If any light escaped into the entrance hall it would flash like a beacon across the night sky. There were no German planes flying overhead as yet, but they would come. Everybody knew bombing was inevitable. Good God – they'd had to build an Anderson shelter like everybody else, hadn't they?

He heard a tap on the door. He'd have to tell her she didn't need to knock; this was her home. 'Come in, Barbara,' he shouted, causing his wife to spill her sherry onto her fingers.

* * *

Barbara heard the shout and grinned. She already loved Grandpa. He was everything a grandfather should be. She flashed the beam of her torch across the doors, searching for the knob. She turned it and slipped in, closing the door quickly behind her. She found herself in darkness but her grandparents were clearly visible, illuminated as if in the limelight. Grandfather was in his dinner jacket; black-and-white suited him, made him seem younger, in control, elegant even.

Her grandmother was standing next to him. She saw a tall, thin woman, with grey hair swept up into an elaborate arrangement on top of her head. Her sharp features – exaggerated by the light – made her birdlike; not a friendly sort of bird, more like an eagle or vulture. She smiled at the absurdity and began her long walk down the drawing room, pleased she had excellent deportment, something all Thistledown girls were taught.

As she approached she studied Mrs Sinclair's evening dress. The gown was close-fitting with a beaded bodice and capped sleeves. The colour was black. Perhaps this was what had made the image of a vulture flick through her mind.

Grandpa stepped out of the circle of light and came towards her, his arms out in welcome. 'Come in, my dear girl. You look absolutely splendid. Where did you get that frock? It's perfect on you, isn't it, Elspeth?' His fingers closed around hers and gave her the faintest of squeezes as he drew her forward.

'Good evening, Grandmother. I'm so pleased to meet you after so long.' Barbara hesitated. 'I love your evening dress; did you get it in London? I'm so looking forward to going clothes shopping with you whenever you have time to spare.'

Her grandmother smiled but didn't offer to embrace her granddaughter. 'Thank you, Barbara. This one is a favourite of mine and yes, it did come from London.' She stepped closer to examine Barbara's dress. 'That is a nice frock, but not quite right; however it will do for now. Get Barbara a small sherry, Edward. I wish to talk to her.'

Barbara acquitted herself well, answered the endless questions politely, remembering not to speak unless spoken to. The evening was an ordeal and she was relieved when, at nine o'clock, she was allowed to retire, claiming fatigue after her first night up. Grandpa had obviously not informed his wife about her excursion on his bicycle.

She hung her dress up carefully; this was all she had to wear for dinner until grandmother was able to fit a shopping trip into her busy schedule of bridge mornings, WVS and WI meetings. She believed she'd not proved too much of a disappointment as Mrs Sinclair had mentioned intending to invite over the Farleys and various other local families, as soon as she had the requisite clothes. Simon was bound to make it clear they'd already met, which might prove to be a problem, but she'd worry about that when it happened.

* * *

'Well, what you think of our granddaughter?'

Elspeth's thin lips curved slightly. 'She is well spoken and polite. With the correct clothes and a little polishing she'll do. In fact she should do very well.' She smiled, looking years younger. 'Edward, in spite of my serious reservations, I think I might actually enjoy having her here.'

'She told me she's intending to join the Land Army. She wants to do her bit for the war effort.'

'Land Army? I should think not. I hope you told her so, Edward. A Sinclair working like a common labourer on a farm? Whatever next!' She stood up. 'I've other plans for her. She will do very well for dear Simon. I can't wait to introduce them. I think I shall arrange an informal lunch party for next weekend. I shall have sorted out Barbara's wardrobe by then.'

'Yes, dear. An excellent idea. Please excuse me; I have an early start tomorrow.' He didn't kiss her cheek, merely nodded and strode off, smiling to himself. His wife was in for a shock if she thought she could manipulate young Barbara. His granddaughter had resolved to volunteer and he'd lay odds on her doing just that whatever his wife might think. He chuckled as he closed the drawing room door.

He didn't use a torch; merely paused to allow his eyes time to adjust to the gloom. By moonlight he went upstairs to his own apartment where he had slept alone for the past eighteen years.

8

The day of the dreaded lunch party arrived. Barbara had been taken to Rosebery's and up to Town and, in spite of shortages and talk of clothes being rationed in the New Year, she had a closet packed with suitable garments. Far more than she thought necessary but Grandpa had given Grandmother permission to spend what she felt was appropriate, which meant more clothes than Barbara expected to wear in a lifetime, let alone a year.

Rosie was in the dressing room with her. Mrs Sinclair was too busy supervising the kitchen arrangements to notice the absence.

'But which one shall I wear, Rosie? Grandmother said this lunch was informal, but I'm sure that doesn't mean slacks and a jumper, does it?'

'Crikey, no, miss. Madam's idea of informal just means guests get sandwiches and bits, not a sit-down meal. They'll be dressed up all posh.'

'Not dinner jackets and long frocks, surely?'

'No, that's for evening, but not slacks – that's for sure. Let's have a look.' Rosie pushed the garments along the row. 'Here, this is nice. A bit like your navy dress, but classier.' She removed the plain cream silk with a V-neck and matching belt. 'This is just the ticket.'

Barbara dived into her shoe rack. 'I've got shoes that match, and

Grandpa gave me some pearls the other day and I've not worn them yet. They'll be perfect.'

'I'd better get back downstairs, miss; today I'm to act as parlour maid and waitress and I've got to change into my black dress before people start turning up.'

Barbara examined her reflection in the floor-length mirror. With her curls restrained in a French pleat, a smart dress and court shoes, she no longer recognised herself. This was the same feeling she'd always had when she'd put on her school uniform. She became a stranger, a different girl, who behaved in a certain way, constrained by the rules the clothes imposed.

The outfits Grandmother had chosen were lovely, but they weren't her. She was an outdoor girl, happier in slacks and jumpers raking about in the countryside, not making small talk at 'informal lunch parties'.

She frowned as the babble of conversation rose from the entrance hall. This was, according to Grandmother, her opportunity to impress the Farleys. She had no wish to impress anyone, apart from Grandpa, and he loved her unconditionally already.

She was now the proud owner of a newish bicycle, which she was sharing with Rosie. She hesitated in the gallery, absently stroking the carved head of a unicorn, wishing she could avoid this event. The sun was shining on the fields and the sweet chestnuts were ready to be gathered.

'Hello, Miss Sinclair. I've been waiting for you to come down.' Simon hovered at the bottom of the stairs, his expression hopeful, but his eyes wary as if expecting to be rebuffed. She understood that feeling.

'Hello, Mr Farley. How are you? Have you managed to get the bicycles repaired?'

'They're as good as new, Miss Sinclair, and will be delivered tomorrow.' He beamed. 'I didn't tell the parents about the accident after all, didn't need to; Father had cancelled the meeting because he had to go to Town unexpectedly.'

'Dr Sinclair knows all about it, but not Mrs Sinclair.'

'Best it stays that way, don't you know. There's no one else our age in there. Shall we escape to the orangery?'

'I think I'd better put in a brief appearance. My grandmother wants to introduce me to your parents. She's hoping we'll hit it off and is convinced we'll make an ideal couple.'

'And we won't?' He looked puzzled. 'I thought we could be chums.'

'We can, but never anything else, I'm afraid. I shall tell you a secret: I have a young man in the RAF.'

'That's all right then; if we can be friends, go out sometime to the cinema or up to Town, it will keep the parents happy and maybe they'll stop pushing young women under my nose.'

'That would suit me too. Why don't you go back in, but remember you have to pretend you've never met me before. I'll follow you.' He waved and disappeared through the open drawing room doors.

'Barbara, there you are at last.' Mrs Sinclair's tone made her disapproval clear. 'Come along, there are several people who have been waiting to meet you.' She grasped her elbow and led her towards a tall, middle-aged man and a small anxious woman. 'Reginald, here she is at last. Barbara, this is Mr Farley and his wife, very dear friends of mine.'

Barbara held out her hand to the woman, who smiled and nodded. 'Delighted to meet you, Miss Sinclair; heard so much about you from your grandfather.' The voice was soft but no eye contact was made.

'Pleased to meet you, Mrs Farley.' She turned to the man and her smile faltered. He was smiling, his fleshy lips curled back revealing even white teeth, but his eyes – so dark that they appeared black – pinned her with an unnerving stare. He gripped her hand, shaking it vigorously.

'You're the image of your father. No doubting your parentage, is there?' She pulled back her hand, disliking the contact, not sure how to reply. 'Do you ride, Miss Sinclair?'

'Yes, I do, but until my mare arrives I can't do so.'

'I'm glad to hear it; not enough women ride to hounds. I'll expect to see you at the Boxing Day meet.'

He loomed over her, his swarthy face uncomfortably close. She was about to nod, agree, but something about this man made her skin crawl. 'Actually, sir, I don't ride to hounds. I don't agree with any kind of blood sports.'

If she had announced that she was a devil worshipper she couldn't have caused more of a sensation. Heads turned, banal conversations halted and she was in the centre of a ring of accusing faces.

'Well done, my dear. I've always thought fox hunting a barbaric sport myself.'

She stepped closer to Grandfather's protective presence, away from the hostile stares; the most baleful of which was from her grandmother. Chatter resumed, the guests turning their backs on Barbara, dismissing her as an unwelcome irritation, an irrelevance.

She tried to ignore the snatches of conversation.

'Such a shame. Poor Elspeth.'

'What a trial!'

'The girl won't fit in with an attitude like that.'

She was in disgrace with everyone apart from Grandpa. On the way out she met Rosie, looking like a nippy from a Lyons' Corner House in her black dress, cap and frilly apron.

'You've gone and done it now, miss,' Rosie said with a broad grin. 'Madam's hopping mad. But the doc's on your side and so am I. You shouldn't have to hunt if you don't agree with it.'

'But I shouldn't have said so, not in front of all those people. I've ruined the lunch party and she'll be beastly to Grandpa now, as if it's all his fault.'

'I say, Miss Sinclair, are you off to the orangery? Can I come with you?'

Either Simon hadn't heard of her *faux pas* or he didn't care. 'Yes, please do. I'm *persona non grata* in there.'

'I don't hunt either. Father calls me a coward, but I'm not. I just hate seeing foxes torn apart by hounds.'

'You're the first person who agrees with me, apart from my grandfather; it's good to have an ally.' She turned to Rosie. 'I don't suppose you could steal us a plate of something and bring it out, could you? I don't feel like going back in there.'

'I'll do it now. You run along with Mr Farley. I'll bring you a couple of lemonades as well, unless you want a sherry or gin and tonic?'

'Lemonade would be lovely, thank you.'

They sat in the calm of the glass conservatory until the last guests had driven away. 'I must go, Barbara. It won't do for Mrs Sinclair to know I've been in here and not doing the rounds in the drawing room.'

'Of course, you go, Simon. I've really enjoyed this afternoon. You've told me so much about your family, your factory and the area that I don't feel quite such a stranger.'

'And you will come to the cinema on Wednesday, won't you?'

'I'm looking forward to it.'

He was a nice young man, kind and attentive, as open as a child about his home life. He was obviously bullied by his father and ignored by his mother, but it didn't appear to bother him overmuch. But something he'd talked about had filled her with misgivings. She needed to see Grandpa and get his opinion.

Should she return the tray of dirty plates and glasses to the kitchen? Better not – she might meet her grandmother. In the entrance hall there was the sound of raised voices coming from the drawing room. Her grandparents were having an argument. She had to cross the space in order to reach the stairs. This meant passing the open doors. She didn't want to eavesdrop, but she had no choice.

'After all the time I spent traipsing around shops in order to make sure she was well turned out and this is how she behaves? It will be all over the neighbourhood by tonight that your granddaughter's a Bolshevik!'

'Bolshevik? How in God's name did you come to that ridiculous conclusion? Barbara doesn't like hunting; she didn't declare herself a supporter of Karl Marx.'

'Everyone supports hunting and shooting. It's part of our English lifestyle. It's what we're fighting this war to protect.'

'Stuff and nonsense! We're fighting fascism, not to make sure men in red coats can continue to slaughter foxes.'

'I don't understand you, Edward. Your family can trace its line back to the Normans. You should be as shocked as I that Barbara showed herself not to be one of us.'

'But I suppose that smarmy bastard Farley is? Have you any idea who his friends are? The crowd he mixes with in London?'

Barbara moved closer. She wanted to hear the answer to that question.

'His business associates and their wives, I suppose, charming people, all of them. I meet them often when I stay at Claridges.'

'He's little better than a gangster; that factory at Chelmsford could not possibly produce the income they need to maintain their lifestyle. Where does the rest come from? Not inherited wealth – we know that much.'

'Reginald's family go back as far as yours. They weren't as wealthy but they were respectable. Charlotte's grandfather was a duke, so your accusations are absurd, Edward. You are more of a snob than I am. Your family have never liked people who get their income from trade. Not every family is as lucky as you; they didn't inherit a massive trust fund.'

'Hmm... but I also have a worthwhile job saving people's lives. That man's dangerous. His business methods are suspect and so are his cronies. I wish you would drop the connection before you become tainted by association.'

'I shall do no such thing.'

There was the sound of heels clicking on the parquet. Barbara ran for the stairs and managed to reach the gallery just as Mrs Sinclair emerged, twin spots of colour on her normally pale cheeks, and stalked across the hall in the direction of the kitchen. Barbara hoped Rosie and Mrs Brown had left or they would be on the receiving end of Grandmother's ill humour.

In her room she removed her dress and then hung it back on the rail in her dressing room. Ten minutes later she was on her way downstairs in her old slacks and jumper. Herself again. The drawing room was empty, a few overflowing ashtrays and a strong smell of expensive perfume the only sign there had been a party. Grandpa was probably in his study, one place he could be sure his wife would not disturb him.

The door was firmly closed but she could hear him moving about inside. Should she risk it? She had to after what she just heard him say about Simon's father. She knocked loudly and waited to be barked at.

The door swung open and she recoiled from the fury in his face. 'Good grief! It's you, my dear. Sorry, I didn't mean to frighten you. Come in, I need someone sensible to talk to.'

A pall of expensive cigar smoke hung over the room and a half-full tumbler of whisky sat on the leather-topped desk. She quite liked the smell of Grandpa's cigars, unlike the pipe Mr Evans had smoked. She froze. Why had she thought of him?

He mistook her unease for distaste. 'Wait a minute, child, I'll open a window. Can't expect you to breathe in my smoke.'

'No, Grandpa, I like it. It was something else.' She paused, not sure if she wanted to explain. 'It reminded me of the pipe Mr Evans smoked; I hated the smell of that.' There, she'd mentioned her stepfather for the first time. She must be getting over her past.

She curled up on the battered leather Chesterfield in front of the fire. 'I couldn't help overhearing what you said about Mr Farley. I have to tell you something Simon told me.'

He collected his cigar and drink and joined her on the sofa. 'Go on, my dear, what did he say?'

'You know what he's like. I was asking him about his job at the factory. Rosie mentioned her husband worked there and that they used to make machine parts but are making munitions now. She's hoping to get a job there as conscription is taking away all the young men.'

'The unions don't allow women to work on munitions – not at the moment anyway. But that's beside the point. What has young Simon been saying that's got you so stirred up?'

'Well, he said the factory was working twenty-four hours a day so workers had to work in shifts. He's supposed to oversee the factory when his father isn't there, but is not allowed to work the night shift. His father, or one of his associates, always does that and the men who work this shift are not locals either.'

'The boy's probably not up to working at night. He might fall asleep; he's not very bright, is he?'

'He knows that – he understands his limitations. But he wanted to prove to his father that he could do a late shift and drove down there the other night. He said there were strange cars in the office car park and vans and lorries outside the factory loading boxes. Why would they be doing that at night?'

'Good grief! What did he make of this?'

'He thought it was "jolly exciting". He thinks his father's involved in secret government work, but I thought it all sounded very suspicious. I don't like Mr Farley. There was something about him.'

He sipped his drink and puffed his cigar, in no hurry to answer.

'Well, Grandpa? Do you think there's something illegal going on?'

'Almost certainly, my dear. But it's none of our business. The man's a rogue but not a traitor as far as I know. My advice is to stay away from him – he's a fascist – a Mosley supporter, as are all his friends. If you're going to go around with Simon, only meet here. He's a nice boy, and whatever his father is up to he won't be involved in it.'

'So you don't think we need to report his night-time activities to the police?'

'No, my dear. I expect they'll be well aware of what's going on in Chelmsford if he's making munitions. They'll keep a close eye on his factory. He'll not be allowed to sell anywhere apart from to the government.'

'But what was he doing in the middle of the night?'

'God knows! I expect he's using his factory to manufacture other things and is selling them on the black market. No doubt the authorities will turn a blind eye as long as he produces what they want every week.'

'It doesn't seem right. Mrs Mullins told me you can be fined for showing a light at night, or not having your ID card on you, so why should he get away with breaking the law? It's one law for the rich and one for the poor.'

'I don't like to hear you talking such rubbish, Barbara. Everyone has a place in society; that's how it should be. The Farleys, whatever my personal feelings, are essential to the prosperity of this country. It won't be people like us who win the war, my dear, it will be the common man and businessmen like Farley. They will get richer but it's in a good cause.'

She had to leave it there. Her grandmother already thought she was a closet Bolshevik just because she hated blood sports. Now her radical views had upset her grandfather. 'You're right. I don't know much about politics. I was just repeating what Mrs Mullins has been telling me. It must seem hard to someone like her, having to make ends meet on so little, whilst we live in luxury.'

'It's how things are, my dear. Always have been, always will. My advice is not to get too involved with the staff. Always leads to difficulties, that sort of thing.'

'But I'm joining the Land Army after Christmas; then I'll be staff at someone else's house. Will they regard me in the same way?'

He ignored her question. 'Have you sent off your papers already? I thought you were going to discuss the matter with me before you committed yourself.'

'I asked Mrs Mullins to post them yesterday. I have to do something. The government has asked women to help with the war effort and I certainly don't want to join the WVS. You don't want me to join the services, so that only leaves the land.'

'As it's a fait accompli there's nothing else I can say. At least I'll have you here every day until the New Year. And your mare should arrive tomorrow. Mr Thorogood rang to say he'd found someone prepared to drive her up.'

Impulsively she threw her arms around him. 'Thank you, Grandpa. I can't wait to see Silver again. Her stable's ready and I believe there's a farm in the next village that will let me have hay and straw whenever I need it. I'm going to bike over to see them tomorrow.'

'Which farm is that? Is it Home Farm, the Evertons?'

'It is. Mountnessing's only two miles from here, isn't it? Simon mentioned they use farm horses and also have a dairy herd, so I'm hoping there will be enough fodder and bedding to spare.'

'Would you like me to drive you over tomorrow after church?'

'No, thanks. I'd rather cycle. I'm intending to go to eight o'clock communion, not matins, then I shall have time to change.'

* * *

Barbara's new bicycle was a Rolls-Royce of its kind. As Rosie now had her own bike back she had exclusive use of her new cycle and this would be her first real run.

She pulled her beret down over her ears using kirby grips to secure it, then, wrapping her long stripy scarf several times round her neck, she tucked the loose ends into her riding mac. In spite of the expenditure on a wardrobe full of clothes, she still didn't own a winter coat suitable for riding a bike on a cold November morning.

The horsebox was expected to arrive at three o'clock. She'd found a couple of old bales of straw and hay in the barn, which would last a few days. Today was supposedly a day of rest, but farmers worked every day. When she was a land girl she probably wouldn't have her Sundays free.

She was glad she'd posted her application; the sooner she started work the better. Her grandparents were still not speaking to each other and Mrs Sinclair wasn't speaking to her either. It was a good thing The Grove was vast; it was easy to avoid anyone you didn't want to see.

The church clock struck ten as she pedalled through the village. She'd been given instructions for finding Home Farm. This was the only farm in the lane that ran down to the railway bridge. She dismounted in the farmyard and bent to stroke the heads of two friendly Border collies that rushed out to greet her.

'Hello, lovely dogs, is your master home, do you know?'

'Beth and Ollie are clever, but I don't think they have quite mastered conversation yet.'

She turned, grinning, to face the speaker. He was a young man, about twenty or so, red gold hair, green eyes and wearing the distinctive blue grey of an RAF officer.

'Oh, good morning. I'm Barbara Sinclair, from The Grove, Ingatestone. You must be Mr Everton's son?'

He nodded and walked over, hand outstretched. She balanced the bike against her knees.

'Alex Everton, delighted to meet you, Miss Sinclair.' His grip was firm. He seemed reluctant to release her hand. 'My parents and brothers are not back from church. Can I help you?'

Aware her face was red and her beret down over her eyebrows in a most unflattering way she pulled a hand free and snatched her hat off, surreptitiously wiping the sweat from her face as she did so.

'Actually, I've come to see if I can order a load of hay, clover if you've got it, and another of straw, not barley. My mare eats that.'

She straightened her bike; she'd accomplished what she'd come for.

Mrs Brown had told her there was to be no hot Sunday lunch today so there was no reason to hurry. 'I have to be getting back, Alex. I don't want to hold you up.'

'Please don't rush off. Why not come in and have a coffee? I'm back to base tomorrow and you're the first pretty girl I've seen all leave.'

She was unsure how to react to this charming young man, although not much older than John, he seemed more mature. She smiled nervously, but still accepted his casual invitation.

The warm interior immediately made her feel at home. It reminded her of Brook Farm: large welcoming kitchen, long scrubbed table, big kitchen range, even a tortoiseshell cat curled up on a battered armchair beside it. The quarry tiles were muddy from farm boots. Mrs Everton, unlike Auntie Irene, obviously didn't insist that visitors remove their footwear.

'Are you happy to sit in the kitchen? I can light the fire in the front room, but it's much warmer in here.'

'No, the kitchen's fine. Are you sure your parents won't object to you inviting a total stranger into their house?'

He smiled directly into her eyes and she caught her breath. 'You're not a stranger. You're Barbara Sinclair, the granddaughter of Dr and Mrs Sinclair. They'll be as delighted as I am to meet you.'

She averted her gaze, looking anywhere but at him. He made her feel quite uncomfortable, flustered. John never did that to her.

'Tea or coffee? Black or white? Sugar or not?' She could tell from his voice that he was finding her nervousness amusing. She wished she hadn't agreed to come in, wanted to find an excuse to leave.

'Tea, milk, no sugar, not too strong, if that's possible.'

'Do you want the fancy stuff – smells like cat's pee and tastes even worse – or the common or garden sort?'

She relaxed; maybe he wasn't so intimidating after all. 'Earl Grey do you mean? I hate it. Ordinary tea please.' This man was at ease in the kitchen in his shirtsleeves, having discarded his jacket when he came in. She rather liked him after all. Whilst his back was to her she slipped off her riding mac and hung it on the back of the chair, then hurriedly stuffed her hat, gloves and scarf up a sleeve.

'Where are you stationed, Alex? Or is that a state secret?'

He glanced over his shoulder with another of his flashing smiles. 'No, of course it isn't. I'm at Hornchurch, less than an hour from here by car, so I can get back when I have leave. Not much happening at the moment. It's all training flights and getting to know the new bods as they join us.'

The sound of running feet and boys shouting interrupted their tête-à-tête. 'My parents and brothers. I'd better put an extra spoonful in the pot.'

She stood up, turning to face the door, her confidence evaporating at the prospect of being discovered, uninvited, in Mr and Mrs Everton's kitchen.

9

Mrs Everton was smiling as she removed her gloves. 'Pleased to meet you, Miss Sinclair.'

Alex interrupted. 'Barbara's come to buy bedding and fodder for her horse, so I'm hoping that means the move's permanent.' He handed her a steaming mug of tea and treated her to another stomach-churning smile.

She blushed. 'I'm hoping to join the Land Army next year and could be posted away.'

'Perhaps you could come and work here; we've applied for some girls to replace the two men we've lost,' Mrs Everton said.

Alex nodded. 'That would be ideal – then I can see you whenever I come home on leave.'

'I'm not sure we actually get a choice, but if we do I'll certainly ask for Home Farm. It would mean I could live at The Grove and still be able to ride Silver Lady.'

Mr Everton came in. Barbara stood up to greet him.

'Sit down, love, and drink your tea. I'm James Everton. Pleased to meet you.' The tall, middle-aged man, propped himself against the range, warming his backside on the oven. 'Our Jim says you're after bedding and hay?'

'Yes, please, if you have any to spare.'

'Plenty, we had an excellent harvest this year. I'll bring a load over tomorrow.' He reached round for his mug. 'What's she like, this horse of yours?'

'Just over fifteen hands, dappled grey, like a huge rocking horse. She's sweet-natured, clever and brilliant cross-country.'

'You'll be hunting then?'

'No, actually I won't. I never have; it's not something I enjoy.'

'Fair enough, each to his own. I shoot the foxes here, much easier and less damage to my fields from bloody great hunters and a pack of hounds.'

The chat continued as the tea was drunk and then Mr Everton stood up, breaking up the group. 'It's time I got changed. I've got work to do before lunch. Come along, boys, you need to get out of your Sunday best. You can load the trailer for Barbara. Perhaps Alex will have time to drive it over after lunch.'

'It doesn't have to be today, Mr Everton, and Alex is in his uniform. He can't drive a tractor dressed like that.'

'He has to be back before dark, James, and it's eleven thirty already.'

'Don't worry, Mum. Dad's right: I'll go and put on some other togs then help the boys load.' He grinned at her. 'If you're not in a hurry, Barbara, you could come out to the barn and give us a hand; then we can deliver it after lunch and be back in time for me to leave.'

Mrs Everton's word was law when it came to food and Barbara happily accepted an invitation to join them for Sunday lunch. She was left alone as the family rushed off. Jim, the eleven-year-old, was back first, in holey jumper, knee-length flannel trousers and collapsing brown knitted socks.

'We've got boots in the cubbyhole, Barbara. We're ready – come with us. Alex takes ages; he's always looking in the mirror, just like a girl.'

'I heard that, cheeky brat,' Alex said as he emerged, in thick navy blue sweater and brown corduroys. Laughing, Jim and his younger brother ran ahead leaving Barbara and Alex to follow.

They were all covered in loose straw and hay by the time the trailer was loaded. 'You've got enough here to keep you going for a few weeks. I'll put on a couple of bags of barley, and one of oats, before we leave.'

'Thanks, Alex.' Without thinking, she reached over and pulled a stalk of straw from his hair. His hand captured hers, holding it against his hot cheek.

'My pleasure, sweetheart. Anything I can do for you, you only have to ask.' His eyes were dark, his hand hard on hers. She was transfixed. She felt a strange sensation in the pit of her stomach and her knees trembled.

He drew her closer. He was going to kiss her. He shouldn't, but she couldn't stop herself walking into his arms.

'Go on, Alex, give her a smacker.'

She shot backwards, tripping over a pitchfork to vanish beneath a pile of loose hay. Jim and Ned collapsed in a fit of giggles whilst Alex aimed a half-hearted blow at their bobbing heads.

'Bloody hell, Jim. Did you have to do that?'

Jim couldn't answer. He was laughing too hard. Barbara sat up, spitting bits from her mouth, not sure if she was amused, offended or embarrassed.

'Up you come; sorry about that – hazards of having younger brothers with a warped sense of humour,' Alex said, grinning ruefully.

'I'm glad really. I should have told you, I have a boyfriend; he's in the RAF too. We're thinking of getting engaged.'

Alex's smile faded. 'I'm frightfully sorry, Barbara. I'd never have dreamt...'

'That's all right, Alex. That was as much my fault as yours.'

'Don't believe a word of it, Barbara. Alex is a right one for ladies. Different girlfriends every time he comes home.'

'Shut it, Jim. Joke's over.'

'We'd better get this over to The Grove or you won't be back in time to leave before dark, Alex.'

'We've got to have lunch before we go. Mum would never forgive us if we sloped off.'

She wasn't sure about staying to eat. Alex was smiling but he was tense. The boys had vanished. Did they expect him to turn on them for their prank? The barn seemed to close in on her and he stood between her and safety.

'Mum says lunch is ready. Alex, Barbara, come and get it,' Ned's voice carried in from the yard.

Alex smiled and strolled off, picking straw and hay from his hair as he went. She hurried after him, flapping her arms and stamping, hoping to dislodge most of the debris before she reached the back door. This time she stopped to remove her outer garments and boots. She wanted to wash before eating; there had to be a scullery somewhere.

'Barbara? Where are you? Lunch is getting cold,' Ned shouted from outside the wash-room door.

She gave up the attempt to improve her appearance and came out. 'Sorry, I'm here. I was trying to tidy up before we ate.'

Ned grinned. 'You look like a dryad. You know, one of those woodland nymphs, with wild curly hair and things.'

She smiled. 'Thank you, Ned, I think. Now, lead the way. My nose tells me our food is waiting.'

* * *

An hour later Alex stood up. 'We have to leave, Barbara, if I'm to get back in time. No slackers allowed here.'

'Are you two coming as well?' she asked the boys.

'We have to come. Alex's too feeble to unload on his own,' Jim said, grinning at his older brother.

'I'll bear that in mind next time you want me to mend your bike.'

'Thank you for a delicious meal, Mrs Everton. I'm going to have difficulty pedalling back, I'm so full.'

'Come again, love. Why don't you ride over tomorrow, let me have a look at your mare. I don't ride myself, but I love horses. If James had his way Molly and Ben would have gone to the knackers yard years ago.'

'You can collect the bill when you come over next. Doris will have worked it out by then.'

Barbara recovered her bicycle and set off first. By pedalling furiously she managed to arrive in the stable yard minutes before the tractor. She dropped her bike and hurried to open the barn doors. Puffed and red-faced she stood by the wall to wave Alex and the boys inside.

The noise of the tractor reverberated round the empty space, making conversation impossible.

He switched off the engine. Jim and Ned, who had had travelled face down on top of the bales, jumped up ready to unload.

Alex came to stand beside her. 'We'll do this, Barbara. You look exhausted. Just tell me where you want it, then you can go in and get a rest before your mare arrives. We'll shut the barn before we leave.'

'Thank you, Alex, that's kind of you. Put the hay on the left and the straw on the right, if you would.' She hesitated, not sure what to say. 'Thank your parents for the lovely lunch and tell your mother I'll be over to see her soon, possibly tomorrow.'

'Will do.' He turned his back and shouted up to the boys, 'Start throwing the bales down, lads. I want to get away from here quickly.'

'Cheerio, Barbara, see you soon.' Ned was the only one to say goodbye.

Shoulders drooping, she hurried back to the sanctuary of her room. She ran an inch of tepid water in the bath. A wash would make her feel better, take her mind off things. Afterwards she pulled on her old jodhpurs and battered jacket, intending to keep her new riding clothes for best, whenever that might be.

Warmly dressed, her teeth finally still, she realised she had an hour before the expected arrival of the horsebox. She wanted Silver Lady to feel welcome so she had no choice – the stale bedding and fodder had to go.

The loose box she'd selected for her mare was adjacent to the tack room and the tap was just outside the double door. The sun was setting; it would soon be too dark to see without a lantern. She refilled the net with fresh, sweet-smelling clover hay and then added an extra layer of straw from one of the Home Farm bales. She checked the water bucket for bits and then retired to the tack room where the barley and oats had been tipped into the fodder bins. There was no time to boil the barley; she'd do that tomorrow.

After cutting up two apples she dropped them into a clean bucket and added two handfuls of bran, one of oats then mixed it with her hands. Satisfied everything was ready, she checked her watch. Nearly three.

They could be here any moment. She lit the lantern and hung it at the back of the small room. She started the paraffin stove; it was too cold to sit around without heating.

Inside she pulled up a battered pine chair and sat as close to the stove as was safe. Apart from the pungent smell of burning paraffin, it worked perfectly. The flat circular top was ideal for boiling a kettle, or making toast, if you didn't mind the strange taste.

She closed her eyes, relaxing in the warmth, pleasantly full from her lunch and happy her beloved horse would soon be here. It had been a lovely day so far. The Evertons were nice, very like Auntie Irene and Uncle Bill. The boys were lovely too; so like Tom and David it made her heart ache. She smiled; her brothers must have received her letters by now. She hoped they were as happy as she was. Maybe she'd get a reply soon; it must be over three weeks since she'd written to Mrs Peterson.

Had John received her letters? Where was he? At least he was safe for the moment; the RAF had already suffered losses over Germany and his preliminary training would be completed by Christmas. She had no idea if this meant he'd join a squadron or be sent somewhere else. Alex was already a pilot – she'd noticed the wings on his collar. He could tell her how long it took aircrew to be ready for active service.

She scowled. She didn't want to think about him; he confused her. First he flirted, then almost kissed her but had sent her away as if she was of no interest. Perhaps he was just being a gentleman, respecting her commitment to John. He made her feel fizzy and tingling inside and, if she was honest, she'd really wanted him to kiss her.

She wished John made her feel that way. She loved John. She wasn't even sure she liked Alex. He was handsome, with his flashing green eyes and auburn hair, and could be charming and kind, but he'd showed a different side when the boys had teased him and in the way he'd turned his back on her.

She wasn't a pretty girl; had been told often enough over the years she was fat, clumsy, and plain. John loved her as she was. They had grown up together and appearances didn't matter to either of them. She might wear something new next time she met Alex, then perhaps he wouldn't dismiss her so casually.

The sound of a lorry grinding its way up the drive roused her. She dimmed the lantern and rushed out to receive her mare.

* * *

Next morning normal relations appeared to have been restored and both grandparents greeted her when she came in late for breakfast.

'Sorry; I've been out to Silver, to see how she's settled into her new home.'

'Is she content?'

'She is, thank you, Grandpa. She's eaten her hay and feed and was eager to poke her head out and look around the yard.'

'Excellent. Did you order what you needed from the Evertons yesterday?'

'It's already in the barn. They invited me to stay for lunch and I met Alex Everton. He was home for the weekend.' She flushed. What had prompted her to mention him?

Grandmother's antennae twitched. 'Alex Everton? That's a young man you'd do well to avoid, Barbara. He has a reputation locally for being, how can I put it, a touch casual in his relationships with young ladies.'

Before she could reply Grandpa interrupted. 'Good grief, Elspeth, young Everton wouldn't look at Barbara. She's not his type; he goes for a more ornamental variety.'

She felt a lump in her throat. So he thought her unattractive as well? Well, it didn't matter; she was going to be land girl where hard work was wanted, not glamour. Her appetite vanished and she replaced the empty plate on the sideboard.

'Actually, I'm not hungry. I ate so much yesterday I'm still full. I'm going to take Silver out for a gentle hack. Explore the area a bit.'

They exchanged glances. 'You will be back for lunch,' her grandmother said. This was not a question.

'Yes, Grandmother. Has there been any post today?'

'There has, but nothing for you.' Seeing her expression her grandfather continued. 'Don't worry, your brothers and friends will write soon. The post's a bit haphazard at the moment, I expect.'

'I've written three times to Tom and David; last time I sent a stamped addressed envelope for them to reply. I'm getting really worried. If I don't hear tomorrow, can I use your telephone and ring the school, ask if everything's all right?'

'Why don't you ring your mother and stepfather, Barbara? Surely they are the ones to supply such information?'

'Left under a bit of a cloud, didn't you, my dear; best not to communicate with them. Let the dust settle.'

'Can I use the telephone tomorrow, please?'

'Yes, you don't have to ask, my dear. This is your home; you can do whatever you like.'

* * *

Silver Lady was surprisingly fresh and danced down the drive like a two-year-old. The ground was firm, but not too hard for a short gallop and several exhilarating canters. Barbara cut across the fields, jumping the hedges and ditches she met, breathing in the crisp November air.

She found herself in a lane that looked vaguely familiar and she realised this was the one that led towards Home Farm. She hadn't consciously opted to visit the Evertons, but now she was so close she could hardly ride past without calling in.

The two dogs bounded up, barking at the unexpected equine visitor. Silver was used to dogs; Brook Farm had three collies. Mrs Everton poked her head out of the kitchen window.

'Put your horse in the box at the end and come in for a cuppa. The kettle's just on the boil.'

Barbara had been there long enough to drink her tea and managed not to ask after Alex. She desperately wanted to know when he was due to come back on leave again. Something prompted her to mention she was going to the cinema with Simon on Wednesday.

'He's a nice enough lad, but stay well clear of his father. He has a nasty reputation hereabouts.'

'What do you mean, Mrs Everton? I certainly didn't like him when I met him.'

'I shouldn't spread gossip, but I must tell you. His name has been linked with a couple of local girls. Ruined their good names. Their families didn't want to know them after they found out. Both of them were forced to leave the area, and goodness knows where they are now. No one in the village has heard from either of them, not even their brothers and sisters. They just upped and left. Vanished into thin air.'

'Do you mean Mr Farley had an affair with these girls? But he's a married man. That's shocking.'

'It is. They should have had more sense, but he showered them with money and gifts and they couldn't say no.' Mrs Everton paused. 'Well, that's what people say. I didn't know either of the girls very well. But both were very pretty, glamorous they were. Alex went out a few times with one of them, Ruby Smith, but this was before she took up with that man. He never brought her home.'

'Why would pretty girls want to become the mistress of someone like him? He's old and ugly.'

'You've a lot to learn about life, my dear. Some girls put money before morals; not quite tarts, they don't stand on street corners, but they're prepared to sell themselves nevertheless.'

'How horrible! I can't imagine anything worse. I'd rather starve than do that.'

'I should hope so too! So would most nice girls. But a few hundred pounds is a lot of money to someone living in a back-to-back with ten other people.'

'Anyway, you don't have to worry about me, Mrs Everton; even my grandparents think I'm plain. Men like Mr Farley wouldn't look twice at me, thank goodness.'

'You don't make the best of yourself, love; in a pretty frock, with your hair up, I bet you look a treat.'

'But I hate looking like one of Grandmother's friends. I'd rather be me; if a man can't see past the outside, I'm not interested in him anyway.'

'Good for you. Our Valerie's the same. "They can take me as they find me, Mum," she used to say. And Peter Miller found her soon enough, at a social at Ingatestone. They met last year and now they're married.'

'I like the sound of Valerie; is she older or younger than Alex?'

'She's nineteen – Alex is twenty-two. I'll invite Peter and Valerie over for Sunday lunch next time he's back and you must come as well. I'm sure you'll get along like a house on fire.'

'When will that be, do you think?'

'Oh, Alex's got a weekend pass at end of the month, but I hope you'll come to see me before then.'

'Of course I will. Before I go, there's something I'd like to know. How does he have his wings already? War only started two months ago.'

'He joined up straight after school. He's a regular – a flight lieutenant – and I expect him to get promoted before long.'

'That's amazing – you must be so proud. Sorry but I really have to get moving.'

Mrs Everton admired Silver, and Barbara left fizzing with excitement. Alex was coming back soon. She'd persuade Grandpa to drive her over and then she could wear one of her new outfits.

She cantered into the yard to find Mrs Mullins leaning on the wall, smoking a cigarette, obviously waiting for her.

'Rosie, what is it? I hope there's nothing wrong?'

10

Barbara dismounted, flipping the reins over Silver's head.

Rosie grinned. 'Nothing to worry about, miss. I'm taking a quick break; madam's talking on the telephone. I've got a message for you from Mr Farley.'

'Is that all? I thought it was something important.' Barbara ran a hand expertly down each of the mare's legs.

'I'd better tell you what I came out to say. I've got to get back in a minute.'

'Sorry, yes, of course you do. We were supposed to be going out on Wednesday but I expect he's changed his mind.'

'He hasn't. He said I was to tell you he's picking you up here at eleven thirty and taking you out to lunch at the Swan and then to the flicks, to the matinee, to see *The Great Dictator*.'

'*The Great Dictator*? Is that being shown at Brentwood? I've heard so much about Charlie Chaplin. This is his first talkie, isn't it?'

'I think so. I wish I could go and see it. I reckon it looks really good.'

'Do you know, I've only been to the cinema once before and that was to see *Snow White* with John.'

'Who's John? Another boyfriend?'

'No, Rosie, he's someone I grew up with – a family friend, nothing else.'

'None of my business anyway, Miss Sinclair. Pardon me for asking, I'm sure.' She turned away, offended. 'I must be getting back. I've not finished my work yet.'

'Rosie, don't go. I'm sorry, I didn't mean to snap. It's just talking about John brings back memories.'

'That's all right then. I understand, miss. You'll come to no harm with young Mr Farley, but stay away from his dad.'

Barbara pulled the rug over the mare, buckled it, checked there was sufficient hay and water and bolted the bottom door behind her.

'Hang on a minute, there's something I want to ask you about Mr Farley senior. Mrs Everton told me he'd been involved with two local girls. Do you know anything about that?'

'Mavis Goodwin, the first of the two girls, lived next door to me when we were growing up. She was a corker: natural corn-coloured hair, big blue eyes and a figure to match. She could have had any boy in the neighbourhood. But she wasn't interested. She started to go out on her own, staying out late, all that sort of thing.

'Then she had new clothes, jewellery, started to act as though she was something special. When I asked her about it she told me she had a rich man friend and he was buying her a flat in Romford.' Rosie stopped, her expression serious. 'I told her she was mad, told her to give him up, guessed he was married, but she wouldn't listen. Then one day she vanished.'

'Good heavens! Didn't her family make enquiries? Contact the police or anything?'

'I reckon she was in the family way and that's why she went. I just hope Mr Farley took care of her.'

'What made people suspect him? Did Mavis say anything?'

'No, not in as many words, but someone from the village saw them together in London at a nightclub and we just put two and two together.'

'And Ruby? Mrs Everton mentioned the other girl.'

'Ruby was more recent, but she was young like Mavis and had the same kind of looks. I didn't know her so well, I was married and had moved away; I reckon this was about four years ago. No one ever saw Mr Farley with Ruby but when she told a friend she was moving to her own flat in Romford, well it doesn't take much to work it out, does it?'

'Ruby went out with Alex Everton; couldn't it have been him she was having an affair with?'

'Alex Everton? Never! He's not got the kind of money Ruby was flashing about. But it's true, she did go around with him just before she went away. Funny that, now you mention it. Ruby must have been going around with Alex and her fancy man at the same time.'

'And she disappeared too?'

'Said she was going to make a fresh start. She'd no reputation left in the village anyway, so it was the best thing for her.'

'How long ago was this?'

'Let me think... about two years ago, no more than that.' The church clock start struck twelve. 'Good Gawd! I've been out here twenty-five minutes. Madam will skin me alive. See you tomorrow. Bye for now.'

Barbara had an hour to wash, change, and present herself in the dining room for lunch. She went in the back door, leaving her boots neatly together on the rack and her mac square on its peg. She raced up the backstairs and along to her room; she must leave her slippers by the boot stand in future.

The dining room smelled of beeswax polish and the floor was so slippery she was forced to grab the door frame to avoid an embarrassing, feet-first entrance. Her grandparents were already seated, but Grandpa stood up to greet her.

'Did you have a good ride, my dear? I dropped in to say hello to your mare. She's a sweetie. I can see why you wanted her here.'

She sat in the chair, conspicuously pulled out, opposite Grandmother and to the right of Grandpa, who sat at the head of the table.

'I rode over to Home Farm and had another chat to Mrs Everton.'

'Excellent! She's a delightful lady, salt of the earth.'

Mrs Brown came in with a steaming tureen of leek and potato soup and placed it in the centre of the table. Then she returned with a basket of freshly baked rolls and a dish of butter. The smell reminded Barbara of her last meeting with John, and her eyes filled. She dropped her head and surreptitiously wiped her face on the corner of the starched white napkin.

'Would you like some soup, Barbara? There's game pie to follow; would you prefer to wait for that?' her grandmother enquired frostily.

'Soup, please; leek and potato's a favourite of mine.' The liquid sloshed into her bowl but she didn't raise her eyes. A roll arrived on her side plate but neither grandparent commented on her silence. She drank her soup half listening until Mr Farley senior was mentioned. She looked up.

'Actually, I'm going to the cinema with Simon on Wednesday so I won't be here for lunch.'

'Good show! Make sure you're back before blackout. Driving with the amount of light we're allowed is a dangerous business. Do you know I've treated dozens of injuries caused by the blackout? It's done more damage than the Germans.'

'Don't be ridiculous, Edward. That can't possibly be true or I would have heard about it at my WVS meetings.'

Her grandfather's jaw tightened and for a moment Barbara thought the fragile peace would be broken, but he nodded, ignoring his wife's rudeness. An uneasy harmony settled over the table until she spoke, her voice seeming overloud.

'That was delicious; would you like some more, Barbara? Edward?'

'No, thank you, Grandmother. But I did enjoy it.'

He dropped his spoon noisily into his empty bowl and folded his arms. 'No, Elspeth, thank you.'

Grandmother rang the little brass bell she kept beside her and Mrs Brown hurried back to retrieve the tureen and remove the bowls. The atmosphere thawed a little when they tasted the game pie.

'Good God! That woman's learning to cook at last. This is splendid. Don't you think so, Barbara?'

'I do, Grandpa, and baked potatoes and tomato relish are perfect with it.'

They munched happily and all had a second helping. The meal had softened his mood and he smiled across at her.

'Your grandmother and I would like a little chat with you after lunch, if you can spare us the time?'

'I have nothing special to do until about four o'clock when I have to go back to the stable.'

'Come to the study whenever you're ready. I shall have coffee served there.' He shrugged. 'I've only a couple of pounds of beans left and I doubt there'll be any more. Those blasted U-boats are stopping the ships coming in.'

'You'll have to make do with tea instead, Edward. We all have to make sacrifices when there's a war on, you know.'

Barbara could almost hear his teeth grinding but he didn't react.

'As there's no dessert, would you excuse me, please? I want to write a quick letter before I join you in the study.'

'Run along, my dear. We shall expect you in twenty minutes.'

There wasn't time to go upstairs and write the mythical letter so she resolved to hide in the orangery. She was unlikely to be disturbed in there. She opened the door but the sweet sickly scent of orange and lemon blossom made her recoil. The perfume was too much for someone already feeling queasy. Where? The only place she could think of was the stables. Forgetting she would have to return to the study in clothes redolent of horse, she held her breath and ran through and out the garden door.

Barbara heard Silver whickering a greeting before she reached the yard. She smiled; it was uncanny how horses knew you were coming before you appeared. The mare's head was stretched over the stable door, ears pricked forward, eager to see her.

'Lovely girl. You don't worry about how I look, do you?' The horse nodded as if in agreement and rubbed her head on Barbara's shoulder. 'I'd better not come right in, Silver, I'm wearing indoor shoes. I shouldn't really be out here at all.'

She buried her face in the rough mane and felt the scalding tears seeping out from the corners of her eyes. She knew why her grandparents wanted to talk to her; she was going to be asked to leave. She didn't fit in. She was plain and outspoken, not suitable for The Grove.

'You love me, don't you, Silver, darling? You wouldn't ask me to go, whatever I did, would you?'

She hadn't heard her grandfather's approach. Didn't know he was there until he placed his jacket around her shoulders.

'And neither would we, my dear child. I can't believe that's what you thought. I've told you this is your home – nothing you can do or say will ever change that.'

'I've over-reacted again, haven't I?' She pulled his jacket closer. She loved his smell: a strange mix of cigar smoke, carbolic soap and lavender. His jacket was warm, comforting, but he needed it more than her. 'Grandpa, you've no coat on. You'll catch your death. It's freezing out here.'

'That's because you're wearing it, my dear. I could hear your teeth chattering from the house.'

'I'm warm enough now. At least I've got a jumper on. We'd better go in; Grandmother will be wondering where we've got to.'

He chuckled and Silver threw her head up in surprise. 'I rather think Elspeth will know exactly where we've been, my dear, don't you?'

She raised her arm and sniffed it. 'Oh dear! Yes. Will there be time to change before we go in?'

'Absolutely not! Good God, we have to change for dinner; twice a day's more than enough.'

Arm in arm they returned to the house. 'Grandpa, why don't you have any animals? There's not even a cat here.'

'Your grandmother doesn't like animals, Barbara, but if you'd like a pet, you shall have one.'

She was tempted to accept, but it wouldn't be fair. 'Thank you, Grandpa, but I couldn't be sure I'd be able to look after it once I've enrolled in the Land Army.'

They both stamped and scraped their shoes and Barbara went into the scullery to wash her hands and face, checking her eyes weren't red. She didn't want her grandmother to know she'd been crying. She kept her shoes on; they were as clean as when she'd gone out, all traces of the stable removed with a wet cloth. Unfortunately this had made her jumper damp but hadn't removed the smell at all.

The study door was open and she could hear the welcome crackling of the logs in the open grate. The massive boiler – which supplied the hot water and the radiators – was running on low, keeping the house from freezing but not sufficient to make the rooms comfortable.

Her grandfather smiled warmly. Her grandmother ignored her, sniffing loudly.

'Would you like coffee, my dear? It will warm you up.'

'Yes, cream and sugar please.' She moved to the opposite side of the fire, filling the awkward pause by rubbing her hands together close to the flames. To her horror steam started to rise from her sleeves.

She snatched her arms back. Good grief! She was going to smell like wet washing as well. Hoping her slacks were dry she curled up in a winged armchair, kicking off her shoes, tucking her feet under her, and removing her arms from view.

'Here you are, Barbara.' He held out a cup of coffee and reluctantly she extended her arm to take it. She raised her head and wrinkled her nose in the direction of her sleeves.

'Good God, child, your jumper's on fire!' She laughed, but grandmother's shocked exclamation ruined the moment.

'On fire? What next? That girl is a walking disaster, Edward.'

Her coffee slopped into the saucer as she put it down. 'I'm sorry, Grandmother, I'm going to change. Please excuse me. I'll be as quick as I can.' She didn't wait for permission; she was out of her chair and running across the room in her socks before anyone could call her back.

She was tempted to remain in her room, not return, but now Grandpa had told her she wasn't to be asked to leave, she was curious to discover exactly what the little chat was to be about.

She dropped her smelly slacks and jumper on the floor. She pulled on a clean pair and one of her new jumpers – the fawn one with an intricate black pattern around the neck, cuffs and bottom edge. After pushing her feet into some soft leather shoes she raced downstairs. Her coffee was where she'd left it and was still hot.

'Sorry, I'm clean and ready.' She was about to curl up in the chair as before but saw her grandmother's mouth tighten, so she refrained; instead she sat with ankles and knees together, feet neatly on the floor as she'd been taught at school. She bent down and retrieved her coffee, took several sips, before smiling brightly.

'What is it you wish to discuss with me, Grandmother?' She saw a flash of disdain and her smile slipped a little.

'Your grandfather will explain, Barbara.'

He winked at her and she was forced to bury her face in her cup to disguise her smile. 'It's about your trust fund, my dear. It has been reinstated. Your birth certificate has been returned along with the documents you need to sign.'

'Oh, is that all? What a relief, I thought it must be something awful, having to come here like this.'

'All? Barbara, your trust fund is hardly something to treat so lightly.'

'It's only money, Grandmother.'

'I told you, Edward, she has no idea how to go on in our world. She's too much like her mother to fit in properly.'

'That's enough, Elspeth. If you can't be civil, I suggest you leave us.' His voice cut the air and she saw her grandmother flinch.

'Very well, I shall go.' Carefully replacing her cup and saucer, she stood up, smoothed down her skirt and sailed out, head erect, looking at neither of them.

Barbara sank deeper into her chair, crushed by the comments. Was she like her mother? Her head started to pound and an involuntary shudder rattled her cup.

'Ignore her, my dear. I do – it's the only way to remain sane in this house. Here, child, drink your coffee. It's hot and sweet; it will help.' She shook her head. 'Trust me, I'm a medical man.' To please him she took a mouthful of coffee. 'Swallow, child, or you'll choke.'

Obediently she swallowed and the coffee went down, but she put the cup back in its saucer on the floor. Her eyes closed and her mind drifted. He wouldn't mind; he was a medical man.

Her lips curved as she remembered Auntie Irene saying exactly that. She thought about John. The soup today had reminded her of him. She wished she could sift her memories, rejecting the unwanted ones and only allowing the nice ones through. She opened her eyes. Her grandfather was beside her, his face creased with concern.

'I'm fine now, Grandpa. Too many memories and not all of them pleasant. I expect they'll fade after I've been here a bit longer.'

'If you feel like sharing them, I'm always here. Sometimes talking helps – you never know.'

'No, I would hate to, but thank you for offering. I just want to put it behind me. I think I'm over it, then something reminds me and it all floods back.' They both knew she meant someone and not something.

'I'll not push you, my dear. Would you like some more coffee? There's still some in the jug.'

'Yes, please. It doesn't taste as good when it's reheated.'

They sat in companionable silence drinking lukewarm coffee, he watching her, obviously waiting for the right moment to introduce the subject of money again.

'Right, back to the trust fund. I understand exactly what you meant – money's not important to you – but I'm afraid you have to accept the fact you're wealthy and you have responsibilities and decisions to make about how to invest your funds.'

'I'm happy to leave all that to you, at least until I come of age.'

'Excellent! That's what I hoped you'd decide. Your annual income is a little over two thousand pounds. That's a great deal of money, my dear.'

'Heavens! I only need a few pounds a week for clothes and keeping Silver. The rest can go to charity perhaps?'

'No; you can give your money away when you're twenty-one, not before. I could invest it in war bonds, which would be helping the country. What do you think?'

'That's a good idea. Could you arrange to transfer five pounds a week for me, Grandpa? With the money I have in my account already, I should have more than enough. In future I shall buy my own clothes. In fact I'm going to get a winter coat and a new dressing gown when I go to Brentwood tomorrow with Simon.'

'I thought you bought everything when you went to London with your grandmother?'

'We didn't get a warm coat for riding my bike or any new nightwear. I have far too many grand clothes and not enough for everyday use.'

'Well, my dear, you get whatever you want. By the way, I spoke to a chap I know in London and found out a bit more about the Land Army. It seems there's an option to be billeted at home and work nearby, but this is not the norm.'

'So I can work locally if I want. Is that what you're saying?'

'I believe so. You could live here and cycle to somewhere like Home Farm. I expect you would prefer that to sleeping in a dormitory with other girls?'

'Actually, I rather liked sharing when I was at school. It was reassuring hearing the girls breathing and murmuring in the darkness. Kept the nightmares at bay.'

'Are you still having nightmares, my dear?'

'No, I love it in father's old room. I feel absolutely safe, as though he's watching over me.'

'Excellent! I should have added, the powers that be are only just re-establishing themselves; they won't be calling you until the New Year at the earliest.'

'Good. It will be lovely to be able to ride and things. Does Grandmother do anything special for Christmas?'

'Good God! I should say so. The house is decorated, there's a huge tree in the hall, carol singers call round, we all have to stir the pudding, and always a dozen or so for lunch on the day itself.' He frowned. 'I doubt it will be like that this year as there's a war on. Not enough staff for a start. But we'll make it special for you, never you fear.'

A knock at the door interrupted them. Mrs Brown came in. 'Do you mind if I clear the coffee things, sir? I need to get off soon.'

Barbara stood up. 'I really do have to write a letter to John's parents, so please excuse me.'

* * *

Tuesday was bedroom and bathroom day. Now she had her horse to exercise the cleaning would have to be done after lunch. She didn't mind the task; it gave her a sense of belonging, of being part of The Grove, not just a guest. She was dressed to ride, intending to go out immediately after the post came. She heard the knock on the front door as she was on the stairs and ran across to answer it.

'Mornin', miss, lovely day. You going out on that little horse of yours?'

'Yes, Mr Giddings, I am. Shall I take the post? Is there anything for me?'

The man beamed. 'There is: two letters, I think.' He handed them over and with a cheerful wave, jumped onto his old black bicycle and pedalled back down the drive.

She sifted through the pile until she found one with her name on. It was thick and official-looking and she didn't recognise the handwriting. She held it up to the light, but the postmark was too blurred to read. The second letter was thin. The spidery scrawl and the postmark indicated this was from St John's Wood. She heard the clack-clack of her grandmother's heels.

'I have the post here, Grandmother. Would you like me to sort it out for you?'

'No, I'll take it, Barbara, thank you.' An imperious hand came out and the letters were handed over. 'I take it those are addressed to you?'

'Yes, they are. One is from an old friend and I think the other could be from the solicitors. I shall read them both when I get back from my ride.'

'Very well. I shall be out for lunch and dinner and, as it's Mrs Brown's day off, you will have to cook for your grandfather yourself. Can you manage to do that?'

'I can. But I think Grandpa told me he was going to London for a medical meeting and won't be back until tomorrow morning.' Her grandmother pursed her lips. 'I'll make my own supper as well. It's no trouble. I love to cook, especially in such a well-equipped kitchen as yours.'

'I shall be home around ten thirty. I'm dining at Mountney Hall. Mr Farley is sending a car. Please leave the back door unbolted. I shall lock it when I return.'

'Would you like me to wait up? I don't think I'd hear if anyone broke into the house if I was in my room.'

'Broke into The Grove? Who could possibly want to do that? No, Barbara, you go to bed as usual.' She looked through the letters and glanced up. 'You haven't forgotten it's Tuesday have you?'

'No, Grandmother, I haven't. I shall do my chores after I've exercised Silver Lady and mucked her out.' She saw the look of disgust – she really must remember not to mention manure again.

It was three o'clock before she was curled up in front of the fire in the study. This had become her favourite downstairs room, apart from the kitchen. It was informally furnished and always had a cheerful apple-wood fire burning in the basket grate. She began by opening the letter from John.

Dearest Babs,

Would you believe it – we're training in London. We had to go to Lord's cricket ground first; I had my interviews in the Long Room. Can you imagine, I actually walked on that hallowed ground? We're doing all the written stuff, navigation and so on, before we're sent away to Scotland to learn to fly Tiger Moths.

I'm staying in a hotel. The food is good and the chaps I've met seem likeable. I've discovered that only three out of five of us will progress to the next stage, and only two out of five pass the flying tests. I hope I'm one of them. I suppose I'll be happy enough to be a navigator, or radio operator, but I really want to be a pilot.

The letter continued in the same vein, giving her the details of his day, and saying how much he missed her. He ended by telling her he expected to get leave when he'd finished his preliminary training. He intended to come and see her before going home to Hastings. John here? She wasn't sure she wanted her two worlds to collide like that. They could meet in London and that way there would be no embarrassing explanations to make.

He wouldn't recognise her in her new clothes. Smiling at the thought she turned to the thick envelope. She pulled it open. Her mouth dropped as all the letters she had written to her brothers tumbled out unopened.

11

Why hadn't the letters been opened? Barbara sifted through the pile until she found a single sheet of handwritten paper.

Dear Miss Sinclair,

It is with deep regret that we are obliged to return your correspondence. Mr and Mrs Evans have instructed us that you are to have no contact with Thomas and David. Therefore I must insist that you do not write to them again.

However, I'm certain you are anxious to know how the boys are. They have settled in well and apart from asking every day if there is a letter from their big sister, there have been no problems. We showed them your letters and explained why they couldn't be given to them.

Although you must not communicate with the boys directly, we have decided that it would be in order for us to write to you in order to pass on any news and information and you may do the same. One letter each half-term will be acceptable.

We remain,

Yours sincerely

Mr and Mrs Hardcastle, Principals of Downton School

Her fingers curled and the constriction in her throat relaxed. It wasn't so bad; the boys knew she had not broken her promise. But how could they wish to involve the boys after so long? Was it guilt? The image of the kitchen, that final night, was still vivid. Mrs Evans sitting slumped and defeated, old, a different person from the one who had terrorised her for fifteen years. She wasn't afraid of her any more.

And Mr Evans, when he'd driven her away for the last time, his demeanour had changed. He was no longer in command, more a crumpled old man unable to cope with life.

She pushed her unopened letters back into the larger envelope. She was sad the boys hadn't been allowed to read them but pleased they had settled in at school. They were children. None of this was their fault. Pure spite had prompted the ban; she was sure of that.

Somehow she would get round it; her brothers wouldn't be allowed to suffer because of her. Mrs Peterson might be prepared to help and allow Barbara's letters to go in with letters to Mary and Charlie.

It took the operator several minutes to connect her to the vicarage. 'Mrs Peterson, it's Barbara. How are you?'

'Barbara.' The vicar's wife sounded far away, as if she was talking to her whilst standing in a field. 'What a lovely surprise. I'm very well, thank you, but how are you?'

There was some anxiety in her question. 'I'm fine, Mrs Peterson. It's lovely here. My grandfather, Dr Sinclair, has done everything to make me welcome. He's even paid for Silver Lady to come and join me.'

'I'm so glad to hear that; we have been worried about you.' Mrs Peterson paused. 'Mrs Adams spoke to me after church the Sunday after you left so suddenly.'

Barbara gripped the handset. She had difficulty speaking. 'What did she say?'

'She said that you had been hurt, were very upset, and what a shame it all was.'

'I'm quite well, now, Mrs Peterson, so please could you tell anyone who's interested to forget all about it.'

'Yes, of course I will.' The line was quiet apart from the sound of breathing.

Was there more unpleasant news to come? 'Is something wrong, Mrs Peterson?'

'Yes, my dear, I'm afraid there is. I'd better tell you the whole. Mr Evans came round to see us the day after you left and told us you had attacked your mother and they had been forced to ask you to leave. He blackened your name and tried to give the impression you were a danger to society.'

Barbara's head spun and a wave of nausea rocked her. For a moment she couldn't answer.

'Are you there, Barbara? Please believe me, we never accepted this story for a minute.'

'Thank you.'

'Then, when Mrs Adams spoke to me, and to several other members of the congregation everything changed. You could see people staring at your mother and stepfather, realising the story they'd been telling was untrue. You had been the one attacked, not Mrs Evans.'

'What happened next?'

'In a matter of minutes they were being ostracised. People turned their backs and they both hurried off. They haven't been to any services since then.'

'How awful! The church was their life. Whatever happened is between us, Mrs Peterson; it's not for others to judge. I don't want Tom and David dragged into this.'

'You're quite right, my dear. Mr Peterson went round but Mrs Evans wouldn't answer the door. He has tried several times. I've spoken to the WVS committee but she hasn't been to any meetings.'

'What about Mr Evans? Has anybody seen him?'

'I haven't, but Mr Peterson went down to the bank and could see him in the back office. However, he refused to come out, just sent a message that he was too busy.'

'If my mother isn't going to church or to the WVS meetings, has she still been to the WI?'

'No, I went myself last week and everyone was saying this was the first meeting your mother had ever missed.'

'Has no one seen her at all? Not out shopping, or in Hastings having tea with her friends?'

'I'm afraid not. Groceries are being delivered to the house. It's all very worrying. We asked Dr Reynolds to call round, but he was turned away by Mr Evans who insisted your mother was well.'

She knew what was coming next and wanted to fling the telephone back on the table and run away. 'I can't possibly come down, Mrs Peterson. When I left I vowed never to go back. That part of my life is over.'

'I can imagine how you feel, Barbara, but don't you think you have a Christian duty, whatever has taken place between you and your family, to make sure your mother is in good health? Could you ever forgive yourself if she was ill, or worse, and you had done nothing?'

'Why don't you call the police? Surely they would force an entry, get in to see for themselves?'

Mrs Peterson sighed. 'Yes, but we had hoped to avoid that. However, if you really can't come down we shall have no option but to inform the authorities.'

Everyone thought Mr Evans had injured her; therefore the absence of her mother would make them believe he had done the same to her. It would serve them both right if the police were called. She could stop all the speculation by explaining it had been her mother who assaulted her, not her stepfather, but she couldn't bring herself to do this.

'I'm sorry, Mrs Peterson, but I'm no longer part of their lives. I'm sure I would be the last person they'd want to see. If you're genuinely worried about my mother you must take whatever steps you feel are necessary. My only concern is for my brothers.'

'Well, my dear, if that's how you feel, I won't pressure you any further. But could I ask you to think about it overnight and perhaps telephone tomorrow morning with your final decision?'

'I won't change my mind, but I will certainly ring you tomorrow morning. I'm sorry, I have to go now. There's someone knocking at the door.'

She dropped the receiver back. All desire to telephone Auntie Irene and Uncle Bill had evaporated. They would also know about her injuries, would want to talk to her about them, and she couldn't face that. The very thought made her stomach roil.

She wished Grandpa was home; he'd understand and would ring and explain why she couldn't come. He was a doctor; they would have to accept his opinion. He wouldn't be back until tomorrow morning. The thought of having to face her mother again brought back terrible memories. She could feel the panic, the black fear, start to take hold. Not here, please God, not here.

She stumbled out of her chair and ran blindly for the door. She had to get out, find somewhere safe, and the only place she knew was the stables. No one ever came to hurt her there.

She ran through the empty house, indoor shoes silent on the parquet and ignoring the coats hanging in military precision. She fumbled the back door open, forgetting to close it behind her. Silver greeted her when she arrived in the yard. She was barely able to unbolt the box before falling inside and pulling the door shut. She didn't rebolt it. She did as she always did when running away from her terror: crumpled against the far wall, under the manger, dropping her head into her lap and covering it with her arms, as if warding off blows. Her mare was well used to these sudden appearances and placed her bulk between her mistress and the door, protecting her from possible attack.

The cold eventually roused her from her stupor. She opened her eyes but could see nothing. Everywhere was black, not even a moon to give a glimmer of light. She tried, unsuccessfully, to straighten her arms, and her teeth began to click. The mare lowered her head and pressed a whiskery muzzle into her icy face, breathing a welcome draught of warm air over her.

Five minutes passed before she could control her teeth and reach out to bury her fingers in Silver's wiry mane. As she hung on, the horse raised her head and stepped back, bringing Barbara slowly to her feet. She rested, absorbing the animal's body heat, until she was sufficiently thawed to attempt to move.

'Good girl. Stand still, let me lean on you.' She felt the horse brace herself. With closed eyes she fingered her way towards the door. She was horrified to find it swinging open. Silver could have wandered off. She had to pull herself together; if she stayed outside much longer she could literally catch her death.

'Stay here. I'll be back with your supper in a little while.'

Silver nudged her between the shoulders as if encouraging her to go outside and fetch the promised feed. The tack-room door was no more than a yard from the stable; if she faced the wall and kept her hands on it she was bound to find the entrance. This time she remembered to bolt the door. The iron burnt her ungloved fingers.

She cracked her knee on the outside tap but didn't pause to rub it, just continued groping her way sideways. At last her fingers felt the latch and she grabbed it, pulling open the door. She always left the lantern at the back, on the shelf, and the matches would be beside it.

It would be easier to keep her eyes closed and not strain to see in the inky dark. She sidled painfully down the length the room, barking her shins on various protuberances and almost upsetting the large paraffin stove, but eventually located the precious matches.

Fumbling the box open she struck one and in the small flare was able to find the lantern. Terrified of setting the whole place alight with a dropped match she opened the front and wound up the wick. Only when she could feel the dampness of the paraffin did she attempt to light it. She pushed a second match into the storm lamp and it lit, instantly throwing a golden glow around the space.

She was so tired and wanted to curl up and sleep. She couldn't think clearly, or force her limbs to move. Her mare stamped impatiently next door and it galvanised her into action. She had to get Silver's supper, fill her hay net, give her fresh water; she couldn't go to sleep until she'd completed these tasks.

There was something she should do, something very important, but she couldn't think what this was. She stared round. Her mouth curved. The paraffin stove, that was it; she had to get it started, then she would be warm. Her fingers were clumsy and the small aperture through which she had to push the match was almost too much. It took four matches to light it, but immediately the room felt warmer.

What next? Something to put on over her thin jumper. She held the lantern up. Feed sacks – grabbing one she pulled it round her shoulders.

After a few minutes her brain started to function. She found the knife used for cutting the string on the bales and slit a hole in the top of the sack and one on each side. She dragged it over her head like a coalman's jerkin.

Her feet were numb, but at least her top half was covered. She no longer had the urge to fall asleep in a corner, just wanted to get inside in the warm and thaw out. But first she needed to find the fodder bucket. Where was it? Her gaze rested on a battered enamel bowl; she would use that instead. Her hands were too stiff to cut apples and carrots. Bran, oats and boiled barley would have to do.

The tack-room door was open, a large wedge of light spilling out into the yard, but hopefully too far from the lane for the vigilant ARP warden to spot it. She carried the lantern outside and put it on the ground whilst she filled up the spare water bucket. She stared down at the bowl full of food and the water. What else did Silver need? Hay – she had to fill the net as well.

The horse, smelling her food, started to kick the stable door and snort. 'Right, I'm coming. Step back, let me in, silly girl, and I'll give it to you.' She emptied the hard feed into the manger and went to bring in the water. Leaving the half-door open, she fetched a couple of rounds of hay from the barn. She couldn't manage the neck of the net so dropped it on the floor. Silver would eat it if she was hungry.

This time she remembered to lock both doors and close the tack room. She collected the lantern and holding it in front of her, down by her knees, she headed for the house. She was shocked to find the door open, but too cold to agonise about it. She slammed it and hurried up the backstairs to her bedroom.

She clicked the light on, glad the blackouts were already closed, and only then did she extinguish the lamp. She ought to have a hot bath, thaw out, go down to the kitchen and make herself something to eat, but was too exhausted. All she wanted to do was fall under the covers and sleep.

* * *

Barbara didn't stir when Mrs Mullins came in with a mug of tea. Even the rattle of the shutters being opened didn't penetrate her dream. It wasn't until Rosie shook her by the shoulder she opened her eyes.

'Good grief, miss, you're still dressed and you're wearing a sack.'

'Am I?' She glanced down, grinning. 'Do you know, I think I've got my shoes on and they're filthy as well.'

Rosie placed the mug in her hands. 'Here, you drink this, Miss Sinclair. I'll go and run you a hot bath; you'll feel much better after that.'

She sipped the tea, her legs dangling over the side of the bed, not sure how she felt. She could hear the roar of the geyser and the water thundering into the bath tub and knew Mrs Mullins was giving her far more than the stipulated five inches. The tea was nice, sweet and hot and not too strong, just how she liked it.

Her eyes drifted down registering her filthy slacks and mud-caked indoor shoes. Why was she in bed with her clothes on? She didn't remember coming to bed. Her mind was blank from the moment she'd put the telephone back. She heard Rosie returning.

'Your bath's all ready, miss. If you hop in I'll nip down and get you a tray of something.'

Barbara slid from the bed, grateful for the steadying arm as her legs threatened to buckle.

'Wait a moment, get your bearings, then we'll walk ever so slowly into the bathroom. Are you ready?'

It took all her concentration to force one leg in front of the other and they were both relieved to reach the cork-topped stool by the bath.

'Here, perch on this for a mo.' Rosie helped her to sit down. 'There, that's the ticket. Now, miss, do want any help to get undressed?'

'No, thank you, I can manage from here. What time is it, Rosie?'

'Just after eight o'clock, a bit later than usual, but still plenty of time to take that horse of yours out and get back for Mr Farley.'

'Good – don't worry about a tray up here, thanks, Rosie; I'll come down.'

The cold marble of the steps made Barbara shiver and she clenched her teeth to stop them chattering. She sat on the edge of the bath, swinging first one leg and then the other over the side, being forced to lift them individually, like an old woman. She slid under the hot water, sighing with pleasure. She rested her head on a folded towel and relaxed.

She stretched, closing her eyes, letting the warmth seep into her body. She could stay like this forever, floating, peaceful and warm at last. After fifteen minutes the water began to cool; she must get out. She drew her knees up and gripped the sides of the bath and pushed, but her arms had no strength. For the first time she regretted the depth of the bath tub. After wallowing like a beached whale she was forced to turn on to her hands and knees in order to get out. She couldn't understand why she felt so weak or why her teeth kept chattering.

She stood in front of the fire whilst she pulled on her riding clothes. This strange amnesia was familiar, but this time there was something different. Whatever was it that was eluding her woolly brain? If she didn't try, maybe the answer would drift in on its own. Yes! This time she didn't hurt anywhere, had no bruises or cuts; that was the difference.

Her mouth filled with bile as memory flooded back. Mrs Peterson wanted her to go back to Crabapple Cottage and was expecting her to ring this morning. She couldn't go. She needed the bathroom. She dashed across the room just reaching the WC before being horribly sick. Clammy-faced and faint she sat on the floor, leaning against the wall whilst she recovered.

Now she remembered. Like an idiot she had run outside in her indoor clothes and fallen asleep in the stable. What had possessed her? She had broken free; she mustn't let the past ruin her future. But she still had to make that telephone call to the vicarage.

She stood and went to the sink to wash her mouth and clean her teeth. She was used to these sudden attacks of nausea; had suffered from what Auntie Irene called 'a nervous stomach' all her life. She didn't want to go back to Hastings, not on her own. That was it! She would ask Grandpa to go with her and then she could do it.

Mrs Peterson was delighted Barbara had changed her mind and promised not to tell anyone of the intended visit until it was confirmed. Mrs Brown and Rosie were waiting expectantly in the kitchen to hear her explanation for her curious nightwear. She gave them an edited version.

'You were very lucky, Miss Sinclair; there was a hard frost last night.

You would have frozen solid if you'd stayed in that stable all night,' Mrs Brown said. 'What you need is someone to help you with that horse. It's not right a young lady like you should have to do all that hard work.'

'If you know someone suitable, Mrs Brown, then I'd be delighted to employ them.'

'I do. As it happens, my son Joe's leaving school this Friday. He'll be fourteen at the weekend. He's not very good with writing and such but give him anything practical, or anything to do with animals, and you'll have no complaints.'

'He sounds perfect, Mrs Brown. Bring him up with you tomorrow and I'll have a chat with him and introduce him to Silver. If they get on, the job's his. It won't take him more than a couple of hours every morning but I'm sure there's plenty of work in the garden and around the house he can do the rest of the day.'

'Thank you ever so, Miss Sinclair. You'll not be sorry; he's a good boy and a hard worker.'

Barbara looked at her watch. 'I'd better be getting on or I'll not be back in time.'

'Do you know what time Dr Sinclair is coming home, miss? Will he be wanting lunch, do you think?'

'He told me he would be back mid-morning, Mrs Brown, so I imagine he will. I'm afraid I have no idea whether Mrs Sinclair will be at home or not. She was out all yesterday and I haven't actually seen her today.'

'I don't think she's here, miss. She must have gone out very early because the door was unlocked.'

'I left it open when I went to bed. I wonder if she decided to stay the night at Mountney Hall. I'll just run upstairs and check if her bed's been slept in.' She knocked but received no answer. She tried the handle and it turned. Her grandmother always locked the door when she was in. The room was empty, the bed neatly made. She hurried downstairs to the kitchen to tell them.

'I shouldn't worry about it, miss. Madam often stays over when sir's away. I expect she didn't think to telephone.'

'I think I'll ring Mrs Farley and make sure she's there, Rosie. She asked me to leave the back door open so I think it's very strange she didn't call to tell me to bolt it.'

'I expect you were down in the stable or fast asleep in bed when she did,' Mrs Brown said helpfully.

She was becoming an expert on the telephone and soon found herself connected to Mountney Hall by a helpful operator. 'Good morning, it's Barbara Sinclair. Is Mrs Sinclair with you at the moment?'

'Just one moment, miss, I shall go and enquire.'

The butler put the phone down and walked away. Moments later she could hear the tell-tale click-clack of her grandmother's high heels approaching.

'Barbara? Is there something wrong?'

'No, Grandmother. Mrs Brown would like to know if you will be in for lunch or dinner today?'

'I am going up to Town for lunch but will be back for dinner. Could you inform your grandfather when he returns?'

'Yes, if he's not back before I go out with Simon I'll leave him a message. Goodbye, Grandmother, I hope you enjoy your lunch.'

The phone went dead. Pleased there was nothing sinister about her grandmother's absence overnight she returned to the kitchen to relay the information to the staff.

* * *

Barbara clattered back into the stable to find a boy wheeling an overfull barrow of dung across the yard. 'Hello, you must be Joe Brown. I didn't expect to see you today.'

The boy grinned. 'Ma popped home and fetched me, miss. Thought it might help you decide if I got on with it; show you what I can do, like.'

She dismounted. 'Why don't you come over and meet Silver Lady?'

Joe dropped the barrow and wiping his hands on the seat of his trousers walked confidently to the horse, hand outstretched. 'You're a pretty girl, ain't you then?'

Silver, recognising a friend, lowered her head to nuzzle him. Instant rapport was established.

'Do you know how to untack, Joe?'

'Never done it, miss, but I reckon you'll only have to show me once. It don't look too complicated. Not like the harness on Mr Billings's milk cart and I've done that often enough.'

She demonstrated how to remove a bridle and slip on a halter without losing the horse. She tethered Silver to the metal ring embedded in the brick wall outside the loose box, before showing him how to remove the saddle and put on the rug. Satisfied the boy was comfortable around horses, she left him to finish mucking out and preparing the stable.

She had over an hour to wash and change before Simon arrived to collect her. She still hadn't settled on what to wear and was reviewing her wardrobe as she pulled off her boots in the boot room.

'Excellent! There you are, Barbara, my dear. I got back earlier than expected so now we have time to have a coffee together before you go out.'

'Grandpa, I'm so glad to see you. Can I come to the study like this, or do you want me to change first?'

'Come as you are. I like the smell of the stable.' He led the way back down the passageway and Barbara, wearing socks on the slippery wooden floor, found it difficult to keep up. 'Here we are. Would you like anything to eat? Riding always used to make me hungry.'

She shook her head. 'I had a huge breakfast, thank you. Coffee would be lovely, though.'

Barbara explained about the returned letters, her mother's disappearance and Mrs Peterson's insistence she go to check for herself that nothing untoward had happened.

'I told Mrs Peterson I would come down if I could persuade you to come with me. Can you spare the time to go to Hastings? We would have to stay overnight, but I'm sure there'll be places open where we can get rooms.'

'I should be delighted to accompany you, my dear. Speed is of the essence, I take it? I have to be at the hospital this afternoon and tomorrow, but I have Friday and the weekend free.'

'That would be wonderful. I'll ring and tell her we're coming. I'd like to introduce you to Auntie Irene and Uncle Bill whilst we're there, if we have time.'

'Excellent. Leave the travel arrangements to me, my dear. You go and ring the vicar's wife and then run upstairs and get ready. I hope you can get changed quicker than your grandmother or you're going to be keeping young Farley waiting.'

She chose the navy spotted dress she'd bought in Brentwood. She didn't feel uncomfortable in this and she was only going to a matinee and lunch at the Swan, not to dinner at the Ritz. He arrived exactly on time dressed casually in navy blazer and grey flannels, a cravat tied jauntily round his neck. Not waiting for him to knock, she grabbed her bag and ran out to greet him.

'Hello, Simon. I'm so looking forward to seeing *The Great Dictator*. It's very kind of you to take me. Shall we go, or do you want to come in and speak to Grandpa?'

'No thank you, Barbara. Let's get off. You look absolutely spiffing. That little hat with the feather suits you; I didn't think you were the sort of girl to wear a hat like that.'

She laughed. 'Well, I could hardly wear my beret with such a smart coat, now could I?'

He double declutched expertly and they roared off down the drive. 'I expect you'll be wanting to do a bit of shopping before we have lunch, won't you?'

'Yes, actually I would like to buy a few things, if you're sure you don't mind waiting.'

'I have to collect a couple of parcels from the station so I can do that whilst you're in Rosebery's.'

She selected a serviceable dressing gown in heavy red flannel and three equally unflattering warm nightgowns. The coat she chose was moss green tweed with a tie belt of matching material.

'That coat looks a treat on you, miss,' a shop assistant assured her. 'Green goes with your eyes.'

'I'll take it. Can you put it in with the other things, please? I'm in a bit of a hurry; someone is waiting for me outside in his car.' Clutching her parcel she hurried out to meet Simon who was leaning patiently against the bonnet. 'I'm so sorry; I was as quick as I could be.'

'I'm used to waiting for my mother and she takes far longer than you.' He removed the parcel from her arms and tossed it on to the back seat. 'Are you ready to eat, Barbara? I'm starving and they do a first-rate steak and kidney pie at the Swan.'

The afternoon sped by and Barbara enjoyed every moment of it. Simon was good company, considerate and polite, and his deafness proved no obstacle to conversation. She discovered he could follow perfectly well if he could see her when she spoke. As they drove out of Brentwood the light was fading.

'Thank you so much for taking me out today; I've really enjoyed it. The film was wonderful. It's a long time since I laughed so much.'

He grinned. 'To tell you the truth I couldn't understand what was going on most of the time.'

'Well, I think it was noble of you to sit through the whole film without complaining.' She looked up, puzzled. 'Simon, this isn't the way we came.'

'No, my father insisted I bring you back for tea. We won't stay long, and even if it is dark, it's no distance from Mountney Hall to The Grove.'

12

Barbara shifted nervously on her seat. 'I really don't think I have time to visit your parents today, Simon. Grandpa was most insistent I get back before the blackout.'

'I promised them, Barbara. Please say you'll come with me. We only have to stay for one cup of tea.'

He glanced sideways and there was fear in his eyes. 'Very well, but I'm not staying for more than fifteen minutes. When I say I have to leave you mustn't argue.'

'Agreed. Thank you.'

The car began to slow as they approached a pair of wrought-iron gates that were the equal of those that flanked the entrance to The Grove. The drive passed through an avenue of naked lime trees and turned sharply right, crossing a stretch of fiercely manicured parkland in which sheep and deer grazed.

'Do you eat the venison or are the deer for ornament only?'

'Pa shoots one whenever we want the meat. I don't care for it myself – too gamey – but he likes to shoot things and we have to eat it.'

She swallowed. 'I like venison in pies, but not on its own.' Why were they talking about meat? He swung the car round the final curve and Mountney Hall was revealed in all its Georgian splendour. Her eyes widened. 'Good heavens, Simon, I'd no idea your home was so grand. It's magnificent.'

'As fine as The Grove?'

'Almost! At least here you can go in through the front door and not have to creep in round the back.'

The car glided to a halt at the base of the steps. Before he had time to open the passenger door she was out of the car. 'It's a lovely house, Simon, in perfect proportion. I can just imagine how long it took you to put the tape on all those window.'

As they mounted the steps the door swung open and the butler, resplendent in black tails, greeted them. 'Good afternoon, Miss Sinclair, Mr Simon. Mr and Mrs Farley are waiting in the drawing room.'

Simon flinched. 'How can we be late? We came here as soon as the film finished.' She stretched her hand out intending to offer her support but he shrugged it off, not looking at her. Embarrassed she stepped away to stand in front of an impressive, gilt-framed mirror, checking her appearance.

Should she remove her coat as well as her gloves? And what about her hat? If it was her usual beret it would come off easily, but this creation was firmly attached to her head by matching glass-topped hat pins. They were only staying for a short while, no point in removing anything apart from her gloves.

He was standing outside double doors waiting for her. He glanced down, his brow creased. 'You haven't given Carstairs your coat and gloves, Barbara,' he hissed. 'You can't go in for tea with your coat on.'

'As I'm not staying for tea, just calling in to say hello, it's not worth taking it off, is it?'

The butler opened the doors and announced them formally. If she hadn't been so nervous she would have found the whole experience amusing. She was visiting a businessman and his wife, not the queen! Mr Farley was on his feet and came forward to greet her.

'Welcome, my dear Miss Sinclair. I'm so glad you can spare a few minutes to call in to see us.'

The significance of her coat had been noted. She extended her hand

and it disappeared in his. His grip was hard, dry, not fleshy and damp as she'd anticipated.

'I promised my grandfather I would be back before the blackout so I'm afraid I can't stay for tea, but perhaps I could come another time?' Good grief! She had just invited herself for a second visit, a definite faux pas, but he didn't seem a bit bothered. In fact he beamed.

'Of course. We quite understand. Perhaps you could you join us for lunch next Sunday?'

She removed her hand and smiled. 'I'm afraid I'm going to see my mother tomorrow and I might not be back by the weekend, Mr Farley.'

She saw a flash of something in his eyes and instinctively stepped backwards. Simon cleared his throat, making her jump.

'Barbara, Ma has a cup of tea for you over here.'

'Thank you, Simon.' She turned and smiled at Mrs Farley. 'How are you, Mrs Farley? It's kind of you to invite me. I'm sorry I can't stay long.'

Mrs Farley nodded and waved vaguely in the direction of a seat. 'Please, won't you sit for a moment, Miss Sinclair? Drinking tea standing up is so tiresome.'

Barbara took the chair indicated, neatly crossing her ankles and placing her handbag on the floor. Simon brought her a delicate porcelain cup and saucer, the china so thin the light shone through it. She took it, with a smile of thanks, and the unmistakable aroma of Earl Grey wafted up. It made her think of Alex and she smiled, wishing she was back in the kitchen at Home Farm.

Mr Farley subsided onto a matching Chippendale and Simon went to sit beside his mother on the *chaise longue*.

'Did you enjoy the film, Miss Sinclair?'

'I did, thank you. I'm so glad Simon offered to take me.'

Mrs Farley nodded but didn't respond. An uneasy silence fell on the drawing room. Mr Farley broke it, his voice overloud.

'I saw you crossing the fields behind The Grove yesterday, Miss Sinclair. That grey mare of yours has a massive jump and you're an excellent jockey. It's obviously not fear that stops you hunting.' He stared pointedly at his son, who flushed.

She remembered Grandpa telling her Simon was a bruising rider so the inferred criticism was unjust. She jumped to defend him. 'Simon is coming out with me next Wednesday afternoon. He's promised to take me over some really exciting country.'

'Has he indeed?' Mr Farley raised his eyebrows.

Simon raised his head and the hate in his eyes shocked her.

'Yes, I have. Why don't you come along too, Pa? If you think you can spare the time?'

Was something going on here that she didn't follow? Was Simon actually challenging his father to a cross-country ride, or was she imagining it?

'I should like to accompany you, if you have no objection, Miss Sinclair?' Mr Farley smiled, not allowing her to voice an opinion of any sort. 'Shall we ride over or will you meet us here?'

'I'll come here.' She gulped down the unpleasant drink and stood up. 'I'm really sorry, but I have to leave.' She caught Simon's eye and he nodded.

'Yes, I have to get Barbara back before dark.'

After placing her cup and saucer on a convenient side table she collected her bag. 'I shall be here around one o'clock, next Wednesday, Mr Farley. That should give us at least two hours before I have to head back.'

'I shall look forward to it, Miss Sinclair.' He half bowed, a smile playing around his mouth. Simon had to step round him in order to reach the door. For a moment father and son were standing shoulder to shoulder; physically they were almost identical.

Both had wide shoulders, the same-shaped head, slicked-back dark hair, and both wore smart navy blazers with a cravat. Then Simon moved past and the resemblance vanished. His carriage was less erect, his expression less commanding. The similarity was superficial; they were two different men entirely. He was kind and friendly, no threat to anyone, but his father was formidable. Anyone who crossed him would live to regret it.

Carstairs, the butler, was waiting in the corridor to usher them back down the hall. It wasn't until the front door closed she was able to relax.

'It's not quite dark, Simon. I'm going to be back before Grandpa starts worrying.'

He paused, an odd expression on his face. His question was abrupt. 'Why did you say we were riding together next week?'

'I'm sorry, I should have asked you first. But your father seems to think you're frightened of big fences and I know you're not.'

'And how do you know that?'

'My grandfather told me.' She was finding him a little intimidating, as if some of his father's aggression had rubbed off. 'I can ring and cancel if you like. I was only trying to help. I didn't mean to cause a problem for you.'

He grinned, the old Simon back. 'I'm being silly. It's Pa – he seems to annoy me every time. It would be absolutely spiffing to go out with you. Thanks so much for suggesting it.' He ran down the steps and flung open the passenger door with a flourish. 'Your carriage awaits, my lady.'

She giggled. 'This place does make me feel like royalty. I'm not used to such things. My life, until I arrived in Ingatestone, was rather ordinary.'

'Well, I must say one would never know you're not to the manor born.'

The car started first time and they roared off down the drive, the speed pinning her to the seat and making conversation impossible. When they reached the lane he decelerated and she was able to catch her breath.

'I'm going to Hastings tomorrow afternoon with my grandfather. My mother's unwell.' Somehow saying the words, hearing them out loud, helped to make the visit seem nothing special.

'Sorry to hear that, old thing. Hope it's nothing serious.'

She hoped it was. 'No, I don't think so. But grandfather thinks it's time he met my mother; after all, she was once married to his son.'

'Tricky business, relatives and all that. Will your RAF chappie be there?'

For a moment she was confused. Why should Alex be in Hastings? 'Oh, no, John's in London, but we're meeting next month. He's got leave before he goes up to Scotland.'

She felt him tense. 'Not bringing him down here, are you, old girl?'

'No, I'm not. Too soon for the grandparents to meet him.' She heard him sigh. 'Don't worry, as far as everyone round here is concerned you and I are seeing each other. It's good cover for us both.'

'Good show. As long as they think you're interested they'll leave me alone.'

'And it will please my grandmother as well, so everyone's happy.'

She didn't tell him Grandpa knew about John or that she was going to Sunday lunch at Home Farm when Alex would be there. That was none of his business. Their relationship was mutually beneficial, but it didn't mean they were close, or that she had to share confidential information with him.

They crunched up the drive in the dark and the pinpricks of light from the headlamps were barely enough to see. She was glad to be home. He was a dear boy but his driving was a trifle reckless.

'Thank you so much for taking me out today. I shall see you next week at Mountney Hall.'

'My pleasure. Cheerio, Barbara.' He waved and the car sped off into the darkness. She flicked on her torch and made her way around the house to the back door.

* * *

'Will I look overdressed in this, Rosie?' Barbara held up a fine wool suit with a box-pleated skirt and long, slightly waisted jacket.

'That's lovely, miss. You have to hand it to madam; she knows how to pick clothes. Green's perfect on you. And with that jacket you won't need a coat. You could take an umbrella instead.'

'I like this outfit better than the others because it's less fussy, more practical.' She removed it from the rail, adding the dark green brogues and small felt pillbox hat that completed the ensemble. 'There, all I need to decide is what else to take. We're only staying overnight, so I thought clean underwear, a nightdress and perhaps a spare blouse would be sufficient.'

'I should wear a cardi under that jacket; it's big enough. What about the gold cashmere? Then you'll not be cold. There was a hard frost last night, and the trains don't have heating now, do they?'

'You're right, and I'll wear heavy lisle stockings to travel and take silk stockings for when I get there.'

'What time are you leaving, miss?'

'Grandpa said he'd be back from the hospital by nine thirty. I think the train leaves at ten thirty.'

'If you get ready, I'll nip down and make a quick cuppa. There's something I want to ask you before you go.'

Barbara carried her leather overnight case and handbag down to the kitchen. Rosie and Mrs Brown greeted her with shrieks of admiration.

'My, Miss Sinclair, don't you like a treat! No one would know you for the young lady who arrived a few weeks ago,' Mrs Brown said.

'That's what I'm afraid of. These clothes make me feel like different person.'

'You look like one, miss. Ever so smart, and a real lady.' Rosie pushed a steaming mug across the scrubbed table. 'Just the way you like it.'

She carefully pulled her skirt straight under her bottom before sitting. 'What is it you wanted to ask me?'

'It's like this. My Auntie Lil, from Hornchurch, has written to my mum and asked if she can take my cousin Marigold in for a while. It seems she's seeing too much of the RAF boys and Uncle Ron is getting right narked and is threatening to throw her out.'

'I don't see how I can help.'

'I was wondering if you could ask madam if Marigold could come here as upstairs maid. She could live in, do the bedrooms and bathrooms and such, look after your personal laundry and ironing.'

'She's not in any sort of... trouble... is she, Rosie?'

'Good Gawd! Not likely, but I reckon if she stays around the RAF base much longer she very well could be.'

'How old is she?'

'Seventeen, eighteen next March. She's been working as a daily with Auntie Lil, so she's had experience of being in service.'

Grandpa's car draw up outside and the horn sounded impatiently. 'Sorry, I have to dash. But I should think it's worth asking my grandmother, especially as she was talking of cancelling Christmas Day this year because there aren't enough staff to do it properly.'

'Righty ho! I'll give it a go when I collect my wages this afternoon,' Rosie called after her.

Barbara grabbed her bags, checked her stocking seams, and ran out.

'Come along, my dear, don't want to miss the train.' He leant across and pushed the passenger door open. 'Hop in. Throw your bags with mine on the back seat.'

She did as she was told and banged the door seconds before the car rolled forward. 'I spent ages deciding what to wear today, Grandpa. I do hope I've got it right.'

He glanced sideways. 'Excellent choice, my dear girl. Elegant and practical. You look lovely.' He changed gears noisily before continuing. 'Young Joe has settled in with your mare, has he?'

'He's wonderful. She'll hardly know I'm gone with him fussing over her.'

The car covered the six miles in record time. 'Here we are, Barbara, and five minutes to spare.'

They had to wait a further ten minutes for the London train to steam in. First class was relatively empty, but second and third were heaving with service personnel and bulging kitbags.

'I'm glad we can travel in comfort, Grandpa. It's standing room only everywhere else.' The train stopped at every station and was almost twenty minutes late by the time they reached Liverpool Street.

'We'll have to hurry, my dear, or we'll miss our connection to Hastings. Let's hope there's a cab waiting.'

There was, and they arrived at London Bridge Station with minutes to spare. She found it difficult to keep up the required flow of small talk and feigned sleep. As the train steamed closer to Hastings her confidence faded. She couldn't go through with it, even with Grandpa beside her. The train shuddered to a halt.

'It isn't going to be as bad as you fear, my dear girl. Facing a nemesis is half the battle. Once you've accomplished that your nightmares and things will slowly subside.'

She forced her eyes open. 'I don't want to go back to Crabapple

Cottage. Could you arrange for them to come down to see us at the hotel?'

He chuckled. 'The main reason we've come is to try and encourage your mother to come out of the house. We have to visit her; there's no other way.'

She checked her hat was still at the correct angle, her lipstick unsmudged and then, pinning on a bright smile, she collected her bags and followed him on to the platform.

'Coooee! Barbara – over here.' Mrs Peterson rushed forward to greet them.

The smile became genuine as she greeted the vicar's wife. 'Hello, Mrs Peterson. It's so good to see you. May I introduce my grandfather, Dr Sinclair, to you?'

'How do you do, Mrs Peterson; kind of you to meet us.'

'It's no trouble at all, Dr Sinclair. I have the car outside. I didn't know if you would want to go straight to Crabapple Cottage, or leave it until tomorrow morning when it's light?'

'Tomorrow morning, I think, Mrs Peterson. Best not to turn up unannounced in the blackout.'

Barbara breathed again. She was to have a short respite. 'Actually, I would very much like to go and see Mr and Mrs Thorogood. I told them I would call in tonight if I got here in time. Would it be possible for you to drive me there?' She turned to Grandpa. 'You don't have to come with me, unless you want to. You could stroll down to the hotel and check us in; make sure that they're able to serve us dinner tonight.'

He nodded, apparently understanding her sudden reluctance to introduce him to a couple who believed her to be in love with their son and were eagerly anticipating the wedding.

'Sound idea. I shall order dinner for seven o'clock, which gives you plenty of time; I hope this farm isn't too far away.'

'About fifteen minutes, no more. I'll be back long before seven. Don't worry, Grandpa.'

Mrs Peterson pulled up outside the front door of Brook Farm. 'Do you need a lift back, Barbara, or will Mr Thorogood run you to the hotel?'

'Uncle Bill has offered to take me. Thank you so much for the lift.

We'll call in and speak to you before we go home tomorrow, let you know what happens. I want to catch up on all the news from Downton School.'

'Of course you do. I shall be in all morning. Goodnight, my dear, and God bless you for coming.'

Barbara flicked on her torch to find her way up the path to the front door. Although she was expected, they wouldn't have heard the car as they always sat in the kitchen and normally she went in that way as well. She hammered on the knocker, stamping her feet to keep warm. She wished she'd chosen to wear her new winter coat. Even though it didn't quite match her smart image she was unpleasantly cold without it.

Someone was coming. A hesitant voice called out, 'Is that you, Barbara?'

'Yes, Auntie Irene, it is. Sorry I didn't come round to the back. It's just too dark.'

'Just a minute, then. This blooming door always sticks; I reckon it's because we only open it on high days and holidays.'

There was the sound of a key turning and then a bolt being slid back and a flash of white as Auntie Irene peered out. 'Come on in, dear. Uncle Bill's in the kitchen.'

She slipped inside and as soon as the door closed the light was switched back on. John's mother stared, open-mouthed.

'Good heavens! I hardly recognised you, Barbara, you look so fine. Like someone from a magazine, not the girl who used to run in out of here in gumboots.'

'My grandmother insisted I had a new wardrobe, Auntie Irene. This is the only outfit I feel remotely comfortable in. All the rest make me feel like a debutante.'

The kitchen door opened, flooding the gloomy passage with more light. 'Come along in, Barbara. I want to hear all your news.' She ran forward to give him a hug, but on seeing her he shied away, as if embarrassed. 'You don't want to be touching me, not in those clothes. I've been out in the yard just now. I'll go and light the fire in the front room, Irene love. Barbara won't want to sit in the kitchen, not tonight.'

Barbara stiffened. 'I would prefer to stay in here, Uncle Bill. It's where we always sit.'

He shook his head firmly. 'No; things are different, Barbara. I didn't realise until I saw you. Respect where it's due, I say.'

He vanished to light the fire in a room no one ever used. 'I'm no different, Auntie Irene. Please don't let these clothes make you believe otherwise. I don't want to feel you have to do anything special for me; I want it to be like it always was.'

Auntie Irene had hastily removed her apron and was surreptitiously moving unwashed mugs and old newspapers out of view. 'But things aren't the same, Barbara. We've talked about it and seeing you has just confirmed what we already knew. You move in a different circle to us – you're gentry now.'

They stood in uneasy silence. 'I'm meeting John in London next month, when he finishes his preliminary training.' She hoped this was a safe topic.

'Yes, he said so in his last letter. I've only been to London once in my whole life.'

'We're going to have lunch somewhere nice, then do a bit of Christmas shopping.'

'I expect the fire's burning nicely now. Let's go and get comfortable in the front room, Barbara. Pity to dirty your nice suit on one of our old chairs.'

They were all relieved when she stood up to leave. They were partially correct – she had changed. She was more confident – an adult, not the nervous girl they had known so well. They didn't ask her to call in again before she left. Uncle Bill drove her down to the Royal Victoria in an awkward silence and she was pleased when the car pulled up.

'Thank you for the lift. Don't wait, I'll find my way in. I've got my trusty torch.'

'Right you are, Miss Sinclair. Goodbye.'

She watched the car reversing and waited for it to drive away. The visit had been a disaster. Wearing her new clothes to Hastings had been a bad idea. Perhaps in her old slacks and jumper Auntie Irene and Uncle Bill would have welcomed her in as they always did. She heard footsteps approaching from the town and saw it was a group of diners. Good; she could follow them in. That way she would feel less conspicuous.

* * *

Over a mediocre dinner consisting of brown Windsor soup, roast pork and apple sauce with overcooked vegetables, followed by treacle tart with solid custard, Barbara described her evening.

'It's inevitable, I'm afraid, my dear. You've moved on, grown up, and they believe you've left them behind.'

'But, Grandpa, I'm the same person. I love them; they've been like parents to me and now they're treating me like a stranger. You know, they didn't even mention John. I expected them to be talking about a possible date for the wedding. It was as if they were talking to someone else, not Babs Sinclair at all.'

'Well, it's up to you to show them that money hasn't changed you in any substantial way.'

'How can I, if they won't see me?'

'Do it through your young man, John. I doubt he'll treat you any differently. He loves you, hopes to marry you. If he's got any gumption he'll be thrilled that his fiancée is a wealthy young woman. He won't see it as a threat, but a positive bonus.'

'I hope you're right, Grandpa. I don't have enough friends to keep losing them.'

He folded his napkin and smiled. 'We have to discuss what's happening tomorrow, my dear. I know how apprehensive you are about the visit. I think you'll feel better if we talk about your fears.'

This was the last thing she wanted to do. She didn't want to lie to him. Equally she had no intention of telling him it had been her mother who had systematically abused her, not her stepfather.

'Actually, I don't want to think about it, let alone talk about it. I just want to go to bed and forget everything. Tomorrow's soon enough to worry.'

'As you wish, my dear. I've arranged for a cab to collect us at nine. Mr and Mrs Evans have been informed of our visit. They must realise their isolation is likely to stop if their friends know you've been there. If you, the supposed victim, don't appear to hold any grudges, then why should they?'

'You're right. Personally, I don't care if no one ever speaks to them again, but I don't want my brothers dragged into this. They'll find it hard enough not having me there, without being the centre of unpleasant gossip.'

'I understand. We'll do our best to put things right for David and Thomas. I'm going into the bar for a cigar and whisky before retiring. With any luck they'll have the nine o'clock news on the wireless. I'll bid you goodnight. Sleep well.' He stood up and she kissed his leathery cheek.

'Goodnight. I'm dreading tomorrow; but, with you there, I believe I can get through it.'

13

Barbara ate no breakfast and refused a second cup of tea. 'I feel bilious, Grandpa. I'll eat afterwards.'

'Very well, my dear. One day without breakfast won't harm you. We don't have to stay long and I'll do the talking if you like.'

'I've nothing to say to either of them. You know why I'm here.' She pushed her chair back. 'It's only eight o'clock. Shall we stroll round the town, let people see us? I'll speak to anybody I recognise and announce to all and sundry that we're here for a flying visit especially to introduce you.'

'That's an excellent idea. I agree the more we're seen the better. However, it's still freezing out there, too cold to go out without a warm coat.'

'I know. I wish I'd worn one, but remember I'm used to getting cold. I have gloves, a warm scarf and sensible underwear. I'll not freeze to death.'

'If you insist, but we'll have to walk briskly and if there's a café open, it's straight in for a hot drink.'

'The Copper Kettle opens at eight; it's where my mother and her cronies gather. It's the most likely place to meet them.'

The biting onshore breeze almost made her change her mind and retreat back inside the warmth of the hotel lobby. 'It'll be less cold if we cut through the back streets, get away from the beach.'

He nodded, putting one hand on her arm and the other on his hat to prevent it disappearing out to sea. 'You lead, I'll follow. This is your patch – you know your way around.'

Heads down, the wind propelling them forwards, they almost ran down the little streets before turning back towards the sea and the café she sought. Her feet and legs were freezing but the rest of her was reasonably warm.

Miss Whiting wouldn't be presiding over the Copper Kettle so early but there were two tables already occupied. 'Good morning, Mrs Bryant, Miss Riches. It's nice to see you again.'

The two middle-aged ladies nodded politely but obviously failed to recognise her.

'It's me, Barbara Sinclair. I've come down for a quick visit to see my parents. Allow me to introduce my grandfather, Dr Sinclair, with whom I'm living in Essex.'

Mrs Bryant recovered first. 'Pleased to meet you, sir. I hardly knew you, Miss Sinclair, you've changed so much.'

'I'm delighted to meet you, Mrs Bryant, Miss Riches. Barbara was most insistent I come down and meet Mr and Mrs Evans. After all, Crabapple Cottage was her home until recently.'

She addressed Mrs Bryant, staring directly at her as she spoke. 'I gather my mother has been indisposed. I came down immediately I heard. Hopefully she'll be well enough to attend church after our visit.'

'We'll call in for her tomorrow morning, won't we, Sheila? Make sure she comes.'

'Thank you, Mrs Bryant. It would set my mind at rest to know her dearest friends are looking after her in my absence.' Mission accomplished, she turned and headed for her usual table in the window. 'John and I always sat here – you can watch the fishing boats heading out – even though the beach is too low to see the waves break on the pebbles.'

He pulled out a chair for her and she sat, smiling her thanks. 'That walk has restored my appetite. I'm going to have a toasted teacake, if they've got one, to go with my cup of tea.'

They stayed twenty minutes and by the time they left, she had been able to talk to a further three acquaintances. Word would be round Hastings by lunchtime that she had come back to visit her sick mother. A taxi was waiting outside the hotel but the driver was absent. 'I expect he's gone in to find us, but we have to collect our bags and I must pay the bill. He'll have to wait,' Grandpa said.

'I'm sure he'll be happy to; extra time is extra money and there are few fares around at this time of year.'

She began to regret her teacake as the car turned into the lane that led to her previous home. A gloved hand squeezed her arm. She glanced up at her grandfather and he smiled, giving her confidence. It looked the same: the hedges neatly clipped, the porch swept clean. The outside hadn't been ignored in her absence. The taxi had been booked for the whole morning and was to return them to the station in time to catch the twelve thirty to London.

'You can't sit here, my dear girl. Come along, let's get this over with. Remember, you're with me; what happened here is past, finished. No one can hurt you again.'

She unclenched her hands and forced her feet to move. She couldn't answer. Her heart was hammering too heavily in her chest, her stomach churning unpleasantly. She'd vowed never to return. What was she doing? Why was she dragging up these terrible memories? There was a gentle push in the small of her back and she was forced to step out of the car.

Up here it was warmer, no icy breeze, and as she hesitated, unwilling to move closer to the cottage, the sun came out, bathing the red bricks in a golden glow.

'It's a pretty little place, my dear, and well sheltered.' He put his arm firmly around her waist and guided her towards the door. She wanted to scream her protest, turn and run, but she allowed him to move her closer. Would the door open or would they have to knock? Surely her mother and stepfather must have heard the car arrive, heard their footsteps on the gravel?

'Damned strange! Why haven't they opened the door?'

Hearing her grandfather swear in earshot of her mother gave her courage. 'I expect they're hiding, too ashamed to open up. I'll bang on the door, but if they don't come, I'm not hanging around. I'm going to get in the cab and go to the vicarage.'

She stepped up to the hated entrance and her knock reverberated through the house. For a moment there was no response and then they heard footsteps approaching. She held her breath, bracing herself. The door swung open.

'Please come in. I apologise for having kept you, I was on the telephone with the bank; a minor problem needed my attention.'

This was a lie; the phone was in the hall. If he'd been there they would have heard him speaking. How had she ever seen him as an authority figure? He was scarcely taller than her and his demeanour was not that of the man she remembered.

Her grandfather stepped around her. 'Mr Evans, I'm Barbara's grandfather, Dr Sinclair. How do you do?'

They shook hands briefly as if the contact was disliked by both. She still hadn't spoken; she had nothing to say. With her grandpa's arm for support she walked into the house that filled her nightmares. The hall was as she'd left it: the telephone on the table, the floor polished, no evidence of a decline in standards of cleanliness. Where was she? Would she come out to speak to them or remain hidden upstairs?

Mr Evans opened the door to the sitting room. 'Would you care to go in? My wife is preparing the coffee. If you would like to sit down, make yourselves comfortable, I shall tell her you've arrived.' He backed out, leaving them alone in the room.

A cheerful log fire blazed in the grate and they graduated towards it. She was cold, wished she'd not allowed vanity to overcome common sense and had worn her sensible winter coat, perhaps then there wouldn't be ice flowing through her veins.

'This is a fine room, Barbara. And mercifully warm. Come and stand closer to the fire. I can hear your teeth chattering.'

She had to find her voice. She couldn't spend the entire visit mute. She cleared her throat, coughed. 'This was always out of bounds to me. I don't think I've been in here more than a dozen times in my life.' Her voice sounded strange, rasping, unnatural. She forced herself to smile, but it was a poor attempt. 'If we're getting coffee, that will be a first too. But I don't think it's me they're trying to impress, do you?'

'You're wrong, my dear. They need you to speak well of them. The balance of power has shifted; they need your approval, not the other way round.'

She stiffened as she heard footsteps returning and the rattle of china on a tray. Instinctively she moved closer to him and they turned to face the door. Mr Evans was carrying the tray, his wife following behind. Her eyes widened. Surely this wasn't the woman she'd been terrorised by for fifteen years? The slim, smartly dressed woman, immaculately made up and with a smile of welcome on her lips, was a total stranger. What had happened to that other person? Why was this woman masquerading as her? Then the stranger spoke and shattered the illusion. She would never forget that voice.

'Dr Sinclair, Barbara, how kind of you to take the time to visit us. Please, both of you, do sit down.'

Barbara wanted to run away, to hide in the stable, but something stopped her; was it the look of apprehension in her mother's eyes? The voice was the same, but her grandfather was right: the balance of power had shifted.

'How are you? Mrs Peterson has been worried that you haven't been going to church lately.' The words hung in the room unanswered.

Mr Evans replied, 'Doreen is fully recovered now, thank you, Barbara. Influenza kept her in the house for the past weeks, but, as you can see, she is now quite well.'

She subjected her mother to a searching stare before pointedly turning her back and walking casually across to sit on an upright, bentwood chair in front of the window. Her posture remained erect, her expression closed; she said nothing.

Mrs Evans smiled at Grandpa. 'Would you like coffee, Dr Sinclair?'

Barbara felt perspiration break out on her forehead. It was the voice; if only that woman would keep quiet, she could get through this.

'Thank you, Mrs Evans, a small cup only. Barbara doesn't want any.' None had been offered. 'I believe I'll get straight to the point. Barbara only came back because Mrs Peterson asked her to. She is anxious that her brothers are not involved in all this.' He took the cup and saucer from Mr Evans. 'We have spoken to several of your acquaintances this morning, made it clear that Barbara holds no grudges and Mrs Bryant and Miss Riches are intending to call for you tomorrow and walk with you to church.'

Something passed between her mother and stepfather. He continued. 'In exchange, I expect my granddaughter to be allowed to write and receive letters from her brothers, and for them to be able to visit her at The Grove.'

Her mother's face contorted. 'Out of the question. They are Evanses, not Sinclairs. We wish them to have no further contact of any sort with each other, ever.'

Barbara shot to her feet. 'How can you be so cruel? They're little boys. What happened was not their fault. Why should they be punished because of your dislike for me?'

Grandpa moved to intervene, but was too late. The barely suppressed animosity exploded.

'Dislike? I hate you. I've always hated you, ever since you were put, red-faced and screaming, into my arms. If it hadn't been for you, my life would have been different.'

'Good God! That's quite enough of that, Mrs Evans.' Grandpa stepped between them hoping to defuse the situation.

Mr Evans stood wringing his hands, pleading ineffectually with his wife. 'Doreen, this won't help. Doreen, you promised me.'

Barbara was too stunned to move. The vitriol seeped into her brain, freezing her will to walk away.

Mrs Evans hadn't finished. Maybe seeing her standing, dressed in clothes she could only dream of owning, looking elegant, aloof, totally removed from her influence, was too much for her fragile hold on sanity.

She bent down and snatching up the coffee pot threw it directly at Barbara. It exploded on her chest sending scalding liquid up into her unprotected face. Finally Mr Evans reacted. He launched himself at his wife and dragged her, spitting and screaming incoherently, from the room.

Grandpa moved even faster. He picked up a vase of late autumn flowers and, tossing the blooms on to the carpet, tipped the water over Barbara's head. The burning pain instantly subsided as the icy water cascaded down her cheeks.

'Sit down,' he said briskly. 'I'm going to soak a cloth and I want you to hold it against your face. Understood?'

She nodded, speechless. A wet cloth was pressed on her face and her hands were placed on top to hold it in position. 'Stay put, my dear. I'll be back in a moment.'

Where exactly did he think she was going to go, soaked to the skin? Vaguely she could hear shouting and banging, hear feet in the hallway. Grandpa was using the telephone; she hoped he'd asked permission. She couldn't hear everything, only snatches of conversation drifted in. Ambulance – she'd definitely heard that. Why did they need an ambulance? Probably a precaution, just in case her burns were worse than he'd thought.

'Good girl.' He was back. He removed her fingers and the wet antimacassar was replaced with what felt like a folded towel. 'The cloth is removing the heat from your face. I'm pretty sure I caught it in time, but I'm taking no chances. Does it still hurt?' She shook her head. 'Good!' He turned the material over and she flinched. The cold was becoming too much. She attempted to remove her hands, lower the towel, but he prevented her.

'No, Barbara, this needs to stay on for twenty minutes.' He felt the used side and smiled. 'Excellent – hardly warm at all.'

'It's too cold, Grandpa, and I'm soaked through already.' Her voice was muffled.

'I know you are, but I'm not letting you take it off until I'm sure your face won't be scarred.'

At the mention of scars she stopped protesting. Her face was already marred. She didn't want to add more damage.

'Right, put this fresh one on your face. It will be the last, I promise. Then we can do something about your wet clothes and your minor cuts and abrasions.'

After twenty minutes the pad was finally removed. He crouched down beside her, tilting her face from side to side, examining the skin carefully, then ran his fingertips over it. 'Well done! No warmth. This could have been very nasty, very nasty indeed. But it's not even going to be sore.'

She blew out her cheeks, opened and shut her mouth and wrinkled her brow. 'It's fine, Grandpa. It doesn't hurt at all.' She sniffed, her nose curling in distaste. 'What's that awful smell? Surely it isn't me?'

He grinned, as he used the chair arms to push himself upright. 'I'm afraid the nearest cold water was from a vase of rather ancient flowers. And I have to agree, you do smell distinctive.'

'My lovely suit's ruined. Coffee and flower water – what a combination.' She raised her fingers to touch her hat and they came away green. 'Good grief! My hat's running.'

'Allow me to remove it for you.' He pulled out the hat pins and dropped the sodden, unrecognisable object onto the floor.

'That was a very smart, extremely expensive, pillbox, Grandpa. Look at it now.'

He chuckled as he nudged it with his toe. 'I shall buy you another ensemble, my dear, never fear.'

'That's all very well, but I've nothing to change into now. What am I going to wear to go home in?'

'We'll organise something. You shan't have to travel back in your undergarments. Never fear.'

She giggled and began to feel better. 'Your face is fine apart from two faint patches of pink, one across your forehead and another on your chin.'

'What's that banging? Is there someone knocking to come in?'

'I'm afraid not, my dear girl. It's your mother. We've had to lock her in the downstairs cloakroom.'

'Oh my God! She tried to kill me. I always knew she'd try and do it one day.'

He pulled over a chair and sat beside her. 'It was your mother, not your stepfather, who abused you, wasn't it?'

'Yes, but he endorsed it; he knew what was happening and never stopped her. I suppose, in his defence, he did send me away to school, and I was safe there. And he bought me a pony and then Silver Lady so I could hide in the stable.'

'Your mother's ill, Barbara; I believe she has been unwell since you were born.'

'That can't be true. She's quite normal with the boys. They've never been slapped, not once. It was only me she attacked. Surely, if she was ill, she'd have abused all of us?'

'Possibly. You say she never smacked your brothers, but did she ever show them any affection, kiss them or hug them?'

'Definitely not. They always came to me when they were hurt or happy. She used to say "boys don't cry" or "don't make a fuss, you're a big boy now", and all that sort of thing.'

'And Mr Evans? What was he like with them?'

'Much the same. Patted them on the head when they were good and sent them to bed without supper when they weren't.'

'As I thought. I'm sorry my dear…' He was interrupted by the clang of a bell as a vehicle screeched to a halt outside. 'Please excuse me; I have to speak to the doctors.'

She felt as if a second vase of icy water had been thrown over her head. The significance of the ambulance, her mother being locked in the cloakroom, it all made sense.

'The ambulance is for her, isn't it? Is she mad? Are they taking her to an asylum?'

He patted her shoulder. 'Yes, my dear, I'm afraid they are. It's possible, with the new treatments available, that she might recover, but I doubt it.'

'But the boys? What will happen to them?'

'They're not your responsibility; they still have their father and he must provide suitable care. But they may come to us in the holidays. You will have to forget all this Land Army nonsense; your brothers will need you to be at home.'

He strode off giving her no chance to ask anything else. How could he say they could come to The Grove? Hadn't it been made clear the boys were to have no further contact with her? Mr Evans would never allow it. She believed she had no choice. She would have to come back, somehow persuade Mr Evans to allow her to return to Crabapple Cottage and try to be a mother to the boys and a housekeeper to her stepfather. She would leave her new life and move back to Hastings, however much she hated the idea.

She sat in misery listening to the voices in the hall, the screams from her lunatic mother, then the horrible silence after they injected her with a sedative. The stretcher, with the blanket-shrouded shape, vanished into the ambulance. Two white-coated men jumped in after it. The driver slammed the doors, ran round to the front and it disappeared down the drive. The abuse was over – forever. Her mother had gone – removed from circulation – placed where she could do no further harm to anyone.

She wriggled; her knickers were sticking to her bottom. She was wet and smelly but physically unharmed. A hot bath and clean clothes would restore her appearance but she knew her life was irrevocably changed.

She scrambled out of the chair, the soggy skirt clinging to her thighs, her blouse and cashmere cardigan as wet as the jacket that covered them. She could have a bath, but what was she going to put on when she got out? Better to stay in her wet clothes, stand in front of the fire and let them dry on her.

If she sat on the footstool, stretched out her legs, pulling her skirt flat across her knees, it might dry. But her jacket, cardigan and blouse must come off. The top of her petticoat and brassiere were as decent as her new evening gown; she could sit in those. She was tempted to step out of her skirt, but thought being seen in her knickers and petticoat would be too much. Grandpa wouldn't mind, after all he was a medical man, but Mr Evans was different.

She froze, her arm half out of her blouse sleeve. Her mother had been taken away alone. Her stepfather had not gone with her, had not even followed in the car. Surely he loved her? Hadn't he protected her for years? Why hadn't he gone to comfort his wife at her lowest moment?

She pulled the smelly blouse back on. The ruined cardigan went over the back of one chair, the jacket over another. The hall was empty but someone was in the kitchen. She ran down the corridor, shivering in her thin blouse and wet skirt and knocked on the door. Without waiting for an answer she burst in.

'Ah! Good, Barbara, my dear, come and join us. There's a cardigan here. Mr Evans fetched it for you. Slip it on to keep warm.'

She grabbed the garment eagerly. The thick hand-knitted wool was just what she needed. But it smelt of her mother. 'No, thank you, Grandpa. I'd rather not.'

'Then sit by the range. Open the oven doors, get some warmth on you.'

She did as he suggested, ignoring the pathetic man crouched over a mug of tea at the far side of the table. Grandpa poured her a cup and added several lumps of sugar.

'Here you are, drink this. You need something to help with shock.'

She took the tea and dragged a chair noisily across the lino to a position beside the range. The warmth from the open ovens was welcome and, combined with the hot sweetness of the tea, she began to feel a little better, more in command.

'Grandpa, why hasn't he gone with her?' She nodded towards her stepfather. 'Did he even pack her a bag? She'll need nightclothes, toiletries and so on.'

'Not where she's going, my dear; personal possessions are not allowed. If she recovers sufficiently then I expect she'll be moved somewhere less draconian.'

'I see. So that's it? An ambulance comes and takes her away and no one will ever see her again?' Her voice rose. 'What about David and Tom? What will they be told? It's Christmas next month. They'll be coming home expecting to find her waiting, Christmas presents under the tree. What's going to happen to them then?'

'Drink your tea, Barbara.' His voice was stern. She blinked, but swallowed obediently. 'All of it and don't say anything else until it's finished.'

She kept drinking and by the time the cup was drained she'd calmed down. His jacket dropped around her shoulders and she inhaled the familiar smell of cigar smoke and lavender.

'There you are, my dear child. Take a deep breath – that's right – through your nose. Now, expel it from your mouth. Excellent! Do you feel better?'

She nodded. 'Sorry, it all got a bit much. I'm fine. But I do want to know what's going to happen to my brothers now... now...' She couldn't bring herself to say the word 'mother'. She thought she'd never be able to say it again. A faint noise from the huddle at the table made her glance round.

'I can't cope with children. I've never been any good with them. I don't even like them. I want you to have them, Barbara. You can afford to keep them, pay for their school fees; you're a rich woman. I want nothing more to do with any of you. Not you, not them, not her.'

14

Mr Evans glared at Barbara, his eyes small grey pebbles behind his spectacles. Grandpa shook his head.

'Good God, man – you can't hand over your children as if they were parcels. You have responsibilities. You're their father. They've lost one parent; do you expect them to lose another?'

Mr Evans ignored him, keeping her pinned under his stare. 'If you don't want to take them, I shall have them fostered out. I'm going to sell this place and move away.'

'Of course I'll take them. I love them. They're my brothers. I always thought it was her that was cruel and heartless but you are far worse.' She looked at Grandpa for support. 'You'll have to act as their guardian until I come of age. Will you do that for me? I shall understand if you don't want to. After all they're not your blood relations.'

'I shall be delighted to have them as part of the family. The Grove full of children after so many empty years? What a wonderful thought. But it will have to be done legally, Evans. Do you have a solicitor we can contact today?'

'I do. I'll ring him immediately; tell him to draw up the papers.' He stood. 'I want all their things removed from here forthwith. I intend to put the house on the market today.'

She nodded. 'In that case I suggest you move out, go to stay in the town, then I can remain here and organise things.'

Grandpa nodded. 'Perhaps you could get Mrs Peterson and Mrs Thorogood to come over and help you? The cab's still waiting outside. I'll go down to town with Evans and start things moving on the legal front. If you tell me what you need, I'll buy you something to wear.'

'I'll write it down, then you can hand the list to the girl and she'll sort it out.'

He smiled. 'Wise move; bit embarrassing a chap my age having to ask for young ladies' clothing.'

Mr Evans made his telephone call then went upstairs to pack. She didn't want to be anywhere near him so remained in the kitchen.

'I'm going to tell everyone the truth, Grandpa. They need to know why Tom and David are never coming back here.'

'I think it will make it easier for you if you do. Having it out in the open after all these years is a healthy move. You don't have anything to be ashamed of. The fault was never yours.'

'I think I'm beginning to understand that events were always beyond my control. I think that was Mr Evans leaving. I hope he's left the key.' She handed over the hastily scribbled list of her requirements.

'I'll ask him for you. I'll do this shopping and speak to the legal bod then come back here.'

'You don't have to; Grandmother will be expecting us both back tonight. I doubt if there are any trains tomorrow. If you don't go today you might not be available for your surgery first thing Monday morning.'

'Mmmm... that's probably true, but I'm not happy about leaving you alone here, not after everything that's happened.'

'As long as I am alone, there's no problem. I can get everything packed up and arrange for a removal firm to bring them. And another thing, you have to explain to Grandmother that not only has she a real granddaughter to contend with, but two adopted grandsons as well.'

'That should be an interesting conversation.' He smiled. 'Elspeth might surprise us both. She has always wanted more children. She had two miscarriages, one before, one after Charles. She wasn't always so... so austere. When we first married she was always smiling, happy, full of fun.'

She found that hard to believe but nodded sympathetically. 'The Grove's big enough to accommodate a dozen extra children. With luck she'll hardly notice the boys, and they're away most of the time now. It's the holidays we have to worry about.' Her expression changed as an awful thought occurred to her. 'I suppose I'll have to join the WVS if I'm not going to join the Land Army.' She shuddered theatrically. 'I can't imagine anything worse. Bandage rolling and cups of tea in a room full of ladies just like my grandmother.'

He was still chuckling as he opened the front door. 'I'll send the cab back with your things, my dear. Let me know when you expect to be home, won't you, and I'll come and meet you at the station.'

She hugged him. 'Of course I will. With any luck I'll be back Monday, by lunchtime. Will my train ticket still be valid?'

'It will, which reminds me, I haven't given it to you.' He unbuttoned his coat to rummage in his inside pocket, extracting his wallet. 'You had better have some cash. I don't suppose you brought much with you.'

'I didn't, thank you, Grandpa. Do you know where the solicitor's office is?'

'No, but I'm sure the taxi driver will. Take care, and I'll ring tonight when I get home; tell you what happened with Evans.'

She waved the car down the drive before going back inside. The house felt different. It no longer had that sense of foreboding. For the first time she felt safe, able to think clearly, move about freely.

Picking up the telephone, she glanced over her shoulder as if expecting a reprimand. There was nothing to worry about any more. Mrs Peterson picked up the receiver.

'Barbara, I have been expecting a call. Is everything all right up there? Mrs Bishop called in with some eggs and said she saw an ambulance leaving Crabtree Cottage.'

'She did. I was ringing to tell you about it.' She explained the situation. 'So, you see, Mrs Peterson, David and Tom are to be my responsibility from now on – or rather my grandfather's and mine.'

'I don't know what to say, Barbara. I'm shocked rigid. I'm so sorry. If only we'd known what was going on... To think of what you've had to suffer all these years!'

'Please, I want to move on – forget about it. I have to consider the boys' well-being. I want their lives to be happier than mine. Today they've lost both parents. I can't imagine what they will feel when I tell them.'

'Children are resilient, my dear. The boys will soon adjust. They have been more unhappy about not being able to see you than homesick, I can assure you. Living at The Grove will suit them – why shouldn't it? They'll have you and their adopted grandparents. Dr Sinclair seems a wonderful old gentleman. I'm sure he'll be good to them – take them to his heart.'

'I know he will. It's my grandmother who's the problem. She hasn't taken to me – thinks I'm common. So I hardly think she's going to be thrilled to have two boys foisted on her that have no blood connection at all.'

'Well, you can keep them out of the way. They're good boys and I'm sure they'll not be a nuisance. Now, would you like me to come over and help you pack up their things?'

'Yes, please. I'm going to ask Auntie Irene as well. Between us we should be able to get it done before Monday.'

'I'll bring any spare boxes and tea chests I can find. Be with you in about an hour.'

Barbara immediately rang Brook Farm. She felt nervous, not sure if she should be asking for help after her reception yesterday, but this was an ideal opportunity to mend matters. Once Auntie Irene and Uncle Bill knew everything, surely they'd forget their reservations?

'Brook Farm,' Uncle Bill answered.

She took a deep breath. 'Hello, Uncle Bill, it's Barbara. I need your help.'

'What is it? Is there something wrong over there? We heard an ambulance going down your way earlier.'

She smiled, glad for once that news spread rapidly in this neighbourhood. She quickly told him what had happened and, as she'd hoped, he was eager to help.

'Irene and I'll be along immediately. We have a few boxes and such-like; we'll bring them with us. What a dreadful thing! I'm real sorry we didn't know. I would have had you here to live with us right away.'

'Thank you, Uncle Bill. It's not anyone's fault. I was too young to realise I could ask for help. Anyway, it's finished now. I want to forget about it. My main consideration is the boys.'

'Right enough, Babs, love. You're a good girl and no mistake. Our John's lucky to have you.'

Thoughtfully she replaced the receiver. What would John think about all this? He had offered to marry her, not care for her two brothers. She couldn't expect him to take on the extra responsibility. She would talk to him about it when she saw him in December and give him the chance to break off the engagement. It wasn't the financial burden – there wouldn't be one; she had more than enough to keep them all – but the fact that most young men wouldn't want to rear someone else's children. Look how Mr Evans had reacted to her. She would be asking him to be father to two boys who were his brothers-in-law.

No, it wouldn't work. Money was no compensation. She was certain he would want to end things when he knew. An image of Alex popped into her head. He had two younger brothers, almost the same age as Tom and David. What would he think? Would he be prepared to take them on? Good grief! Whatever was she thinking? How did Alex Everton become mixed up in all this? He was an attractive man, but a stranger, and thinking of him and marriage at the same time was risible.

She was in the boys' room when the Thorogoods arrived. She'd left the front door ajar and they came straight in.

'Babs, shall we bring up the boxes or leave them in the hall?' Aunt Irene called from the bottom of the stairs.

'Bring them up, please; I've already got a pile of things sorted.'

She beckoned them into the bedroom. 'All the clothes that still fit are in one pile, outgrown but good in another and jumble in a third.'

'Well, I never did! Is this where your brothers slept? Where are all the toys, puzzles and things? Did they take them to school with them?'

'No, everything they've got is here. They have a farm, a box of Dinky cars and a few books and puzzles.'

'It's a crying shame, that's what it is, and all of our John's things stored up in the loft. They could have had them to play with, if only we'd known.'

'That's enough now, Irene love. Can't you see you're upsetting our Babs? What's done is done. I reckon the little lads will get plenty of toys when they move to Essex.'

Barbara came to a decision. 'I'm going to make this the best Christmas they've ever had. I always did their stockings, otherwise they'd not have had any, but this year I shall pull out all the stops. I know there's a war on, but everyone's saying that we should make this a season to remember, aren't they? Show Hitler we're not letting him ruin our holiday time.'

'Good for you, Babs. We've got rationing to cope with in the New Year, and lots of things in short supply already. Those as can afford it have been driving round buying up sugar, tinned goods and such, and poor folks will do without, you mark my words. If you've got the money you can always get what you want.'

She flushed. Was she one of the uncaring rich to whom he was referring?

'Bill, it's you upsetting Babs now. It's not her fault she inherited all that money. She's still the same lovely girl she's always been and we're silly to think of her as anything else.'

'Maybe you're right, Irene love. And without the money, what would have become of the boys? At least Babs can bring them up properly; give them a good start in life.'

The sound of another car pulling up outside alerted them to the arrival of Mrs Peterson. Barbara hurried to the landing and shouted down: 'Come on up, Mrs Peterson. We've got three boxes of clothing for the church. You're collecting for the evacuees, aren't you?'

Mrs Peterson staggered up carrying a tea chest. 'Here they are, Barbara, and there are two more in the car.' She smiled. 'Would you go and get them for me, Mr Thorogood? Thank you so much.'

'Pleased to, Mrs Peterson. Shall I take a couple of these boxes down and put them in your boot whilst I'm about it?'

Mrs Peterson stared round the bedroom; the bedding packed away, shelves empty. 'Looks as though you've finished without me. Is this all there is?' She nodded at the three tea chests.

'Yes, not as much as I thought. It hardly seems worth getting a carrier for so little. I'm going to take the clothes I'm keeping with me in that suitcase over there. They've grown out of most of their things and they don't have many toys.' Barbara smiled as she remembered. 'They do have bicycles and cricket things and a few other bits and pieces in the garden shed.' She rubbed her back. 'We've finished in here. If Uncle Bill carries the tea chests down, they can wait in the hall.'

The ladies exchanged glances. 'Why don't you go and make us all a nice cup of tea, Babs dear, then Mrs Peterson and I can pack up your mother's things.'

She'd never even considered doing that. There was no way she was going into that room or touching those clothes. 'I'm not concerned with anything apart from Tom and David's things, but please go ahead. Everything can go to charity, or in the ragbag. I certainly don't want anything from in there.'

Mrs Peterson placed an arm on her shoulder. 'Will Mrs Evans not need anything in hospital?'

'She's gone to an asylum, Mrs Peterson, not a hospital, and they don't allow personal possessions.' She sounded hard and the vicar's wife flinched and dropped her hand.

'Very well, Barbara. But I think I'll keep a suitcase of clothes for your mother, if you don't mind? She might need them later on; it's a shame for her things to be thrown away. I can think of several families in the village who would be grateful to have them.'

'I've already said, Mrs Peterson, please take them. I doubt if Mr Evans will care. He made it quite clear he wants nothing more to do with any of us.'

They heard Uncle Bill trudging back upstairs. 'Bill, take the boxes into the main bedroom. We're packing up Mrs Evans's things next.'

'Righty ho! I could murder a cuppa, Babs. Any chance of making us one?'

'Of course. I was just going down to do it.'

They were all sitting with mugs of tea when a third car pulled up outside. 'Good heavens, are you expecting any one else, Barbara?' Mrs Peterson asked.

'Yes. It should be the cab with my clothes.' She grinned down at her ruined suit. 'These have dried on me; I rather think they'll only be fit for the ragbag now.'

'Such a shame. That was a lovely suit, and I bet it cost a pretty penny as well. Maybe I can do something with it. I'm a dab hand with laundry.'

'Thank you, Auntie Irene. I'll give it to you when I've changed.' She held up the misshapen gold cardigan. 'Don't suppose you can save this for me?'

'Good heavens! No. That's past redemption, I reckon.'

She remembered to tip the driver generously and arranged for him to collect her early on Monday morning. She intended to catch the eight o'clock train. With her three parcels clutched in her arms she ran upstairs and went into her bedroom to change. She froze at the door, couldn't stop the scream. The hideous sound echoed throughout the house.

Uncle Bill arrived first. She was blocking his view of the room, arms braced on either side of the door. 'What is it, love? Let me see what's upset you.' Gently he unfastened the fingers on her left hand and stepped round her. 'Bloody hell! Come along, Babs, out of here; no point staring at this mess, is there? You can change in the lads' room, can't you?'

She recovered her voice. 'Why would she do this? I'd left here, had no intention of returning. This wasn't even my room any more.'

Mrs Peterson guided her away from the havoc. 'Your mother was ill, mentally disturbed. She couldn't help herself.'

'But to slash all the curtains, tear the mattress to pieces, break up the shelves – it doesn't make any sense.'

Auntie Irene closed the door, shutting out the unpleasantness. 'That in there has nothing to do with you, my love; it is all to do with your mother's insanity. It doesn't make sense to any of us, but it did to her.'

'I'm sorry if I scared you. I'll change and be down in a few minutes.'

She closed the door, glad to escape the suffocating sympathy and leave the circle of anxious faces. They meant well, but she was unused to anyone caring and found it overwhelming.

She ripped the brown paper from the two small parcels, eager to see what Grandpa had selected. To her delight and astonishment, his choices were exactly right: a pair of heavy twill dark green slacks, a long-sleeved cream linen blouse with Peter Pan collar, and a moss green round-neck jumper. He'd even included two pairs of green socks. The larger package contained a warm, hip-length, loose-fitting coat, in green and brown flecked tweed.

She stripped off her wrinkled clothes and dressed in the fresh ones. As she was tying the laces on her brogues, she smiled. Fancy Grandpa remembering to match her outfit to her shoes and to purchase socks as well!

Auntie Irene was waiting outside the door. 'We've been talking, Babs love, and think it best if you don't sleep here tonight. You come back with us to Brook Farm. No point in staying by yourself when you can be with friends, now, is there?'

She wanted to argue, insist she was not a child, could quite easily look after herself for one night, but something held her back. Auntie Irene was making a gesture, re-establishing the closeness. Refusing might jeopardise this.

'This cottage is freezing and I doubt that there's anything to eat in the pantry either, so thank you, I'd be delighted to come back with you.'

'There's not much left to do, is there?'

'No, just the outside things to collect together. I haven't arranged for anyone to bring them to The Grove. Do you think Uncle Bill might know of a suitable firm?'

Mrs Peterson met them in the hall. 'Mr Thorogood and I have filled up my car with boxes. I'll come back after morning service tomorrow and collect the rest.' She paused. 'Are you coming to church tomorrow, Barbara?'

'I am. I've been going to Ingatestone church with my grandparents, but I don't really know anyone. It's not the same.' Her lips curved as Mrs Peterson was about to protest. 'Yes, I know, churches are for worship not gossip. But I used to really enjoy Reverend Peterson's sermons. The vicar at Ingatestone is getting on and tends to repeat himself. Do you know, last week he read the same passage three times. I think we'd have been there all day if the verger hadn't gone over and told him.'

'Sounds like a stuck record; perhaps all he needs is winding up?'

'Bill, that's enough. You shouldn't talk about the reverend gentleman like that.'

He winked at Barbara and nodded at his wife. 'I've locked the back door, Babs. Do you have the key to the front?'

'I do now. Grandpa sent it up in one of the parcels.'

* * *

Monday morning found Barbara outside Crabapple Cottage, dressed and ready, a large suitcase of her brothers' clothes and her overnight bag at her feet. The packing had been completed and the carrier, Mr Perks, had called Sunday afternoon to collect the tea chests and bicycles. She had locked the door and pushed the key back through the letterbox.

The taxi was coming up the lane. She bent to reclaim her luggage. She was pleased she'd been given a second chance to leave here and this time on her terms.

When she arrived at the station, Mr Adams came out himself to collect her cases. 'Good morning, Miss Sinclair. I'll take your things in for you. I can hardly believe the difference since you last caught this train.'

'I'm not frightening your passengers this time, Mr Adams. I doubt I'll be back in Hastings for a while; in fact not at all, unless I come to see Mr and Mrs Thorogood. I expect travel is going to become increasingly difficult. I believe it will have to be essential journeys only in future.'

'I reckon you're right, miss. What with the shortage of fuel and all, folks will have to make do with local company until this blooming war is over.'

'People said it would be over by Christmas, but it's hardly even begun and already it's the end of November.'

'Well, miss, let's hope they assassinate that blighter Hitler and then maybe the Germans will think again.'

A mournful hoot warned them the train was approaching. She followed the stationmaster through the ticket office and out onto the platform. Once comfortably settled into a ladies only compartment in first class, she sat back in the corner, enjoying every moment of the journey. The train was on time and she found a taxi outside Bridge Street station to convey her to Liverpool Street. She arrived in Ingatestone to find Grandpa waiting outside.

'Welcome home, my dear. Everything sorted out satisfactorily in Hastings?'

'Yes, thank you, Grandpa. The rest of the boys' things should arrive in a day or two.' She climbed into the car and slammed the door. 'I decided not to contact David and Tom. I've spoken to the principal at Downton School, but have just told him the boys are coming home with me this Christmas vacation. Mrs Peterson's going down to the school but I'm meeting them at Paddington on the 16th of December. I intend to tell them face to face.'

'Excellent notion, my dear. It's what I was going to suggest. The legal matters will take a while to be completed, but I'm able to act in loco parentis until then.'

'I've been thinking about the financial side of things. I shall have to use my trust fund to pay their school fees. I know I said originally I only wanted five pounds a week, but that won't be nearly enough now.'

'Don't worry about any of that. Until you come of age I shall be glad to pay all their expenses. When you're twenty-one we can sit down and decide how you want to arrange things.'

'Are you sure? What about Grandmother? How will she react to your supporting two children who are nothing to do with her?'

He chuckled. 'I told you she might surprise you. Believe it or not, she's thrilled Tom and David are coming. She's already opened up the nursery floor, and the new girl, Marigold, and the lady from the village – I forget her name, but she comes in to do the heavy work – are busy scrubbing and polishing.'

'Marigold? Mrs Mullins's cousin? I didn't realise she was coming so soon. Rosie told me about her on Friday.'

'Elspeth was delighted to have a live-in maid again and now we have two extra in the house, the girl will be a godsend.'

'What's she like? Is she small and dark like Mrs Mullins?'

'The exact opposite. She's tall, with corn-coloured wavy hair and big blue eyes. A lovely girl. I can see why she caused a stir at that RAF base.'

'Well, being honest and hard-working is more important if you're a maid. Luckily there's no sort of base anywhere near us.' She hated the way she'd sounded, more like Mrs Peterson than a girl of eighteen.

'I like her, Barbara. She looks you right in the eye when she speaks, nothing shifty about her.'

The new girl was waiting in her room when Barbara went up to change. 'Good afternoon, Miss Sinclair. I'm Marigold, Rosie's cousin. Madam says I'm to help you unpack.'

'Hello, Marigold. I'm glad you're here. When my brothers come home for Christmas there'll be a lot of extra work.' She looked round; the room seemed to be welcoming her. 'I can manage my few things, thank you, Marigold, but there's a case downstairs with my brothers' clothes in; perhaps you could put those away for me?'

'Certainly, miss. Madam's put them in the nursery. Joe's whitewashing the walls and it's all been scrubbed. It's going to be lovely up there. The sweep's coming later this week to do the chimneys, then the fires can be lit. It'll be like a palace when it's finished.'

Marigold might not look like her older cousin but she certainly talked as much. 'I shall come up later to see for myself.'

The gong for lunch was rung at one thirty, half an hour later than usual, the meal delayed especially for her arrival. She flew downstairs not wishing to keep her grandmother waiting a moment longer than necessary. The dining room door was open, both grandparents standing by the fire talking.

'Thank you so much for keeping lunch back.'

Grandmother came forward, the first genuine smile Barbara had seen on her face. 'It's our pleasure, Barbara. Come along in. I asked Cook to prepare leek and potato soup as I know it's a favourite of yours.'

'Thank you, Grandmother. That's thoughtful of you. I'm so pleased you've agreed to allow my brothers to make their home here. They're good boys and both very intelligent.'

'If they're anything like you, then I'm sure they are, my dear. Now, have the seat nearest the fire; travelling so far in this weather might well have chilled you.'

Barbara sat, bemused by this *volte-face*. What had caused her grandmother's change of heart? She beamed down the table at her grandfather, feeling for the first time that she was wholly welcome and not an intruder.

They were halfway through the soup when her grandmother spoke again. 'I've started to arrange the boys' accommodation, but thought you would like to choose the soft furnishings, curtains and so on.'

'Please don't buy new; the boys aren't used to a fuss. Haven't you got something in the attic that would do? I know there's no rationing on cloth at the moment but I still think we ought to try and reuse as much we can. Buying new should be a last resort.'

'Well said, my dear. My WVS group would applaud your sentiments. Shall we go up later and have a rummage around; see what we can find together?'

'I'd love to come, Grandmother. And it's strange you should mention the WVS as I was wondering if I could join you there? I want to help with the war effort, and obviously I can't join the Land Army now, and I don't want to sit about doing nothing.'

Grandpa almost choked in his soup. 'Well, my dear girl, I'm astonished and delighted. An extra pair of hands is always needed, especially young ones like yours.'

'Yes, we'd be absolutely thrilled to have you, Barbara. We're not doing much at the moment; mainly knitting and first aid, but believe me we'll be busy when this war finally gets going.'

'I'll have to write and withdraw my application for the Land Army. I'll do it first thing tomorrow.'

'That reminds me, Barbara, young Farley rang this morning about the ride you've arranged for Wednesday afternoon. There's been a change of plan. It seems they are coming here at nine o'clock instead. Elspeth has invited them to stay for lunch after you've been out.'

Barbara's eyebrows shot up and inadvertently she glanced at her grandmother. To her surprise she laughed.

'I know, you will all smell dreadfully of the stable, but if we sit in the breakfast room, the dining room furniture won't suffer.'

'That's a lovely idea, Grandmother. Is Mrs Farley coming as well?'

'She is, yes. We have a WI meeting in the village and it seems a shame not to all get together afterwards.'

As Barbara returned to her room Marigold bustled past, golden hair under her scarf, wrap-around apron tied securely about her minute waist, a pile of clean linen balanced in her arms. She smiled as she passed and it was only then Barbara realised what had been worrying her about the new maid.

Her appearance fitted, exactly, the description of both the young women Mr Farley senior was supposed to have had an affair with and who had subsequently disappeared, and he was invited to lunch on Wednesday.

15

'My, Silver Lady looks a real picture, miss. I reckon I could plait her tail for you next time. It don't seem too hard.' Joe slapped the mare's gleaming, dappled rump. 'Good girl, you'll do us proud today.'

Barbara rubbed her oily hands on her jodhpurs. 'She will. Now that I've clipped her she looks very smart, but you must make sure she's well rugged up and she'll need a deeper bed in future.'

'She'll not get cold because of me, miss, I promise. What time are the gentlemen coming?'

'At nine, which gives me thirty minutes to go and change into my best. I'm even going to wear my new hat.'

He grinned. 'Hope you don't need it. The ground's hard.' He glanced up at the leaden sky. 'I reckon we're in for snow later.'

'Hope it's not whilst we're out. Don't worry – Silver always looks after me; she'll not attempt a jump she can't manage. It would be sheer bad luck if we came to grief.' She stroked the horse's nose. 'You won't let me down today, will you, lovely girl?' She gave her one last pat and left the loose box, calling back over her shoulder to Joe, 'Don't forget, the boxes for the Farley hunters must be ready by ten thirty.'

She didn't hear his reply but knew he would have the stables done long before they were needed. Mrs Brown's son was a natural with horses and was already an indispensable member of the staff.

At five minutes to the appointed hour she was mounted and ready to leave. Silver, sensing her excitement, stamped and skittered around the yard. 'Stand still, silly thing, or you'll pull a tendon before we've even set off.' The horse calmed and Barbara straightened her hat.

Joe was watching from the archway. 'I can see them. Mr Farley's on the chestnut and Mr Simon's on a big bay.' He scampered back to her side, grinning up at her. 'Reckon both horses are well over sixteen hands. Are you going to go and meet them, or wait in here?'

She laughed. 'I'm not hiding, Joe, not really. But I've never ridden out with hunters, and Mr Farley likes to jump huge fences. I'm worried Silver won't be able to keep up.'

'Your mare might be smaller but she's the equal of any horse; that hedge you jumped yesterday was over six foot, I reckon, and the ditch...'

'You're right, Joe. I'm off; no point in them coming all the way down.'

She squeezed her knees and Silver responded instantly; her ears pricked and her neck arched. She trotted out of the yard and down the drive to meet her riding companions. Silver saw the geldings and immediately cavorted towards them.

'Good morning, Miss Sinclair, lovely day for a ride.' Mr Farley touched his hat with his whip handle. 'That mare of yours looks splendid. I'd not realised she was so tall. I doubt she'll have any trouble staying with us today.'

'Good morning, Mr Farley, Simon. Sorry about Silver; she's not used to meeting other horses. My mare doesn't kick and I'm sure she'll settle down in a moment.'

She was fully occupied staying in the saddle as her mount bucked and shied like a two-year-old in an effort to impress the massive hunters. Simon pushed his bay alongside.

'Sinbad's smitten already, Barbara. Look at him; he's flexing his muscles for her.'

Silver shook her head, the grey plaits down her neck bouncing, and Sinbad snorted his approval. Mr Farley eased his chestnut up on the other side and she began to feel hemmed in, riding boot to boot with the two men. Luckily both geldings were gentle giants and Silver Lady enjoyed the attention and lengthened her stride to match them.

She forced her hands to relax before her nervousness communicated itself to her horse. 'Which way do you want to go, Mr Farley? I thought we could go through Ten Acre Wood as there's a bridle path and then cut across the fields towards Mountnessing.'

'Plenty of hedges and ditches that way, are there?'

'Yes, several, and good gallops as well. The ground's hard, but not so bad we can't enjoy ourselves.'

'That's the spirit. We'll let you take the lead; you can show us the way.'

She glanced across at Simon. He looked quite different. His inane grin and slouch had gone; he looked totally in command. In fact, every inch his father's son. When she turned her head Mr Farley was staring at her, something unexpected and unwelcome in his eyes.

'You ride well, Miss Sinclair. I don't think I've seen a better seat in Essex.'

Heat flooded her cheeks. She dug her heels in, wanting to get away; knowing that today she'd unwittingly aroused his predatory interest. Silver broke into a collected canter; at least if he was interested in her, Marigold would be safe from his attentions.

She could hear the sound of hoofs but, as promised, both men kept behind her, leaving her to set the pace. Half a mile ahead was the five-barred gate that led into Ten Acre Wood. Normally she'd open it but this morning she decided she wouldn't. She'd demonstrate just how good her horse was. This set the pattern for the ride.

Silver started to slow down, expecting to be asked to halt whilst the gate was negotiated. 'No, darling, we're going over it today.' She shortened her reins, giving the horse the necessary impulsion. She steadied, keeping Silver at an extended canter, not allowing her to break into a gallop.

As they thundered down the path she stared ahead, between the horse's pricked ears. Using her knees to urge her horse on, she leant forward – they soared into the air, clearing the gate with feet to spare. They landed perfectly and she allowed the horse to slow, waiting for the Farleys to catch up, praying they were both as good as everyone said.

She heard first one, then the other, land safely and glanced over her shoulder to see it was Simon leading, an exultant grin on his face. They had jumped a dozen more obstacles and raced at a full gallop along the riverbank when her mare stumbled and she was forced to pull up. She waved the two men past, pointing down; they galloped on, throwing up plate-sized divots of mud as they passed.

'What have you done, Silver? Let's have a look.'

She lifted the mare's hoof and saw a small stone lodged under the shoe. Expertly she flicked it out then walked the horse up and down to check she wasn't lame. 'You're fine, no problems. Shall we see if we can catch them up?'

She looked round for a suitable something to stand on, but seeing nothing she lengthened a stirrup leather to swing herself aboard. Silver stamped, tossing her head, eager to chase after her new admirers.

'Hang on. I've got to sort myself out before we go.' Once both feet were firmly back in the irons she patted her mare's sweaty neck and urged her forward. She had assumed the two men would wait at the end of the field. When she arrived at the foot of the massive hedge that bordered it, they weren't there. The exit was a hundred yards down, through a gate. This one had to be opened as it led directly into a narrow lane, which allowed no room for a horse to jump safely. So where were they?

She reined in, standing in her stirrups to scan in both directions. Had they veered off and gone somewhere in the vast meadow? Puzzled, she trotted Silver down to the gate and, to her horror, realised the missing men had jumped the hedge. All she could see of them were two small shapes vanishing over the horizon – too far away for her to catch them up. She might as well head for home.

On the way back she walked, allowing her horse to cool down properly, which gave her ample time to think about what had happened. She couldn't imagine what had prompted Simon and his father to take such a risk. She had not considered Simon foolhardy. However, today – when astride a horse – he'd metamorphosed into his father, matching him stride for stride, jump for jump, completely out of character. She clattered into the yard to be met by Joe.

'You're early, miss; hope Silver's not pulled up lame.'

Barbara's legs gave way after she dismounted. She steadied herself. 'Good heavens, I hadn't realised how tired I was.' She patted Silver's neck. 'She got a stone in her shoe. Mr Simon and Mr Farley went on without me so I decided to come home.'

'Does she need walking or can she go in?'

'She's fine. She can have a drink straightaway and she'll only need unplaiting and rubbing down.'

'The other boxes are ready. Am I going to need to rub the hunters down as well?'

If they'd kept up their punishing pace both animals would return in poor condition. 'They've been riding hard so it's possible both horses will need cooling. You won't be able to do both, but I'm sure Mr Simon will stay to do his own mount.'

She handed her reins to him. 'You should have plenty of time to do Silver before they arrive.'

Inside it was delightfully warm and as she hooked off her boots and hung up her hard hat and jacket, the kitchen door opened.

'Barbara, I thought I heard you come in. Are the others with you?'

'No, Grandmother. I had to come back early. The Farleys were galloping off into the distance the last time I saw them.'

'Men! What boys they are!' She smiled. 'You have time to take a lovely hot bath and change before lunch, but I shouldn't put on anything smart – we're eating in the breakfast room.'

'I thought slacks and my new green twin set?'

'Exactly right, my dear. Now run along, you'll get chilled standing around in your socks in this freezing passageway.'

Barbara, as usual, took the backstairs and met Marigold on her way down with the dirty linen. 'Hello, how are you settling in?'

'Lovely, thanks, miss. My room's ever so grand. I'm not used to having one to myself. And a bathroom and toilet inside, no po to empty in the morning.' The girl smiled. 'It's a bit remote like, The Grove, but Rosie says as I can go to hers when I have time off.'

'My old bicycle will be arriving from Hastings today. Would you like it? Then you could pedal into the village to see Rosie, and maybe to Brentwood, when you get a couple of hours' free time.'

'Cor! That'd be something! Me own bike? I reckon I've fallen on my feet here. All I needs is a nice young man to take me to the pictures and I'll be like a pig in clover.'

'I believe they hold a social at the village hall every month. I think Rosie said it's this Saturday, but because of the blackout it's being held in the afternoon. Isn't that your free afternoon?'

'It is. Thanks, miss. I'll go, if madam says it's all right. I've only been here five minutes, she mightn't want me to be going gallivanting.'

'Mrs Sinclair was in the kitchen a minute ago. Why don't you go and ask?'

'I'll do that. Cheerio, and thanks.'

* * *

Barbara was in the drawing room talking to Mrs Farley when her grandfather arrived.

'Sorry; am I late? Got held up, nasty accident in Brentwood this morning.'

'No, Edward, you're not. We're early, or rather Barbara is.' Her grandmother handed him a dry sherry. 'Simon and Reginald have only just returned. I think lunch will be a little later than planned.'

He smiled warmly and went over to kiss her on the cheek. Barbara noticed how much happier he seemed, almost rejuvenated; a spring in his step that hadn't been there when she'd first arrived. The atmosphere had definitely thawed since her return from Hastings.

Twenty minutes later they heard male voices approaching.

'Ah! Time for lunch.' Grandmother arrived at the door in time to prevent the hot, muddy men from entering. 'Good, you're here at last; we're just on our way to eat.' Expertly she ushered them back across the hall and into the small, less formal breakfast room.

Barbara noticed Simon hanging back, allowing his father to stride ahead, who was talking loudly about the exciting ride, the jumps and ditches he had taken.

'I say, Barbara; I'm most frightfully sorry about leaving you like that. Sinbad rather takes hold, you know. I just have to hang on and hope for the best.'

It wasn't how she'd seen it, but she let the comment pass. 'I'd had enough and so had Silver. I can't believe you jumped that hedge; you could have been killed.'

For a second he looked like his father, hard, uncompromising, then the usual self-effacing Simon came back. 'No choice, old thing. Pa went, so I followed. I closed my eyes and left Sinbad alone.' He grinned. 'No one was more surprised than I to find myself in one piece galloping across the stubble.'

'Did you know there was a field on the other side and not a narrow lane?'

He shrugged. 'No idea! I expect Pa did. He hunts all over this area, doesn't he?'

Everyone seemed in a good mood and even Mrs Farley smiled occasionally. Barbara was relieved Mrs Brown and Rosie served; she didn't want Mr Farley to set eyes on Marigold.

'Will it be all right to leave the horses here overnight, Edward? Simon can come over tomorrow to collect them.'

'Is that possible, Barbara? Can Joe cope with three animals?'

'Yes, Grandpa; Mrs Farley brought over their rugs and we have plenty of feed so they'll be fine. Silver will love it; she's not used to having handsome male company.'

'Which reminds me – as you're not leaving us in the New Year and the boys are coming, Elspeth and I thought it might be nice to get a couple of puppies for you. Joe tells us he knows of someone with a litter that might be suitable. What do you think?'

'Puppies? That would be wonderful. Tom and David will be thrilled. Thank you so much, Grandmother. I know you don't like dogs much, but I promise we'll keep them outside.'

'I've no objection to you taking them to your own rooms, using the backstairs of course, as long as they don't come into the main part of the house.'

'They won't. But they'll be perfectly happy out in the stables with Silver; they don't need to come into the house at all.'

To her amazement Grandmother laughed out loud. 'Remember, Barbara, I had a son. I know exactly what small boys are like. Those puppies will be upstairs in the nursery whatever the rules; so I've decided to accept the inevitable and give permission straightaway.'

The lunch party finally disbanded at three o'clock. It was dusk and Mrs Farley, who was driving, wanted to get back before the blackout. Simon joined Barbara by the window.

'There's a social in Ingatestone village hall on Saturday. Would you care to come with me? Everyone goes; they're jolly good fun. Party games for the children, whist for the old folk and dancing for everyone else.'

'I'd love to. I've never been to a social. In fact, I've never been to anything. But I warn you, I've not danced in public and only know the waltz, quickstep and foxtrot. If they do any of the new American dances, I'll be quite lost.'

'The jitterbug? That's easy. If you can foxtrot you can do anything. I'll collect you at midday on Saturday.'

'Lovely, but I'll see you tomorrow, won't I, when you come over for the horses?'

He scowled. 'I'd forgotten about that. Someone has to drive me over, so I don't know what time it'll be.'

'Surely another morning off is a good thing? I know where I'd rather be, and it's not in a factory, not when the sun is out.'

'You're right. It's just that my father always tells me; never asks.' He smiled. 'May I call in for a coffee before I take the horses? Will you be here?'

'Yes, Silver will need a day off. I shall be busy making curtains for the boys' room. I'd love to see you for coffee.' He really was a sweet boy – well not actually a boy; he was twenty-four, older than either Alex or John, but he seemed younger somehow, easier to manage.

Her grandmother came back from waving off her guests. 'Well, my dear, that was enjoyable. Are you coming into the drawing room or do you have things to do upstairs?'

'I've nothing special to do, only finish hemming curtains, but I can do that anytime. There's still plenty of time before the boys come home.'

She kicked off her shoes and curled up in an armchair, then remembered and started to remove her feet.

'No, please be comfortable. Sit the way you want, my dear.'

Surprised, she settled back. She was, finding her grandmother's behaviour puzzling.

'My dear, I owe you an apology. I have behaved appallingly and I hope you can forgive me? Could we possibly start again? I promise I'll do better this time.'

'Of course. You've nothing to apologise for. These last few weeks have been strange for all of us.'

Grandmother wiped her eyes. 'When Edward told me what you'd suffered all these years I felt so bad; it could have been so different if only I hadn't sent my boy away all those years ago.'

'It was not anyone's fault, it happened, and it's over. Now I want to look ahead, not back.'

'I'm sure you do, but if Charles had still been in contact, he would have brought you down to us when things started to go wrong. We could have had you here; you wouldn't have had to endure so much.' She sniffed. 'When Edward told me, we sat and cried together. We'd never shared our grief for Charles, and have, as I'm sure you'd noticed, become estranged. But now I feel we have broken down the barriers at last and can start to enjoy each other's company again.'

'What wonderful news. I know Grandpa's not been happy – neither of you have. If my problems have brought you together, then that's a good thing.'

'I can't tell you how thrilled Edward and I are to have your brothers here to live. We wanted a big family, and finally we're going to have one.' She patted the sofa. 'Come and sit here, my dear, next to me. It's warmer by the fire.'

Barbara unfolded her legs and, in her socks, ran across to curl up beside her. 'I was lucky, Grandma... sorry, Grandmother.'

'No, I like Grandma – it sounds less formal. I want to be close to you, Barbara, try to be the mother you never had.'

'That's good, as there's something I want to ask you. Simon has invited me to the village social on Saturday and I know Marigold's going to go as well. Would it be all right to offer to give her a lift? I'm not sure about this sort of thing.'

'Would you like to take her?'

'Yes, it seems mean for her to have to ride her bike when it's so cold and Simon and I are driving.'

'Then ask her. At least I can be sure she'll get home safely. I promised Mrs Mullins I'd keep an eye on her; make sure she didn't get into mischief.'

She felt a strange bubbling sensation inside, a warm glow, and she smiled. 'You know, Grandma, I believe I'm feeling truly happy for the first time in my life. It's as if I'm going to explode, or shout for joy.'

'I'm delighted, my dear. Edward and I have spent so much time talking about you and Tom and David. But he said I wasn't to bombard you with our ideas.'

'Go on, please, what are they?'

'Well, we wondered if you'd like to transfer them to Brentwood School? Charles went there as a weekly boarder; it's an excellent school and takes day boys. They could start in the New Year, be home all the time. What do you think?'

'I think it's a smashing idea. I expect it's going to get more difficult to travel once the war really starts, isn't it? I'm sure they'll be much happier as day boys. I didn't know they had a prep school as well.'

'Yes, they do. I'll ask Edward to get things organised straightaway. There's only a while left to this term after all.'

'What do I have to do, Elspeth, my dear?'

'Edward, I do hope you won't be cross, but I had to tell Barbara about transferring the boys to Brentwood. She thinks it's a smashing idea.'

He looked from one smiling face to the other. 'How can I be cross with my two favourite girls? I'll go and ring them now. I expect we'll have to pay the fees for Downton next term as we've left it so late.'

'I'll pay them from my allowance, Grandpa.'

'You'll do no such thing. I told you, Elspeth and I are taking responsibility for Tom and David for the next three years.' He smiled. 'So, have you told her my other suggestion yet?'

'No, Edward. Shall I tell her now?'

'I rather think it's my turn to be the bearer of good news.'

'What is it, Grandpa? What's the other good news?'

'We'd like your brothers to be known as Sinclair; to be our grandsons in the fullest sense. What do you think?'

'We'll all have the same name? I think that will make everything perfect. They can start at Brentwood as Thomas and David Sinclair; they'll be able to put things behind them.'

'Excellent. I'll get things moving. Shall I ring Downton for you?'

Barbara thought. 'No, better not; the boys don't know what's happened yet. I'll tell them everything when I see them.'

* * *

The following morning Barbara opened the blackouts and gasped. During the night it had snowed. The grass had vanished under a sparkling white coat. She shivered; there was ice on the inside of the window. It looked magical. A tap on the door interrupted her frosty fantasy.

Marigold appeared. 'Mr Simon has rung up, miss, and says they're snowed in and he won't be able to drive over to collect the horses.'

'Thank you. I was just going down to help Joe. I'll tell him. Just a minute, Marigold. Mr Farley and I are going to the social on Saturday. Would you like a lift?'

The girl's expression transformed. 'Really? In a car? That'd be grand, miss. That's if you're sure. I'd not want to upset anyone.'

'Mrs Sinclair suggested I ask you, so no one is going to be upset.'

'Crikey! My mum won't believe it. Going to a social in a car!'

'How deep is the snow? Have you been outside this morning?'

'No fear. I hate the stuff; all wet and cold and it melts in your shoes. I've never seen the fascination. But neither Mrs Brown nor Rosie have turned up so I reckon it's too deep for bicycles.'

She met Grandpa in the hall. 'Good morning, Barbara my dear. No going out anywhere today, I'm afraid. The snow's drifted to several feet in places. The drive and lanes are totally blocked.'

'That means no Joe, so I'm off to do the horses. I'll have breakfast when I'm finished.' She stopped to pull on thick socks and gumboots, her riding mac, gloves and scarf.

'I'll come out and give you a hand, my dear. Those horses are too much for a young girl to do on her own.'

'No, thank you, Grandpa. You stay in the warm. I like the cold and after all a paid groom does for half a dozen horses, so three's no problem.'

The back door opened easily but an icy blast whistled up the passageway, bringing a flurry of snow in with it. She tugged on her old beret and, head down, ventured out. In places the snow was over her boot tops and by the time she'd struggled round to the stables she was frozen. She found a shovel and began to clear the yard. With the snow piled up she couldn't even open the stable doors. The three horses heard her outside and began to stamp and whicker impatiently.

'Hang on; I'm nearly there. I'll have your food soon, don't worry.'

In the end she was forced to abandon her attempt to remove the drifts and settle for opening the boxes and tossing in two rounds of fresh hay. Next she scrambled over into each box in turn to remove their water pails and refill them. She was glad all three animals were easy to handle and had no objection to her unorthodox entry. By the time she'd finished she was filthy and freezing, but the horses were comfortable and fed. She was stacking the tools neatly in the barn when someone spoke behind her.

'What ho, Barbara? Am I too late to help?'

She dropped the pitchfork with a clatter. 'Simon, how on earth did you get here? The roads are totally blocked.'

16

Simon pointed to his feet. 'Snow shoes. I've always wanted to use these. Pa had them in the barn, along with skis and ski poles too. Pity there aren't enough hills for skiing.'

'Good grief! I'm impressed.' Barbara replaced the pitchfork she'd dropped. 'But you didn't have to come. I've managed on my own.'

'Well, I wasn't sure if your boy would get into work and it's not right you having to look after our horses.'

'I've done it now, but you must be frozen. Come in. I think I'd better see if Grandpa has any spare clothes you can borrow.' She grinned. 'You look like a yeti. I think you actually have icicles on your eyebrows.'

'Not to worry. If you're sure everything is done out here, I'd be glad of a hot drink and a thaw-out in front of the fire.' He banged ineffectively at his clothes to dislodge some of the impacted snow. 'I'm so much broader than Dr Sinclair, but we're about the same height, so a loose jumper would probably fit me.'

She led the way back to the house explaining how she'd had to climb into the stables as the bottom doors wouldn't open. They were laughing so hard they almost fell inside in their eagerness to get out of the arctic conditions.

'Simon, leave your boots and things in here, then go through into the kitchen. I'll find Grandma and she can sort you out something dry to wear.'

'Right ho! Have Mrs Brown and Mrs Mullins made it to work today?'

'No, but we have her cousin, who lives in, and she's around. If you ask nicely, I'm sure she'll make you a cup of tea.'

She left Simon at the kitchen door and ran through the house. Even with the boiler on minimum it was still much warmer inside. She found her grandparents in the library.

'Grandma, Simon's walked over here to help with the horses. He's in the kitchen trying to thaw out. I said I'd ask you to find him something to wear whilst his clothes are drying.'

'I'm not sure what you've got, Edward, that might fit Simon. Shall I go up and have a look?'

'Go ahead, my dear. I think there are sweaters and some old cords and a couple of winceyette shirts that could be large enough.' He raised his eyebrows. 'I take it you're going straight up to change as well? You're dripping on the carpet, my girl.'

She looked down. 'Oh dear, so I am. Sorry, I'll go and take these things off.'

Elspeth found clothes for Simon that more or less fitted him and when Barbara came down he was in the library drinking a large whisky, wearing brown cords that didn't meet at the front, a voluminous blue shirt and V-necked maroon sweater that was straining at the seams.

'It's snowing again. Simon's not going to be able to go home today. He's phoned and explained he's staying here until the weather improves.'

'That's what I thought. I'll be glad to have someone else to help me this afternoon when I go out to do the horses.'

There was a crackle from the large wireless in the corner and the plummy voice announced the BBC Home Service. They sat to listen to the twelve o'clock bulletin. It appeared that the whole of Europe was suffering from the same extreme weather conditions. They heard the troops in France, guarding the Maginot line, were doing it in several feet of snow.

Grandpa switched off the set. 'I hope they have suitable winter clothing and sufficient bedding out there. I'd hate to think of those young men away from home at Christmas suffering because of the weather.'

'Mrs Mullins will be upset. Her husband's in France, you know,' Barbara told them.

'Yes, we do know that, my dear. There are several young men from the village in the same battalion. They like to keep the boys together if they can.'

'I wonder how John's managing in London.' As soon as she'd spoken she realised her error. Simon wasn't aware her grandparents knew of her relationship. There was an uncomfortable pause before Grandpa stepped in.

'Who is John, my dear – a family friend?'

She smiled her thanks. 'Yes, you remember, Grandpa, I told you he's Auntie Irene and Uncle Bill's only son. I grew up with him. Their letters are always full of news about what he's doing. I couldn't believe it when they told me that the RAF sends all their new recruits to Lord's cricket ground for their preliminary interviews.'

'I know a chap called Johnny. He's training to be a pilot in Scotland. Bally cold up there in the Cairngorms, I should think. But at least they've got mountains to ski down.'

Grandma stood up to collect the dirty coffee cups and saucers. 'I'd better go and do something about lunch. I doubt Marigold can cope on her own.'

'Please, let me do it, Grandma. I love to cook and have hardly had the chance since I've been here.'

'If you're sure, my dear, I'd be delighted. You do the lunch and I'll do supper. Simon, why don't you and Edward go and play billiards whilst I finish hemming the curtains for the nursery?'

Barbara left them at their various activities. She would much rather cook than sew. She pushed open the door to find the maid already there. The girl was in tears.

'What's wrong, Marigold? Are you unwell?'

The girl blew her nose loudly. 'No, miss, it's not that. It's just I can't cook and Mrs Brown's not here to do lunch and I ain't got a clue what to prepare.'

'I'm here to do it, so please don't upset yourself. Can you do vegetables and things?'

'I can peel a spud, if that's what you mean, but that's about it.'

Barbara hurried into the pantry to discover the small room bursting with hams, sides of bacon, braces of pheasants and boxes and baskets of every conceivable vegetable. Slabs of butter and trays of eggs jostled for position with jugs of cream and milk. What there wasn't, was bread, at least fresh bread. There was half a stale loaf; that would have to do. She found an empty basket and filled it with cabbage, potatoes and onions.

'Here we are. I'm going to do bubble and squeak, bacon and eggs and fried bread. What do you think?'

'It sounds grand, miss. I love a bit of bubble and squeak. I don't reckon that's cooked here very often.'

'Well, it's what they're getting today. I think it's ideal for a cold, snowy day. If you peel potatoes and cut them into small pieces, I'll do the cabbage and bacon.'

'What will you do for afters? Mrs Brown always does afters at lunchtime.'

'I think there's time for me to make an apple pie.'

They worked well together and by twelve thirty everything was ready. She sent Marigold in to lay the table, checking first that she knew where things were and how to put them out. Fifteen minutes later, when the girl hadn't returned, she went in search of her. She could hear voices in the dining room. Who was holding up her helper? She walked in to find her deep in conversation with Simon. They both looked round guiltily.

'I'm ever so sorry, miss, but I've not done it yet. Mr Farley was asking me about my family and such.'

Barbara frowned at Simon; he had no right to waylay the staff, and what was he doing in the dining room anyway?

'I know, mea culpa. I came to see if I could help and then I met Marigold. She's new, isn't she? It's my fault. I held her up.'

'As the table's still not done, you'd better do it yourself, Simon. We're both needed in the kitchen.' There was no need wait to see if he did as instructed. He would do it; after all he was very obliging.

At one o'clock she was ready. 'I'm going to ring the gong. Marigold, can you wait a few moments and then bring the plates in? I'll come back and dish up the pie; it will be done by then.'

'It looks lovely, miss. You're ever such a good cook.'

'You must have yours whilst we're eating; it seems silly to let it get cold.'

* * *

The gong was clearly heard by her grandparents. 'Come along, Elspeth, and please remember, whatever Barbara has managed to prepare, we shall tell her it's delicious.'

'She told me she likes to cook. It might not be our usual fare but I'm sure it will be tasty.'

She looked round. 'Where did Simon get to after your match, Edward?'

'I've no idea, but he'll have heard the gong and turn up for his lunch.'

They walked into the dining room to find their missing guest placing the last of the crystal water tumblers on the table.

'Good heavens, Simon. We didn't realise you were helping Barbara.'

'Only to lay the table, Mrs Sinclair. I hope I've got it right. It's a long time since I've been asked to do this.'

She scanned the place settings and nodded. 'Perfect, Simon. Shall we have wine with the meal, Edward? Is there something suitable or do you need to go down to the cellar?'

'There's a decent claret decanted. We can have that. I hope what we're getting merits it.'

'Now, Edward, remember what I said. Here's our chef. Shall we sit down, Barbara, or would you like some help?'

'Sit down, please, Grandma. Everything's ready. I've plated it today; makes it simpler for Marigold to carry out.'

The girl came in, a plate held carefully in each hand. She gave the first to Grandma and the other to Barbara. The aroma of crisply fried bacon filled the room. She stared at her plate on which was a perfectly fried egg, two rashers of bacon, a portion of bubble and squeak and a slice of fried bread coated in caramelised onions.

'My dear, I'm speechless. This looks and smells absolutely delicious.'

The plates arrived for the men and Grandpa poured them all a glass of wine. After the first mouthful there was no more talking until the plates were clean.

'That was amazing, Barbara. I've never had cabbage and potatoes served like that. Does it have a name? I'll ask our cook if she can make it for me,' Simon asked.

'It's called bubble and squeak, but I'm not sure which ingredient is which. I'm so glad you enjoyed it, Simon. This meal's a favourite with my brothers.'

The apple pie and cream were equally well received. Barbara was impressed by his willingness to help. He even offered to wash up but Grandma was adamant that wouldn't be necessary.

'Marigold can manage that, Simon, thank you. Let's all go back into the library. Shall we play rubber or two of bridge?'

'I've no idea how to play, Grandma. And anyway, Simon and I have to change and go outside again shortly.'

'Yes, the horses – I'd forgotten. Simon, I'm having a bed made up for you in the green room, but I'm afraid there's no fuel at the moment for bedroom fires.'

'Jolly good. Thanks, Mrs Sinclair. We don't have heating upstairs at Mountney Hall, so I'm used to a spartan existence.'

As the temperature had dropped Grandpa decided it would be sensible to use only the kitchen, breakfast room and library and not attempt to keep the other rooms warm as well. Therefore supper was eaten informally and prepared by Grandma and Marigold. The nine o'clock news said the country had ground to a temporary halt but the army had most of the main roads cleared and trains were running normally. The snow was expected to thaw by the weekend. There was no news of any further aggression from Germany.

* * *

Barbara decided to sleep in her socks and was glad she'd made herself a hot-water bottle. The radiators in her bedroom were barely warm and without her usual fire she was sharply reminded of her bedroom at Crabapple Cottage. She snuggled deep under the covers, leaving only the tip of her nose out, and tried to sleep.

Her mind was too busy. She'd discussed ideas for Christmas with Grandma and they were in complete accord. Even Grandpa had said it was important not to be seen to be cowed by Hitler's progress across Europe. Grandma had also suggested a trip to Brentwood, if the weather improved, to buy some 'in between' clothes, things that could be worn around the house and to visit friends. Harrods and Hamleys were also mentioned as places to buy presents for the boys. After years of having no personal money, and nothing to look forward to, her life was suddenly overflowing with excitement.

Eventually she fell asleep but her hot-water bottle, now cold, woke her. She tossed it out, but was wide awake and needed to get up. Her bed was so warm she tried to ignore the clamour of her overfull bladder but was forced to scramble out and, torch in hand, scamper across to the bathroom.

She pulled on her thick dressing gown and found her slippers. She wasn't going back to sleep without help. What she needed was a nice mug of cocoa. There was plenty of milk in the pantry so she would creep down and make herself some and refill her hot-water bottle at the same time.

Her breath condensed in a silver cloud in the beam of her torch. She was shivering as she hurried through the silent house, downstairs and along to the kitchen. The range was always hot so in less than twenty minutes she was on her way back, hot-water bottle under her arm, mug of cocoa in one hand, torch in the other.

As she reached the gallery she thought she heard a noise and slopped her drink over her fingers. Who was it? She prepared to call out. It had to be Simon – her grandparents slept at the other end of the house. Then she was certain she heard the sound of a door closing.

Puzzled she shone her torch down the empty passageway. Why had Simon been creeping about? He had his own facilities and had no need to come out in search of a WC. She must have imagined it. She was over-tired and her ears were playing tricks on her. The sooner she got back to bed the better.

* * *

The next morning she'd forgotten about hearing unidentified noises in the corridor. Dressed in her oldest and warmest clothes, she raced through the house to the kitchen. Simon was there already, a mug of tea in his hand.

'Hope you don't mind, old thing, but I've made myself a cuppa. There's plenty in the pot.'

'Thanks, just what I need. Shall we do the horses before breakfast? Get it over with?'

He put down his mug and smiled. 'I'm game. I've not poked my nose outside since yesterday afternoon, but at least the sun's shining.' The sky was blue, the snow soft underfoot.

'I think it's thawing, Simon. We should be able to shovel it away from the doors.'

'Good show! I think I might be able to take Sinbad and Bee back later.'

The yard was already clear, the boxes open and a cheerful whistling could be heard from the barn.

'Joe's back, thank goodness. That must mean the lanes are clear.'

The stable boy appeared, a broad grin on his face. 'Morning, miss, sir; sorry about yesterday. We were up to our armpits in it. But the lanes are fine now, at least for a bicycle.'

'We managed, but I'm really glad you're back, and you've worked hard. What time did you get here?'

''Bout seven o'clock. Didn't take long to shift the snow. Have you come for your hunters, sir? Shall I tack them up for you?'

'Yes, will you do that, Joe? I'll get off whilst it's sunny. If a bicycle can get along the lanes then so can a horse.'

With the snow shoes strapped to his back, astride Sinbad and leading Bee, Simon set off a short while later.

'This white stuff will be gone before Saturday so I'll be here to pick you and Marigold up at midday as planned,' he called as he left.

'Good. I'm really looking forward to it. Take care, and please ring when you get back so that we know you've arrived safely.'

'Will do. Cheerio. See you on Saturday.'

Simon had refused to come back in for breakfast, but she was starving. If Joe had got here that should mean Mrs Brown and Rosie would be here as well. She shut the back door and stamped the snow from her gumboots. Yes, two extra sets of boots and two winter coats hung in the boot room.

As promised the snow melted and by Saturday everything was clear. The trip to Rosebery's was completed successfully and Barbara's dressing room was now filled to capacity. Saturday morning, over breakfast, Grandpa was worried.

'The temperature's dropping sharply, Barbara; more snow is forecast for this weekend. I'm not sure you should be going out this afternoon.'

'Edward, don't fuss, my dear. Simon is taking them in his car and it's only two miles to the village. If it starts to snow they would be home long before the lanes were blocked.'

'And I'll make sure we take boots and wear thick coats in case we have to walk home.'

He chuckled. 'That's very reassuring, my dear girl. Although having seen the way young Farley drives, I'm not sure walking wouldn't be the safest option.'

'I hope it isn't too bad next week because I'm invited for Sunday lunch at Home Farm. Mrs Everton's daughter, Valerie, and her new husband are coming. I'd really like to meet them.'

'Next Sunday? That's a long way off; even if it does snow tonight they'll have the lanes open long before then. That reminds me, I must get Joe to fill up the log store and remember to call the coal merchant and order a load for the boiler.'

'Will you drive me over there, Grandpa? I want to wear something decent and I'll not be able to ride my bicycle if I do.'

'Delighted to, my dear. You're going up to Town next week with your grandmother aren't you, to do some Christmas shopping?'

'We are, Edward. We're going to make this an extra special time for the boys. I rather fear that this might be the last time, for a long while, anyone will be in a position to celebrate in style.'

'Are we still having guests on Christmas Day? And going to the Boxing Day party at the Farleys'?'

'Of course, Edward. Now we have a live-in, and Mrs Mullins and Mrs Brown and Betty have all said they'd be glad of the extra money and are happy to work on Christmas Day, there's no reason to cancel it.'

Barbara smiled at the thought; parties of any sort were a novelty for her. 'I'd like to buy presents for the Mullins children; with their father away it's going to be hard for them this year. Would that be all right, do you think?'

'Yes, that's a kind thought. Edward and I always do them a Christmas box, then Mrs Mullins can use the money as she thinks fit. Perhaps we could be a little more generous this year, my dear, in the circumstances?'

'Excellent idea. Now, please excuse me, I have to go into the surgery this morning. I expect you'll have gone before I get back, Barbara, so have a good time.'

By midday Barbara had changed three times before finally settling on a pretty cotton shirt-waister, one of her most recent purchases. The full skirt of palest gold swirled around her legs. She loved it. She wore a darker gold cardigan and had her matching court shoes in a cloth bag to take with her. Her hair was up and she was wearing the right amount of makeup. Too much and she would look flashy. She had decided to wear her heavy, full-length tweed overcoat, and collected a scarf, gloves and woolly hat to go with it. In the kitchen, Marigold, similarly dressed, was waiting for her.

'Hope we don't have to walk home, miss, but I've got a thick cardi on and warm socks just in case. I can shove my boots on when Mr Farley arrives.'

'You haven't forgotten you'll need your shoes as well? I've got mine here.' She dangled the bag.

'Good Gawd! Court shoes. I'll look a right lemon dancing in me socks, won't I? I'll nip up and get them. I'll not be a tick.'

She vanished and Barbara could hear her running up the uncarpeted backstairs. It was five to twelve. She hoped Simon wouldn't be late. Marigold returned, breathless, triumphantly waving her red shoes.

'Is he here? Am I late?'

'No, he's not and no, you're not, but I think that's the car pulling up now. Shall we get our boots on and go and meet him?'

Simon flung open the rear door of his vehicle with a flourish. 'In you go, Marigold, too bally cold to hang around today.' The girl ducked her head and slid across the leather seat. He banged shut the door and, quite forgetting about Barbara, jumped back into the car leaving her to walk round and get herself in.

'Are we ready, ladies? Then off we jolly well go.'

The car shot forward and Marigold squealed in excitement. Barbara gritted her teeth and clutched the strap. How typical! A pretty face and Simon was showing off, driving even more recklessly than usual. She didn't breathe normally until the car skidded to a halt in the open space outside the village hall. He jumped out and ran round to open the front door.

'Sorry, old thing, forgot to do it last time. Brain like a sieve.' He held out his arm and she smiled, her good humour restored.

This time he left Marigold to climb out unaided and the girl was happy to do so. 'Cor! Sounds lively in there already. Have they got a band?'

'Heavens, shouldn't think so. Unless some local lads are prepared to play for nothing. It's a gramophone, turned up loud.'

With Barbara on his arm, and Marigold trailing behind, they went in, dropping their shillings into the saucer as they walked past. A plump lady in purple gave them a peg, with a number stuck to it, for their boots.

'Put your coats on the rail and your boots along the back, but remember your number, or you could go home in the wrong ones.'

The hall was already half full of locals of all ages and descriptions, but there was a noticeable absence of young men. Those who were there, were in uniform. Simon appeared to be the only man of his age in civilian clothes. Barbara wondered if he was aware of that.

She looked around with interest. The hall was decked out with tired bunting and a few bunches of balloons. The small stage at the far end held the gramophone on a trestle table, a boy of about fourteen guarding the pile of records.

There were plain wooden chairs around the edges, hard up against the wall, and card tables had been set out at the back, near the entrance. The floor in the centre was clear, ready for party games and the promised dancing. She scanned the chairs. Already many were occupied, and she nodded and smiled at faces she recognised. The postmistress was there, and the postman, also the entire Mullins and Brown families.

Marigold shouted across the noisy hall, 'Here I am. I arrived in style, I did. Ain't this grand?'

The girl ran across the room, her red-spotted dress flaring out around her long legs. Barbara saw every pair of male eyes from nineteen to ninety swivel to watch. The girl lit up the space; there was no doubt about it, she was stunning.

Well, she supposed as she had three young men in her life, and one who actually wanted to marry her, perhaps being beautiful wasn't essential. She sighed. It would be nice to be as lovely as Marigold. Then she noticed the growing circle of assorted males gathering like bees around a honey pot and decided that she was happy to be as she was. She would hate to be gawped at by strange men. She felt a light touch on her arm.

'Barbara, come and meet some friends of mine.'

Simon led her over to a cluster of smartly dressed young people, two men, both officers – one in blue, the other khaki – and three girls with excellent deportment and crystal-clear diction.

'Amanda, Eliza, Harriet, I'd like to introduce you to Barbara Sinclair. She's living with her grandparents at The Grove, you know.' The three girls smiled and closed ranks around her. Barbara felt the evening was very much a matter of 'them and us'. The two men, Jasper and Henry something or other, were polite but rather distant and she began to feel *de trop* and wished she could change camps and join in the far livelier group surrounding Marigold and her family.

The village hall prided itself on its indoor lavatories, provided by her grandfather and the Farleys she'd been told. She was powdering her nose, halfway through the afternoon, when she got into conversation with Harriet, who was hopping about from one foot to the other, waiting for the cubicle to empty.

'Simon seems very attracted, Barbara. Are you serious?'

She was about to shake her head but remembered their agreement. 'We are going around together, but it's not serious, at least not yet it isn't.'

'Thought so; he's obviously warned the other two off. They know better than to poach on his preserves.'

The lavatory door opened and Harriet rushed in. 'Excuse me, I'm desperate to spend a penny. I'll catch up later.'

Barbara returned to the hall worrying about Harriet's remark. Why should Simon warn off Jasper and Henry? And why would they take any notice if he did? Then, she caught a glimpse of her escort laughing, his arms around the shoulders of his friends, and understood. Of course they wouldn't flirt with her, not if they believed she was close to Simon. They wouldn't want to upset their friend. He had told her how difficult he found it to attract the right sort of girl. His deafness put them off.

Pleased she'd solved that puzzle she rejoined her new friends and was soon swept away by Simon to dance a riotous polka. By three o'clock, when the event finished, she was exhausted. She'd joined in all the party games and danced every dance with Simon.

There were large flakes of snow falling as people began to pour out of the hall.

'Stay in the warm, Barbara; I'll start the car first. She's sometimes a bit tricky in the cold.'

Marigold appeared behind her, cocooned in a balaclava and thick coat. 'What a lovely do, weren't it, miss? My feet are killing me after all that dancing. Two fellows have asked me to go to the flicks with them when they're on leave next time and I said yes. I love the pictures—' Her monologue was interrupted as Simon's car roared into life.

'Right ho! Come along, ladies, your carriage awaits. Let's get moving before the snow's any heavier.'

He promised to ring during the week to arrange another outing and Barbara went in satisfied that her first social had been a resounding success. Both Harriet and Amanda had promised to get in touch as well. Marigold quickly hung up her coat.

'Thanks ever so, Miss Sinclair. I'm back on duty in half an hour. I'm serving dinner for madam tonight, so I've got to go up and change.'

Barbara went to the library to share her experiences with her grandparents.

'Harriet Chilvers and Amanda Hope-Grainger are both delightful girls. They are exactly the sort of families we would like you to get to know better, aren't they, Edward?'

After listening to the nine o'clock news, Barbara excused herself. She wanted to write to the boys, and to John, before she went to bed. Fires were once more allowed in bedrooms and she knew it would be as warm upstairs as down. She went into the kitchen to collect her hot-water bottle from Marigold and found her wiping down the table.

'I had a nice time this afternoon, miss. You and Mr Farley make a lovely couple. Are you walking out or anything?'

Without thinking she replied, 'No, we're just friends. I have a young man in the RAF.'

The girl handed her a filled hot-water bottle. Barbara was so concerned she had just broken her promise to Simon she didn't really register Marigold's next remark. As she was undressing she thought she might have heard her say something about "it not mattering". To what Marigold was referring she'd no idea and was too tired to worry about it.

17

'I'm sick of snow and even if it means we're going to have a white Christmas, I still wish it would disappear.'

'Think how much worse it is for our troops stuck in France, Barbara my dear. Our lanes are usable and the buses and trains functioning and we have sufficient fuel to keep us warm all winter. How many others can say the same?'

'I know, Grandpa, I shouldn't complain; there's a war on. But Silver hasn't had a good gallop for a week, and I'm supposed to be going out to lunch at the Evertons tomorrow. If it's too bad, Valerie and her husband might not be able to come.' Or Alex – but she kept that thought to herself.

'I said I'll drive you; I've been going into hospital with no problems all week. Is Mrs Everton's daughter coming by car?'

'I've no idea. But I expect so. Farmers are about the only people who still have petrol.'

Her grandmother came in, her face anxious. 'Marigold didn't come home last night. I've just been up and her bed hasn't been slept in.'

'Is Mrs Mullins in today?'

'It's her day off, Edward. I'm very worried. I know Friday was Marigold's day off this week, but I did expect her to come home.'

Barbara stood up. 'I've got to take Silver out for some exercise. Shall I ride over to Mrs Mullins and see if Marigold's there.'

'Would you? Thank you, my dear. Did she say anything about where she was going yesterday?'

'She mentioned a couple of soldiers had invited her out while she was at the social. I expect she went to the pictures with one of them.'

'Have you checked in the boot room, Elspeth?'

'No, I haven't. She wouldn't wear gumboots to go out, surely?'

'No, but he she'd take them with her if she intended to cycle home this morning.'

'Did someone pick her up yesterday morning?' Barbara asked. 'Because if they didn't, she would have had to go to the village to catch a bus and would have worn her boots. I'll check on the way out.'

The hall and corridors were, as usual, barely above freezing and she ran from the library to the boot room in an effort to keep warm. Two sweaters and a thick vest were not enough in this weather. As she passed the kitchen door she heard Mrs Brown moving about, preparing breakfast. Perhaps the cook knew where the missing girl was. She opened the door.

'Morning, miss. Right parky it was riding over here, I can tell you.'

'Marigold! We were all worried about you; your bed hasn't been slept in.'

'Sorry. By the time the bus got in yesterday it were dark and I didn't fancy a bike ride. I stayed with Rosie. Good thing her Graham's away – it left room for me in her bed.'

Barbara was about to ask why the girl couldn't have rung, then remembered the call box was over a mile away from where Rosie lived. 'I'll tell my grandparents you're here. Don't lay up for me – I'll have something in the kitchen when I get back from my ride.'

She explained to her grandmother why the maid had stayed out all night.

'That girl ought to come back after her day off. She's a live-in servant; she's our responsibility. If it was too dark to walk she should have caught an earlier bus.'

'Grandma, if she'd done that she wouldn't have been able to see the end of the film.'

'Don't worry, my dear. She's back safely; no harm done. You could suggest next time that she makes certain she's back before dark. Maybe it would be safer for her to stay with Mrs Mullins as she did last night?'

'Very well, Edward. I suppose that we're lucky to have a live-in girl. I don't want her to leave, not with Christmas almost upon us.'

* * *

In the rush to attend the eight o'clock service, return, eat breakfast and prepare for her lunch at Home Farm, Barbara didn't have time to speak to Mrs Mullins. She still didn't know who Marigold's escort had been.

The sun was out, but the temperature was below zero and the lanes treacherous. A fresh layer of ice appeared every night and she was worried her grandfather would refuse to drive her over.

She had selected her outfit the previous day. Remembering how her couture clothes had embarrassed Auntie Irene and Uncle Bill, she had settled for something from her 'in between' range. She was happy that the pair of well-cut, pale green slacks worn with a matching long-sleeved linen blouse were exactly right. She loved the dark green cardigan, with embroidered flowers around the yoke, she'd chosen to wear over them.

The jade combs Grandma had given her held her curls back from her face. She didn't want it up today, too formal for an invitation to lunch. A dusting of face powder and a smudge of red lipstick and she was ready. She sniffed her hands. Did they still have a whiff of the stable? No, just lemon soap. She wished she had some French perfume, or any perfume. Lemon soap was such a young thing to smell of.

Grandpa was in the hall waiting for her, his topcoat and gloves already on. 'You look lovely, my dear girl. I hope you're intending to wear a warm coat?'

'Of course I am, Grandpa. I learnt my lesson in Hastings. I want to look nice, but not freeze to death.'

Her grandmother was at church; Mrs Farley had called for her earlier. Barbara rather thought Grandpa was relieved to have an excuse to miss the service. 'I'll telephone if I need a lift home, Grandpa. I'm pretty sure the Millers will be coming this way and will be able to drop me off and save you having to come out again.'

'I'm not going anywhere. The news bulletin said there's a thaw on the way. With any luck the road will be clear by tomorrow.'

She stared out of the car window at the frost-encrusted trees. 'It's really beautiful, all this snow, but I shall be glad to see the back of it. It was horrible in London, not Christmassy at all, just freezing.'

'Your grandmother said Harrods' toy department was deserted, no children to be seen anywhere, and with the windows taped and no Christmas lights, it must have seemed rather bleak for the festive season.'

'It certainly was, but we bought everything we wanted. It's going to be delivered sometime this week. They even wrap gifts and label them for you. All we have to do is put them under the tree on Christmas Eve.'

'That's what you pay for, my dear. Did you find everything you wanted for the boys?' He didn't wait for her answer. 'Although judging by the number of parcels and bags you brought back with you, I'm sure that you must have.'

'We did. But I've also got something for the Everton boys and Mrs Mullins's children. Grandma bought up half the food hall. Honestly, I can't believe we'll eat all the exotic things she's ordered.'

The car skidded violently and conversation ceased as Barbara was thrown sideways, banging her head on the side window.

'Bloody snow! Are you all right, my dear? No injuries? What about your head?'

'Honestly, I'm fine. Are we stuck? Do you want me to get out and push, or anything?'

He shook his head as he rammed the car into reverse and pressed the accelerator. The rear end shot sideways, the wheels slipping on the ice. 'Hang on, I'm going to try that again.' The car swerved from side to side before finally crunching out of the rut and back onto the cleared central strip. 'I'll take it more slowly from here; we don't want to end up in a ditch.'

She was grateful to arrive without further mishap. The yard at the farm had been swept clean and two cars were parked in the open barn.

Her heart flipped over. Alex was here. She'd been so worried he might not have made it; it was a long way from Hornchurch.

'You're right; it's thawing, Grandpa. Hopefully it won't be so hazardous coming home.'

She waved to him and then, box of chocolates under her arm, picked her way carefully across the yard to the back door. Jim spotted her approach and raced through the house to greet her.

'Come in, Barbara. Everyone else is here already and you had the least distance to travel.'

'I know. I'm sorry, but we skidded off the road and it took a while to get going again.'

He took her things and hung them up. She handed him the chocolates and he beamed with delight. She wiped her shoes clean on the rag he passed her.

'We've been sledging down the hill by the river on Mum's tray and Alex helped us build an igloo.'

'How exciting. I went to London to do my Christmas shopping and hemmed three pairs of curtains. I think it sounds as you if you had far more fun than me.'

Jim didn't stop at the kitchen. 'We're all in the front room. Dad lit the fire last night and it's lovely and cosy in there. Mum likes to have plenty of room when she's cooking a big lunch.' The boy beamed up at her. 'We always use it when there's more than just us here. Don't look so worried. It's my favourite room, apart from the kitchen.'

'Do you think your mother would like any help? With eight of us to feed there must be a lot for her to do.'

The front room door swung open and Alex stood framed by the firelight, the blue-grey of his uniform making him appear larger. 'Good, you're here. Come in, Barbara, and meet my sister Valerie and her husband Peter.'

He was matter-of-fact, no hint of appreciation in his eyes, and she felt her chest squeeze with disappointment. If she had known he was going to treat her like his little sister she wouldn't have bothered to dress up. The other occupants of the substantial beamed room stood up to greet her warmly, their enthusiasm making up for Alex's lack.

A girl of middle height, unmistakably an Everton, with her sparkling green eyes and russet hair, rushed over to embrace her. 'I'm so glad to meet you at last. I've heard of nothing but Barbara this and Barbara that, for weeks. Come and meet my husband; he's just been told he's exempt from call-up, at least for the moment, which is a great relief.'

Ned handed her a glass of sweet sherry and returned to his seat in the window, where he was struggling to complete a complicated jigsaw puzzle of the Tower of London. Jim vanished back to the kitchen – today his turn to help.

Mr Everton smiled. 'You look a picture, Barbara. Doesn't she, Alex?'

Her face coloured. She looked down, fiddling with her glass.

'You're embarrassing our guest, Dad,' Valerie said laughing. 'But you're right: I love that outfit. Green goes so well with your dark hair.'

Alex laughed. 'Who's embarrassing Barbara now?' His smile made her stomach lurch.

Barbara went even pinker as she wasn't used to compliments. Taking a deep breath she raised her head. 'Thank you, all of you. It's nice to know my efforts to impress have been appreciated.'

Mr Everton chuckled. 'You don't have to impress anyone here, my dear, but a bit of glamour never went amiss, not with our Alex anyway. Always an eye for a pretty girl has our Alex.'

Alex shifted uncomfortably and she enjoyed the moment, joining in the general laughter. They sat, sipping sherry, discussing the war, the possibility of invasion, the annoyance of carrying a gas mask and the appalling weather, until Jim arrived to call them for lunch.

She was relieved to discover the meal was to be eaten in the kitchen around the huge oak table and not in another, less friendly place. She liked Valerie and agreed to go to visit her in Romford after Christmas. At two thirty the party broke up, everyone agreeing it had been an enjoyable afternoon, but no one wanting to drive on the ice when it got dark.

Alex tapped her on the shoulder. 'I'll run you home, Barbara. It's hardly out of my way and it will save Dr Sinclair having to come out again.'

Not quite the way she'd hoped he'd offer but she smiled her acceptance. 'Mrs Everton, may I please use your telephone to let them know that I've got a lift home?'

'Go on, love. Alex will show you where it is.'

The low-ceilinged corridor was dark and Alex too close behind her, making her feel unsettled.

He reached past to open the door, his hand brushing her cheek. She shivered. 'Thank you, Alex. Are the blackouts drawn? I have a torch, so don't worry.'

He placed a warm hand in the small of her back and guided her in. There was no moon; it had clouded over during the afternoon. It wasn't dark enough to need her torch but searching for it gave her something to do.

'The telephone's on the desk. I'll go and fetch your coat and bring it back here.'

She rang and told her grandmother she was getting a lift home but didn't specify with whom.

'Is it Valerie and her husband bringing you?'

'Actually it's Alex, Grandma.'

'How nice. Why don't you ask him to call in. It's so long since I've spoken to him.'

'I'm afraid he won't be able to stop as he has to be back at his base in Hornchurch. Perhaps another time?'

'Of course, my dear. How silly of me. I keep forgetting he's in the RAF. A pilot isn't he?'

'He is. He flies Spitfires and he says he's going to fly over us next time he goes up. The bad weather has kept them on the ground recently.'

She heard his footsteps in the passage outside. 'I have to go. See you later.' She replaced the receiver and turned to face the door. She disliked having him behind her; she wanted to see him, know what he was going to do. He'd put on his flying jacket. The dark brown leather made him look even more attractive. He held out her coat. She had no option but to step closer and turn her back in order to slip her arms into the sleeves.

She tried to shrug the coat out of his hands but he moved in, not releasing his hold, his hands encircling her throat as he pulled the collar close around her. She shivered a second time.

'Are you cold, Barbara?' His voice, like rich chocolate, gave her palpitations. She swallowed nervously, unable to speak and heard him laugh softly. His warm breath tickled her neck. 'Valerie and Peter are waiting to say goodbye. I suppose we'd better go back to the kitchen.'

'Yes, of course.' Her fingers felt clumsy as she pushed the buttons through their holes and she was relieved when he stepped away. 'I'm ready now.'

'You're not. I still have your gloves, hat and scarf here. Do you need any assistance to put them on?' His tone was light, teasing. He was definitely flirting with her.

'No, thank you, Alex. I'm not a child. I can dress myself.'

'I never supposed you were. You're a very lovely and desirable young woman, as well you know.'

'Alex, Barbara, are you coming? Valerie and Peter are leaving.' Mrs Everton's call broke the spell and Barbara was able to move.

'Let's go, Alex. Your sister has a long way to travel this afternoon.' She smiled, hoping the excitement she felt racing through her body wasn't visible. Goodbyes accomplished, both couples hurried across the yard to the barn.

'It's thawing right enough, Alex. Should be easier driving home than it was coming,' Peter called, as he turned his car over with the starting handle.

'Drive safely. I shall write to let you know when it's possible for me to visit you, Valerie. I was so pleased to meet you both.' She jumped as Alex's car burst into life beside her.

He opened the passenger door and she ducked her head to climb inside. 'Your mother made a lovely lunch, Alex. I've really enjoyed this afternoon. It's a shame you can't get any more leave before the New Year.'

His features were indistinct in the semi-darkness. 'I've volunteered to be on duty over the holiday. It's fairer if the chaps with families get home and I've had more leave than the poor blighters in France.'

She was about to apologise but shrugged instead. 'Do you have a rug? Something for my knees?'

'A rug?' Her request had thrown him. 'No, I don't, sorry. But it's not far – you'll hardly have time to freeze.' His hands stretched across and brushed her cheek. He was wearing his gloves. The unexpected contact sent a jolt of something strange down her spine. She was no longer feeling cold.

They had to wait for the other car to reverse out of the barn and leave the yard before they could go. He engaged the gears and sent them shooting backwards, a spray of dirty water cascading up on either side. She grabbed the strap and braced herself as he spun the wheel again, sending the car sideways, before straightening with expert control to send the car hurtling through the gate.

She released her breath and opened her eyes. 'Heavens, Alex! Is this how you fly your Spitfire?'

He glanced at her, his grin white in the gloom.

'Sorry, couldn't resist showing off. I promise I'll behave. I'd forgotten you ended up in a ditch on the way over.'

'It wasn't that bad, but we did skid. The road must still be slippery; the ice can't have melted already.'

'You're right. In fact the surface is treacherous: water on ice, lethal combination.'

'Should you be driving all the way back to your base tonight, if the roads are dangerous?'

'I'd rather risk a skid than be arrested for being AWOL.'

'I keep forgetting you have no choice in these things.'

His explosion of amusement filled the freezing car. 'Good God! I've been dressed in uniform both times you've met me. That's a bit of a clue, you know.'

She wasn't sure if he was laughing at her and was defensive. 'You changed into cords and jumper last time when you brought the hay over.'

'I did indeed.' He paused, as if choosing his words. 'About that time... I think I was a bit offhand with you. I didn't mean to be. The boys set my teeth on edge. I don't usually mind their banter, but, well...' Another pause. 'I didn't want you to think I was a philanderer, not to be trusted.' He cleared his throat. 'Hope I didn't offend you.'

Happiness bubbled up inside. Alex felt the same way, or at least she thought that's what he was saying. She didn't know how to answer so said nothing.

'Barbara?'

She detected hesitation in his voice, an emotion she didn't associate with him. It prompted her to speak. 'Of course I wasn't upset. Why should I be? We'd only just met and I'm almost engaged to someone else.' This wasn't what she'd intended to say but her misgivings had made her say what was in her heart. She felt his withdrawal.

'I see, well, that's that then.'

He didn't speak again until the car turned through the gates of her home. She felt wretched, but couldn't think of any way to put things right. She'd said no more than the truth. She wasn't free to become involved with him and he knew it. Why, it'd be a bit like committing a deliberate act of sabotage if she took up with Alex whilst being engaged to John.

Doing the right thing was hard, but it was better to stop things now before they went any further. She wished her stomach didn't curl and her pulse race just thinking about him.

'Where shall I drop you? Didn't you say you don't use the front door any more?'

'Round the back, there's a turning circle and you won't have to reverse.'

He pulled up close to the wall, in the shadows, at the far side of the area. She didn't wait for him to open the door; she fumbled with the handle, ready to scramble out.

'Thank you for the lift, Alex. Have a lovely Christmas, and I hope we meet again in the New Year.' She knew her voice sounded artificial, her words insincere, but she wanted to get away, go inside, before he could question her response.

He'd parked so she couldn't open the door properly and had to squeeze out sideways. When she emerged from behind the car he was waiting for her, blocking her path. He looked powerful, almost dangerous. He opened his arms and, in spite of her reservations, she couldn't stop herself walking in.

He pulled her against him, nestling her inside the warmth of his jacket. His heart pounded against her breasts. Her arms encircled his waist and she tilted her face to receive his kiss. His lips were hard, cold, nothing like John's. They didn't coax a response – they demanded one.

As heat poured through her she forgot everything: her promise to John, the cold, that she'd only met Alex once before. All that mattered was the pleasure he was creating as his tongue explored the moistness of her mouth. She didn't want him to stop. She wanted him to... wanted him to do what? She had no idea, but whatever it was, it wasn't the sort of thing a good girl did.

She brought her hands round to his chest and pushed. Reluctantly he raised his head. Even in the dark she could see the glitter in his eyes, feel the excitement pulsing out of him. She shook her head, trying to focus, make sense of what had taken place.

'Barbara, darling, I've wanted to kiss you like that from the moment I set eyes on you. I knew you felt the same way. I can always tell.' She pushed harder and he released her.

'Always, Alex? I take it you find yourself in this kind of situation quite often then?' She sounded harsh, brittle, but couldn't stop. His casual comment had doused her passion.

'I didn't mean anything. God! Don't be like this. I meant – oh sod it – you're too much of a child to understand anyway.'

'Please, Alex, just go. Let's forget this ever happened. I already have. Goodnight; thanks for the lift.'

She stepped round him and walked away, every step harder than the first. She wanted to turn and run back, feel that heady, intoxicating passion again. If he called her would she go? Was she strong enough to ignore him?

The car door slammed and the engine fired into life. Blinking back scalding tears she ran the last few yards, no longer caring if he saw her distress. The backstairs were deserted; she met no one on her dash to her bedroom. She closed the door but didn't turn on the light. The fire was enough to see by.

Angrily she wiped her eyes. Why was she crying? She should be happy she'd not made a complete fool of herself. Hadn't Rosie warned her Alex had a reputation with the ladies? His father and brother had said the same. He was no gentleman. Unlike John or Simon, he'd taken advantage of her inexperience. He had forced his unwanted attentions on her. Good heavens, how might it have ended if she'd not called a halt? Would he have seduced her in the barn and... and done what?

Girls got into trouble if they let boys take liberties, but she had no clear idea of what taking liberties actually meant. Of course, she knew getting into trouble meant you were having a baby, that a man had to put his thing inside a woman to make her pregnant, but how it was accomplished she couldn't imagine.

Over the years she'd bathed the boys, helped them undress, seem them unclothed; knew what the male form looked like. She'd never really considered how intimacy between a man and woman worked. This was hardly a topic of conversation she could broach with Grandma.

She frowned. This wasn't something she'd considered when kissing John. Why did a kiss from Alex make her think of the next step? She loved John. She'd known him since she was a little girl; he'd always looked out for her, but for some reason a stranger had triggered this wildness. She washed her face, pleased to see there was no imprint of her wanton behaviour on her features. Her grandparents must be wondering where she was.

* * *

'Edward, I'm sure I heard a car outside some time ago. Where do you think Barbara has got to?'

He had a shrewd idea. 'I expect she's saying goodbye to Alex Everton, Elspeth. What do you expect? He's a handsome young man and a Spitfire pilot as well.'

'Edward!' Her shocked exclamation made him regret his flippant response.

'Don't worry, my dear. I'm sure she's in no real danger from him. A goodbye kiss won't do her any harm.'

'If you're quite sure there will be no more than that. I have high hopes of her making a go of it with dear Simon. They seem to get on so well. He becomes almost animated in her company, don't you think?'

'I'm very much afraid you're going to be disappointed there. I think I ought to tell you, Barbara is involved with a young man from Hastings. Do you remember she mentioned someone called John the other day?'

'John, you mean the son of the farmers?'

'That's the one. It seems he proposed before he joined the RAF and she accepted him.'

'Why doesn't she wear a ring? If she's engaged she shouldn't be going out to socials or parties with Simon, or indulging in a goodnight kiss with Alex Everton.'

'It's complicated, my dear.' He explained and she listened.

'That's so typical of Barbara. Such a kind thing to do, but it's not a real engagement is it? She's not in love with the young man, is she?' She put down her embroidery frame. 'I think I can hear her coming now.'

'Elspeth, you mustn't mention this. She told me in confidence. And remember, she's not hurting young Farley but helping him, giving him someone to take out and keeping his father off his back.'

* * *

Barbara pushed open the library door, forcing a smile to her face. 'It's thawing, did you realise? With any luck the snow will be gone by tomorrow.'

'Good show; did you have an enjoyable time, Barbara?'

'Oh yes, thank you, Grandpa. Valerie was great fun and we hit it off at once. I'm seeing her in the New Year. She lives just outside Romford so it shouldn't be hard to get there.'

'Good, we wanted you to make new friends. Has Alex got any leave over Christmas? Considering there's a war on that young man seems able to come and go as he pleases.'

Barbara swallowed before finding her voice. 'I've no idea, Grandma. I certainly didn't ask him. Do you mind if I put the wireless on? It's ITMA in a few minutes.' She hoped her false brightness fooled them. She didn't want to answer any more questions about Alex. Things were too complicated at the moment and she just wanted to forget about all three of the men in her life.

18

Grandpa drove her to the station to catch the early train to Liverpool Street. It had snowed during the week and the lanes had only been cleared the day before. The car shuddered to a standstill outside Ingatestone station beside a pile of dirty, grey snow.

'I have to go in to the office, Grandpa. I haven't bought my ticket yet.'

'Damn nuisance, all this snow; can't remember a winter as bad as this and it's not even Christmas.'

'Never mind, I've never seen a white one and neither have the boys, so there's a good side to everything.'

'Stuff and nonsense, my dear, you don't like it any more than I do. Your mare hasn't had any real exercise since she went out with the Farleys.'

'That's true. Don't get out – it's too cold. We'll be back on the three thirty. I can't wait for you both to meet David and Tom.'

Her gas mask was hidden inside a smart velvet case and held in one hand and, with her handbag in the other, she hurried in to join the end of the queue. This train was obviously a popular one for both shoppers and service personnel returning home after leave. The waiting room was crowded, no one willing to stand on the open platform. The 'ladies only' room was less busy; she still didn't feel comfortable in crowds.

The train steamed in five minutes later and she found herself a seat facing forwards. The compartment was almost as cold as the platform. She turned up the fur collar of her coat, wrapped her scarf around her face then pulled the sides of her coat tight across her knees and hoped a few more travellers would join her and raise the temperature. She heard voices in the corridor and two elderly matrons slid open the door and came in.

'Good morning, my dear. My goodness, it's cold in here.' The plumper of the two, in sturdy brown brogues, heavy brown stockings and what looked like a mink coat, settled into the window seat opposite.

'Good morning, I'm so glad someone else has come in. It should be a bit warmer with three of us.'

The thinner lady not only had a long fur coat but a matching Cossack hat as well. 'Are you going Christmas shopping, my dear?'

'No, I'm collecting my brothers from boarding school.'

'How splendid. Gels today, traipsing about on their own, joining the Army, Navy, even the Air Force, just like the last war. They can't manage without us when there's war on, can they?'

She assumed the lady meant the government. 'I was going to join the Land Army, but my family circumstances have changed and I've joined the WVS instead. I've already knitted six balaclavas and done a basic first aid course.'

'Good for you. My gel, Primrose – silly name but my great-aunt offered to leave us her money if we agreed to call her that...'

Barbara hid her smile in her collar. These two were priceless. It would make the journey seem shorter being able to listen to them.

The plump lady continued. 'Anyway – Primrose has joined the WAFS and vanished to train somewhere in the midlands. Won't even get any leave at Christmas.'

'Well, Elizabeth, there's a war on. We all have to do our bit.'

Barbara pretended to doze, hoping the two would continue to entertain her. She almost shot upright when she heard the name Farley.

'Well, Elizabeth, I wasn't mistaken. It was Reginald Farley up to his old tricks again.'

'I can't believe it, not after all the fuss last time. I thought he would have more sense than to risk his marriage again.'

Barbara kept her eyes shut and listened closely.

'Well, Elizabeth, I'm certain it was him. I only saw his face from a distance but I saw the girl, that new maid from The Grove, quite clearly. You couldn't mistake her. There aren't many young girls with that corn-coloured hair – and not out of a bottle either.'

'Well! I'm not going to breathe a word of it. I promise no one shall hear it from me.'

The train jolted to a halt and two more well-dressed women joined them in the compartment. Barbara sat up, delving into her handbag so she didn't have to make eye contact with either Elizabeth or her friend.

She was stunned by the knowledge Marigold had been dragged into the depraved clutches of a monster like Mr Farley. She was tempted to get off the train, catch the next one back and go and warn Rosie, warn Marigold. Then the guard waved his flag, blew his whistle and she'd missed her chance. The pleasure in her excursion had gone, ruined by this piece of gossip.

She was still undecided about her course of action when the train arrived in London. She checked her hat was securely pinned, pulled on her gloves and followed the four older women from the train.

'Babs! Sweetheart – it's been too long.'

'John – what on earth are you doing here? I thought we were meeting at Fortnum & Mason's later, that you only had a couple of hours?'

'It's a surprise. Now I've got a six-hour pass, so I spoke to Mrs Peterson and she told me you were catching this train.'

She'd intended to ask John for more time before their engagement became public, but with his arms around her, holding her close, and his dear face smiling down, she was swept away by his joy. His mouth covered hers and without thinking she responded as Alex had shown her. His kiss deepened and she forgot everything.

A porter with a trolley, finding his way blocked, interrupted. 'Here, you two lovebirds, a man's got to earn his living. Save the canoodling for somewhere private, why don't you.'

John raised his head, slackening his hold enough for her to step back. Her face was hot. Her lips tingled from his kiss.

'John, how could you? What if someone saw us?'

'I should think several dozen people saw us, darling. We're standing in the middle of the platform. Don't look so cross, I'm teasing. I know what you mean, but if an acquaintance of your grandparents saw us, so what? We're engaged, for God's sake; it's perfectly acceptable for us to kiss anywhere we damn well please.'

She tried to pull away, remove her hand from his but he was too strong and kept a firm grip. He didn't understand. How could he? She'd been worrying about Alex's friends or relations, not her own. John guided them through the busy station and out to the taxi rank. The road was empty. All the cabs had been taken.

'We can wait here for the next one or walk to the hotel. Which do you want to do?'

She shivered. 'What hotel?'

'I thought we could go to the Grand Midland. It's not far from here or the station. We could have lunch together.'

'I was intending to visit a museum or two, but I'd much rather have lunch with you.'

He tucked her arm through his and guided her through the crowd. He seemed different, more confident, older and it wasn't just the uniform. In the weeks since she'd seen him, he'd grown up, become a man, as she'd become a woman.

'What do you think of the uniform? Very smart, isn't it?'

'It is. So much more attractive than khaki.'

'I can't believe the difference in you, Babs. I hardly recognised you when you got off the train. You've changed and it's not just the smashing clothes.'

'So have you, John. You're more assertive somehow. I can't imagine you would have kissed me in public six weeks ago.'

He stretched out and brushed a stray curl from her cheek. 'Everything has changed.' His face became serious. 'When Mum told me what you'd had to put up with all these years, I couldn't believe it.' She could see tears in his eyes. 'You should have told me; I could have helped. Stopped it, done something. No one, and especially a little girl, should have had to…'

'Stop it, John. It wasn't your responsibility, or your fault. It's over. I want to forget about it. I have to think about Tom and David now. I'm the only family they've got.'

'You're wrong, sweetheart. I asked you to marry me and you accepted. Tom and David are a shared responsibility. I've always wanted younger brothers; I can't wait to get more involved.'

'We don't have to worry about that until I'm twenty-one. Grandpa is their legal guardian for the time being.'

During the short walk from Liverpool Street to the bus stop he kept a tight hold on her arm, making sure she didn't slip on the icy pavement. When they arrived at the Midland the liveried doorman jumped to attention and saluted as they approached.

'Good morning, madam, sir.' They smiled and walked past him, through the circulating doors and into the pillared vestibule.

'Let's order coffee straightaway. Do you want anything to eat or wait until later?'

'Could we have lunch soon? Straight after coffee?'

He slipped his arm around her waist and brought her closer. 'I can't believe my luck. I'm engaged to the most beautiful girl and have just passed my prelims and can go on to further training. And I haven't told you, I'm not going to Scotland now; I'm doing two months on a flight simulator in Epsom.'

'That's terrific news. Does that mean we'll be able to meet again before you leave for Scotland?'

'It does. I don't start in Epsom until the New Year. I have to report back to St John's Wood this afternoon.'

'What about your visit to Brook Farm?'

'Mum and Dad don't mind because I've got leave over Christmas. I was rather hoping I could come down and meet your grandparents, spend some time with you and the boys. What do you think?'

'Please do come down. You're quite right: it's time we made this official. Will you come to us first and then go on to Hastings or the other way around?'

'I'm on leave from the 23rd. What about if I come then and stay the night? I can still get home for Christmas, if I'm lucky.'

'That would be lovely. You can help us decorate the tree. I gather it's a big tradition at The Grove.'

'I'd enjoy that. Good – here's the coffee.' He spoke briefly to the waiter. 'That's arranged. The dining room is open already.'

She watched him and her lips curved. The weeks of strenuous physical training had made him athletic. He was such an attractive man and he loved her. Perhaps it wasn't going to be so hard pretending she was in love with him.

'Darling, the waiter chappie is going to organise a special tea for you and the boys. He's putting in whatever they've got spare. I told him to include a couple of bottles of ginger beer.'

Impulsively she reached across and kissed him. 'Thank you, John, what a lovely idea. Why didn't I think of that?'

* * *

After a leisurely lunch she dropped her napkin on the empty plate. 'I must powder my nose, John. Shall I meet you in the foyer afterwards?'

He reached over and captured her hands. 'Before you go, Babs, I have something for you. It's not your Christmas present, and I was going to wait, but I think you should have it now.' He opened her palms and she felt something small and square drop between them.

Her heart sank. She stared at the small leather box. Her eyes brimmed. This was so wrong, taking his ring when she felt the way she did.

'Please, don't cry, darling. I know we have to wait a while before we can be married, but I wanted you to have a ring, make everything official. I want to be introduced to your grandparents as your future husband, not an old friend from Hastings.'

Her fingers clenched and she withdrew her hands. She raised her head. He was looking so serious, his eyes dark. 'Thank you, John.' He flicked open the box and she saw an emerald and diamond circle. 'It's lovely, exactly right. Is it a family heirloom?'

He nodded. 'It belonged to my grandmother. Here, let me put it on. I want to see it on your finger.'

She held out her left hand and he slid the ring on. 'How did you know it would fit?'

'An educated guess. There's a gold chain at the back of the box, so you can have it round your neck and not on your finger if that's going to be easier for you.'

Had she inadvertently let him know she had reservations? Embarrassed she scrambled to her feet. 'I must go. See you in a minute.' When she came out of the ladies' room she stopped, horrified.

'Miss Sinclair, what an unexpected pleasure. Are you here alone?'

'Mr Farley...' She was tongue-tied. She could hardly tell him she was with her fiancé as that would cause trouble for Simon, but if she told him she was alone? 'I'm about to leave to collect my brothers. Is Mrs Farley with you?'

He loomed over her. She could smell his expensive aftershave, see the long black hairs in his nose. She stepped away but he followed. Her back was pressed against the wall. 'Why don't you come and have lunch with me? A pretty little thing like you shouldn't eat alone.'

'Thank you, but I've already eaten. Please excuse me, I really must leave.'

Reluctantly he stood aside, but in order to get past she was forced to press against him. Once free she fled to the reception area, her stomach churning. She was going to be sick. Clasping her hand over her mouth she looked around desperately, praying there was somewhere she could go.

A firm hand gripped her elbow and she was whisked through a door and all but pushed into a cubicle. Someone rubbed her back and murmured words of comfort as she retched.

'Babs, I'm here, don't worry. You'll feel better in a moment.'

Eventually she slumped back on her heels, her stomach empty. Her face was cold and sweaty. She felt faint, not sure she could stand safely.

He reached up and pulled the chain. 'Come along, let's get you out of here.'

She wiped her mouth on the handkerchief John gave her and he heaved her upright. She needed the support of his arm. As she turned, the door opened and she came face to face with a furious bespectacled gentleman.

'Great Scot! What the devil are you doing in here, young lady?'

'An emergency, sir. My wife's in a delicate condition – you know how it is in the early months.'

Immediately the man smiled and stood to one side. 'Quite so. Take care, my dear.'

Not sure whether to laugh or hide her face in shame she said nothing until John led her to a comfortable chair in a discreet corner. 'I'm so sorry, John. I had a nasty shock and you know what that does to my digestion.'

'What happened? I'll find the bastard and knock his teeth out.' His face was hard; he looked like a stranger. She wasn't sure if she was impressed or dismayed by his fierceness.

'No, please don't do anything. I expect the man was drunk. He didn't touch me, just made me feel uncomfortable.'

'In which case, darling, I'll not press you for more details.' He grinned. 'Pity about the lunch. Never mind, you've got a picnic tea to eat on the train.'

'How could you? I don't want to think about food at the moment, thank you very much. Is there time for a cup of tea before we go?'

19

Whilst John ordered the tea Barbara closed her eyes, allowing the tension to slide away.

'Babs, before you dashed off we were talking about the ring.' Her eyes flew open. 'I don't want to confine you to barracks for the next few years just because we're engaged.' He smiled at her confusion.

'You don't mind if I go to the pictures with Simon Farley or to a social?'

'Of course I don't. From what you've told me, he's a decent chap and understands the score. We won't put an announcement in *The Times* – not now – but I would like to make it official with your grandparents.'

Did he believe that by telling them they'd keep an eye on her? See that she didn't do anything rash... such as kissing another man... kissing Alex? Her nausea threatened to return. 'That's very thoughtful of you. Simon's pleasant, not like his father.' She swallowed hard. 'Mr Farley's a dreadful man.'

'Then make sure you keep away from him. Good, your tea's arrived.'

She glanced at her watch. 'I think we need to get a move on. If the train's on time it'll be here in twenty-five minutes.' She slipped the ring off her finger and replaced it in the box, ignoring the gold chain. 'I've enough to explain to Tom and David today. I think our news can wait until tomorrow, don't you?' He scowled. 'John, please try and understand. They've got to be told their mother's a lunatic and their father has turned his back on them. If I tell them I'm getting married they might well think I'm going to abandon them as well.'

'I told you I want to be involved.'

'I know you did, but I can't take the risk that they might see it as another rejection. I'm sorry if you don't like it, but that's the way it's going to be. My brothers come first and if you don't accept that...' She left her sentence hanging as she gathered her belongings leaving him to carry the picnic basket. He strode beside her in stony silence all the way to the station.

The forecourt was cold, full of steam and floating soot. The hissing from the engines, and the banging of the shunters as they hooked up to the empty carriages to take them away to be cleaned, made conversation impossible.

Mrs Peterson had told her the platform she wanted and she walked briskly in that direction assuming John was behind her, but not prepared to glance behind to check. She couldn't understand why leaving the ring in the box had upset him; he'd given her the gold chain to wear it round her neck after all, so must realise the ring wouldn't be on her finger all the time.

Good grief! That was it! Without thinking she'd put it back in the box when she should have asked him to thread it on the chain and fasten it round her neck. Was it too late to do it now? She stopped and waited for him to catch up. When he didn't appear at her side she finally turned.

He was nowhere in sight. She scanned the area, certain, even in the crowd, she would spot him. There were only a handful of RAF uniforms so it shouldn't be too difficult. She checked each one but didn't see him. Where had he gone? The hoot of a train arriving at the platform reminded her the boys were here. Looking for John, and more importantly the picnic case, would have to come later.

How could he ruin their day by being so petulant? He seemed more mature than that. She swung back. First things first: Tom and David were her main priority. She hadn't time to buy a platform ticket so waited impatiently on the concourse. The steam from the station engine made it hard to see, but she heard them calling.

'Babs, Babs, here we are.'

Two grey-uniformed boys, gaberdine macs flapping round their knees, shot under the barrier and hurled themselves into her arms. She held them close and they spun round in a circle, laughing and crying with happiness.

'Stand still, boys. Let me look at you properly.' She stood back. 'Good heavens, Tom, you've grown an inch since I saw you in October. It won't be long before you're as tall as me.' She straightened David's peaked cap. 'And you're growing too, but you're both too thin. Haven't they been feeding you at that school?'

'The food's absolutely filthy. You wouldn't believe the muck they expect you to eat,' Tom told her, grinning widely.

'Tapioca three times a week and ghastly brown stew with gristle and stringy bits,' David added gleefully.

She looked suitably horrified. 'Well, you'll have lovely food at The Grove. Where are Mrs Peterson and Mary and Charlie?'

Tom waved vaguely in the direction of the train. 'They're coming. Mrs Peterson had to catch a porter. We couldn't wait to see you, so we ran ahead.'

'I hope you told her that you were running off?'

They nodded.

'Look, here they come.' Tom pointed to Mrs Peterson and her children following behind a porter with four cases and various parcels and boxes.

Only then she noticed her brothers were not wearing their gas masks. 'Tom, David, you must have your gas masks on you at all times. It's the law. They're not much use on a porter's trolley if there's a gas attack, are they?'

David's face fell and he grabbed her hand, glancing anxiously up into the pigeon-infested roof.

Tom laughed. 'There's not been a German bomber over here. Our house master said that Hitler's too scared of our air force to come.'

Mention of the air force reminded Barbara she still had to locate John before they could look for a taxi. She'd abandoned her idea of a bus when she'd seen how much luggage the boys had.

'Mrs Peterson, how are you? Thank you so much for collecting these two rapscallions. I'm sorry they ran off without their gas masks.'

'Never mind, my dear, they can put them on now, can't they? You look well. That's a very smart outfit you're wearing, I must say.'

Tom nodded. 'You look like a toff, Babs, and it suits you.' His jaw dropped as he peered round her. 'Why's John running over here with a picnic basket in one hand and a bunch of flowers in the other?'

'I think the flowers might be for me, Tom. We had a few words earlier. I expect he's apologising.'

John held out the bunch of hothouse blooms, a sheepish grin on his face. 'Thank you, John. I wondered where you'd gone. I was worried.'

'Thought I'd absconded with your tea? I had a devil of a job finding these. That's why I've been gone so long. Am I forgiven for being stupid? I do understand and shouldn't have reacted like that.'

She couldn't help noticing his breathing was as even as always; the mad dash across the station hadn't affected him at all. He really was an attractive man and fighting fit. She held out her hand, forgetting they had an attentive audience.

'It's forgotten. We can talk about it when you come down next week.'

His gloved fist tightened round hers and, in spite of the onlookers, he bent and brushed his lips across hers. His almost kiss made her mouth tingle his lips were so cold.

'Look at that, David, they're canoodling.'

She shot back, her face crimson. 'John has to get back to base. Say goodbye to him, boys.'

They chorused their farewells. 'Don't worry about meeting me on the 23rd. I'm not sure what time I'll be at Brentwood, but it'll be before dark. I'll walk if I have to; it's not that far is it?'

She shook her head. 'A fair distance, five miles at least. Try and cadge a lift. Anyone can tell you where we live.'

He ruffled the boys' hair, deliberately knocking off their caps, and strode off, his gas mask swinging in one hand.

'Barbara, have you and John an understanding?' Mrs Peterson enquired quietly, making sure no juvenile ears overheard.

'We have, Mrs Peterson, but, well, we can't say anything until everything else is sorted, if you know what I mean.'

The other woman understood. 'Definitely not, more than enough for them to take in at the moment.'

The four children were clambering over the trolley, removing their gas masks as instructed, out of earshot.

'The boys are not going back to Downton, Mrs Peterson; they're transferring to Brentwood School. It takes day boys as well as borders and I think they'll be happier at home.'

'You're right, my dear. We're going to leave our two there. They seem settled, and there are few mixed boarding schools available.'

'They must come and stay with us in the summer holidays if travel is still possible by then. We've enough room for a dozen guests.'

'That's kind of you. They'll be delighted.' Her eyes filled. 'Their father's pointed out that if the air raids start the children will have to stay at Downton. It's going to be far too dangerous return to Hastings and cross London like we're doing now.' The conversation ended as the porter arrived behind them.

'Where to, madam? The taxi rank?'

Mrs Peterson wiped eyes. 'Yes, thank you.'

Barbara listened to her brothers chatting whilst they stared avidly out of the cab window at the London streets. She thought they looked pale, not how boys of their age should look. Not like the Everton boys, who were brown and lithe, full of good food and fresh air. Her brow creased as she tried to remember if they'd always looked peaky and decided they probably had. Well, things would be different now. They would have plenty to eat, friends to play with and a loving family around them. She decided not to tell them anything until they were on the train. Whilst they were engrossed in the food she'd give them the bad news.

The cab pulled up outside Liverpool Street and she remembered to tip generously. She looked round for a porter. The boys were capable of carrying their own cases but she thought, as it was Christmas, she ought to spread her good fortune around, and over-tipping was one way of doing it. Their trunk would no doubt be sent on.

'A porter's coming. Can we ride on the trolley as there's only three cases and a few boxes for him to take?' David asked.

'Don't be silly, David. The man couldn't push us as well; we're too heavy,' Tom told his brother.

She doubted the two of them added up to one large case, but didn't say so.

'Where to, madam?' the young man asked her as he stacked their belongings neatly in his trolley. He was lame, which must be why he wasn't in the services.

'The ticket office first, please, then the three thirty to Colchester. First class, non-smoking.'

'Hop on, boys, plenty of room for two tiddlers.' They didn't need telling twice. With broad grins they scrambled on top of the cases. 'Hold very tight, please. No falling off allowed.' The young man winked and she returned his smile.

The compartment selected was in the middle of the long train and fortunately this was empty. The boys jumped down and waited politely to see if they were to carry their own cases.

'Go in, boys. Our porter will bring in the luggage.' They vanished into the train and she could hear their shrieks of excitement as they raced up and down the corridor. The pound note she gave for a tip was excessive but she wanted to make someone else as happy as she was.

'Thanks, miss. Merry Christmas.'

She watched him examining the note as if he'd never held one before and was glad she'd done it.

'Sit down, boys. I've got tea here. John had it made up at the Midland, and even asked for two bottles of ginger beer to wash it down.' She pulled out the table and secured the supporting leg. She removed the bottles, placing them beside the smart picnic box.

'There. Shall we wait until the train leaves or start now?'

'Now! We've had a mouldy sandwich and it's ages since we had breakfast. It was only lumpy porridge and I'm starving,' David added.

'You're making Downton sound like something out of a book by Charles Dickens. Are you sure you didn't have gruel as well?'

'Like Oliver Twist? No, but the soup was pretty thin sometimes.'

She unfastened the buckle holding the box closed. The lid fell open and they gazed, round-eyed, at the contents.

'There's chocolate éclairs,' David breathed.

'And sticky buns and sausage rolls,' Tom said.

She was more impressed by the inclusion of damask napkins, which had been carefully wrapped around three cheap glass tumblers.

'Sit down, both of you, and I'll give you a napkin. Spread it on your lap and use it as a plate.'

Two white squares flapped over four grubby knees and, like eager nestlings, they sat open-mouthed to be fed. She waited until they were munching cheese straws and sausage rolls before tackling the tricky subject of their future.

'Boys, I've something to tell you. I hope you'll think it's not all bad news.' She had rehearsed this speech over and over but now it was time to say the words they wouldn't come. They remained stuck in her throat. She took a sip of the ginger beer. 'In future you're going to live with me and you're not going back to Downton School. You're going to a prep school in Brentwood that takes day boys.'

Tom finished his mouthful before answering. 'With you? Forever?' She nodded. 'That's definitely good news. Boarding's all right, but we'd much rather come home every night.'

'What about you, David? How do you feel about living at The Grove in future?'

'If you're there, then I'll like it best. We didn't want to go back to Crabapple Cottage if you weren't there any more.'

Tom asked the crucial question. 'Why are we living with you now, Babs? What's happened to Mother?'

'Your mother's ill. She's been ill for years it seems, and is in a hospital. She won't be out for a long time. It's best if you're here with me. And Dr and Mrs Sinclair want to be your grandparents as well. They want you to call them Grandma and Grandpa as I do.'

'What about Father? Won't he be lonely on his own?' David asked, his face creased with concern.

'Mr Evans decided it would be better for you to be with us. He's selling Crabapple Cottage and moving away.'

Tom threw his half-eaten sausage roll into the box. 'He never liked us much anyway, so we won't miss him, will we, David?'

She removed the napkins from their laps and crossed the compartment to sit between them. 'Men find it hard to show their feelings. I'm sure in time he'll realise how much he loves you both and come to see you.'

'He needn't bother. We don't want to see him. He was never any fun and neither was she. You were the only nice one at Crabapple Cottage and now we've got you to ourselves.' Tom turned his head to stare out of the window; he was fighting back his tears.

'Grandpa wondered if you'd both like to be known as Sinclair from now on? Make a fresh start. What do you think?'

The little boy sniffed and dried his eyes on his sleeve. 'Might as well. He doesn't want us so we don't want his name.' He smiled, his eyes wet, and offered his hand to her. 'How do you do? I'm Thomas James Sinclair.'

She shook his hand. 'Pleased to meet you, Master Sinclair. I'm Miss Barbara Sinclair and this other young person here, please would you introduce him to me?'

David loved playacting. 'I'm David Edward Sinclair. How do you do, Miss Sinclair? I do hope you are quite well?'

She nodded regally. 'Absolutely splendid, thank you, but I shall be a great deal better when I've eaten an éclair.' She darted a hand into the box and waved a cake in front of them. 'There are only two left. If you don't hurry up I shall eat them all myself.'

Shoving and giggling the boys snatched a cake and were soon mumbling in ecstasy as fresh cream and crisp choux pastry filled their mouths. She forced a mouthful down then hid hers under the napkin. Her act had served its purpose but the boys' recovery could only be temporary. It would take more than a chocolate éclair to erase the bitterness of being abandoned by both parents, unwillingly by one, but deliberately by the other.

The basket was empty long before the train started its deceleration. Their appetites had returned and the boys had eaten the lot. It didn't take long to tidy the compartment by putting everything into the container. The bottles could be returned to the local grocer to reclaim the deposit; the glasses, napkins and basket reused.

'David, Thomas, put on your caps, pull up your socks properly and tuck the belt ends in on your macs.'

They were too excited to argue. Satisfied they were presentable, she hooked a gas mask over each of their necks and handed them a case and a box to carry. 'Right, we're ready. Shall we wait by the door? Then we can be sure we won't be left on the train.'

Tom insisted he knew all about the intricacies of leather straps, windows and door handles so she left it in his capable ten-year-old hands. The train shuddered to a halt and he pulled up the leather strap, released the window, and leant out to grab the handle on the outside. He turned it, pushing the door with his hip. She was unable to catch him as he flew out and was left dangling from the door.

Laughing she pulled the door closed and removed him. 'I thought you knew all about train doors, Tom.'

'I didn't say I'd actually opened one, did I?' He rubbed his armpit. 'I'm not doing that again. I shall have a massive bruise under here.'

'Serves you right for being a show-off,' David chanted.

'Enough, you two. Hurry up and get out. David, slam the door shut behind you. The guard's waiting to blow his whistle.'

Spotting a litter basket she dropped the rubbish in as they passed. 'That's better; I've a hand free for anyone who wants to hold it.'

David grabbed it, grinning at his brother, who stepped in close on the other side. Flanked by her two siblings she emerged from the station to see Grandpa striding towards them.

'Excellent timing,' he shouted. 'I've just arrived myself.' He picked his way carefully across the compacted snow that lined the road. The boys tensed.

'I'm Dr Sinclair, your sister's grandpa, and I hope yours as well from now on.' He offered his right hand to Tom. 'How do you do, Tom, welcome.'

The boy straightened his shoulders.

'I'm fine, thank you. May I introduce my younger brother, David?'

David stuck out his right hand, but didn't release Barbara's. 'How do you do. I'm pleased to meet you. Thank you for inviting us.'

'Excellent!' He winked at her before continuing. 'I was expecting a couple of little boys but can see that I was mistaken. Two fine young men have arrived instead.'

She saw the boys squirm with pleasure. Grandpa was in his element. 'Come along, your grandmother is prowling round the house waiting for you. We're going to have high tea at six thirty and you'd better be hungry, that's all I can say.'

She relaxed. Food and praise, that's all it took to win their hearts. In the car they bounced up and down on the rear seat asking non-stop questions about the village, countryside and their new home. The car slowed as it approached the wrought-iron gates.

Tom craned his neck to stare up. 'Blimey! Is this where we're going to live? It's very posh isn't it?' After that there was silence behind her.

'Do you know, boys, we can't go in the front because of the blackout. We all have to go in and out of the back door.'

'Why?' She knew Tom would be intrigued.

'Wait and see. I'll show you as soon as we get out, and you'll love your new rooms; I can't wait for you to see them.'

To her astonishment Grandma came to welcome her brothers. She couldn't help remembering the contrast to her own arrival.

'Welcome, Tom and David. I'm your new grandma. Come along in out of the cold. Give your things to Marigold and she'll sort them out for you.'

The boys handed over the cases and boxes. The girl winked at them and they grinned, liking her openness.

'I expect Grandpa told you high tea is at six thirty. Cook's been busy all day baking.' She smiled when she saw Barbara's expression. 'It's being served in the drawing room today as it's such a special occasion.'

Grandpa chuckled.

'Shall I take the boys up, let them have an explore? They're eager to see where they're going to be living in future.'

'Yes, my dear, do that. You've got an hour and a half before tea –

plenty of time. Off you go with your sister. We shall have a lovely chat then and you can tell me all about how awful the food was at school,' said Grandma.

They followed Marigold up the backstairs.

Barbara was close behind them. 'It's far quicker this way especially if you're going outside or to the kitchen. I'll take you down the grand way and you can tell me why we have to use the back door and why we need to use torches indoors at night.'

Tom clattered ahead of her. 'How did Grandma know about the food at school?'

'I expect all boys think the food's horrible; she made a good guess.'

He laughed. 'It was. I like her and Grandpa. It's going to be good fun living here with you.'

'I hope so, Tom. It's certainly going to be the best Christmas. You know they have a huge tree and a Yule log.'

'What's a you'll log, Babs?' David shouted from the rear.

She was still explaining when they reached the second floor. The backstairs emerged onto a wide landing with windows overlooking the park. The boys ran over, scrambling on the window seat to stare out.

'Is all this Grandpa's? It's as big as the playing fields at Downton.'

'It's even bigger than that, Tom. And there's so much snow we could make a huge snowman and even an igloo.'

'We can do all that tomorrow but now you must come and look at your rooms,' she told them. 'Look. The far door is Marigold's room, strictly out of bounds. The one in the middle is the schoolroom, but now it's more of a playroom and this one here leads into your bedroom.'

Tom pointed at the last door. 'What about this one? Who lives in there?'

'No one; it's the bathroom and lavatory.'

The maid appeared from the bedroom door. 'Hello, boys, have you come to have a look and see where everything is?' She stepped to one side as Tom and David rushed in.

'Bagsy the bed by the window,' David screamed as he flung himself on top of it.

'You can have it. I like being next to the light switch.'

She went across to the walk-in cupboard. 'Come and see this, boys. It's a wardrobe you can walk in.'

'Where did all these clothes come from?' Tom asked when he saw the rails.

'Grandma and I have restocked your wardrobe. The far end is your new school uniform, the middle section is for best, and clothes at this end are for every day. The left-hand side is yours, Tom; the right-hand side yours, David.'

'Look, Tom, there's shelves with shirts and jumpers and things, and boxes with shoes in.'

Barbara was satisfied they were happy with everything she'd showed them so far. Her mouth curved as she imagined their reaction when they saw the rest. 'Come along, you can get into your playroom through this connecting door.'

Marigold opened it for them. 'I reckon it's like Father Christmas's workshop in here. I've never seen so many wonderful things. Right spoilt you two are going to be, that's for certain.'

Two small bodies shot past and she was forced to jump out of the way. Barbara could hear them exclaiming and shouting with excitement. She watched them without comment for a moment, her heart full, praying having all this would begin to compensate for what they'd lost.

'Well, boys, what you think of your very own playroom?'

Tom was already kneeling on the floor setting out a set of lead soldiers perfectly painted as the troops of the Emperor Napoleon Bonaparte. David was doing the same with a box that contained Wellington's soldiers. Tom glanced up, his eyes shining.

'This is amazing, Babs. We always wanted an army and there's everything here. Look at this horse – it's got all the details on it, right down to the captain's regiment.' He held up an exact miniature of a war horse for her inspection.

'They're wonderful. I take it you're not going to budge from there for a while. Don't you want to look at all the rest of the things before you get involved in a battle?'

They both shook their heads and, ignoring her, continued to set out the troops. She went to sit on a comfortable upholstered armchair near the safety-guarded fire and Marigold followed her. She wiped her eyes. 'I needn't have worried; all it took was a set of lead soldiers and they're content.'

'That's boys for you, and men for that matter. They don't go much for the lovey-dovey side. As long as there's good food and plenty to do, they're happy most of the time.'

'Sit down for a minute, if you're not too busy.' Barbara pointed at the matching chair on the far side of the fireplace.

'Madam said part of my duties now was to look after the boys. If they wake up at night I'm only through there.' She pointed at the door at the end of the room. 'They're lovely nippers, so it'll be no hardship.'

'That's a relief. I was worried they might be frightened up here on their own.' This was an ideal opportunity to mention the gossip from the train. 'Marigold, I hope you don't mind me mentioning this, but when I was travelling up to London earlier I overheard two ladies talking about seeing you out with Mr Farley, Simon's father.'

The girl's disgust would have been hard to feign. 'Good Gawd! It weren't me. Never in a month of Sundays. He's old enough to be my grandfather.'

'Thank goodness. I didn't think it could be. I'm so glad; he's got a horrible reputation. I've been worried ever since I heard.'

'You don't need to be. I might be only seventeen, but I know how grass grows, miss, and I'm not one for looking over a fence to see if it's greener on the other side.'

Barbara laughed. 'But you do have a young man, someone nice to go to the pictures with?'

'I do.' She lifted her apron and slipped her hand into her skirt pocket. 'Here, look at this. He gave it me last Saturday.' She held out a powder compact with matching lipstick case. Barbara took it and was relieved to find it was EPNS and not solid silver. A pretty gift but not extravagant, exactly right from the sort of young man Marigold would go out with.

'These are lovely. I haven't anything as nice.' She handed them back and watched the girl polish them on her apron before restoring them to her pocket.

'I've never been given anything like this before. I'm not letting them out of my sight, that's for sure.' The girl stood up. 'I'd better get on. I've the boys things to hang up before I go down and help with the tea.'

'Shall I help you? They don't need me here.'

'No, miss, it's not your job. You sit and watch your little lads enjoy themselves.'

Barbara stretched out her legs in front of the fire mulling over Marigold's answer. She was convinced the girl had been genuinely shocked by the suggestion. The ladies on the train had obviously got it wrong. Mr Farley would never give such a cheap gift; if the items had come from him they would have been the real thing. She shuddered and she remembered her brief contact with him. How could any woman want that man?

'Babs, come and play with us. You know all about the Napoleonic wars, don't you?'

'Of course I will, Tom, but I warn you it's ages since I did history at school.'

The longcase clock in the corner struck six. 'Is that the time? Come along, boys, I want to show you around the house before tea.' The two children prepared to scramble up leaving the toy soldiers all over the rug. 'No, put these away, please. You know the rules: always clear up after yourself.'

There were so many tiny figures, horses, cannons and bits and pieces that it was fully ten minutes before the velvet-lined boxes were safely back on the shelves.

'Something else, you must always bring your torches with you when you leave the bedroom. Can you think why that might be? It has something to do with not being able to use the front door at night.'

The blackout curtains had been drawn and the shutters closed on the landing so she was able to switch on the light. 'Remember I told you we're going the proper way this time.' She led the way down the faded maroon carpet, pausing at the bottom of the stairs. 'I'm going to turn out the light. Switch on your torches; you're going to need them.'

She plunged them into darkness before pushing open the door that led on to the first floor where the main bedrooms were situated.

'Don't we have electricity up here?' David asked, grabbing hold of the back of her jumper.

'Yes, we do, but there's a special reason why we can't use it at night. I'm waiting for one of you to tell me what that is.'

Tom shone his torch along the wide corridor, the thin beam flickering across dark brown family portraits making the eyes appear to follow him. 'I don't like it much up here. It's creepy.'

This wasn't going well. The last thing she wanted was for either of them to be nervous about moving around the house. 'Shine your torches up at the ceiling. Can you see anything at the far end of the corridor?' Three yellow lines pointed into space.

'There isn't any ceiling up there. Where's it gone?' Tom asked incredulously.

'It's the surprise I was telling you about in the car. The reason why we can't switch on the lights. The centre of the house has a glass dome and it can't be blacked out, so until the war's over we all have to creep around using torches because otherwise we'd be breaking the blackout rules.'

'That's amazing! Come on, Dave, let's go and have a deco.'

David released his clutch on Barbara's jumper and transferred it to his brother's before trotting behind him to look at the rotunda. Both boys agreed it was worth the bother of no electricity.

'I wouldn't like to meet a bad man up here without my torch,' Tom said.

'Don't be ridiculous, Tom. Nobody's ever going to meet a bad man up here. Stop frightening your brother, please.'

20

Friday disappeared in a flurry of activities and when Tom and David finally went to bed Barbara was certain she had made the correct decision. They had been an instant success with both her grandparents, and Joe – the stable boy – had already taken on the role of older brother.

Dressing for dinner had, thankfully, been dispensed with. The house was far too cold to wander around in evening dress. She only had to brush her hair and put on a little lipstick before, torch in hand, she headed for the breakfast room. Meals were being eaten there until the temperature rose; this was a small room and much easier to keep warm. Her grandparents were waiting for her.

'Sorry, am I very late? I didn't like to leave them until I was sure they were asleep. It's only their second night in a strange house after all.'

'Would you like a sherry, my dear? Or a glass of claret?'

'Wine please, Grandpa. I've decided I don't really like sherry.'

Her grandmother patted the empty space beside her. The small sofa that had been moved into the room was positioned next to the fire. 'Why don't you come and sit with me, and tell me what you have been doing all day? We've hardly seen you.'

'We built three enormous snowmen and dressed them. The boys are determined to make a whole family before the snow goes. I've told them they can build the rest of them on their own. My fingers are still numb.' She flexed them in front of the flames. 'Grandpa, I'm afraid they've rather adopted Joe.'

'He's a good lad; no harm in the boys spending time with him. He'll keep them out of mischief.'

'They need to mix with boys from Brentwood School, make friends their own age. You could invite the younger Everton boys to spend the day here tomorrow.'

'What a good idea, Grandma,' she said even though she had hoped to keep contact with Home Farm to a minimum. The fewer reminders of Alex the better. 'Do I have time to telephone before dinner? Jim and Ned could cycle and I could ride and meet them; Silver needs the exercise.'

'Jolly good idea. The cycles that came from Hastings aren't safe for the weather conditions. It would be far better if you went on your horse.'

Ned and Jim were thrilled to be asked to spend the day at The Grove. Mrs Everton was happy to allow them to cycle, as long as she was there to escort them.

After the nine o'clock news bulletin Barbara put down her book. 'I think I'll go up now. I'm worn out.' She went over and kissed Grandma. 'It's Marigold's day off tomorrow, isn't it? Is she staying in the village with Mrs Mullins again?'

'Yes, I've agreed it would be safer. She's a reliable girl and I'm sure she'll be back in time on Sunday morning.'

'That's what I thought. I hope Tom and David are sufficiently settled to be upstairs on their own.'

'I'm sure they are, my dear. Tom said they'd only looked at half their toys so far. They've have got plenty to occupy them,' said Grandpa.

'I know that. The daytime's no problem, but what if they wake? They could be scared. Especially David – he's not as confident as Tom, Grandpa, as I'm sure you've noticed.'

'Leave a light on in the playroom and the bedroom door ajar. I'm sure if they can see, then they'll be fine.'

'Grandma, are you sure?' The thought of leaving a light burning unnecessarily was shocking.

'Just this once, it won't matter, my dear. And don't forget we're saving fuel by not having lights on in the passageway and hall, aren't we?'

'I suppose we are. Mrs Holroyd, at the last WVS meeting we went to, was so insistent we must economise to help the war effort. I feel guilty every time I throw something away just in case it could be reused somewhere else.'

'You're enjoying the meetings now, are you?'

'I am, Grandpa. I thought I'd hate them, but it's not at all how I imagined it would be. Mrs Mullins and Mrs Brown have just joined and there are lots of other women from the village as well. I like being part of a team, feeling that all of us can make a difference.' She stopped and laughed. 'Oh dear, on my soapbox again. I'm sounding like a recruitment poster. I'd better say goodnight. I'm going straight over to Home Farm tomorrow, so I'll not see you at breakfast.'

* * *

The Everton boys were waiting at the farm gate when Barbara trotted up the next morning. 'Good morning, Ned, Jim. I'm glad to see you're well wrapped up. Are you ready? Do you have to go and tell your mother that you're leaving?'

'No, she's watching from the window. All we have to do is wave,' Ned said.

She turned their into the yard and waved to Mrs Everton. 'Right, let's get going. You go on ahead. Stick to the middle of the lane; it's slippery but less bumpy than the edges.'

When they arrived they were met by David and Tom dancing around in the stable yard waving shovels. She handed her reins to Joe.

'Silver will need a good rub-down; we trotted all the way back so she's got quite warm.'

'Righty-ho, miss. Morning, Jim, Ned, good to see you.' Joe knew both boys from the village school. She'd intended to introduce the children but they'd vanished into the park to build more snowmen to join the three already huddled in front of the house. 'I'm going in,' she called. 'I'll ring the bell when it's time to come in for a hot drink. Don't go anywhere else will you?'

'We won't, Babs,' Tom shouted back. 'Unless we go in the barn with Joe. That's all right isn't it?'

'Fine. But nowhere else.'

The boys came in an hour later, frozen but happy. Four more snowmen had joined the group. Barbara gave them mugs of steaming cocoa and cake and sent them upstairs to play. When she went to fetch them for lunch they were engrossed in a massive battle. The floor was covered with soldiers and they were reluctant to leave their game.

'It's Sinclairs versus Evertons, a blood feud, Babs, and we're winning at the moment.'

'You're not, Tom,' Jim said. 'We're biding our time. We'll surround your troops with a surprise attack later on, just wait and see.'

The snow returned in a cloud of white as they were finishing lunch in the kitchen.

'Cor, look at that! It's a blizzard out there. We can't cycle back in that, Babs,' Jim said.

'No, you can't. I think you'll have to stay the night. I'll go and ring your parents and see what they say.'

Mr Everton agreed to drive over and collect the children next morning, at nine o'clock, which would give all of them time to get ready for morning service. Barbara ate in the kitchen with the boys and joined them upstairs for a riotous game of Monopoly that lasted until bedtime. She waited by the fire, reading, until she was certain they were all asleep and she could join her grandparents in the library.

Grandma looked up from her embroidery with a smile. 'Are they all asleep?'

'They are. No trouble at all. It's a good thing those beds are large. They didn't need to go top to tail; they're quite comfortable side by side. I put a bolster down the middle of each bed so there shouldn't be any fighting during the night.'

'Excellent, well done. Would you like a nightcap? We're having a whisky.'

'No, thanks, Grandpa. I dislike spirits. I'll get myself a cocoa later on when I fill my hot-water bottle.' Her grandparents were looking happier each day. She wondered if having the children running around the house was the reason. 'I hope the boys didn't disturb you with their high spirits earlier, Grandma?'

'Not at all. I was tempted to join in. Don't look so surprised, my dear. I do enjoy myself sometimes.'

'We love hearing the children playing. This house has been quiet for too long. It's a house full of joy and promise now, and that's all down to you, my dear girl. If you hadn't come to find us…' He stopped and cleared his throat a few times. 'The Grove is a home again and your grandmother and I are going to make damn certain it stays that way. One doesn't often get a second chance and we're not going to spoil this one.'

'I'm glad you're both happy with how things are. I am, you know that, and neither Tom nor David has mentioned Hastings even once. I'm not sure if that's a good thing or not.'

'Plenty of time later for them to grieve for their parents, but now they're celebrating finding you and enjoying the excitement of a new life here. I expect there will be a few tears when school starts, but let's enjoy things as they are, shall we?'

'Well said, Edward, my dear. I do hope the Everton boys come over and stay often. They are charming and so polite, exactly the right sort of playmates for our two.'

Barbara smiled at the possessive tone. 'They were enacting a battle this morning and it was Sinclairs versus Evertons. No mention of Evans at all.'

'Excellent. Now, my dear, it's time for the news. I pray there's nothing more than the weather to report.'

* * *

She was up early, knowing the boys would be down wanting a cooked breakfast and Sunday was Mrs Brown's day off. Marigold could make edible toast and a pot of tea but that was her absolute limit. Barbara clattered down the backstairs and scurried along the freezing passage into the kitchen. The blackouts were closed, the range low and no sign of the girl. She raced around, drawing back the heavy curtains, and daylight flooded the room.

Was it the snow? It must be too deep to even walk through; that's why Marigold was late. The range was soon back to cooking heat and within thirty minutes the kitchen was warm and the kettle on.

She was glad there was no sign of the boys as this would give her longer to do all the extra chores. She had the table to lay in the breakfast room for her grandparents, and the kitchen table to do for herself, the boys and Joe (who always came in for a second breakfast).

She settled on something simple as she was on her own. It would be porridge with milk and sugar, followed by hot toast, butter and either marmalade or jam. She glanced at the wall clock: almost seven thirty. Marigold was nearly an hour late.

If the snow was deep, Joe wouldn't have come either. She would have to race upstairs after breakfast and change into jodhs, then go and sort Silver out herself. That meant no church for her this morning. She heard voices on the backstairs and hurried into the kitchen to check the porridge was ready.

Tom arrived first. 'Where's Marigold? She said she'd be back for breakfast this morning.'

'I don't know, but I think the snow must be too deep for her to get here. We'll have to manage on our own. I'm going to look after Silver as Joe won't be here either, so you'll have to attend church without me.'

All four boys pulled faces; church was not an uplifting experience for them.

'We could help with Silver and do the washing-up. Grandma and Grandpa could go to church without us just this once,' Tom said hopefully.

'Good try, Thomas, but it won't work. Church parade for us, I'm afraid.'

Four heads turned in unison.

Tom grinned. 'Never mind, Grandpa, it was worth a try.'

Jim asked to leave the table. 'Can I go and see how deep the snow is, please, sir? I'm worried that Dad won't be able to come over this morning to fetch us.'

'He could use the tractor; that'll go through anything,' Ned said. 'I like riding on that.'

'Not in this weather, young man. Far too dangerous.'

There was the sound of feet in the passageway and Joe appeared. He stopped, his cheerful grin fading as he sensed their surprise. 'Bit inconvenient this morning, miss? I don't mind. I'll go back out.'

Barbara recovered first. 'No, of course not, Joe. Come in. We thought the snow was too deep for you to come this morning.'

He scratched his head. 'It's not deep – no more than a few inches, I reckon. Right easy to walk through but I didn't bring the bike.'

Grandpa frowned and the boy began to back out thinking he was at fault somehow. 'It's not you lad. Please, come in and sit down. Your breakfast is ready.'

Joe shuffled in, and sat at the table nodding at the boys, but too shy to speak again.

'It's Marigold, Joe, she's not come into work. We thought it was because of the snow. Now we're a bit concerned,' Barbara assured him.

'Oh, is that all? I reckon she's like you. After the blizzard she'd have thought it would be too thick and not bothered to get up and check. She'll be along in a bit, all smiles and apologies, you wait and see.'

'I expect you're right and we're worrying unnecessarily. Grandpa, are you ready for your porridge?'

'Bring it through in five minutes. Your grandmother's not down yet.'

She gave the younger boys the toasting forks and opened the front of the stove. 'Could you do the toast and I'll do the porridge, the tea and coffee.'

'What shall we do?' Tom asked.

'You can take it in for me. It's a responsible job.'

After breakfast the boys ran back upstairs to play a final game before Mr Everton arrived to take Jim and Ned home. She piled the dirty crockery in the sink, hoping Marigold would arrive to do it. Her grandparents were content with their meagre breakfast, which gave her time to finish the letter she was writing to a school friend. Sarah and she weren't close, but she wanted everyone to know how happy she was with her change of circumstances. She also thought they might send Christmas cards to Crabapple Cottage.

She was on her way to the library when she heard the telephone ringing and increased her pace. She picked it up on the third ring.

'The Grove, Barbara Sinclair speaking.'

'It's Rosie, miss. I was just checking that Marigold got home last night as she didn't come to mine like she said she would.'

Barbara's stomach clenched. 'She's not here. We thought she was with you.' She couldn't think of anything else to say. The enormity of the situation overwhelmed her. Marigold was missing; she'd been out all night in below-freezing temperatures. How could she have been so stupid as to try and walk home in the dark? She could hear Rosie crying but could think of no words to comfort her.

She heard her grandfather come into the room. She shoved the receiver into his hands. 'Marigold isn't with Mrs Mullins; she didn't come home last night.'

He took charge. 'Mrs Mullins, return to your house. Stay in the warm. I shall organise a search party immediately. Have you contacted the police?'

'No, sir, I thought she was with you until just now.'

'Very well, you mustn't worry. Marigold's a sensible girl; she will have found somewhere to spend the night. If we get off now and find her soon, everything should turn out well. Is there any chance she might have stayed in Brentwood with a friend?'

'She doesn't have any friends round here, sir. She's not been with me long enough to make any.' Barbara could hear her crying. 'I'm going to hang up now, Mrs Mullins, and get things moving. Do I have your permission to contact the police? They can mobilise the Home Guard and we'll soon have dozens of men out searching for her.'

He replaced the receiver, his face grim. 'This doesn't look good, Barbara. I doubt anyone could have survived out in the open last night. I'm going to be busy organising a search party; would you go and tell your grandmother what's happened?'

She nodded and ran to the breakfast room to break the news. 'I don't think Grandpa holds out much hope; I can't believe anything bad can have happened to her. She's such a lovely girl, so full of life.'

'We must pray she found somewhere warm to wait out the night.'

'Then why hasn't she arrived this morning? She must be too cold to move or...' Her voice faded. She couldn't complete the sentence, couldn't bear to speak the words they were both thinking.

They heard the sound of Mr Everton's car crunching down the drive on the way to the rear of the house to collect his sons. 'The boys! They can't know about this – they're still fragile from their own loss. Do you think Mr Everton would take them back with him? They could stay there until all this is resolved.'

'I'm sure he would. If you go up and pack them some clothes I shall go out and talk to him, explain the circumstances.'

Barbara raced upstairs, pausing on the landing to compose herself. 'Tom, David, would you like to go and stay with Jim and Ned? You seem to get on so well and it will make the time between now and Christmas pass more quickly.' The idea was received with a resounding yes. The case was packed and toiletries found. 'Do you want to take any games or toys with you?'

Jim answered. 'They don't need to, Babs, we've nearly as much stuff at home as they've got here. And they can help with the animals so there's a load of things to do.'

'That makes things easier. Boys, I've put in mostly old clothes as I imagine you'll want to get dirty.' She snapped the case shut and handed it to Tom. 'Come along, you lot, we mustn't keep Mr Everton waiting. He's a busy man and has lots of work to do on the farm.'

She was sure she'd concealed her fear successfully and that her brothers believed their unscheduled visit to Home Farm was no more than she said. She deliberately escorted the boys down the backstairs as she didn't want them to overhear anything that might be said in the library. She found Grandma waiting in the back hall with Mr Everton. They smiled, but she could see the worry hidden in their eyes.

'Are you ready, lads? This is a lark, isn't it? I hope you're coming prepared for some hard work?' He nodded at Tom and David.

'Yes, sir. We've never been allowed to help on a farm before. It's going to be good fun isn't it, Dave?' His younger brother nodded, too excited to do more.

'Get your boots and coats on quickly whilst I put your slippers and spare shoes in a bag.'

She had to restrain herself from hugging the boys; she knew they'd hate it, especially in front of their friends. 'Grandpa will come over and collect you. Behave yourselves. Don't do anything silly.' As soon as the door closed behind them she turned, tears spilling down her cheeks.

'Grandma, this is so dreadful. I can't bear to think of Marigold lost in the snow somewhere.'

She took Barbara's hands. 'Now, my dear, we have to be strong. It won't do anyone any good to give in. If anything terrible has happened, Mrs Mullins and her family are going to need all our support.'

'Did you explain to Mr Everton that we don't know exactly when the boys can come home?'

'Yes, I did. He understands and is quite happy for them to stay there as long as necessary.'

The house was going to be full of policemen and that was the last thing children needed to be involved with. Grandpa was still on the telephone and she sat down with Grandma to listen. He was talking to a Captain Smith of the Home Guard.

'Yes, precisely. I have only a stable boy working today; my two gardeners have the weekend free. Very well. The police are already on their way and I have contacted the hospital and they have arranged for the ambulance. Yes, I agree. We shall start the search from this end; your men can start from the bus stop in Ingatestone.' He replaced the receiver, but didn't, for a moment, acknowledge their presence.

Barbara watched him. She could tell from his face that he believed the search was too late.

'Grandpa, Marigold couldn't possibly have survived outside, could she? Please, be honest.'

He nodded sadly. 'I'm very much afraid you're right, my dear. But, it's Christmas time, and perhaps miracles can happen. I must go and get my medical bag. The police contingent should be here anytime.' He walked over to his wife and rested his hand on her shoulder. 'Do you think you should go down to the village and sit with Mrs Mullins, my dear? She's going to need all the support available.'

'Of course I will, Edward, if you think I should. But won't her mother be there with her? I know they're a close family and Marigold is her youngest cousin, I believe.'

'Hmm... well, in that case, remain here next to the telephone, just in case there's any news.'

Barbara couldn't sit still and wait. She had to do something. 'I'm going to change and start searching on Silver. I'll be able to see over hedges and into ditches that people on foot might miss.'

'Good girl! I should have thought of it myself. Elspeth, give the Farleys a call and get Simon and Reginald to come out on horseback too.'

* * *

She continued to search but found no sign of the missing girl. The three horses must have covered the areas the men couldn't reach but there were no footprints, nothing to show Marigold had attempted to walk home.

She was peering over a hedge when Silver threw up her head, almost unseating her, and whickered loudly.

'Good morning, Miss Sinclair, this is a sad business.'

'Yes, Mr Farley, it is.' Somehow she kept the fear from her voice. 'Have you seen any sign of Marigold?'

His knee was pressing into her thigh. He reached down and grabbed Silver's reins. They were quite alone. If she screamed no one would hear her.

'Been thinking about you since the other day, my dear. You're a fine young filly. Far too good for that idiot son of mine.'

This was too much. 'Simon is a charming, pleasant person – unlike you.' Using her free heel she dug in hard. Silver, unused to such treatment, shot backwards covering her in snow. Farley's gelding reared and deposited him on his backside. Leaving him shouting obscenities at her and his horse, she cantered away.

How could that awful man make advances at a time like this? Was he involved in Marigold's disappearance? Did he already know she wouldn't be found? Should she tell Grandpa? No, it was too far-fetched to even consider that man had abducted her. Those women on the train had thought he was involved, but she'd believed the girl when she'd told her she wouldn't be seen dead with him.

Silver stumbled and she lost both stirrups. She must put these fears aside and concentrate on the search, at least for the moment. She was relieved when at one o'clock the police inspector decided to call it off. She was freezing and exhausted and more than ready for lunch.

Later Captain Smith and Grandpa joined the police inspector in the library. She hovered outside deliberately eavesdropping, desperate to hear good news, but knowing in her heart Marigold was probably dead.

'Well, gentlemen, I think we can safely assume the young lady did not attempt to walk home last night. Between us we have covered every inch of the ground and there's no sign of her. I'm very much afraid this investigation has now become a police matter.'

This meant the inspector thought Marigold had been abducted or worse. Her heart pounded. Could her earlier wild imaginings actually be the truth?

The policeman continued, his voice sombre. 'I have sent for CID. Inspector Galloway and his sergeant are on their way and will take over the investigation.'

Her knees buckled and she slid in a heap to the floor. She raised her knees and lowered her head, hoping the sick dizziness would pass. The last thing anyone needed now was a fainting, feeble female. She took several deep breaths, the way her grandfather had told her, and slowly her brain cleared. She heard footsteps coming, headed for the open library door. She had to get up, but she was too late.

'My dear girl, I suppose you heard that? Come along, let me help you.' A surprisingly strong arm encircled her waist and she was hoisted to her feet. 'Let's go and sit in the kitchen. I'll get you a hot cup of tea. In fact I'll get us all one.'

'No, Grandpa, you don't understand. I know something terrible; I've got to speak to the policeman. I've got to tell him what I heard on the train.'

21

'I should wait until the detectives arrive, Barbara. I'm sure you don't want to have to go through your story more than once.'

'Won't Inspector Bailey think I'm concealing evidence?'

'I doubt anything you have to tell him will make a difference to the outcome, my dear.'

She clenched her hands and straightened her shoulders. 'In that case, I'll make that tea you mentioned earlier.'

The room seemed empty, no longer friendly and welcoming. The absence of the happy, laughing girl was more noticeable here than anywhere else. Marigold had only been working with them for a couple of weeks, but she'd blended in so well she'd become part of the family.

Grandpa had gone to explain to Grandma what was going to happen next. The house was about to be invaded by men with big clumping feet who would poke and pry into every corner and want to interview everyone. Marigold's room would be torn apart, her things examined in minute detail, her privacy invaded in the worst possible way.

As she assembled the cups and saucers, and fetched the milk from the pantry, Barbara stared out of the window. The sunshine reflected gold and pink across the snow. The beauty of the landscape failed to penetrate her misery. Her eyes focused on the ring of snowmen the boys had built. These were unable to move, trapped, just as she was. Nothing would ever be the same. Evil had touched their paradise.

The kettle whistled merrily on the hob, recalling her to the task in hand. She made two pots of tea: one to take into the library for the police inspector and his two constables, the other for the breakfast room. She wasn't sure if she should knock. The library had been invaded; the room was no longer hers to enter and leave as she pleased.

'I've made you some tea, Inspector Bailey. Shall I put it on the desk?'

The small, balding man smiled tiredly. 'Yes, thank you, Miss Sinclair. This is a bad day, a very bad day. As soon as Inspector Galloway and his men arrive I shall hand over to them. I'm afraid they will want to interview everyone here, search the house and so on, but it has to be done.'

'We understand – you have a job to do. If you wish to speak to us we're in the breakfast room; it's at the end of this corridor, on the left.'

Scarcely twenty minutes later a black car pulled up outside. Grandpa got to his feet.

'I think Inspector Galloway has arrived.' She prepared to follow him.

'No, child, I'll speak to him first. Give him all the background information I have. He'll send for you when he's ready.'

She watched him go, thinking how old he looked, how bowed down. He'd been sitting with Grandma, holding her hands, offering what comfort he could. At least something positive could come out of this tragedy; they would spend their declining years in a more loving relationship.

She hadn't been asked to reveal what she knew. She dreaded the moment when her grandmother discovered the husband of her closest friend could possibly be a murderer. Poor Simon – how would he cope with the scandal? He didn't like his father, but she was sure he would be devastated to discover... She couldn't finish the thought. She prayed she was wrong, that the whole thing would turn out to be a terrible accident.

She jumped as the door opened. 'Shall I come? Does he want to speak to me, Grandpa?'

'He does. Would you like me to stay in with you? Give you some moral support?'

'No, thank you. This is going to be hard enough without you hearing it as well.' She wondered whether he already suspected what she had to tell the policeman. After all he had warned her about going to Mountney Hall. He was well aware what sort of man Reginald Farley was.

The sergeant was waiting at the door. 'Miss Sinclair, please come in. We gather you have some information pertinent to our inquiries?'

He ushered her over to a hard-back chair placed directly in front of the leather-topped desk. The man, standing politely on the other side, offered her his hand.

'I'm Inspector Galloway, as you've probably gathered. Thank you for coming forward. I can imagine how difficult all this must be.' He waved at the chair and she sat, crossing her legs at the ankles, placing her hands in her lap, feeling like a schoolgirl summoned for an interview with a head teacher.

The inspector was, like his uniformed counterpart, a man in his forties, but there the resemblance ended. The man sitting opposite her, waiting attentively for her to speak, was an eagle not a sparrow. If anyone could solve this mystery it would be him.

'What I have to tell you is hearsay and gossip. But I'm sure you can sift the truth from the exaggerations.'

He didn't interrupt to ask questions; he allowed her to finish her story before speaking. 'Thank you, Miss Sinclair, that must have been very hard for you. Obviously we must corroborate the information about the previous two young women. Do have any idea who the ladies on the train might be?'

She shook her head. 'No, but I'm sure they don't live in the village or they would belong to our WVS group. They got on the train at Brentwood so I expect they live there. I'm sure my grandmother would know who to ask. Would you like me to fetch her?'

Inspector Galloway stood up. 'That would be most helpful. My sergeant will write up your statement and get you to sign it. I'm afraid I shall probably have to speak to you again. I'm sure I don't have to remind you, Miss Sinclair, that it would be better if this information remained confidential.'

She returned to the breakfast room. 'Inspector Galloway would like to speak to you both. He'll tell you what it's about; if you don't mind I'd rather not talk about it any more. I think I'm going to make a huge pot of soup for lunch. It will give me something to do and stop me thinking.'

'Your grandmother and I have been talking. We thought we would shut all the rooms downstairs apart from the kitchen, this one, and the library. We can eat in here and the children and the staff can eat in the kitchen. The library can become the drawing room. Hopefully the police will return it to us by the end of the day.'

'I think that's a jolly good idea. It will be much easier to keep warm if we only use a few rooms.' The real reason was that they were going to be short-staffed. It was unlikely Rosie would return either. 'What about asking Mrs Brown and Joe to move in? I know it's hard for them to get here every day and, since her husband died two years ago, she's finding it difficult to manage the rent on her cottage.'

'Joe could have the box room on the nursery floor and Mrs Brown could use the two rooms that adjoin the kitchen. They used to be the housekeeper and butler's domain.' Her grandmother smiled for the first time since the phone call. 'I shall ask Joe to go home and speak to his mother. If she agrees then they can start moving in as soon as the rooms are ready.'

'Fred's in the boiler room at the moment. I'll go down and ask him if he'd like to increase his hours, become full-time.' Grandpa helped her from her chair. 'We'll get through this, my dear, if we all work together and support each other. We're a family now. Nothing can take that away.'

Barbara returned to the kitchen, her heart full. Grandpa was right: it would be easier for them. Marigold had only been with them a short time. She could only imagine the pain Rosie and her family must be going through. Their Christmas would be ruined; they wouldn't be able to skirt round the tragedy like they were doing.

How were the boys were getting on at Home Farm? She was missing them already. Whatever happened she would ask them to return tomorrow. The police should have finished their business; the house would be back to normal. Tears pricked and her throat clogged. Things would never be normal again. People were expected to die in a war, but not like this.

She immersed herself in vegetables and stock, glad to have something to occupy her time. When the soup was made she turned her attention to a chicken and ham pie to be eaten, if anyone had any appetite, for supper. Like evening dress (which had been dispensed with) dinner had now disappeared to be replaced by supper. Night was falling before she was called back to sign her statement.

'Have you finished here, Inspector?'

'We have, Miss Sinclair. I have been able to confirm all the information you gave me and we shall now continue our inquiries elsewhere.'

She quickly scribbled her signature on the bottom of the sheet and hurried out. The detective's penetrating stare unnerved her. She'd hate to be a criminal facing interrogation by him.

Joe had returned with the good news that he and his mother would be moving in the next day. He had spent the rest of the afternoon with Fred, the boiler man, clearing the two rooms his mother was going to occupy. Barbara went to see how he was getting on.

'Good heavens! I can't believe the difference.' The room that was to be Mrs Brown's sitting room had been transformed. 'I had no idea these rooms were here. I'm sure your mother will love this, Joe.'

The boy grinned, pushing back his hair. 'Madam found the blackout curtains and Dr Sinclair sorted out the furniture. I reckon it's better than we've got at the cottage. Come and see the bedroom – it's grand.' He took her through the communicating door and gestured towards the double bed with matching wardrobe, chest of drawers and dressing table. 'Just look at that, miss, the full set. Ever so smart.'

'It's lovely, Joe. I can't believe you and Fred have done this in an afternoon.' Her grandmother came in, a green candlewick bedspread and several small cushions in her arms.

'Oh, there you are, my dear. I just looked into the kitchen and was worried when you weren't there.' She placed the things on the bed. 'What do you think? Will Mrs Brown be comfortable here?'

'I'm certain she will, Grandma. The police have gone so we've got the house to ourselves again. Do you realise none of us have eaten since breakfast? Shall I serve supper soon?'

'I don't suppose any of us are hungry, but we must eat. Yes, we shall eat in an hour.'

Barbara turned to Joe and Fred. 'Would you like some soup and chicken pie before you go home? It's all ready. I can dish it out straightaway if you want some.'

By the time she'd cleared away she barely had time to rush upstairs to change into a clean jumper and have a quick wash. Although they weren't changing she didn't feel appearing for the evening meal in a top covered in pastry would be appreciated, however extreme the circumstances.

Nobody wanted to use the library until it had been cleaned and aired. It had the aroma of policeman, something they wanted to forget. The sofa that had been brought into the breakfast room seated two comfortably. Grandpa was content to pull up a dining chair.

'What happens now, Grandpa? Inspector Galloway told me they were "pursuing their inquiries elsewhere", but he wasn't any more specific than that.'

'I imagine he has constables talking to bus conductors, villagers and so on. He will want to get his facts straight first.' He carefully didn't mention who the inspector would be speaking to next.

'It's all right, Edward. You can say what we're all thinking. The police will be searching Mountney Hall and the factory at Chelmsford even as we sit here. I rang this afternoon but the operator told me the number was temporarily unavailable. Do you really believe that Reginald could have murdered dear little Marigold?'

'I don't know. Being an unsavoury character, a profiteer, and a philanderer doesn't make someone a murderer. I'm hoping the girl will be found to have died from hypothermia and no foul play has been involved.'

They were all talking as though Marigold's death was a fact. 'This is horrible. I can't bear to think she's dead. However it happened, it's a tragedy. Did you go down and see Mrs Mullins this afternoon, Grandpa?'

'Yes, I did, but the house was closed and the next door neighbours told me the family have gone to stay in Hornchurch with her sister. It seems they have accepted that the girl's dead as well. Now the police have finished I want Tom and David back. They only met her a couple of times; they'll hardly notice she's gone, especially as Joe will be living upstairs with them.'

'I agree, Edward. There's nothing we can do. We must get on with our lives, try to make this a happy Christmas for the boys.'

'I shall go and telephone the Evertons when I finish my coffee. But before I do, Elspeth, I think you must ring and cancel the invitations. I don't think it would be appropriate to hold a large party at the moment.'

Barbara had been looking forward to a house full of people. The noise and chatter might help to fill the void that Marigold's absence would inevitably leave. Even with Mrs Brown and her son living in the house, it would still seem empty with no Rosie or her cousin working there.

'Grandma, I was wondering if it might be possible to invite the Evertons instead? I know that they're on their own this year. They aren't close friends, but I really like them and it would be lovely for the boys. What do you both think?'

'There's certainly enough food arriving from Harrods. I think it's a good idea, but if you're not happy, Elspeth, then we'll enjoy ourselves on our own.'

'You're right, both of you. It's the boys' first Christmas here and I want it to be one they will remember. At the moment it could be memorable for all the wrong reasons. Yes, I'll go and make the phone call to the Evertons, Edward, and ask them if they'd like to join us on Christmas Day.'

He waited until they were alone before speaking quietly to Barbara. 'You realise things could be even worse by tomorrow? If Farley is arrested for murder, Mrs Farley will leave and go and live with her daughter. That would leave Simon on his own over the holiday. I think we ought to consider including him; he could be at Mountney Hall with only the staff for company.'

'Grandpa, have you forgotten John's coming to stay on Thursday? Simon might feel awkward being here once he knows I'm engaged to someone else.' She shifted uncomfortably. 'I know it sounds uncaring, but having Simon here will just remind us all about something we're trying to forget, at least over Christmas.'

'I understand how you feel and you're probably right. Family must come first. He might well find someone else to run the factory and move away with his mother. Let's say no more about it.'

Grandma returned looking better than she had all day. 'It's all arranged. Mr Everton will return the boys tomorrow morning. He insisted. And they are coming to join us for lunch on Christmas Day. Mrs Everton seems a charming person. I think I might come to like her.' She rejoined Barbara on the sofa. 'Do we have gifts we can give the Everton children? I'm sure there's something suitable for their parents in the things coming from Harrods.'

'We bought far too much for our two. They will hardly miss a couple of things. Did you say the delivery's tomorrow?'

'Yes, or Tuesday. Edward, whatever happens, tomorrow I think we should continue with the plans we've made. We will still take the boys to the pantomime on Wednesday.'

'I didn't know you'd got tickets. Are you going up to Town or is it a local show?' asked Barbara.

'Oh dear, what with everything that's happened we forgot to tell you. Edward and I thought you might like the afternoon alone with your young man before he had to meet us.'

'That's kind of you, Grandma. I'm not sure when John's arriving, but it will be before dark. What time does the pantomime finish?'

'Like everything else, it finishes before the blackout. We should be back by four o'clock.'

The nine o'clock news bulletin, which had just finished, had informed listeners Canadian troops had arrived in Britain. Barbara hoped these new additions would help the war effort. She was on her way to the kitchen to make them all a mug of cocoa when she heard the phone ringing in the library.

'I'll get it, Grandpa; you stay in the warm.' She hurried along the passageway, one hand trailing along the panelling the other shining the torch in front of her. She had to agree with Tom the house was rather creepy in the dark. She lifted the receiver and waited.

'One moment, I have a call from Inspector Galloway for you.'

Her heart plummeted. It could only be bad news. No one rang at this time of night with anything else. She groped for the chair that had been used earlier in the day. It might be better to be seated before she spoke to the inspector.

'Inspector Galloway here. Could I speak to Dr Sinclair?'

'It's Barbara Sinclair. Can you tell me please?'

22

'Good evening, Miss Sinclair. I'm afraid I must insist on speaking to Dr Sinclair.'

'Yes, of course. I'll fetch him. Please wait a moment.'

'It's all right, my dear. I'm here.' He picked up the handset. 'Why don't you go and keep your grandmother company? I'll be along later.'

She wanted to protest, but he was right. Her place was in the breakfast room offering comfort. If a blackout curtain was hung from floor to ceiling in the passage they could have the lights on and everywhere would be much warmer.

She stopped and shone her torch back along the corridor. The ceiling was high, but Joe would be able to reach it on a stepladder. There had been at least one more blackout curtain upstairs in the sewing room. It should fit the space perfectly. Pleased she had something else to discuss, she rejoined her grandmother.

'Grandpa is taking the call. The inspector wouldn't talk to me.'

'I should think not, Barbara. What he has to say will not be suitable for your ears or mine. Far better your grandfather deals with it.'

She was too restless to sit, but pacing the room was not an option. Her suggestion for the corridor was well received.

'I think that's a splendid plan, my dear. What a clever girl you are. I shall ask Joe and Fred to hang it up. They're going to be busy moving Mrs Brown's bits and pieces but I'm sure they'll find half an hour to do that. The Christmas tree is arriving sometime tomorrow, so they've got to bring that in as well.'

'We never had a tree at Crabapple Cottage. Decorating one is a treat I'm going to share with the boys. I've always wanted to do it.' Her brow furrowed. 'I have a vague memory of a tree, with sparkling glass baubles and candles, but it certainly wasn't in Hastings.'

Grandma cleared her throat. 'My dear, it would have been when your father was alive. He always loved Christmas and he would have continued the tradition with you.'

Barbara's eyes filled. 'That must be it. It also explains why trees were not allowed after he died. She wouldn't have anything in the house that reminded her of him.'

'This makes it even more important that we celebrate properly, whatever the circumstances. It will be in your father's memory, as well as to welcome you all to your new home.'

'I was wondering, Grandma, if the puppies could be brought home tomorrow, not left until Christmas Day? Having them to play with might lessen the impact of the bad news.'

'I'm sure that could be arranged. We already have the baskets and newspaper for the floor.'

'Thank you. I'm glad you agreed they can live at the far end of the boot room until it's warmer. It would be difficult getting outside to the stable to feed them four times a day with all this snow.'

The conversation faltered as they heard footsteps outside. She joined Grandma on the sofa and they linked hands, watching the door anxiously. His face told them everything.

'I'm so sorry, my dears, it's the worst possible news. Poor child. What a thing to happen.' He dabbed his eyes. 'Inspector Galloway's men searched the factory and found a patch of recently disturbed snow under the trees on the far side of the site. They found the girl buried there. By tomorrow the fresh fall would have covered the place and she would probably never have been found.'

'How absolutely dreadful, Edward. Such a lovely girl; to be snuffed out like that.' She couldn't continue, and accepted the handkerchief he offered her.

'If I hadn't told them what I'd heard he would have got away with it. No one would ever have known. Marigold would have become another missing girl.'

'That's correct, my dear girl. At least her family can grieve, and will be able to bury her.'

'Has Mr Farley been arrested?'

'No, Barbara, but he's assisting the police with their inquiries. I don't believe he's been charged.'

'What does that mean, exactly?'

'It means, Elspeth, he's being held in custody whilst they interrogate him and continue to look for evidence.'

'Are they treating the disappearance of the other two girls as suspicious, in view of what they've just discovered?' asked Grandma.

He nodded. 'They are. The inspector told me they have several leads they are following.'

'Do you think those other girls are buried at the factory as well?' Barbara shuddered. She hated Mr Farley but couldn't believe he was a mass murderer.

'If they do, they didn't tell me. And they can't dig up the grounds; they'll have to wait until there's a thaw.'

'Maybe Mr Farley will confess, then it can all be settled straightaway. What those families must be going through, and at Christmas too.'

He leant over and squeezed his wife's shoulder. 'What we all need is a stiff drink. No, Barbara, I'm fetching you a brandy, for medicinal purposes. It will steady your nerves.'

She pulled a face. 'I'd rather have my cocoa. I've got it ready; I'll go and make it now.'

She returned with the drinks to find her grandmother cradled in her grandfather's arms. She felt she was intruding and was about to back out when he stopped her.

'Come in, my dear girl. I hope that you've put plenty of sugar in the cocoa.'

She nodded. 'I did. And if I've got to have brandy, can you tip it in this? Maybe it won't taste so bad mixed in.'

'Excellent idea. I think I'll do that for all of us.'

None of them wanted to go to bed. Marigold's ghost hovered in the dark corridors, making them seem alien and unfamiliar.

'Edward, I think I'd like to move into one of the rooms opposite Barbara's. Why don't you move to the adjoining room? We can share the bathroom. That way we'll all be together, the boys and Joe on the second floor, us on the first and Mrs Brown on the ground floor.'

'It will also mean we can turn off the heating everywhere else. We'll be saving fuel and making ourselves more comfortable.' He swallowed the dregs in his mug. 'I think we should all go up. Things might appear less bleak in the morning.'

Barbara, as usual, chose to use the backstairs. In spite of her sadness she was forced to smile when she realised her grandparents would also have to use this narrow, noisy staircase in future. Someone would have to pack the dead girl's belongings, but not now; her death was too raw.

It had promised to be such a joyful Christmas, everyone in the country pretending there wasn't a war on, that Hitler wasn't poised to invade Britain. Complaining about the appalling weather had replaced moans about the shortages and the rationing due to start in January. Mrs Brown had told her conscription was being extended to all men between twenty and twenty-seven and that was starting in January as well.

She tried to concentrate her mind on the war, not on the murder, but this didn't stop her having a broken night. Several times she woke, her heart jumping. She remembered that everything had changed and a wave of misery would sweep over her.

She got up early, glad she had volunteered to do the early-morning chores until Joe and Mrs Brown were in residence. Keeping busy was the answer. She switched off the light, drew back the curtains and opened the shutters. There had been a little fresh snow overnight; she could see it crisp and white on the windowsill. The sun was struggling to come up behind the trees and she stood watching as their silhouettes were edged with golden light. Her eyes filled. How could there be evil in a world as lovely as this? She shook her head angrily and went down to start breakfast.

Mrs Brown and her son moved in before the boys came home. Joe had done his stable duties and was now helping Fred with the ancient tractor and trailer to transport their belongings from the rented cottage in the village.

The cook, ever practical, summed up what all of them were feeling. 'It's a sad day for Rosie Mullins and her family. Marigold didn't deserve to die that way, but she was a stranger to me. She'd been here such a short time I hardly knew her. I'm upset, course I am, but it's not as though she's a relative or anything, is it?'

Barbara agreed. 'I know it's selfish to say so, but it's going to be so much easier to get on with things without Rosie here. I do hope she finds work somewhere else. The family need her income.'

Mrs Brown thumped the bread dough on the floury table. 'Don't fret, miss; Rosie will get a job at a factory, for much better money. She would have gone ages ago, but she didn't like to, seeing she'd been working here so long.'

'That's a relief. Good – that sounds like a car. It must be the boys.'

'Are you telling them, or will madam do it?'

'I'm going to do it. I was hoping my grandfather would be back; it's hard to be sad when there are puppies playing around your feet.'

She pulled on her gumboots and shrugged on her heavy coat. She was going out to meet the boys, not waiting inside. As she got round to the turning circle a strange car, and her grandfather's black saloon, pulled in.

David and Tom jumped out and thanked Mr Everton who waved and drove off, obviously wanting to avoid having to talk about the tragedy in front of the children.

'Welcome home, both of you. Did you have a good time? Did you behave yourselves?'

David ran across to throw himself into her open arms. 'We did, we did, but I'm glad to be back here with you.'

She swung her little brother round. 'And I'm glad you're back. Are you all right, Tom? You're rather quiet this morning.' Had he heard something already? Could there have been a report in the paper so soon?

He arrived at her side and she released David to hug him. This time he returned it, pressing his face against her shoulder like a small child. She whispered into his ear.

'Have you heard about Marigold, Tom?' He nodded and she squeezed him closer. 'I wanted to tell you both myself. Never mind, it can't be helped. I take it David doesn't know?'

Tom raised his tear-stained face. 'No, I heard Mrs Everton talking this morning. It's horrible! Who could do such a thing to Marigold?' He gulped and buried his face for a second time.

Their grandfather had parked and was standing, a cardboard box in his arms. He raised his eyebrows and nodded at Tom. Barbara nodded back. He stepped into action.

'Tom, David, I have an early Christmas present for you both. In the circumstances we all felt it was a good idea for you to have it today.'

Tom straightened and Barbara quietly handed him a hanky to wipe his eyes before he turned round. 'What present, Grandpa? Is it in that box?'

'Indeed it is, but let's go in before you open it. It's damn cold out here.' Both boys giggled, half shocked, half impressed by his profanity.

Tom rushed ahead to open the back door. He stood aside to let him enter first.

David hung back, his face worried. 'What circumstances, Babs? Why's Tom upset?'

She knelt, ignoring the snow on the doorstep. 'It's Marigold, darling. She died. They found her body under some trees.'

His mouth opened in shock. 'Dead? Not alive any more?'

'I'm afraid so. It's very sad, but I'm sure she wouldn't want you to grieve for her. After all, you only met her a couple of days ago. She's nice and warm in heaven now, safe and happy.'

His lips curved a little. 'She is, isn't she? So we can pray for her in church on Sunday, can't we?'

'We certainly can, David. Now, hurry up and get you coat off. Grandpa has that Christmas present waiting to be opened. What do you think it could be? Have you any idea at all?'

David was immediately distracted. Christmas presents in large brown boxes were unusual and early presents unheard of. 'I can't guess. Tom won't open it without me, will he?'

'Of course he won't.'

David didn't wait for his sister but ran ahead to the kitchen. He stopped in the doorway, exclaiming in astonishment. Mrs Brown's enormous tabby cat, Lavender, named after her birthplace, was standing on top of the Aga, her back arched and her tail rigid.

'Look at that! It's a cross cat, Babs. Is that the present?'

Laughing, she pushed him into the room. Lavender had obviously realised what was in the box and disapproved. Tom was dancing from leg to leg, his sadness forgotten in his eagerness to open it. He must have guessed what was inside, but until he could see for himself he wouldn't believe it.

'Now, Tom, you come to this side; David, go on the other.'

The box was moving and squeaking. Tom tore the box open and screams of delight reverberated round the kitchen. 'Two puppies. One each. Oh, look, Babs, they're so sweet.' Tom's eyes were shining as he spoke. The boys crouched on either side of the box, hardly daring to reach in and remove one of the black, wriggling, bright-eyed bundles. 'David, which one do you want?'

'I don't mind. Shall we share them?'

She dropped down beside them. 'I hope I can share as well? I've always wanted a dog, and now we've got two.' She removed the smaller one, who licked her face enthusiastically. 'This one has a white patch on his tummy, shall we call him Patch?'

She placed the squirming bundle in David's arms. He sat cross-legged, crooning to the puppy, his face transformed by happiness.

Tom picked up the larger dog. He held it out at arm's length and it wagged its whip-like tail. 'This fellow has eyes like black buttons. Shall we call him Buttons?'

She kissed her grandfather. 'Thank you so much, Grandpa. I've never seen them so excited. I don't think we'll have any problems now.'

'Makes one wish one was a child again; life was so much simpler then.' He grinned. 'Good Heavens! Just look at that.'

Lavender, having seen the canines were puppies and no threat to her status, had jumped down from the stove and come to investigate. Mrs Brown put the large, cream china bowl of dough to prove on the back of the cooker, smiling proudly.

'My Lavvy loves puppies. She never had kittens of her own – not for want of trying, I might add – and I reckon she'll take those two rascals under her wing quick smart.'

The boys collapsed into fits of giggles. The cook looked perplexed then her plump face split into a grin. 'Oh dear! I forgot, it sounds a bit rude to call her Lavvy. From now on she'll be Lavender.'

'Probably wise, Mrs Brown,' Grandpa said dryly.

Her grandmother arrived, attracted by the unexpected sound of laughter. She'd been supervising the positioning of the blackout curtain in the passageway. Barbara saw her come in.

'Look at the cat – she's adopted the puppies. She thinks she's their mother.'

'How adorable. They'll need their basket in here if Lavender is going to be taking care of them. I can see these dogs are not going to be living in the boot room either.' She shook her head. 'And to think I intended for them to live in the stable.'

David jumped up and threw his arms around her. 'But you don't mind really, do you, Grandma? They're such lovely puppies and we'll clear up the mess. I promise we will.'

Her grandmother stiffened as David's arms touched her. Then, almost unwillingly, her arms moved until she was hugging him back.

'Well, young man, if you and Tom promise to clear up after their little accidents they may remain in here for the present.' She smiled ruefully at Mrs Brown. 'I'm sorry, Mrs Brown, it's not very hygienic having them in your kitchen, but if we put the basket at the far end, away from the pantry, it shouldn't be too much bother.'

Mrs Brown beamed. 'My Lavender will soon have the little chaps house-trained. I put a dirt tray down in the winter; it's too cold for her to be out all night. She'll soon show them how to use it and box their ears if they don't.'

The huge wicker dog basket was more than large enough for two puppies and their surrogate mother. 'Bring the puppies over, boys, and put them in. Lavender will follow. The rug in the bottom will be quite warm enough. They don't have to be near the cooker.'

Watching Buttons and Patch snuggling up with Lavender was heart-warming, exactly what they all needed.

'When do they need feeding again, Grandpa?'

'They were fed at ten o'clock, Tom. They will need another meal around two. That's ideal; we should have eaten our own lunch by then.'

Joe had come in to admire the new arrivals. 'I'll nip out and fill up a large dirt tray, shall I, sir? They'll need to use it any time. Little ones like that don't last very long before—'

'I'm sure they don't, Joe, but please spare us the details. Yes, go and fetch a tray. I hope you can find something suitable. The ground's frozen solid.'

'I'll get some from the orangery, madam, if that's all right?'

* * *

During the afternoon the children helped move their grandparents into their new bedrooms. Grandma was on hand to hang up the clothes as they arrived. By teatime the changeover was completed.

'You know, it's warmer up here already,' Barbara said as she pulled the blackout curtains at the far end of the gallery. 'Cutting off the heat to the rest of the house has already made a difference.'

Grandma agreed. 'I'm going to see if I can find a stair carpet for the backstairs. If we're all going to be using them in future they can't stay as they are – far too noisy.'

'It's not urgent, though. It could wait until after Christmas, couldn't it?'

'I suppose so. Remember, you have to make up the bed in the green room for your guest. I don't imagine Mrs Brown will have time.'

'I want to keep busy anyway. It makes things easier. I have to admit

I've hardly thought about it all day. It's hard to be sad when we have those adorable puppies to play with.'

'You mustn't be sad any more, my dear. Try to put it out of your mind, and thank God this family is untouched by the tragedy.'

* * *

Barbara managed to take her mare out for an hour or so the next morning. Joe was waiting in the yard when she returned.

'I tell you what, miss, it's grand living in, being part of this house and all. When I get called up I'll not be worried about Mum because she's got a good home here.'

Good God! He was a boy; surely the war couldn't go on so long that he would be old enough to be conscripted? 'Heavens, Joe, it will all be over and Hitler crushed, long before you need to join the forces.'

'I'll be seventeen in less than three years, miss, and the last lot lasted longer than that, didn't it?'

With this sobering thought uppermost in her mind she returned to the house determined that this Christmas was not going to be spoilt by despondency and gloom.

She'd expected to find her brothers in the kitchen but when she looked in even Mrs Brown was absent. She crept in to look at the puppies and saw the big tabby cat was taking care of her charges. The sound of purring filled the room.

Smiling, she went in search of her family. She could hear excited voices in the library, now converted into a far more manageable drawing room by the addition of two sofas, two more armchairs, a couple of occasional tables and a card table that doubled as a backgammon board.

The tree had arrived. Unfortunately it had been selected to stand in the drawing room. She couldn't see either her grandmother or her brothers behind the foliage.

'Babs, look at our tree. Its massive,' David shouted. 'Grandpa's got to get the gardener to come in and cut it back. If we leave it like this there's no room to get round it.'

'It is rather large. At least the ceiling is high in here so we won't have to lop the top off as well.'

'It seems such a shame to mutilate it. It's the best one we've ever had.' Grandma appeared from behind the branches. 'There are no brown bits anywhere and it's lovely and green. And look how straight the branches are, perfect for tying on decorations.'

'Good God, Elspeth! We can't leave it like this. It dominates the room; in fact it takes up more than twenty-five per cent of it.'

'I know, Edward, but there will only be nine of us on Christmas Day. Three-quarters of this room is more than enough to fit us all in.'

'Please, please, Grandpa? Can we have it huge? I've never seen such a big tree, not even in the square at Hastings.' Tom rocked back and forth on his feet, his eyes imploring.

David joined in. 'It's the best tree in the whole world and it's here in our library.'

'Well, all right then. I'll have to get the men to move it right up to the far end of the room. I must admit it will look spectacular against the blackout curtains.'

The packages and hampers from Harrods arrived in the afternoon and, although the boys were not allowed to touch, they stared wide-eyed with excitement.

'Are we having a stocking this year, Babs?' Tom asked.

'Absolutely! I'm making one for everybody. We shall hang them up by the fireplace and pretend we believe in Father Christmas. I'm going to do one for Mrs Brown and Joe as well; after all they're part of the household now.'

'What about Buttons and Patch and Lavender?' David added.

'Now, boys, would you like to come with me up to the attic to fetch the tree decorations? Your grandma's spoilt you this year and bought some sets of electric tree lights. Much safer than candles, but shockingly expensive,' asked Grandpa.

Grandma patted his arm. 'But don't forget, my dear, they will last for years. Candles burn out in a couple of hours. Remember, there's a war on and we mustn't be wasteful, now, must we?'

The boys were upstairs playing with their soldiers after tea when the telephone rang. Neither Barbara nor her grandmother rushed to answer it now. Grandpa responded with monosyllables. After replacing the receiver he turned to them.

'That was Inspector Galloway. Farley has been charged with the murder. It appears they found incontrovertible evidence and no longer need his confession to get a conviction.'

Barbara wasn't sure if she should be pleased the monster was caught or shocked that the man was someone she knew.

'I'm glad, Edward. This will mean the family can arrange for her funeral, get on with their lives, doesn't it?'

'It does, apart from the trial, which will be in the New Year. When I delivered your letter to Mountney Hall this morning, Elspeth, the butler chappie told me that most of the staff had been given notice. The house is to be closed up.'

'I wonder what's happening to Simon.' Barbara hated to think of him enduring the shame and gossip on his own and began to regret her request that he not be invited to stay with them.

'Simon's away; he's driving his mother to his sister's house in East Grinstead. The butler told me the three remaining staff are moving to the dower house. That must mean young Farley intends to live there from now on.'

'And the factory? Is he capable of running it on his own, do you think?'

'Time will tell, Barbara. The fact that both Mrs Farley and Simon moved before Farley was actually charged says a lot about their relationship. They must have had their suspicions before all this happened.'

She remembered hearing her grandparents having a heated argument about the Farleys after the ill-fated lunch party soon after her arrival. Grandma had defended him then, had said she enjoyed meeting his friends in London and refused to sever the connection. How could her grandmother not have recognised the depravity of the man when she had been such a close friend?

Grandpa went to sit with his wife. 'This must be hard for you, my dear. You were always too trusting and that man could be charming when he wished to be.'

After supper Grandpa liked to smoke a cigar and drink a brandy so he left the breakfast room and returned to the library.

'Barbara, Mrs Brown and Joe have tomorrow free. They've agreed to do the early-morning chores; this means you'll have to care for your horse in the afternoon. I'm sorry; I had forgotten your friend was coming when I agreed.'

'Doesn't matter. I'll feed Silver early. John's not coming until late afternoon. That means I'll have plenty of time to wash and change before he arrives.'

'However, they'll both be back to prepare and serve our special evening meal. If we have candles, the best silver and glasses I'm sure the room can be made to look suitably festive.'

'Let me do that. I love making a table look pretty. I can do it in the morning, after you've gone.'

'Thank you, my dear. And don't forget to air the library tomorrow or the smell of cigar smoke will linger all day. You have to push up the window; I warn you, they're easy to open, but very difficult to refasten. But don't worry – your grandfather will lock it when he gets home.'

23

The pantomime party departed at eleven o'clock – they were going to have lunch out before going to the show. Mrs Brown and Joe had finished and gone to catch a bus in order to visit friends and family in Brentwood.

Fred had done the boiler, banked all the fires upstairs and left them ready to be lit in the breakfast room and library. He promised he would be back before dark to see to them again. Barbara was on her own in the house. She smiled. Not quite alone; she had the animals for company.

Laying up in the breakfast room took her most of the morning. She used a crisp cream damask cloth and folded the matching napkins into water lilies, a skill she'd acquired at school. She placed an arrangement of holly and sparkling glass balls in the centre and an ornate Georgian silver candlestick on either side.

She lit the candles to see the effect. The crystal-ware sparkled and the heavy silver cutlery and glass baubles reflected thousands of tiny spots of light. She snuffed out the candles, satisfied the table was perfect. It would be the boys' first grown-up meal and she wanted it to be special. Her stomach rumbled; it must be lunchtime. There was soup in the kitchen; she didn't want anything else as they were having a huge meal that evening.

Mrs Brown had shown her the salmon that had arrived from Scotland on the train the day before. Joe had had to cycle to Ingatestone to collect it, bringing it back in a canvas sling balanced precariously from his handlebars. This was to be the first course. Steak and kidney pie would follow. This was Tom and David's favourite meal and she knew they wouldn't really enjoy the salmon. Dessert was sherry trifle for the adults and floating islands for the boys.

She fed the puppies whilst waiting for her soup to heat. The sky was heavy with snow, the sun hidden. She hoped it would hold off until everyone arrived safely.

Silver was pleased to see her and had no objection to being fed and watered earlier than usual. 'Here you are, lovely girl. I expect Joe will look in on you when he gets home, but I'm going to shut the stable door just in case he doesn't.' She gave her mare a final pat and left her contentedly munching. The bolts on the top door were stiff, frozen in their hasps. The snow began to fall softly around her head as she checked the barn and tack-room doors were shut.

She made her way back to the house, glad she didn't have to go out again tonight. As she reached the back door she heard a car turn into the circle. Who could possibly be visiting in this weather? She smiled. It must be a taxi; John had arrived early. She hurried round to discover it wasn't a cab, but Simon Farley's car. Her heart sunk. She didn't know what to say to him.

She hurried across – if he got out she would be obliged to ask him in and she didn't want to do that. She still had to bathe and change before John arrived. The car window was wound down.

'Hello, Barbara. Shocking weather. Won't keep you, but Ma asked me to drop in these gifts for the boys. She'd already got them when... well, you know.'

She was touched he had bothered to bring them when he had so much else to think about. 'Thank you so much. That's so kind. You stay put and I'll get them out. I'm dressed for the weather.'

'Good show – save getting the old shoes muddy.' He turned round and undid the rear passenger door. 'Can you manage? I can easily get out and help, you know.'

There were only two parcels on the rear seat. 'I can carry these, thank you.' She leant in and pushed her fingers underneath and lifted. They were far heavier than she'd expected. 'Sorry, I need to climb in, get a proper grip. They're quite heavy; do you know what's in them?'

'Building sets. You know – the ones with little bricks and things. Keep them busy for hours. A perfect present for Boxing Day.'

'No wonder they weigh so much.' She braced one knee on the leather seat and slid her left arm deep under the parcels. Inadvertently her hand went into the gap at the back of the seat and her gloved fingers touched a small, flat, circular object. Instinctively she closed her thumb and forefinger and pulled. The disc came out.

Her stomach plummeted. She didn't need to look. She knew what she held. It was Marigold's powder compact. She poked it back into its hiding place thanking God she'd had her back to Simon when she'd found it.

'Do you want any help back there, old thing? You're taking a long time.' His voice sounded too close. Had he seen?

'No, I'm fine. Just getting a good grip before lifting.' She was amazed her voice sounded normal. She heaved and reversed out of the car, praying she wouldn't drop them, that he wouldn't feel it necessary to scramble out to assist her. She used her bottom to slam the door shut. The snow was swirling round her, making it impossible for him to see her clearly.

'Thank you, Simon. We're all thinking about you and Mrs Farley. It must be so difficult for you both. I'm going to go in before I drop these. Goodbye.' She imagined his eyes were boring into her, that he was behind her. Delighted to discover she had left the back door ajar, she fell inside, almost throwing the boxes onto the floor in her panic to close it behind her.

Her heart was thundering. Could she turn the key in time? Somehow she managed to ram the bolt across. She was safe. He was outside. He couldn't get in. She leant against the door, in the darkness, swallowing bile, cold sweat trickling down her spine. Her legs refused to move.

How could they have got it so wrong? All the pieces had fallen into place when she'd found the compact in his car. There was only one way it could have been there. Marigold must have pushed it into the seat hoping someone might find it and realise the truth.

She remembered the girl asking if she and Simon were just friends, remembered finding him deep in conversation with Marigold in the breakfast room on the day he'd walked over in his snowshoes. The sound of his door closing that night – the girl's horror when she'd suggested that Mr Reginald Farley might be her escort. It all fitted.

Of course Marigold had been speaking the truth because she was going out with Simon, not his father. It had to have been Simon who'd killed her. Tremors shook her. He was not the meek and obliging young man he pretended to be. His riding, the reaction of his friends, all the clues had been there. He looked just like his father from a distance; he could easily have been mistaken for him from the back. Was it possible he had deliberately framed his father?

Her heart slowed. She pushed herself upright. The blackouts were open; she couldn't risk putting on the lights. Her torch beam was feeble in the darkness. But she was safe. What next? Yes, she must go to the library and call the police. The door was open. She was about to go in when she heard a noise. There was someone in the room. He had pushed up the unlatched window and climbed in to find her. Instinctively she placed her hand over the beam of her torch.

Her legs were trembling. The stealthy footsteps were getting closer. She saw his fingers, ghostly pale, curl round the door. She must move. Had to get away. She flung herself backwards, forgetting the need for silence, and raced for the backstairs. She took them two, three at a time, but was still in the stairwell when she heard him at the bottom.

* * *

John was standing by the train door as it steamed into Ingatestone station. Snow was falling, not heavily, but enough to make him glad he was wearing his greatcoat. He jumped down onto the platform and handed his ticket to the stationmaster.

'I'm staying at The Grove. Could you possibly give me directions?'

The man beamed. 'It's easy enough to find. Just follow the road and take the lane. It's well signposted. It's about a mile through the village but you can't miss it. It's a grand big house, wrought-iron gates with the name on.' The man nodded. 'I reckon that drive will be the worst part. You'll get the full force walking up that.'

'I'm used to it. They have us marching up and down in all weathers. Thanks. Merry Christmas to you.'

He swung his kitbag over his shoulder and checked his torch was in his pocket. He was going to need it before he reached his destination. He lowered his head, pulled up his collar and adjusted his scarf to cover his mouth. In this weather the two miles would take more than thirty minutes, but he didn't care. He was going to see his darling girl, meet her grandparents, have the engagement made official.

Babs was not as committed as he but once she'd slept with him she wouldn't change her mind. Over dinner he was going to make the announcement – she couldn't back out, not when Tom and David knew. Dr Sinclair would fetch champagne and he would make sure she had several glasses.

He smiled, certain his plan to seduce his reluctant fiancée would work. Her grandparents slept in a different part of the house – Babs had told him that – and the boys were on the second floor. He would have no problem slipping in and out of her room undetected. If she became pregnant, so much the better. She'd know before he left for Canada, then she'd have to marry him.

Canada. He hadn't told her that bit of news. All the Epsom chaps were going to be trained as bomber crew. The arrangements had been made after Canada had begun to send over aircrew to join the British pilots. He could sail away happy if she was his wife, safe from marauding servicemen. He was perfectly content for her to remain at The Grove with her brothers until the war ended. He heard a van approaching and stepped up on to the ridged snow, giving it room to pass. It pulled up and a friendly face appeared at the window.

'Hop in, Alex. I'll give you a lift to Home Farm. Has the old jalopy packed up then?'

The driver had mistaken him for someone else. John poked his head into the car. 'Sorry, wrong person. I'm John Thorogood. I'm on my way to The Grove.'

'Oh... Never mind. Would you like a lift anyway? I can take you to the end of the drive.'

'Thanks, that would be kind of you.' John ran round to the passenger door and climbed in, brushing the snow off his clothes as he did so. 'I take it Alex is in the RAF as well?'

The man chuckled. 'Yes, he's a Spitfire pilot, handsome lad, about your build. That's why I thought you were him. Nasty business up at The Grove.'

John's stomach lurched. 'I don't know about any nasty business. I've just got engaged to Barbara Sinclair and I'm on my way to meet her grandparents. I haven't spoken to her this week.'

'Their young live-in girl, Marigold White, got herself murdered at the weekend. They've arrested Mr Farley for it. Nasty bit of work he is. Two other local girls disappeared a few years back and people said he was involved then.'

'God! That's awful! I've been incommunicado all week, unable to make or receive telephone calls. I wish I'd known. What a dreadful thing to happen and at Christmas too.'

'Well, they've got the bastard who did it. The girl had only been working up there a week or so, but her cousin, Rosie Mullins, had been there for years. She's left as well, so the missus tells me.'

He was quiet, trying to digest this appalling news. Babs had mentioned the girl, said she was pretty and vivacious. Thank God Babs was safe. The driver drove on in silence for a while.

'Do you know Alex Everton then? Miss Sinclair spends a fair amount of time at Home Farm. The Everton lads are around the same age as her brothers. She's met all the family, stopped for Sunday lunch a couple of times.'

John didn't like the sound of this Alex Everton. 'No, but Barbara, Miss Sinclair that is, has mentioned them. I'm not trained yet. I don't have a squadron.'

'Young Alex joined as an officer after he left Brentwood School. He'll be a squadron leader before this lot's over; you mark my words. Unless he's shot down, of course.'

'I suppose Alex Everton has a fiancée? Most of the chaps in my group are hooked up with someone.'

'Not on your life! He likes to play the field. Leaves a trail of broken hearts behind him. It's a good thing your young lady is already spoken for or he would be after her. Young Alex never could resist a pretty face.'

The van slowed as it left the village. 'Drop you here, Mr Thorogood. Keep walking and you'll find the house you want at the far end. You can't miss it.'

'Thank you. Saved me a miserable walk. Merry Christmas to you.'

He increased his pace as he reached the end of the drive. The drive was white, his feet making black imprints in the snow. He remembered he had to walk through the archway and round to the gravel circle at the back. The blackouts weren't drawn. That was odd. It would be pitch-dark inside without lights on.

He noticed a parked car. Dr Sinclair must be home. He paused. There was something not quite right. He walked back to have a closer look and noticed the snow was melting on the bonnet. The car hadn't been there long. He shone his torch beam inside and saw the ignition was switched on, the driver's door not quite closed. Someone had got out in a hurry.

Puzzled, but not unduly worried, he hurried round to the back door. He knocked but got no response. Not wishing to stand outside any longer than he had to, he decided to go in and announce himself. He tried the door but it didn't budge. He pushed harder.

Why on earth would she lock herself into the house? His stomach clenched. He shone his torch down the side of the house and saw footprints. The hair on the back of his neck stood up and he gripped his torch tighter. Whoever had arrived in the car had gone round to the front. Why? John was glad he had the solid weight in his hand. It would be a handy weapon. He moved cautiously, still unsure if he was overreacting, making a melodrama out of something simple. Rounding the corner of the building he was almost blinded by flurries of snow. He shone his torch down; the trail followed the path and stopped halfway along the front of the house.

It ended outside an open window. Someone had climbed in; he could see marks of his entry in the snow on the windowsill. The room was dark, unnaturally so, then he realised he was staring at an enormous, undecorated Christmas tree. It filled the end of the book-lined room, its branches almost touching the shelves.

He paused, straining his ears, but heard nothing. He undid his coat and, dropping it quietly into the room, climbed in, crouching on all fours, alert and ready to stop the bastard who'd dared to break into his darling girl's home.

He edged his way past the prickly arms of the tree, cursing silently as they scratched his face, not daring to use his torch in case the intruder was nearby. Fingering his way down the bookshelves, he allowed his night vision time to take over. It wasn't quite dark. There was enough light to see the door. It was open.

Gripping the torch more firmly he approached the gap. He put his ear to the door and listened. Nothing. Hang on a minute, he could hear something. What was it? He relaxed a little – only puppies yapping somewhere further down the passageway. He was certain the intruder wasn't outside the door. He slid round, his uniform making him invisible in the gloom, then stood, his back pressed to the wooden panelling, and listened.

* * *

Simon was waiting. Waiting to hear her move. This gave Barbara a few seconds to decide where to hide. Could she get to her bathroom? That had a lock on the door. Would she be safe in there? She swallowed, but her tongue stuck to the roof of her mouth. She desperately wanted a drink. No, she was going to be sick. Which one was nearest? The one connected to the green room, John's room; that was first on the left as you came out.

Thinking about him calmed her. He'd promised to be here before dark. He would arrive and protect her, keep the monster on the stairs from hurting her. Simon hadn't begun to climb. The first few steps creaked, so she would have heard him. Where she was, on the tiny first-floor landing, the boards were sound. She could tiptoe to the door and then slip through and with luck he mightn't hear her. But when she did this there would be a tell-tale gleam from the corridor.

The central glass dome, which dominated the front of the house, would make it lighter out there. He would know immediately. She counted to ten. Her heart was thumping painfully, her skin prickling. He hadn't moved yet. He must be on the bottom step.

She hated the dark. It was pressing on her, crushing the breath from her lungs. She had to get out of the blackness, into the light. She forgot caution and burst out into the hallway, dashing into the guest bedroom. She slammed the door shut and with frantic fingers searched for a key to turn. The guest room must have a key. It did. Her breath hissed from between clenched teeth. She turned it, the grating sound horribly loud in the silence.

She couldn't hear anything through the thick door. Had he pounded up the stairs and followed her or was he still deciding which landing she'd exited by? Her breathing slowed. She was safe. He'd never break down this door. What about the key? Could he somehow wriggle that out? She snatched it from the lock and, clutching it in her hand, crept across the room to collapse, panting on the bed, her need for the lavatory forgotten.

The blackouts were drawn in here. She sat, regaining her equilibrium, before easing herself off the bed and heading to the bathroom. The door was closed. She shone her small beam of light at the doorknob. It started to turn. The torch slipped from her fingers. It landed on the Persian rug and went out.

With fingers clamped in her mouth she backed across the room, praying she wouldn't fall over any furniture. She slid behind the floor-length curtains, shuffling sideways until her fingers grasped the catch. This room had French windows leading on to a small stone balcony. If she could get onto that she might be able to scramble across to the adjacent one and into her room.

Terror made her brave. Pulling open the window a few inches, she edged through, closing it behind her. He wouldn't think to look here; no one in their right mind would venture outside in a snowstorm even with outdoor clothes on. She pressed herself against the wall and the biting wind and freezing snow enveloped her.

* * *

John moved on the balls of his feet from the near-darkness of the library into the pitch-black of the corridor. He listened. Nothing apart from the restless puppies. Then he heard someone crashing up a flight of stairs ahead of him. He arced his torch along the walls. God dammit! Why did they disguise their servants' doors in the panelling like this? He saw a sliver of yellow. Someone had switched on a light upstairs. He raced along the corridor and pulled open the door, caution no longer important. Whoever this was, he was making so much noise he couldn't possibly hear him.

As he pounded up the stairs he saw a flicker of light ahead as a door was flung open. He reached the landing, was about to throw himself through the door, torch raised over his head, when he hesitated. Surprise was crucial. He had no idea who he was up against, but something told him it had to be linked to the recent murder of the maid.

Had Farley escaped from custody and come here to find Barbara? Could she have inadvertently pointed the police in his direction? He knew it wasn't a burglar. They wouldn't dash up the stairs banging doors; they would be like him – silent.

He'd left it long enough. He pushed open the door, bracing himself for an attack, but none came.

He stood in the wide corridor giving himself time to adjust. No need for a torch here. He rotated – listening – looking for any sign of his quarry or Barbara. He had been close behind; the intruder couldn't have got far. He had to be on this floor, but where?

He put his ear to the first door. He turned the handle and gently pushed. It didn't budge; it was locked. He ran his fingers over the keyhole. It was empty; the door had been locked from the inside. She was in here. He was certain of it. But where was the man looking for her? He moved silently to the next entrance. He froze. It was ajar and he could hear someone moving about inside. Then he heard the voice. It sent icy shivers crawling up his spine.

'Barbara? Where are you? I'm coming to find you but I'm not counting to ten.'

This was the voice of a madman, a childish chant that made his hair stand on end. Who the hell was it? He shifted the torch to his right hand, reversing it so that the heavier, battery-filled end was uppermost. He edged through the door, weapon raised. It was a bathroom, but it was empty and dark. The light was coming from the connecting bedroom. The whispered chanting continued and he prayed he'd get to the man before he found Babs.

The second door in the bathroom opened outwards, making it easier for him to conceal himself. He waited until the voice was on the far side of the room then peered round. He saw a large, broad-shouldered man, approaching the blackout curtains. The closet door was open. He'd obviously already searched there. He would get only one chance. The intruder was tall and heavier than him. If it came to a fight the odds were against him.

He steadied his breathing. Fear for his beloved gave him strength. Surging forward, his teeth bared in a snarl of rage, he struck the man across the head. The intruder crumpled and John watched, horrified, as a puddle of dark, viscous blood pooled on the floor. Christ, he'd killed him. He'd not meant to hit him so hard, only to stop him. For a moment he was paralysed, didn't know what to do; should he search for Barbara or see how badly hurt the man was? Then his training took over and the fog cleared.

Wherever she was, Babs was safe. Her attacker hadn't found her. He dropped to his knees beside the body, calling out as he did so, 'Babs. Babs, sweetheart, it's safe. You're safe now. You can come out. It's over.'

He expected her to emerge from behind the curtains, frightened, but delighted to see him. But she didn't. Where was she? He couldn't go and look for her. He had to try and stem the blood from the wound on the man's head. His basic first aid training gave him the knowledge he needed. He made a pad from his handkerchief and pressed down on the gash with one hand whilst feeling for a pulse with the other.

Thank God! The pulse was weak but regular. He hadn't killed him, at least not yet. Judging by the amount of blood the man was losing, it wouldn't be long before matters became grave. He knew that head wounds bled freely, could appear worse than they were. He prayed that was the case here.

The pressure seemed to be stemming the flow. What he needed was something else to press on top and a belt to tie it firm. He couldn't move; was there anything within arm's reach? He looked round – nothing. There were towels in the bathroom but he couldn't fetch them. The man could bleed to death in his absence. He still had his cap pushed through the epaulette on his shoulder. That would do, not ideal, but needs must. With his free hand he snatched it out and slipped it between his right hand and the blood-soaked handkerchief.

Where the hell was she? He shouted this time, his voice echoing round the room. 'Babs? Where are you? Come out, darling, I need your help.'

Still nothing. She couldn't have been in here after all. The man had made a mistake and had been searching in the wrong place. Now what the hell was he to do? What a bloody awful mess! He sat for fifteen minutes, calling a final time. The room walls were thick. If she was anywhere else, she wouldn't hear him unless she came out of hiding. But she didn't know this bastard was unconscious so would stay put until someone came to find her.

He stiffened. Was that a car? Was someone coming? It had to be the missing Sinclairs and the boys. He began to relax. Thank God! Barbara's grandfather was a medic. He'd be able to sort things out in no time. Shit and derision! They wouldn't be able to get in; the back door was locked. Would anyone think to go round and climb in the window? Had the wound stopped bleeding sufficiently for him to risk removing his hand?

* * *

'We had a lovely time, Grandpa, Grandma. Thank you so much for taking us to the pantomime.'

'Our pleasure, Tom. Come along, David; let's get inside in the warm.' He stopped.

'That's odd, my dear. Why is Simon's car here? Are we expecting him to visit?'

'No, Edward. I thought he was away. We can ask him when we see him. Hurry up, I want to get inside. The snow's freezing.'

The four bundled out of the car and hurried round to the back door. Tom arrived first.

'It won't open, Grandpa. It's stuck.'

'Here, let me have a go.' He pushed. 'It's locked and bolted. Whatever for?'

'Where are Barbara and Simon? The kitchen blackouts haven't been drawn; I noticed that as we came past.'

'I've no idea, Elspeth, but I want you all to wait here. If you huddle together in the porch, it won't be so bad. I'll go round and climb in the library window then come round and let you all in. Thank God that won't be locked.'

He ploughed through the deepening snow to the front of the building, astonished to find the window already open. As he climbed in his feet became entangled with something on the floor, and he stumbled to his knees swearing volubly. Pushing himself up he shone his torch down on the offending object. It was an RAF greatcoat. What the bloody hell was going on here? He jumped as he heard sounds behind him.

'It's only us, Edward; we decided we would come round and climb in too. It's far too cold to stay outside, even with our coats on.'

24

'David, draw the blackouts. Tom close the window. Quickly now, I want to put the lights on.' Edward drew his wife in the direction of the door whilst the boys were busy. 'There's something very wrong here, my dear. Keep the children in the library. I'm going to investigate.'

'Please be careful, Edward.' He bent and kissed her gently on the mouth.

'I'll be fine. You take care of the boys.' He switched on his torch. 'Put the lights on as soon as the door's closed behind me.'

He paused in the corridor. Hearing nothing, he turned and pushed his way past the blackout curtain into the grand entrance hall. The weight of snow on the dome reflected light on the floor and he was able to run across to the sweeping staircase. He listened before he moved. He reached the gallery and immediately saw the triangle of light shining out into the corridor.

By torchlight he made his way to the open door. This was the bathroom. He slipped through the gap and across the tiled floor. He could hear someone in the bedroom. He waited a moment longer then decided, whoever it was, they didn't sound especially dangerous. He stepped into the room to see a total stranger crouched over Simon Farley's body.

The stranger glanced round. 'Thank God! You must be Dr Sinclair.

I'm John Thorogood. This bastard was after Barbara so I hit him. Unfortunately rather harder than I'd intended.'

Instantly professional he dropped down and checked for a pulse. 'He's in no danger; it's weak, but regular.' He didn't suggest John remove his hand. He could see the blood coagulating on the floor. 'Head wounds bleed like the very devil. Stay there, young man. I'm going to get my bag.' He straightened. 'Where's my granddaughter?'

'I don't know. She's hiding somewhere. I've been unable to look for her. I've been sitting here for about fifteen minutes.'

'No doubt she's locked herself in her own bathroom. She doesn't know it's safe to come out.'

He kept a bag in the car and a spare in the library. He slid to a walk as he went back behind the curtain. He didn't wish to alarm anyone.

'Elspeth, I need my medical bag. There's been a bit of a misunderstanding and Barbara's young man has knocked Simon Farley out. Could you ring for an ambulance – probably won't need it, but just in case? Then I should get the boys down to the kitchen and let them play with the puppies. I should put the kettle on as well.'

He smiled cheerfully at the boys, found his bag and hurried back to his patient. As soon as he'd dealt with Simon's injury, Barbara's young man could go and find her. Why she'd felt it necessary to hide he'd no idea. As he'd told Elspeth, all this was probably a misunderstanding.

'I think he's coming around a bit, Dr Sinclair.'

'Excellent. Move your hand. Let me have a look at the damage.'

He watched John do as instructed. The young man stood up, flexing his cramped legs a few times. 'Do you need me or can I go and fetch Barbara?'

'Her door is the one next to this. Off you go, young man. I can cope here.'

The deep gash was oozing blood and would need a dozen or so sutures at the hospital. All that was necessary at the moment was for him to put on a clean dressing and secure it with a bandage. He was pinning the end neatly when Barbara's impulsive young man returned, his face worried.

'She's not there. The blackouts are drawn, but there's no sign of her. I looked in the other two rooms and called, but she's not there either. Where the hell is she? If this bastard has harmed a...'

'That's enough, young man. I think you've caused sufficient damage to Simon Farley for one day. Whatever made you think he was a threat to Barbara?'

He explained how he'd found things, which put quite a different complexion on matters. 'Fetch the cord from the dressing gown hanging on the back of the bathroom door. Quickly, man, he's coming around. I'll tie him up, just to be on the safe side.'

Minutes later Simon's hands were secured in front of him and he had been positioned in the recovery position just in case he vomited. The young man stood up, his face worried.

'I was sure Babs was hiding in this room. The bedroom door was locked from the inside.'

'Sweet Jesus!' His heart contracted. 'I know where she is. She's on the balcony. She has to be.' He raced across to the window and, despite the light restrictions, flung back the heavy curtains. The French windows were closed but not latched. He pushed them open and stepped out into the whirling whiteness.

* * *

Barbara crouched down into the small space where the balcony balustrade met the house wall. She turned her back to the snow, pulling up her collar and unwinding her scarf to retie it over her head, muffling her ears and mouth. She wished that she'd not dropped her thick gloves on the floor when she'd bolted the back door. Still, she could push her hands into her coat pockets. That would keep the edges closed over her knees as well. Her initial horror that she'd freeze to death began to fade. She was warmly dressed, had two pairs of socks and gumboots on. She was safer out here than in the hands of the murderer inside.

John would be here soon, and Grandpa. They'd capture Simon and rescue her. She probably wouldn't be out here more than a few minutes. She couldn't hear what was happening in the room. Snow deadened sound. She'd been half frozen to death in the stable not long ago and that time she'd only had indoor clothes on. If she trapped her body warmth inside her clothes, she'd be fine until someone came out to get her.

The snow settled on her shoulders. Had she become invisible? Part of the landscape, a living snowman? After about ten minutes she began to feel pleasantly sleepy, no longer cold. It wouldn't hurt to close her eyes for a bit. She'd been rushing around all day; a little nap would help her.

Her head sank lower, dropping between her knees, exposing the back of her neck to the elements. A small avalanche of snow, dislodged by her movement, shot down her neck. The icy wetness jolted her awake. She shivered violently and her teeth began to chatter. Something told her she needed to stand, stamp her feet, get some circulation back into her limbs.

Her legs appeared to have frozen solid. They didn't respond. Her arms still worked, thank goodness. She'd use them to pull herself up. She tipped forward onto her knees, putting her bare hands on the window, and attempted to inch herself straight. Within seconds her fingers were beginning to stick to the glass; she tugged them free. The sharp pain as the skin tore was exactly what she needed to help her fight the hypothermia that was sucking her life away.

If she could swing her arms about it might help, but then more snow would get in up her cuffs and through her open coat front. Her boots were full. While she was sitting crouched there'd been a gaping hole and the snow had gone inside. She flopped back against the balcony. Her legs were useless. If she couldn't stand how could she get back in? She closed her eyes and prayed. In the distance she heard voices; then two arms were around her, lifting her up, carrying her into the warm. Her prayers had been answered; John had come to save her.

* * *

John saw the shape against the balustrade and, elbowing Dr Sinclair aside, he dropped down and snatched Barbara up. 'My God, darling, wake up. Babs, don't go to sleep, sweetheart, stay with us. You need to stay awake, darling.'

Ignoring the semi-conscious form groaning on the carpet, Dr Sinclair ripped the covers from the bed. 'In the bathroom. It's warmer in there. We have to get her clothes off, wrap her in the blankets, then start rubbing each limb as hard as you can.'

As he tore her clothes off he could see her skin had a strange blue tinge and he feared they might be too late.

* * *

In the kitchen the boys were playing happily with their pets, the kettle was singing on the stove and Elspeth thought it safe to go and find what was happening. She couldn't imagine why John had hit Simon. An argument over Barbara, perhaps?

'Stay in here, boys. I'm going to unlock the back door and then go down and draw the rest of the blackouts.'

'All right, Grandma. Is Barbara upstairs with John and Simon?' Tom asked.

'She must be. I expect they're in Marigold's room.' This was an inspired answer. Neither boy wanted to follow up there.

She was forced to step over the dropped parcels before she could unlock the door. She picked them up and took them back with her to the library. She lit the fire and then returned to the breakfast room and did the same there. By the light of the flames she drew the blackouts. She smiled at the beautifully arranged table. Barbara had been busy.

She was tempted to investigate upstairs, but Edward had told her to stay with the boys. Her lips curved. She felt like a woman in her prime and not a dried-up old stick. Edward had kissed her, he'd moved into the adjacent room. Could there be a flame rekindling so late in their lives? Did people of their age still have intimate relations? Today anything seemed possible. Glowing with happiness, she returned to the kitchen to make a pot of tea.

'Mrs Brown and Joe will be back any moment. I expect they'll want a hot drink.'

'I bet they'll like a hot-water bottle to stuff up their jumpers if they've had to walk back in his snow,' Tom said, grinning.

'What a good idea. I'll make some. Can you boys go and fetch all the bottles you can find hanging behind the scullery door?'

Filling up hot-water bottles would keep them busy and it would also give her an excuse to go upstairs. She could put one in each of the beds. It took two kettles before the nine hot-water bottles were filled and ready and their crocheted covers replaced. She piled seven of them into a basket and, staggering under the weight, told the boys where she was going.

'You stay here. David, can you give Joe and Mrs Brown their hot-water bottles when they come in? I think I heard a car pulling into the circle. Tom, will you pour out tea?'

The boys nodded, thrilled to have a role to play. 'Can you ask Barbara and John to come down, Grandma? He hasn't met Buttons or Patch. I bet he'll love them,' David called.

'I'm sure he will. Now, I won't be long.'

* * *

'That's it, young man, rub hard, cover it up and move on.' Edward was not sanguine about the outcome. Barbara was too cold; her body temperature not responding quickly enough. What they needed were hot-water bottles and plenty of them. He heard a movement and looked up. 'Good God, Elspeth, how did you know I was praying for those?'

John didn't need to be told. He leapt to his feet and took the basket. Seconds later they were tucked inside the blankets and Barbara was safely wrapped in a warm cocoon.

'We can't do any more with her down here on the bathroom floor, my boy. Let's get her in front of a fire. Is there one in the library, my dear?'

'There is, Edward. It was burning well when I left it.'

'Excellent, excellent.'

The young man scooped Barbara up as if she weighed nothing, and cradled her next to his heart. As he did so he saw her neck stiffen and she opened her eyes.

'John, John, I knew you'd come. Simon killed Marigold and he was going to kill me.'

John tightened his hold. 'Don't worry about that, darling. He's all trussed up like a Christmas goose. You can tell us all about it later.'

Thank the Lord! He couldn't have coped if he'd lost this precious girl. He stepped over and slid his fingers under her chin. 'Good girl – you're coming back to us. Keep talking. We need to keep you awake.' He shone his torch in front of the young man, lighting the way down the grand staircase.

'Is there tea made, Elspeth?'

'Yes, I did it before I came up.'

'Well done, darling. I'll get Barbara settled in front of the fire whilst you fetch the tea. I think we all need it. Did you ring for an ambulance?'

'I did, Edward. I'm sure it will be here soon.'

* * *

Barbara relaxed into John's arms, feeling a delicious warmth thawing her out. They were sitting on the large sofa in front of a roaring fire. 'I prayed you'd come in time, John, and you did.'

He kissed her gently. 'Sweetheart, you shouldn't have gone out there. You could have died.'

She struggled to release her arms and sit up, shocked to see that they were bare. She peered into the blankets.

'John, I've no clothes on!' His gurgle of laughter made her cross. 'It's no laughing matter. I'm so embarrassed. How can I ever look Grandpa in the eye again?'

'My darling girl, he's a doctor, and you've still got your knickers and bra on, so stop fussing.'

She frowned, not convinced. 'Listen, when we stripped you, we were more concerned about saving your life, getting you warm. I can assure you neither of us even thought about your lack of clothes.'

'Good.' She reached up to touch his cheek, feeling the rasp of bristles under her fingers. 'And anyway, you're my fiancé. When we get married I suppose you'll see all of me.'

'God, I should hope I do! Unless you're going to be like my grandmother and dress and undress under your nightie.'

'I thought I heard an ambulance. I'm not going to hospital, so it will have to go away again.' She felt him tense. 'What is it, John? What haven't you told me?'

'I'm afraid the ambulance is for Farley. I clocked him on the head with the torch; he needs stitches and is concussed.'

She sighed and settled back. 'That's all right then; he deserved it.' She shivered. She knew what would happen to Simon. 'I suppose he'll hang? In some ways it would be better if he had died; it will be horrible for his parents when he's executed.' She couldn't understand why he was amused. 'What have I said? Why are you laughing at me again?'

'Sweetheart, if I'd killed him it would be me dangling from a rope. I hope that's not your preferred option.'

She tried to punch him. 'Please don't joke about it. No, what I meant was killing anyone in cold blood seems wrong; in the heat of battle, yes, I can understand that, but well… you know what I mean.'

'I do, and I agree; there's going to be more than enough killing in the next few months.'

They heard the sound of voices outside in the passage and knew Simon was being removed to the ambulance.

'Did Grandpa ring Inspector Galloway and tell him everything?'

'He did. The police are meeting the ambulance at the hospital. They're not coming tonight for any statements; we'll have to do them tomorrow morning.'

'What time is it? I must go and get dressed. There's going to be a special supper tonight. I've made the breakfast room look lovely. I'm not missing it, whatever Grandpa says.'

'I rather hoped tonight might be special for us as well. I want to make our engagement official, tell the boys, put the announcement in the paper.'

'That would be lovely. I'm sure David and Tom would be more shocked if we weren't getting married after seeing me lolling around semi-naked on your lap for the past hour.'

'As soon as the ambulance has gone there should be some more tea coming. Shall we tell everyone then?'

'Yes, let's.' She leant her head on his shoulder and stared into the fire.

Tonight she had no doubts. John was the man for her; he'd saved her life. She must put Alex aside. This was the man she wanted to spend the rest of her life with. 'John, in spite of everything that's happened, I really believe that this is going to be the best Christmas ever.'

BIBLIOGRAPHY

How We Lived Then – Norman Longmate
Christmas On the Home Front – Mike Brown
Wartime Britain 1939–1945 – Juliet Gardner
The Home Front – Marion Yass

These books were an invaluable resource and my thanks to the authors.

ABOUT THE AUTHOR

Fenella J. Miller is a bestselling writer of historical sagas. She also has a passion for Regency romantic adventures and has published over fifty to great acclaim.

Sign up to Fenella J. Miller's mailing list for news, competitions and updates on future books.

Visit Fenella's website: www.fenellajmiller.co.uk

Follow Fenella on social media here:

facebook.com/fenella.miller

x.com/fenellawriter

ALSO BY FENELLA J. MILLER

Goodwill House Series

The War Girls of Goodwill House

New Recruits at Goodwill House

Duty Calls at Goodwill House

The Land Girls of Goodwill House

A Wartime Reunion at Goodwill House

Wedding Bells at Goodwill House

A Christmas Baby at Goodwill House

The Army Girls Series

Army Girls Reporting For Duty

The Pilot's Girl Series

The Pilot's Girl

A Wedding for the Pilot's Girl

Standalone

The Land Girl's Secret

Milton Keynes UK
Ingram Content Group UK Ltd.
UKHW040608071223
433886UK00002B/3

9 781835 186213